Hot Siberian

HOT
SIBERIAN

Gerald A. Browne

ARBOR HOUSE
WILLIAM MORROW
New York

Excerpt from "I've Been Invited to a Party" by Noel Coward. Copyright © 1963 by Noel Coward. All rights controlled by Chappell & Co. Used by permission. All rights reserved.

Excerpt from "Money, Money" by John Kander and Fred Ebb. Copyright © 1972 by Alley Music Corporation and Trio Music Company, Inc. Used by permission. All rights reserved.

Excerpt from "Take My Breath Away" by Giorgio Moroder and Tom Whitlock. Copyright © 1986 by Famous Music Corporation and GMPC.

Library of Congress Cataloging-in-Publication Data

Browne, Gerald A.
  Hot Siberian.

  I. Title.
PS3552.R746H6 1989   813'.54   88-7561
ISBN 0-887-95965-X

Printed in the United States of America

First Edition

1 2 3 4 5 6 7 8 9 10

BOOK DESIGN BY NICOLA MAZZELLA

For my two loves,
Merle Lynn and Maggie

The author wishes to acknowledge those friends and informants who, in one way or another, helped bring this story about. Especially:

Nadya Demisov, Tamara Ustinov, Aleksei Voynovich, Vadim Federovska, Joy Burkett, Joan Tompkins, Reta Alley, Sterling Lord, Alan Williams, Dr. Marvin Belsky, Dr. Richard Coburn, Dr. Ruth Ochroch, Cowboy and Jill, Jeff and Viv Wattenberg, Marcie Egan, Chris Watkins, Harold Blits, Sheldon Rosenfeld, Inessa in Leningrad and Natalya in Moscow.

CHAPTER
❖·❖·❖ 1 ❖·❖·❖

JANUARY 12.

New Year's Eve.

Josep Kislov was nearly as drunk as he'd ever been. It wasn't, however, one of his usual hung-mouthed, grumbling, self-sorry drunks. He had reasons to feel good.

His tour of work at Aikhal was up. Thirty-two months straight, which made him eligible now for six months off. Most of those who came to work at the Aikhal installation didn't stay on the job for that long a stretch. At the end of a year they were quick to take the forty-two days vacation they had coming. Siberia got to them. Its long, awful cold was as confining as a penitentiary, its white waste a depriving absence of color. Just knowing where they were gnawed at them. *The Arctic Circle, three thousand miles from Moscow.* That was how even those who had never lived or been in Moscow measured it. On the map of the Soviet Union they kept imposed in their minds they marked the blank Siberian spot that was Aikhal time and time again, and it made them feel like specks. They had to get away if only to reconfirm their self-importance.

Josep Kislov accepted that it was evidence of his superior mental muscle that he'd been able to endure the consecutive thirty-two. The fact would be impressive in his *trudovaya knizhka,* his workbook. Every working Soviet citizen is required to have such a book. It serves as both a job record and a ledger of deportment to be presented when changing from one job to another, often determining if the move will be up or down. Actually, Kislov no longer gave a damn what his workbook said about him.

For the time being his job classification had him as a sorter and preformer. Metal trays of diamond rough were brought to his workbench, about a thousand carats at a time. They had already been gone over for the larger stones, those removed. Kislov culled them further, sorted out and gathered aside in separate lots all the diamonds of two particular sizes, those which would best finish at a half carat and at one carat. Nothing smaller. He passed the remaining smaller rough on to another sorter.

Only a small percentage of the diamonds that came to him were well-formed octahedral crystals, obvious diamonds ready to be cut just as they were. The rest were lumpy or long, little irregular chunks that bore no apparent diamond shape. Kislov had to grind them down to the acceptable proportions, using a flat high-speed wheel coated with oil and diamond dust. When he'd first been assigned to this job a number of odd-shaped stones had gotten by him. As a result they got lodged in the channels inside the robotic arms of the faceting machines. It was like clogging an artery. The machines had to be shut off and partially disassembled. The men in charge of the faceting, the cutters, hated the bother. Especially since Kislov was new at the job, they blamed and cursed him, ridiculed him with exaggerations about how the blind, feeble woman whose job it was before had never let such a thing happen. The cutters were spoiled, Kislov thought, spoiled by their electronic machines. They simply wanted to program the machines, then stand around taking credit while the multiple robotic arms turned out precisely faceted, perfectly proportioned identical half-carat or full-carat diamonds by the blazing piles.

At the end of each workday Kislov had to hand in a report of the exact number of diamonds he'd sorted and preformed. He knew to the carat how many stones were contained in each of the trays he turned over to the cutters for finishing, exactly how many trays each week. At that time he hoped he'd somehow be promoted to cutter. It would have meant better pay and certain special privileges.

He no longer held that ambition. Something far more rewarding was imminent, he believed.

As a sorter-preformer his monthly salary was four hundred roubles—doubled because of Siberia. He hadn't gambled, but salted away most of it. Twenty-three thousand roubles were waiting for him in his account at the State Bank in Ulyanovsk. He was looking forward to saying a hello and an enjoyable goodbye to those roubles. He'd have a new car, at least a Zhiguli two-door, new clothes from hat to shoes, a careful haircut, and a silver cigarette case that he could snap open smartly. Altogether quite a different person. He wouldn't stay long in Ulyanovsk. He didn't like his city. It was dull, provincial, stagnant despite the perpetual flow of patriots who made pilgrimages there to gawk reverently at one preserved site or another, anywhere that Vladimir Ulyanov, later known as Lenin, was supposed to have done anything, whether it was read a schoolbook or wipe his ass. Kislov would remain in Ulyanovsk just long enough to satisfy his eyes with his only sister and to stroll enough up and down the main way, Goncharov Street, showing off his prosperity. Then he'd get a permit that would allow him to spend some time in Moscow. City paved with privileges, Moscow. There he would go to the Ministry of Foreign Trade and seek out the man of last September.

During the second week of September a group of officials from the ministry had come to the installation on business. That in itself wasn't unusual. Such officials showed up every so often, Kislov had noticed. He had wanted to speak to one of them, but he couldn't get up the nerve or, for that matter, settle on which, judging from sight, would most likely be receptive to what he had to say. Until last September and the one he had heard them call Nikolai. Kislov didn't allow himself a second thought. As swift as the moment he convinced himself that this Nikolai, though younger than the other officials, was his man. He appeared important enough. The others spoke to him respectfully. And being young, he was no doubt ambitious. That would be an advantage.

Kislov saw his chance and took it when this Nikolai happened to be alone in an area just outside the office where the production records were kept. Kislov could not recall later whether or not he had physically maneuvered the man into that nearby alcove but he probably had pressured his elbow a bit to get him in there out of possible sight. Kislov checked to make sure no one was within hearing range, then blurted out in a sibilant whisper as much as he could of what he had to tell, the accumulated information that had become so valuable to him. For substantiation, but really not knowing whether or not they were in any way meaningful, Kislov gave him a paper with the three scribbled addresses on it, along with his name. Throughout, this Nikolai hadn't said a word, kept his mouth and eyes absolutely unreadable. Kislov wished there had been some acknowledgment, any little sign, even a mere single nod would have been encouraging. All he had to draw from was the fact that this Nikolai had listened.

Four months had passed. Kislov hung on to the explanation that because of the seriousness of the matter and the large stakes that were involved it was something that couldn't be rushed. It was being very methodically looked into. He thought it probable that some highly placed toes were being avoided. Anyway, come tomorrow morning he would be on the transportation tractor for 280 miles to Mirny, where he'd catch a plane to Yakutsk, the nearest city of size. There was no need for him to spend time in Yakutsk. He wasn't sneaking out even one tiny diamond to sell there.

"*S'Novim Goddom!*" people were shouting, Happy New Year!

Kislov agreed and was prompted to return the greeting. He howled it, opened his mouth wider than necessary for the words, got redder in the face. Just about everyone at the installation was drunk, all two thousand and some. Since noon there had been the swilling of Georgian brandy and bottle after bottle of *sivukha*, that ugly, poorest man's kind of vodka. Badly distilled, it punished the roof of the mouth and the throat and made the stomach clench, but it was cheap and delivered a fast drunk. Kislov had decided this night was too special for *sivukha*. He was already on his second bottle of *spirt*. Well distilled, practically pure Russian alcohol at 192 proof, *spirt* had the expensive kindness to slip past the palate and get all the way down before glowing like molten silver, sending wires of warmth to the most extreme capillaries. Kislov claimed that whenever he drank *spirt* the fire of his first swallow went right to his asshole.

He and the girl, Erika, had drunk it the proper way to begin with—from small glass tumblers filled only a drop or so short of overflowing. She drank it straight along with him, but requested water to follow it with, and after tossing down four like that she surreptitiously dumped them into her water glass, clear with clear.

This Erika.

Kislov had first taken notice of her an hour ago when he was seated alone at a table off to one side of the recreation area. She had on a happy green dress and black stockings. Kislov watched her pick her way through the standing crowd, saw her brush off advances. He had no reason to more than hope she was bound for him. He wasn't attractive and knew it. He appeared older than forty-six. A narrow-shouldered thin man with a paunch. His features were too sharp and his face too long, and he couldn't smile freely without revealing too much gum.

The way Erika had come and taken the chair opposite him at the table, hadn't asked, just assumed, it occurred to Kislov that there was something of a whore in it. He didn't want to think she was a whore, but, if so, she was better-looking than any he'd ever been with. Early twenties was Kislov's guess, an Estonian or possibly a Pole. Either way, some anonymous World War II German in her. She had clean blond hair and good skin, and was tall, with a conscientiously exercised body. He searched for whore money in her eyes but saw only himself. She volunteered that she'd arrived at Aikhal only the day before and was going to be assigned as a sorter of finished goods. She'd admitted she'd had no experience. Kislov offered to give her some

pointers on sorting, but she wasn't interested, rather preferred easier talk about such things as how cold the weather
got there, allowing Kislov time to get drunker.

Now, with still forty-some minutes remaining in the old
year they'd left the din of the recreation area and were
making their way along one of the extended passageways
that led to and from the sleeping quarters. The passageway
was like a straight tunnel, dimly lighted and windowless,
constructed of welded steel sections, well insulated. Bare
red bulbs just below ceiling level marked the location of
emergency exit hatches.

Whether their destination was his bed or hers had not
yet been decided. It was slow going. Kislov's legs were
unreliable. Every few steps his knees would either lock or
buckle or one of his ankles would twist over. Erika was
patient. She steadied him with an arm around. She was
plenty strong enough. Kislov paused, used the wall for
support while he swigged from the bottle of *spirt*. When
Erika lifted the bottle to her mouth, she pretended, stop-
pered it with her tongue. They continued on, Kislov stag-
gering, dependent upon her.

A short way farther on Erika maneuvered him off to
the side again, so his back was against the wall. He slung
his arms loosely around her. She reached down and took
hold of him through his trousers, kneaded his genitals. He
fumbled for her breasts, roughly. She glanced down the
passageway in both directions and determined that they
were alone. She pressed her body hard against his, ground
him with herself so tight that his hands and the bottle were
pinned between them.

A pair of mechanical clicks were followed by a brief
hiss.

It was the opening mechanism of the emergency hatch,
the surrender of its pressurized rubber seal.

Kislov felt as though his body were passing through the
wall and then there was the panelike barrier where the
inside and outside temperatures fought, a difference of 140
degrees. He fell out the hatch back first and landed in the
snow ten feet below.

At once he looked up to the open hatch. He saw the lighted rectangular shape of it diminish and disappear as Erika pulled the hatch door closed. The frigid air sobered him considerably, cleared away most of the distortions of his drunk. What a stupid fucking thing, he thought as he got to his feet. Thank God Erika was hurrying to get help. But why had she closed the hatch? On the other hand, what good having it open? It was way above his reach, and she couldn't reach down to him. Besides, when they came to get him it would be by way of one of the regularly used ramps. Where was the nearest ramp? From there all he could see was the huge steel pilings that supported the superstructure of the installation. The pilings in a line one after another, uninterrupted. He shouldn't go searching for a ramp, he decided. Not to panic. He'd be more quickly found and taken in if he remained where he was. He hugged himself tightly and tucked his hands into his armpits.

The temperature was seventy below zero. He was wearing only felt boots, trousers made mainly of acrylic fiber, and a flannel shirt. Not even thermal underwear. They'd better hurry, a shiver warned him, a pervasive biting shiver. He glanced to the sky, blamed it for such severe cold. The moon was lopsided and neon-bright, causing a blue cast on the snow. On the rise about a mile off he could easily see the dark departure that was the forest. He could even make out some of the high-reaching trunks of pines. It was from there that the wolves came for the scraps of meat that were thrown out for them. The smell of the meat brought the wolves beneath the installation so they could be shot from above. A wolf pelt was worth one hundred rubles. Kislov scanned the expanse of snow and saw only snow. He wasn't meat, he told himself, and tried to put the wolves out of mind.

The air was so still and cold he could hear the breaths that came from him crackle as the moisture particles in it froze. His breathing was shallow; the lower portion of his lungs had defensively closed off. He couldn't define his toes when he tried to work them. At first his nose and ears had burned from the cold, but now they were deadened.

He remembered having once seen a babushka in Yakutsk whose ears had been amputated because they'd been frozen. He sure as hell wanted to keep his ears. Where was Erika? Were they all so drunk she couldn't make them listen? How long had he been out there? He looked at his watch and saw ten minutes to twelve. He realized the steel case of the watch was stuck frozen to his skin. Fuck this, he thought, he wasn't going to just wait there. He'd find one of the ramps and beat upon a hatch and someone would hear. He took a step. It hurt to move. He was cold to the marrow.

The *spirit*.

His eyes caught upon the bottle where it had landed in the snow no more than a reach away. He'd forgotten about the *spirit*. Of course, the *spirit* would help save him. He picked up the bottle. About half was left in it. His fingers had difficulty unscrewing the cap. He was trembling so he had to use both hands to get the mouth of the bottle to his lips. He took one, two, three, four fast swallows and another for good measure.

The *spirit*, because it was almost pure alcohol, hadn't frozen. However, while it had remained liquid, it had become the same temperature as the atmosphere. Minus seventy degrees. The moment it touched the tissues of Kislov's esophagus it froze them. Working like some cryogenic substance it immediately froze the mucous membranes of his stomach, the walls, blood vessels, and nerves of his stomach. In the adjacent veins and arteries, the vena cava, aorta, and others, it turned his blood to ice.

Within seconds, Josep Kislov was dead, frozen from the inside out.

CHAPTER
◆◆◆◆ 2 ◆◆◆◆

FOUR MONTHS LATER IN LONDON.

Rupert Churcher gazed into his Régence giltwood mirror and detested what he saw. According to his disposition on this day his jowls were decidedly more pronounced than they'd been just last week. There they were, to the left and right of his mouth, swagging like portiers. Where was the gentle demeanor that had been his stock in trade, the collaborative pleasant expression of his features? He used to be able to conceal any amount of cunning behind them. But now . . . well, just look at his eyes! The whites of them were not a crisp, guileless white as they'd once been, no longer helpful in outlining the blue-gray sincerity of his irises. His whites had soured, become creamy, appeared bruised. Such debility could only be chalked up to how much of his well-being he had given to his position. Literal loss of face while striving to save face for the Central Selling System.

Yesterday, Thursday, had been a fair example of these trying times. That odoriferous tribal chief from Botswana and his retinue showing up without notice. The whole black bunch of them strutting right in and insisting they be brought up to him here in his private office on four. What gall, the way they'd dumped a basket of rough in the middle of his Kirman and announced its price.

Back in the better days they wouldn't have been allowed past the ground-floor guard. As things were, he, Churcher, the very head of the Central Selling System, had chosen to choke down his indignation. Oh, how much he'd been tempted to tell those smelly monkeys to pick up their diamonds and get out. Instead, he'd stood there and suffered them, looked down at that sizable heap of rough and put on his grateful face. It was either that or have those diamonds go to the outside market. Too many stones were finding their way from Africa to Tel Aviv. The Israelis were slippery, required watching. They'd like nothing better than to play monopoly, beat the System at its own game. Rather than give the Israelis the advantage of even another carat it was shrewd of him to toady a bit as he had yesterday. Besides, those Botswanan diamonds were well worth the asking price, would bring the System a tidy profit. However, back in better days the System would have set the price and profited more. Naturally, this Botswana chief, like all the others who came toting to London, had wanted cash. So Pulver and a couple of Security Section men had to go to all the bother of fetching the money from the bank. While that was being done, the counting and all, he'd offered tea, and afterward he'd told Pulver to have the damn cups, saucers, and spoons sterilized. Pulver had made the sardonic suggestion that perhaps the firm would do well to invest in a hospital autoclave.

Times had indeed changed, Churcher thought. A frequent thought. His predecessor, Harold Meecham, was fortunate to have retired when he did in 1972. Churcher recalled how delighted he'd been with his appointment to director, the ultimate promotion. Proud as a prince of it. Africa hadn't seemed like so much of a problem then. There'd been some boiling up here and there, in Namaqualand, Zaire, and elsewhere, but nothing that the System couldn't cool down with well-placed and reasonable payoffs. *Dash*, as the natives so aptly called it.

Who would have thought, until it was obvious and too late, that old, subservient Africa would take to presiding over itself so seriously? In some of the new African nations the System's representatives, buyers, mine managers, and so on, had been lucky to get out with their hearts still in their chests. A few fellows stationed really deep in the bush had never again been heard from.

The diamonds belong to the ground, the ground belongs

*to the country, the country belongs to the people, the dia-
monds belong to the people* was the sort of empiric Marxist
babble one was forced to hear. In the same breath the
System was informed that the diamond-mining leases it held
were invalid, since they'd been issued by officials no longer
in power. As well, unwritten agreements, honorable un-
derstandings that had been kept and taken for granted since
as far back as the early 1900s, suddenly stood for nothing.
The slickly structured, neatly overseen way the System had
extracted diamonds from Africa was in shambles.

Could it be restored?

The System believed so, Churcher particularly. He personally went back into Africa with homburg in hand, hoping
to knot new, even tighter ties with the new leaders of the
various African nations. With hardly a chew the System
swallowed its pride and didn't give one damn how transparent were its motives. Straight-facedly contrite, Churcher
admitted regret for the System's part in the inequities of
the past and vowed there would be no such abuses in the
future. An accumulation of things had simply gotten out
of hand on the local level and would be rectified. Good
that they'd been called to mind, Churcher said.

Over the punishment of hundreds of horribly concocted
cocktails and countless plates of inedible food, Churcher
and other emissaries of the System never let go by a chance
to express political empathy. And finally, in the privacy of
those whom they believed to be the right company, they
conveyed how eager the System was to make substantial
amends, the emphasized word being, of course, "substantial."

The fat Swiss bank accounts that the System opened
were intended to secure for it diamond-working arrangements in perpetuity. However, no sooner were millions
deposited on behalf of the solidly perched leader of an
African nation but there would be a coup, an overthrow,
an unscheduled election, an assassination, or whatever, and,
that quickly, an altogether different regime would have to
be financially indulged. It occurred repeatedly. The out-
stretched palms multipled! Before long a frightful number

of ingrate African exiles were way out of place, schussing the slopes of Gstaad, dipping in the waters of Marbella, signing for everything at the Carleton in Cannes, and otherwise living it up at the System's expense.

It was maddening.

The financial drain mattered to the System, but what struck home harder was the prospect that Africa was helplessly out of hand and was likely to remain that way. Mind, diamonds would always be showing up from Zaire, Tanzania, and the like; however, they could not be reliably expected. Such an unpalatable realization! The System had dominated the world diamond market since the turn of the century. Ever devising, ever grabby, it had managed to increase its position to the extent that its hold was imposed over 90 percent of the diamonds that were pulled out of the earth each year. The methods it chose to market those diamonds could not have been more dictatorial.

Ten times each year the System summoned some three hundred diamond dealers to its headquarters, located at 11 Harrowhouse Street, London EC 2. They were virtually the same most important three hundred dealers each time, as only rarely was a new name added to the list. To be so included by the System was a privilege and not merely a matter of prestige, for except in the worst of times, to a dealer it meant sure profit.

In the trade these gatherings in London were called "sights." The dealers who were notified to attend were called "sightholders." Ostensibly, the reason for conducting a sight was to allow sightholders to examine the diamond rough that the System had decided to sell them. However, the dealers were not permitted to pick over their packets, take certain stones and leave others, and pay only for what they took. They had to accept the entire packet or none at all, the bad along with the better, exactly as the System had proportioned it. Nor could a sightholder quibble about price. He might wince, and once in a while even dare aloud some lighthearted comment pertaining to cost, but he made damn sure his tone was unmistakably lighthearted. A troublesome sightholder, one who failed to abide by the

System's criteria, would be excluded from the list. Set adrift, so to speak, put out on his own to scrounge up diamonds wherever he could, a time-consuming, quite often chancier alternative.

The average price the System put on its packets was one million dollars. Three hundred sightholders paid a million each ten times every year.

What it came to was three billion dollars.

Little wonder the System went to so much bother and expense in its attempt to get things back to working order in Africa. Control was imperative. Control of supply enabled control of price.

The System continued to hold its sights on schedule, drawing the diamonds it needed for them from its backup inventory. The sightholders had no idea that anything unusual was going on. The evident turmoil in Africa did not seem to mean a thing. The System was as implacable and efficient as ever. Any rumors that it was having difficulties were swiftly evaporated by its normal arrogance.

For nearly two years, from late 1976 to well into 1978, the System deliberated what move it should make. It couldn't keep up the front much longer; its reserves were close to depletion. Soon it would be forced to cancel sights and let the diamond market, not so figuratively speaking, stone itself to death. The only other alternative was something the System had been putting off like a maiden keeping her legs crossed, and that was to seek rescue from the only possible direction.

The Soviet Union.

After World War II the Soviets were in desperate need of diamonds. They could not rebuild industrially nor hope to keep up technologically without them. Diamonds were essential to drilling oil, making steel, building rockets. With practically no diamond production of their own the Soviets were forced to buy from the West, from the System.

Politically, the men at the top of the System were congenital conservatives. In their view anyone who was even left-handed did not deserve sympathy or trust. They made the Soviets pay dearly for the diamonds they needed.

And whenever the Soviets complained, they upped the price. The Soviets resented being gouged but had no recourse. For the time being they could only grit and pay. The long run would be a different matter.

Soviet geologists went hunting. In, of all places, Siberia. They had noticed the geological similarities between certain areas of Yakut Siberia and the diamond-rich regions of South Africa. Hundreds of geologists tromped back and forth across the frozen Siberian wastes, but it was not until 1954 that a woman geologist named Larissa Popugaieva made the find. In the basin of the Vilyui River she came upon a kimberlite pipe, the sort of extinct volcanic outlet that contains the kind of rock in which diamonds are found. Soon after that initial discovery, numerous other diamond-bearing pipes were found in that Yakut area.

Larissa Popugaieva was declared a Hero of Socialist Labor and awarded the Order of Lenin.

However, finding diamonds was one thing, getting them out of the ground another. Particularly this Siberian ground. It was permafrost, constantly frozen as much as a mile deep, a result of the fierce climate that went to 80 below zero Fahrenheit. Summers there were as brief as a month and, as if overcompensating, presented sweltering temperatures that often exceeded 100 degrees. Such heat transformed the skin of the land into mushy green bogs above which mosquitoes clouded like thick, black, buzzing mists.

Mining had never been attempted under such adverse conditions. The extreme cold changed the molecular behavior of substances, turned lubricants into glue, caused rubber to become brittle as dry bone, and made many metals fracture into fragments when asked to take the merest strain. Machinery was paralyzed. The human machinery as well. Parts balked, muscles lost their elasticity, nostrils clogged with ice.

For eleven years, from 1955 to 1966, the Soviets hacked at the frozen ground, grubbed for their diamonds. Many who worked the open-cut mines died from hypothermia. Pneumonia was almost as common as head colds. Frostbite caused casualty after casualty. There were summer instances when men or women or couples strayed too far from camp. Seduced by the sun to remove their clothes, they were literally driven mad by mosquitoes.

Those who fared best in the frigid climate were the Chukchis. Genetically connected to the Alaskan Inuit and in appearance greatly resembling them, the Chukchis came from the easternmost, northernmost corner of the Soviet Union: the Bering Sea coast and Pegiyemel. They were the last natives of Siberia to submit to Russian rule. Fierce fighters, they held off the Russian army for over a century. While other workers at the mines wore fur-lined hats and gloves, the Chukchis went about with their heads and hands bare. It wasn't that their skins were thicker or possessed an extra, anomalous thermal layer. They just thought of the cold differently. It was to them an old familiar enemy they would never totally give in to. The Russians enlisted as many Chukchis as they could to work the diamond mines, and paid them well. The difficulty was keeping them on the job. As soon as a Chukchi had earned enough to buy the number of reindeer or harpoon points he had in mind, he'd head for home, just walk off across the frozen waste as though he had no doubt of getting there.

Despite the many obstacles, the Soviets managed to dig up more than enough diamonds to meet their industrial and technological needs. In 1965, for example, Soviet production was a million carats. But it was, unquestionably, the hard way to go, and there were those high in the government who thought it a shame that fine, gem-quality diamonds were being used on the studded ends of oil-drilling bits.

It was proposed that an expenditure be made in rubles and manpower to improve the mining methods of the Siberian diamond fields. That the country should take full financial advantage of its diamond resources was the contention. The proposal caused some members of the Central Committee to set their jaws and shore up their minds. They were against having anything at all to do with diamonds. Staunch party hard-liners, they argued that diamonds by their very nature smacked of capitalism, that diamonds and exploitation of workers had always gone hand in hand. It would be hypocritical for Russia, in its role of model Marxist state, to be involved in such business. Instead, to meet its needs, could not Russia manufacture synthetic diamonds at a more reasonable cost?

The debate was bitter and drawn-out. The diehards were eventually thwarted. The Secretariat of the Central Committee approved. Next it was up to Soviet engineers.

What the engineers came up with was a solution that could not have been more simple nor more audacious. Inasmuch as the outside cold was such a physical drawback, then mine the diamonds from the inside. Enclose the mine and erect an installation directly above it, one that could house all the various phases of the diamond-mining process, from the excavation and crushing of the ore to the extracting and separating of the precious stones. The installation would also provide housing for the workers and administrative personnel, complete facilities.

It was asked: What about the permafrozen ground? How would that be dealt with?

With the exhaust heat of jet engines. The temperature and texture of the ground could be brought to a point where it would be normally workable.

In the process of recovering diamonds was it not necessary to wash the crushed ore? Where would such a huge quantity of water, a veritable lake of it, be kept without it freezing?

To answer that problem a new recovery method had been developed, one that used X-rays. As the mixture of crushed ore and diamonds was conveyed along a belt, it would be scrutinized under fluoroscopic light. The diamonds, because of their elemental makeup, would be easily distinguishable. They would show up in various bright shades of blue, green, yellow-orange, or icy white and could, therefore, easily be picked out.

A scale model of the proposed installation was shown to the members of the Central Committee Secretariat, so that they understood how extensive a project this would be. Its structures would cover an area of nearly thirty acres.

So everything would be under one roof, even whatever was needed for cutting and polishing the diamonds?

No. There'd been no allowance for those finishing phases. Why shouldn't the cutting and polishing be done someplace with a more compatible climate, in Kiev or Minsk or possibly even some place as far south as Tbilisi?

Tbilisi? The Secretariat scoffed at the suggestion of mixing Georgians and diamonds, the Georgians with their well-founded reputation for, to put it tactfully, sleight of hand. The unanimous decision of the Secretariat was that the finishing of the diamonds should be done on the spot. The Siberian remoteness would in itself serve as a security measure. Employees would not be going in and out every day the way they did at other workplaces. Mind, at some regular factories in Moscow and Leningrad the pilfering rate ran as high as 10 percent. Such wrongdoing, though not sanctioned, was tolerated, since it increased the workers' satisfaction with their jobs. However, to tempt them with diamonds would be a different matter altogether, actually unfair.

Agreed.

Approved.

The installation at Aikhal got off the ground.

Literally off the ground. The entire thing, except for the mine-shaft enclosure, had to be constructed on pilings that extended twelve feet above the surface. Enormous steel beams were sunk twenty feet deep into the permafrost and held in place by the almost instantaneous freezing of the slush that was filled in around them. More solid than concrete. The pilings were essential to keep human-generated heat from melting the ground and making the installation sink. It was not uncommon in northern Siberia to see wooden houses sunk down into the tundra to their windowsills.

The enormous energy and millions of rubles the Soviets invested in the Aikhal installation were well spent. In 1971, its first year of operation, it came up with two million carats of diamonds, of which 37 percent were gem-quality stones. Soon thereafter, other installations similar to Aikhal were built in and around the Vilyui River Basin. However, Aikhal continued to be the richest deposit. By 1975 Aikhal was producing five million carats a year and showing no signs of depletion. Unlike most diamond-bearing pipes, those at Aikhal seemed to yield more as they were dug deeper.

Typically, the Soviets kept their production figures secret. Why should they let anyone know they were stockpiling? In 1977, the United States Bureau of Mines estimated diamond production of the entire world at just under forty million carats, or almost nine tons. Only slightly more than 25 percent of this production was said to be of gem quality. Little did the bureau know. The Soviets could have tacked on another fifteen million carats. Three and a half tons. The Russians were up to their beards in diamonds.

The old axiom that says timing can be everything was never more fitting.

The period during which the Russians were enjoying such success with their Siberian mines coincided almost to the very year with the time when the System lost its control over its diamond holdings in Africa. By then, 1978, Rupert Churcher had been at the head of the System for six years. While coping with Africa he'd kept an eye on the Russians and was aware of the small amounts of high-quality diamond rough they were bringing to the market every once in a while. Churcher did not know for certain what quantity of such rough the Russians were capable of producing, but he put stock in the formidable figures that the System's security people came up with through its informants. At first the System had viewed the Russian diamonds as merely a potential threat, one that the System with its stranglehold on the marketing aspect of the trade could easily cope with. There had even been some talk early on about profiting from the situation by allowing the Russians to market some of its goods through the System. That met with graven resistance from the board of directors. The very idea! it had huffed.

Then came the African problems and a change of heart.

If the System was to survive, an affiliation between it and the Russians would have to be. Churcher, however, wasn't about to expose his wounds and beg mercy. He tried some finagling.

He promoted the rumor that an important diamond find had been made in northern Australia. It was reported to be a huge field that could be easily and quite inexpensively mined. What was more, the gem yield percentage was phenomenally high, higher than had ever been gotten out of South Africa or even out of Namibia.

This blessed, bountiful Australian find was, of course, a feint. There was some truth to it. There were diamonds in northern Australia. The System had known that for ages. However, it had also known that the diamonds found there were mainly small and of inferior quality. What Churcher hoped was that all the to-do over the Australian find would flush the Russians, get them to come out and ask the System if it would be so kind as to help market their diamonds. The System would, with perfectly measured reluctance, condescend.

The Soviet Minister of Foreign Trade was Grigori Savich. He didn't take the System's bait. He just nosed around it and eyed it carefully.

Churcher casually extended an invitation to Savich to come to London for a friendly chat.

Savich told Churcher to come to Moscow and talk business.

Churcher went.

The Soviets did not mention how the System had made them pay dearly for diamonds right after the war, but no doubt they kept it in mind. They politely permitted Churcher to say his opening piece about how the System with its years of marketing experience and its established setup could be put to profitable use by the Soviets. That was true, and the Soviets agreed. They were most cordial. They agreed to everything up to the point of terms. When it came to stating terms, Churcher was interrupted by Savich. From Savich's unequivocal tone, Churcher gathered that the Soviets knew the System was negotiating from weakness. He just assumed his soft face and nodded.

The deal was cut. All the way to its small print.

The Russians would from then on supply the System with the diamonds it needed for the world market.

The System was saved. Just a few months short of having to fold.

It was never publicized that the System and the Soviets had become such cozy business bedfellows. That would have been bad for business, especially damaging in the West on the retail level. Why give the men in the United States, for instance, a political excuse for not buying a diamond bauble or two for their lady loves? Instead, the System saw to it that Russian diamonds in general were disparaged, said to be on the small side, to be rather undesirably grayish and difficult to cut because they were brittle. Everyone, even the best-informed diamondaires in the trade, bought the scenario.

The Soviets and the System.

Over the years their secret collaboration prevailed.

Rupert Churcher prevailed.

However, on that Friday afternoon in May in the late 1980s, as Churcher studied himself in the mirror above the commode in his private lavatory off his private office on the fourth floor at 11 Harrowhouse, he had doubts that he would last long enough to get his knighthood. Yesterday the Africans, today the Russians, he mentally complained. It was a dreadful much. Just moments ago he had excused himself and left the three Russians seated in the special boardroom, the smaller, more elegant room normally reserved for when the senior members of the board, such as Sir Hubert Brightman and Sir Nelson Askwith, got together for an insiders' chat. Churcher had excused himself because he'd felt he was on the edge and it was giving way. "Nature calls," he'd said with a casual shrug and taken this breather.

Churcher broke his gaze in the mirror, made his eyes avoid his eyes. He glanced down and was astonished to see his fly undone, a portion of his starched shirttail poking out. He didn't recall having unzipped. Hell, he didn't have to piss. That had only been an excuse. Was his mind that far off? He shook his head as if that might rearrange his thoughts to a more comfortable order. He did up his fly

and decided on a splash of Wellington. Sometimes his spirit
could be lifted by a little thing like that. Wellington from
Trumper's on Curzon Street had for many years been
Churcher's cologne of preference.

He twisted the tiny gold crown-shaped cap from the
cologne bottle. The cap slipped from his fingers, dropped
to the marble floor, and came to rest a few inches to the
left of the base of the toilet bowl. When Churcher bent
down to retrieve it he got a close-up look at that white
porcelain convenience into which he defecated each morning. He took such distasteful proximity as another personal
infliction. Fuck the Wellington. It had betrayed him. He
screwed the cap back on and left the lavatory, went through
his office and down the deeply carpeted main hall to the
special boardroom.

For some reason it was set in his mind that the three
Russians would be exactly as he'd left them. Not fixed like
a tableau but still seated in their places at the oval conference table. He found Grigori Savich and Nikolai Borodin
standing at the window, their backs to the room. The third,
Vadim Vysotsky, was also up; he had the glass-fronted book-
case open and seemed to be mildly amused, perhaps by the
fact that the deckled pages of the well-patined edition of
Thackeray he was thumbing through had never been cut.
Evidently Vysotsky had looked into other things; he'd helped
himself to a Havana from the seventeenth-century carved
ebony box on the sidetable. While Vysotsky puffed away
and nearly obscured his entire head with dense Cuban
smoke, Savich and Borodin were speaking in Russian.

Churcher always felt uneasy when the Russians spoke
Russian in his presence. He had resolved any number of
times to take at the least a conversational course in the
language. However, he knew and was brave enough to use
only a few words and phrases that he'd picked up, such as
skolko, "how many," and *pozhalsta*, "please," and *Ty shto
spizdy sarvalsa*, "Where have you been all my life?"—which
Churcher did not realize translated literally to "Did you just
pop out of a cunt?" From the inflections and gestures in
the exchange between Savich and Borodin, Churcher gath-

ered their topic had something to do with the cityscape as seen from that window. Churcher felt ignored, undeservedly insignificant, as he sat down in the petit-point lap of the seventeenth-century winged armchair. Finally, Savich turned partially and acknowledged Churcher by inquiring: "Where exactly is that statue?"

Churcher knew the statue being referred to, the only one that could be seen from that vantage, a half-dozen streets away. "It's on the top of Old Bailey," he replied.

"Old Bailey?"

"The Criminal Court Building." Churcher welcomed the interest, the diversion. "Newgate Prison used to be on that spot. In fact, most of the granite stones of old Newgate were used in putting up the Criminal Court Building."

"So I've heard," said Savich, dismissing the information. "But the statue . . . Nikolai and I were just agreeing there is something wrong with it."

"Oh?"

"It is not wearing a blindfold."

Churcher got up, went over, and squinted out at the robed figure of Justice standing high up on Old Bailey's oxidized copper dome, sword in one of her hands, scales in the other, right enough, but no blindfold. He'd never noticed that before.

"Unusual, isn't it?" said Borodin, a tinge pointedly. "For your Justice not to be symbolically depicted as impartial?"

A capitulating grunt from Churcher. He went back to his chair.

"I wouldn't take it as indicative," said Savich, and in so saying conveyed the opposite. He resumed his place at the conference table directly across from Churcher. Borodin, appropriately, took the chair to Savich's right. Vysotsky sat apart a bit and away from the table, as witness or mere background.

It occurred to Churcher that the statue thing might have been premeditated, intended to put him on the defensive. That Savich himself was there for this regular monthly meeting did not bode well, he thought. The Soviet Minister of Foreign Trade did not just happen to be in London and come to sit in. Normally, business was done with this Nikolai Borodin fellow. Something was up.

Churcher tried to read Savich. He hadn't been face to face with him for two years, but Savich did not seem older or in any way different. The dossier that the System's Security Section had on Savich was extensive, and perhaps back in a more priggish era it would have been meaningful. That Savich at age sixty-two was still a bachelor and an accomplished womanizer did not discredit. If anything it contributed to the testimony that he was very much the man. Females, from youngsters to matrons, found him appealing, a man who would be a challenge to try to resist. He appeared to have strengths, all the various kinds, inward and outward. There wasn't a hint of stoop to his posture, as though not a single day of his life had ever beaten him. He was tall, thickly built, his head set solidly, rather defiantly, in place. One might say he gave the physical impression of being the kind of man who, if condemned to hang, would dangle and kick for an exceptionally long time. The dark brown pupils of his eyes were ringed by black. His eyes never changed, seemed to constantly present the entire emotional spectrum, depending upon what one searched for in them. The Russian broodiness was, naturally, always evident in that rich brown, as was melancholy. Two of Savich's most striking features were his brows. He allowed them to grow long and bushy, and he trained them so they came to a rather sharp peak. The effect was that he appeared to be raising his brows at everything, not necessarily fault-finding, just effortlessly reacting. They were black brows in match with his straight hair, but his brush mustache was variegated gray.

Grigori Savich did indeed make colorful reading, Churcher thought, momentarily admitting to himself a measure of envy. However, he did not approve of Savich's attire. The least Savich could have done was come in a proper suit. Borodin had. As usual, he'd come in a double-breasted navy worsted, acceptable cream shirt, and appropriate subdued tie. Savich, on the other hand, looked dressed for the country. In, of all things, a brown, large-patterned plaid jacket, hard-finished herringbone brown trousers, blue pin-dot shirt, and brown woven silk tie. A small-figured purple silk square was nonchalantly fluffed out of his breast pocket. It did not matter that the jacket and trousers were of fine cloth and well tailored, and that apparently the shirt was also made to measure. They were an impropriety, an affront. Churcher wished he were in a position to let Savich know how put out he was about this. He smiled a slight, tight-lipped smile.

Silence.

Savich sat forward, apparently to get down to business. He seemed about to speak but then, as though following an impulse, he turned and nodded to Nikolai Borodin, deferring to the younger man.

Nikolai hadn't expected that but was ready for it. Without having to collect his thoughts or hyphenate with a fragment of stammer he went right to it. "Mr. Churcher," he said, "the prices of our rough are being increased five percent."

"You want to increase the amount of rough we handle for you, is that it?" Churcher pretended to have misunderstood while he bettered his balance.

"The *prices* of our rough," Nikolai reiterated.

Churcher didn't flinch. "Five percent, you say."

"Five."

Churcher brought his hands together at chest level, fingertip lightly to fingertip, demonstrating lack of tension. "I can't see how we'd be able to agree with that," he said calmly. "Which category of rough are you talking about, anyway?"

"Across the board," Nikolai told him.

Churcher made a negative mouth and shook his head. "Perhaps there's room for an ever so slight increase in the price of bort, but not on gem-quality. Definitely not on gem-quality. As prices now stand on gem our margin is extremely thin."

"I think you should know that our first inclination was an eight percent increase."

That elevated Churcher's voice a notch. "I'm trying to

tell you the profit's just not there. But don't take my word for it. Go over our accounting figure for figure, see for yourselves."

"Computers make marvelous liars," Savich remarked.

"I beg your pardon," Churcher huffed.

"I'm not insinuating that you would intentionally cheat us." Savich's tone softened his stance just enough.

Nikolai admired, as he had numerous times before, how well Savich could do that.

"I should certainly hope not," Churcher said. "We've been square as a block with you on every carat you've ever placed in our hands."

Nikolai told him, "It was only the spirit of partnership that brought us down from an eight percent increase to five."

Churcher reached to a small silver plate on the table and broke the edge off one of the Carr whole-wheat crackers it contained, little more than a crumb, but it served to occupy his mouth momentarily.

At that moment Nikolai discounted Churcher's stuffiness, his duplicitous ways, and allowed a twinge of compassion for this man who, in this instance, could only squirm and lose. To offset such feelings, another part of Nikolai reminded him of the time before his time when the System had had its knee on Russia's neck.

"Assuming that some small percentage price increase was feasible—just assuming, mind you—when did you see it taking effect?" Churcher asked.

"The first of June."

"You know, I find it hard to believe that you're not more adequately acquainted with the way our business is conducted," Churcher said. "If you were, you'd know that June first, two weeks from now, would be impractical." He went on to explain. "Naturally, we would pass a portion of any increase on to our clients . . ."

Portion was bullshit; *all* would be more like it, Nikolai thought.

". . . and our next sight is set for the sixth of June. Packets have already been made up. Rather than jolting our sightholders with a sudden, unexpected increase, we would, as we have in the past, want to let the prospect of such a thing sink in. Make it appear to be information that has inadvertently leaked out and spread. That would give the industry a chance to predigest the bad news."

"For the June and July sights the System could absorb the increase," Nikolai suggested.

"Out of the question!" Churcher snapped.

"Take it up with your board," Savich advised, punctuating the end of the subject.

Churcher didn't say he would or wouldn't. He fumed silently for a long moment, then pinched his thumb and second finger into his vest pocket and brought out something. Tossed it onto the conference table. A diamond. It bounced a few times as though acrobatically demonstrating its liveliness before coming to rest on the highly polished mahogany surface. Directly in front of Savich. It wasn't a large diamond. Only one carat, but it looked lovely just lying there.

"I'm sure," Churcher said, "you're aware of the close watch we keep on the market. We're sensitive to every movement of any consequence. We know day by day what kind of goods are being sold and in what quantities." Churcher paused to blow his nose into a tissue. He balled up the tissue and deposited it delicately, as though it were something valuable, in the ashtray. He sniffed once and went on: "Off and on over the past year and a half—actually a bit longer—diamonds of this quality have been appearing on the market in unanticipated amounts. One time they turn up in Hong Kong, next in New York. The last large lot came to light in Milan a little over a month ago. It consisted of two thousand pieces, all D-flawless investment-type one-carat stones, perfectly identical."

Nikolai did some swift mental figuring. At present prices a D-flawless one-carat diamond, the standard unit by which the trade set its selling and buying scale, was worth eighteen thousand dollars. Times two thousand pieces came to thirty-six million dollars.

Churcher removed a pair of tweezers and a ten-power

magnifying loupe from a drawer and pushed them across to Savich.

Savich ignored them.

Nikolai took up the tweezers and used them to pick up the diamond, which he examined with the loupe. He saw immediately from the diamond's perfectly proportioned cut, crisp faceting, and clear, icy whiteness that it was typically Siberian. Nikolai had witnessed the electronic cutting and polishing of many such diamonds during his annual mandatory visit to the Aikhal installation last September. "It's ours," he informed Savich in a matter-of-fact tone.

"I've held back calling this to your attention," Churcher said.

"So why bring it up now?" Savich said.

"We avoid such distasteful matters whenever we can."

Sure you do, Nikolai thought, knowing otherwise from his six years of experience dealing with the System.

"We had hoped all it would amount to was a few isolated incidents," Churcher said. "However, it is now apparent to us that a pattern is developing. We want it nipped before it gets more serious."

"A thousand or two extra carats now and then won't rattle the market," Nikolai said.

"We just can't have it," Churcher said emphatically.

"I gather you believe if you got to the bottom of this you would find us."

"Well, they are your goods," Churcher retorted.

"That means nothing," Nikolai contended. "Practically all the goods the market is now cutting are ours. The diamonds you're so concerned with could be from any one of a number of sources. Have you considered that?"

"And dismissed it for good reason," Churcher parried.

Savich came back into it. "Perhaps, Mr. Churcher, instead of sneaking about playing Sherlock Holmes, KGB, or whatever, your security people should review the terms of our pact with you."

"That, Minister Savich, goes both ways," Churcher said with more belligerence than he'd intended.

Savich didn't rise to it. Level-voiced, every syllable

deliberate, he told Churcher: "According to our agreement we retain the right to sell certain quantities of finished gems through our trade organization, Almazjuvelirexport."

Churcher nodded.

"Possibly," Savich continued, "your dislike for that arrangement is so intense that you mentally blank it out."

"Possibly," Churcher said rather than all he wanted to say. He knew for damn certain those two thousand Milan carats and, as well, those other prior mysterious lots that had been marketed in New York and Hong Kong were in excess of the stipulated quota the Russians were supposed to sell through Almazjuvelirexport. The System's figures had been gone over and gone over and were indisputable. Churcher had a summary printout of them back on his desk that he'd planned on having brought in to him today at the proper moment. But now, having assessed Minister Savich's response, especially its manner with its notes of defiance and admonition, Churcher decided it prudent not to carry the matter further. He supposed the Soviets would always be leaping over the boundaries of the System's agreement with them. Whenever they needed a few million they would just dip into their hoard of diamonds and go to market. That was the uncomfortable fact the System would have to bear, being reminded time and time again of its subordinate position.

Fucking Russians, Churcher thought for perhaps the ten thousandth time, as he looked across at Nikolai and then to Savich with what felt like that old, soft, friendly film over his eyes.

CHAPTER
♦♦♦♦ 3 ♦♦♦♦

BUSINESS WITH THE SYSTEM DONE, NIKOLAI AND SAVICH were underway on Clerkenwell Road, being driven in one of the Soviet embassy's black Daimlers. About the only amenity of the embassy that Savich took advantage of whenever he was in London was a car with driver. Rather than stay at the embassy he always occupied a corner suite at Claridge's. The reason he gave was an allergy to some undetermined flowering shrub or tree that grew in the embassy's vicinity in Kensington Palace Gardens, which could hardly have been the case in winter. Savich didn't give a damn that his excuse was transparent, nor was anyone injudicious enough to look through it. He stayed at Claridge's, where he could have comings and goings as he pleased, and while he was there the hotel flew the Soviet flag alongside the Union Jack and others on one of the poles above its main entrance.

Now, with the Daimler stopped at an intersection, Savich appreciated the gaits of two attractive girls who were crossing the wide way. It was a warm and windy afternoon, so the girls' light dresses were being blown against their figures and they were letting their hair fly wild. Savich said: "You handled matters well today, Nikolai."

Nikolai thanked him for the compliment. "Churcher will counter with an offer to agree to a lesser increase, probably three percent," Nikolai said. "He'll claim his board wouldn't hear of anything higher, even though he won't yet have put it to his board."

"You know your man."

Another compliment. Nikolai's cup was running over.

Savich told him: "Churcher will be hoping to settle for four. Three if he can but with four in mind."

"We stay firm on five?"

"Absolutely. Those bastards are way out of character playing poor boy. They've plenty of margin. In a couple of years we'll squeeze them again." Savich worked the electric window control switch situated on his armrest, just fidgeting with it, causing the window on his side to lower about halfway, then abruptly reverse direction and close. "It was a bit surprising today that Churcher took us on alone," he said. "I expected some of his troops. The only reason I had Vysotsky along was so we wouldn't feel too outnumbered."

Savich alone could easily have dealt with a whole roomful of them, Nikolai believed.

"You know," Savich went on, "I thought Churcher looked a bit drawn."

"Really? I suppose that's not as apparent to me because I see him so often."

"How are you spending the weekend?" Savich asked.

"I don't know," Nikolai replied. "I seldom know."

The Daimler was again underway, now close alongside a bus. Savich looked up to a window of the bus and caught the merest glimpse of a pretty passenger. A moment later it occurred to him that she was now forever in his mind but lost, and it saddened him slightly. "Are you still seeing your Vivian?"

Nikolai was mildly surprised that Savich remembered her name, had said it as though it were frequently in his thoughts. Savich had never met Vivian, only knew of her. Nikolai told him, yes, he was still seeing Vivian. He wondered what "seeing" included. "We may drive down to Devon tonight or tomorrow," he said. "Vivian mentioned that possibility earlier in the week, but she may have changed her mind by now." Nikolai, out of politeness, almost inquired about how the minister would be spending his weekend time.

"You like it here in London, don't you, Nikolai?"

"Yes."

"After six years it must be getting to feel like home to you."

"Not like home," Nikolai said, because he thought he'd better and it was somewhat true.

"Keeping the System in hand is no easy task. They're such a slippery bunch. It's good to have someone of your competence on top of them. However, if you want to come home and step up, I'd say you've earned such a request."

Nikolai detected a note of pride in the minister's tone. Was it sincere or was he being nicely told that his time in London was waning? He waited a moment before looking for a hint on Savich's face. Savich was turned away, giving his attention to the sidewalk and an outstanding, well-dressed woman, a handsome British type giving up some of her composure to her desperate need for a taxi. Nikolai believed if he hadn't been along Savich would have ordered the Daimler pulled over so he could offer her rescue. Nikolai also believed the woman, despite her unapproachable air, would have accepted.

Savich continued to gaze out the window, although the Daimler's progress in traffic had taken the woman from his eyes. "What did you make of Churcher's complaint?" he asked.

"The excess diamonds?"

"Yes."

"Well, he brought it up at the right moment."

"Those lots of D-flawless one-caraters he spoke of are in his mind, not on the market."

Nikolai agreed.

"No doubt Churcher will bring up that nonsense again, try to use it as a negotiating point against our increase. The only reason he planted it today was so he'd have it to dig up later."

Nikolai said that he'd be aware of the ploy.

Savich smiled and expressed his confidence with a nod. His eyes held on Nikolai's eyes for a moment, but Nikolai felt incapable of correctly reading them. Possibly he was mistaking fondness for professional respect, and even that might be projection on his part.

The Daimler continued westward through congested London on a route made circuitous by many one-way streets. Finally it was on Brook Street. Nikolai expected he'd have to catch a taxi from Claridge's on, but they passed that hotel, went a block farther, and took a right on Gilbert Street to pull over at the entrance to number 39. Evidently Savich had given the driver instructions earlier.

"Have him take you to your Vivian," Savich said with a rakish grin as he got out. Nikolai watched Savich's brown plaid back go at a sprightly rate up three steps and enter the well-kept limestone-and-brick building. He noticed on one of the varnished oak double doors a polished brass nameplate: Atkins & Pomeroy, Solicitors. What business could Savich have with a London law firm? Nikolai asked himself. The obvious, immediate answer was that it probably wasn't business but a personal visit. For all he knew either Atkins or Pomeroy or both were female.

Nikolai told the driver his destination, and just moments later he was amid the scurry of Park Lane and down among the swirl of Hyde Park Corner and, like something centrifuged, spun off into Halkin Street for, almost instantaneously, the comparative repose of Belgravia. At Belgrave Square he felt his anticipation inflating. Each turn of the Daimler's wheel was a pumping up within him, and although he appeared composed when they reached the little triangular private park of Chesham and turned into Loundes Place, Nikolai had the urge to tell the driver never mind, he would run the rest of the way.

The Daimler stopped at the left curb about midway down the block. Nikolai, despite himself, took his time getting out. He thanked the driver and was left standing there to straighten his double-breasted jacket, tug down his shirt cuffs, and admire an arrangement of vivid rununculas through the window of a nearby flat. He casually surveyed the street in both directions. Not a car in motion on it, all its buildings of a past, fine age, their clean cream and white protected by the ominous black-painted wrought-iron spears of five-foot fences. Nikolai read again the sign on the left of the arch at the entrance to Loundes Close: EXERCISING

OF DOGS PROHIBITED. He always thought the phrasing ex-
emplified British obliquity, for what it meant was not to let
one's dog relieve itself there.

From where he was standing Nikolai knew by heart he
had 134 steps to go. He was through the archway and on
the cobbles of Loundes Close before he spotted Archer's
Silver Spirit Rolls limousine with Paggett, his driver, waiting
in it. The sight of it shortened Nikolai's strides, but then
he realized that and lengthened them, all the way to the
tidy three-story white-trimmed brick house at the end.

He let himself in. With the key she'd given him a year
ago after three torturous and ecstatic months of equivo-
cation. The key of penetrability, she called it. How smoothly
it now turned the bolt. Nikolai closed the door louder than
he would have if Archer's car hadn't been there. He went
up the stairs to the living room and them.

Archer was in an upholstered chair with a long drink.
He transferred the tumbler from his right to his left as he
stood to shake hands with Nikolai and say, "Nice to see
you again, old boy," along with a smile that was supposed
to certify that.

Vivian was pacing, which Nikolai knew was a good sign.
She paused long enough to put a kiss on Nikolai's mouth,
just a good wet smack, possessive in its brevity. She immediately resumed her pacing. Her cat, an oriental silver
tabby named Ninja, followed after her, imitating her every
move, quick about-faces and all, just waiting for when she
sat so that he could claim her lap. Vivian usually paced
when things were going well. When troubled she would
find a corner. Today she was even very suitably dressed
for pacing, in a white silk rather sheathy number that, though
split with shameless confidence very high in front, still
somehow cupped the rounds and undercurve of her buttocks. White calfskin open-sling sandals with four-inch heels
also helped. Not that she needed the height. Barefoot she
was five-ten.

Without missing a pace she opened the flap of the flat
black box she had in hand, undid a crinkle of foil, and
broke off a square of Bendick's military-type chocolate, her

most bitter favorite. She plopped the chocolate into her mouth. As though it were snuff, her tongue positioned it between her cheek and gum, where it would gradually melt while not impeding her speech.

"Nickie, darling!" she exclaimed. "Look what Archer brought me. Isn't it god-sent ugly?"

She didn't have to indicate the three-legged Louis XVI table, it stood so removed both in form and place from everything else in the room. The table was about thirty inches tall and two-thirds that around. Some table. It was as though whoever had made it two hundred or so years ago had saved up all his woodworking and aesthetic errors for this piece. Its legs were too thick, so the Louis curve of them didn't achieve grace. Its feet, covered with ormulu, looked like oversize bootees. Practically every inch of its veneered surface was inflicted with some sort of parquetry or marquetry. Its bombé cabinet part appeared painfully swollen, and perhaps in an attempt to compensate for its lack of beauty, its functions were made tricky: an inset curved door slid open, and its top was apparently hinged to lift up.

Vivian demonstrated the top. "It has to be worth at least thirty," she said, closely examining its interior.

"Forty," Archer estimated with authority.

Kopeks, thought Nikolai, but knew, of course, they were talking about pounds in the thousands. He went to the regular unpedigreed side table that served as a bar and helped himself to a scotch neat from a nearly empty bottle of Glenfiddich. Take it in stride, Nikolai advised himself, and Vivian unknowingly punctuated his thought by letting the Louis XVI table's top slam down.

She began happily pacing again, and so did Ninja.

Pages of that day's newspaper were strewn on the seat of a second upholstered chair, where Nikolai wanted to sit. He started to gather up the paper rather carelessly, but Vivian stopped him, took the pages from him, and folded them just so with the racing section exposed. The fields at various racetracks were marked with a red felt-tip pen, personal meaningful circlings and underlinings and cross-outs and scribbled notations. The sure thing her hopes had ridden on yesterday had run out of the money, Nikolai recalled. He asked what she had going today.

"Gareth rang up around noon," she said, as though that were equal to a call from Prince Charles. "He'd been in a trance since eight this morning, was thoroughly exhausted, but he rang me up as soon as he came out of it to tell me what he'd been given." She paused a beat for emphasis. "Eyesore, a maiden filly in the seventh at Doncaster."

Gareth was her tout. But no ordinary tout. A tout with supernatural connections. He himself was not a punter, merely a sensitive, he claimed. It would be a sin for which he would surely be cut off forever if he wagered on a horse that was "given" to him by the "racing angels," as he referred to his otherworldly informants. It was, however, permissible for Vivian, if she so desired, to bet on his behalf an extra tenner or more on the nag, something she invariably did. When one of Gareth's "given" horses lost, the only explanation he offered was that the racing angels were known to be capricious. They had to have their fun too. Couldn't expect them to always be dead serious, he would say whimsically. There were times, such as a short while ago when a "given" horse had been beaten by twenty-two lengths, that Vivian thought perhaps the racing angels, instead of winging it, ought to take at least a peek at the form.

"What time is it?" she asked.

"Four-thirty," Archer said before Nikolai could.

"The seventh's been run," Vivian thought aloud. "I wish I could ring up and get the results." She couldn't, because in keeping with some divine rule only Gareth could impart the good news. When a horse didn't win he just didn't call.

A couple of times Nikolai had expressed his opinion of Gareth. Vivian defended him, saying that indicated how short Nikolai was on faith. Nikolai didn't tell her how clearly he pictured Gareth choosing a race with a field of only five or six horses entered, then telephoning five or six people such as Vivian and touting each onto a different "given" horse. With a bet placed for him on every horse in the race, Gareth was indeed blessed with a sure thing. Vivian didn't mention it either. She also realized that was a possibility, but it just so happened she was perfect for Gareth's game, as much an avid believer in the supernatural as she was a habitual gambler.

Nikolai watched her mouth another chunk of chocolate bitterness and continue pacing. Her every step was provocative, a parting of the high slit skirt front to reveal her exceptional legs and flash of bare inner thigh. Archer had a slightly better view, Nikolai thought, because his chair was directly in line with Vivian's pacing and her turn was right in front of him, well within mental reach.

"Do you honestly think forty?" Vivian asked with a dubious glance at the three-legged Louis XVI monstrosity.

"At least," Archer replied.

"Well." She sighed, just heavily enough. "I'd love to accept it, Archie, I really would, but, as you can see, it just doesn't suit the rest of my things. If only it were Regence or whatever. Do you think it might by any stretch of taste go well enough in the country?"

"I doubt it," Archer replied too quickly. "If anything it would be worse in the country, don't you think, Nick?"

"Yes," Nikolai replied, his single line.

"Then I guess you'll just have to return it," Vivian told Archer. "Surely they'll refund, or if they're stubborn about that just drop it off and cancel your check. I assume you paid by check."

"Cash," Archer fibbed.

"Where did you buy it?"

"A place on Davies Street. It was part of a shipment just in from Monaco."

"They'll refund," Vivian said.

"Their policy is no refunds. They were quite clear on that."

"Or exchanges?"

"Or exchanges."

"Oh dear," Vivian agonized.

"Hell, just shove it in a corner behind a screen, or put

it in the back of a closet," Archer said. "One thing for certain—I'm not about to suffer the embarrassment of trying to return it, nor am I or Paggett going to lug it down the stairs. It's yours," he said, as though the problem had depleted his patience.

Vivian did a little moan, a wordless compound of despair, resignation, and delight.

Nikolai had once been entertained by such charades, but they had long become too predictable. Each time the same play and characters; perhaps variations of the dialogue, yet always the same ending.

Archer Hamlyn-Howe was Vivian's ex-husband. At age twenty-five she had married him, age thirty-eight. She'd married him right enough, but he hadn't altogether married her. For too many years he had been assessed as a most splendid catch. Too long he'd been an automatic on most of the most-eligible lists, pictured time and again looking Savile Row as all get-out or fortunately yachty or eminently horsey or whatever in the magazines in which his sort of people approved of seeing themselves.

The accompanying caption usually went something like: *Archer Hamlyn-Howe, called Archie by his numerous admirers and well-wishers, schooled at Eton, member of Boodle's and Brooks's, a whiz at tennis, refuses to play bridge, reads Greek for pleasure, an ardent lepidopterist, immensely wealthy, for some time now has been on the lookout for a gratifying professional niche, very choosy when it comes to women, says he'd much rather continue hanging about than risk being disastrously married, spends at least half his time at his twenty-thousand-acre family estate in Devon.*

Such billing spoiled Archer. He became stuck on himself, not in the usual vain sense, but rather stuck in the psychological slosh that no woman worth a damn would want him if it weren't for his having been born, as they say, on the sunny side of the hedge.

If Archer had asked Vivian before their nuptials if she was marrying him for his money he could have saved them both legal bother. He put that to her in the middle of a night in the middle of their second week and she was absolutely forthright about it, told him of course his money had been a potent persuasive factor. Archer said nothing more. He got up, dressed, and went to a bed at one of his clubs.

Vivian had expected him to react more rationally. She'd done right in not sparing him the truth, she thought. Because the truth it was. Archer had happened to her at a time when she was especially tired of having to drag herself out of the cold waters of desperate straits. The stipend she had coming in every month from her trust was not enough, would never be enough, to subsidize her tastes and nature, unless she drastically changed both. Then, she felt, she'd no longer be herself, and that wouldn't do, because she liked herself, she genuinely, thoroughly enjoyed being Vivian Holbert. It seemed to her that living right out on the very edge presented a far more engaging scene. So what if she couldn't keep from gambling, was either mortgaged up to her nose or giving in to some irresistible reason why she should be. She was probably the world's most charming borrower, could smile a checkbook out of the tightest pocket. A half hour after meeting someone she could have him lending. She somehow always managed to repay, a bit late perhaps or only a partial payment, but she was never a deadbeat, took pride in that. Money that came into one hand went instantly out the other, as though the condition of being ahead was painful for her. What was solvency, anyway? Just having couldn't compare with the joy of spending. If ever asked what most gave her life its spirit, Vivian might have thought only a moment before replying: "Improvidence!"

Archer wanted the marriage annulled but was somewhat wounded when Vivian so readily agreed to that. Through his solicitors, Archer offered her a generous settlement. "For the inconvenience" was how the settlement papers put it. She had only to sign to be set for life. Archer was certain she would, but she turned it down. It hadn't, she said, been an inconvenience. As far as she was concerned what had been taken had been given, mutually. They were even.

At that instant Archer began really loving her, wanted to undo all that he had undone, but he was a legal document too late and Vivian wasn't one to retrace steps. She returned to spendthrifting and mortgage juggling, hocking and borrowing with renewed appreciation for such vicissitudes.

Archer never understood her preference for profligacy. Nor did it make sense to him that she wouldn't let him outright help her financially. Levitated by love, he opened substantial bank accounts in her name and had her notified. She didn't refuse them, just put that money out of mind, let it lie fallow. Archer gave up trying to give her money. He also gave up asking her to remarry him. Eventually she would come around, he hoped. Meanwhile he devised an acceptable way to contribute to her well-being.

Every so often, when Archer discerned the pressures on her becoming a bit much, he'd buy her a gift. Such as a precious, though homely, pair of Sèvres Rose Pompadour potpourri vases that had belonged to the infamous Madame la Marquise herself, valued at fifty thousand, or a rare English snaphaunce pistol circa 1590, or an antique silk Isfahan runner that was, dash it all, too long for any of her halls.

Vivian always went through the nicety of declining these "gifts" for one reason or another. Didn't need, wouldn't ever use, couldn't stand the sight of. And Archer always went through his obstinacy, refusing to take back. Thus they arrived at the accommodating impasse, with no recourse but for Vivian to dispose of them—in other words, to sell them.

That was the routine they were now just about getting to the end of with the ugly Louis XVI *petite table de salon*.

"It would be a shame to condemn it to storage," Vivian said. "Don't you agree, Nickie?"

Nikolai had his glass to his mouth, so his yes sounded very hollow.

Vivian closed the subject by moving the little table from its position of attention. "Shall we drive to the country tonight?" she asked the moment more than anyone.

Her cat, Ninja, seemed to understand those words. He brought his slanted green eyes up to her, snaked his black-ringed tail slowly, and mewed just once as though saying, "Let's!"

"If we went down tonight we could rise early and do a bit of fishing," Archer said.

Nikolai told himself he should be used to this "we" by now, and anyway, it wasn't really all that much of an assumption on Archer's part, seeing that Vivian's country cottage was situated in Devon, adjacent to Archer's land.

Vivian tried to forecast what would be her mood tomorrow. She decided fishing would be pleasant. As for tonight, however, if she didn't have so much want for Nikolai, she'd almost wish it were her poker night. With the money from the ugly table imminent she'd be flush enough to pull off some uncanny bluffs.

The telephone rang.

It was Gareth, supernatural tout.

Between her hello and ta to Gareth, Vivian issued only a couple of impassive mmm-huhs. But as soon as she hung up she whirled with her big smile and exclaimed: "The maiden is no longer a maiden! She paid eight to one!"

CHAPTER
❖❖❖ 4 ❖❖❖

THE DECISION WAS MADE IN FAVOR OF GOING TO THE COUN-
try that night, as Archer had suggested. Archer also moved
that they make the trip together in his Rolls. It would be
great fun, he said. They would indulge in a bit of banter
on the way, and besides, Paggett had just yesterday restocked
the bar and if he, Archer, rode alone he would be drinking
alone and that invariably led to his drinking too much.

"Poor Archie," Vivian cooed and went to him, and he
lowered his head to receive her peck of a kiss where his
hairline had once been.

Nikolai wasn't opposed to riding with Archer. He fore-
saw Vivian sitting between them, sharing herself to that
degree, but, after some miles and the effect of a drink and
a half, choosing him to snuggle against.

"I think we should go in two cars," Vivian said.

Archer insisted nicely but he gave in when Vivian closed
her eyes and shook her head, which he knew meant her
mind was unswayably set. He said at least they could follow
each other down. Just in case she had some trouble with
her old Bent was his excuse. Vivian could hardly deny that,
and Archer, having achieved what he felt was his best
possible position in this matter, left to go to his townhouse
on Chester Terrace to sort out a couple of things. He'd be
back in a jiff, he said.

Archer wasn't halfway down the stairs on his way out
before Vivian and Nikolai were into a kiss. Having not
really kissed since the night before they were both feeling
deprived. Vivian embraced with both her arms and all her
strength. In her four-inch heels she was equal in height to

Nikolai, so her pelvic mound didn't have to reach, just press and perform. Her enjoyment was inspired by the fact that it had taken so little of her effort to cause him to become so hard so quickly. With her eyes closed she felt a bit whirly in the head, and when their mouths separated and she stepped back abruptly, she was breathing as if she'd just run up a hill. The space between them represented their quandary.

Should they do it now or later, go at it or wait?

They would double-bolt the door. They would ignore Archer's raps and honks. In the cave of their privacy they would undo, they would feed, feast, layer the air with their wants and havings, and float the intermissions with just some part of each other, perhaps only toes, kept in touch.

But if they did now, as much as they felt, it would take a torturous effort to rise and go around midnight, and although traffic on the road might be lighter then the drive would be reduced to a mere drive, an epilogue rather than a part of it. As well, such intense voluntary holding off was a not unenjoyable sort of torment.

Nikolai removed his tie and unbuttoned the collar of his shirt on his way into her bedroom, where he'd been allocated the top drawer of her dresser. He placed the tie in his drawer and decided against changing completely. He hung his suit jacket in his part of her walk-in closet and found a pair of his loafers among her half-hundred or so pairs of shoes on the floor. She was organized enough with her clothes and other accessories, but her shoes were always a satin, peau de soie, calfskin, suede, patent, and silk brocade scramble. Nikolai used his forefinger in place of a shoehorn to get into his loafers. He put on a cotton knit sweater and was ready. No need to take along a razor, toothbrush, and such. He now kept spares of those there at her place in the country, as well as here.

Vivian in the meantime changed into an easier, amply cut dress of white cotton. She shoved its sleeves up to her elbows, and after considerable grumbling and digging in the closet she surrendered some of her height to a pair of flat, special-heeled Italian driving shoes.

"Better pee now if you have to," she told Nikolai.

He did.

Ninja, know-it-all cat that he was, awaited them downstairs at the front door. They went out to Vivian's Bentley. Ninja, like a child or dog finding satisfaction in being first, jumped up and in. Unlike the average cat, Ninja liked riding in a car. He sometimes stretched out across the top of the facia, dividing his hauteur between the driver, the passenger, and the road ahead. Most times his spot was on the rear window ledge between the stereo speakers, where he wrapped his tail around himself, tucked his head down, and was a black-and-gray furry mass being blasted.

Vivian keyed and started the Bentley, a black sedan which in another year would be out of its teens. The car's three previous owners had gotten the best out of it, and Vivian after the first year of diligent care had become indifferent to its various mechanical ills. The car could burp and shudder, smoke and stall all it wanted, she decided, it would get not one penny more of costly sympathy from her. Evidently, the car had conceded to her attitude, as for the past two years it had been running as if in its prime. She pulled the Bent out to the archway of Loundes Close and let it idle there. Within a minute or two along came Archer in his Rolls-Royce Silver Spirit. Beaming, he waved out at them and lifted his drink in a salute to their fealty, their having waited for him.

A quarter hour later both cars were through with the traffic of London proper and westbound on the M4, the Bent leading the way. Nikolai reached into a cardboard carton in the backseat and got a compact disk, just any one of about thirty that were there, all equally favored. He didn't look at its label, let it be a surprise when he inserted the disk into the player and out came the group Weather Report doing "Corner Pocket." Perfect for the moment: happy, brassy, percussive, honest moving music. He turned the volume up and glanced back at Ninja between the rear speakers. Ninja's ears were twitching in time with the beat and his whiskers were vibrating.

Archer, following at an unsafe distance, had his driver

flick the Rolls's headlights, so as not to be altogether excluded. Each time Nikolai turned and looked back or Vivian
glanced into the rearview mirror, those headlights spoke
brightly for Archer. Nikolai didn't mind, really. Archer was
Archer. Well-meaning, not really over-the-nose, just very
British. He had an irrepressible streak of generosity that
was unusual for a wealthy person. Most of his sort were
penny squeezers. And certainly Nikolai couldn't blame the
man for loving Vivian. That would be like blaming himself.
The only strong criticism he could make was that Archer
had once had her and been fool enough to lose her.

Nikolai reached over and gently slipped his hand beneath Vivian's hair. He knew how much she liked having
the back of her neck touched while she drove. And the
lobes of her ears. She smiled, pleased with him, as his
fingertips moved on her skin. She remained profile to him,
intent on driving.

Nikolai took her in.

He thought how each time she came into his eyes she
brought love, more love. It wasn't, the way he saw it, love
that was only assimilated by him, used like fuel. Rather it
was love that also accumulated, mounted up. Sometimes
it was the sort of love that he could neatly arrange, comfortably compile. More often it was love flooded in, shoved
in, heaped in every which way, so much that he was sure
it surpassed his bursting point.

He was reflective as he looked at her now, recalling
the first time he ever saw her. Even then, in that initial
momentary impression, she must have occupied some of
his emptiness, that space in him that he had, until then,
disregarded, at least never given honest attention to.

On an afternoon a year and four months ago.

At Sotheby's on New Bond Street.

In the high-ceilinged main auction room.

The sale being conducted that day featured Russian
works of art, icons, objects of vertu. Nikolai was there only
as an observer with a personal interest. The atmosphere
of the auction room struck him as solemn, suitable for the
auction itself, which was a sort of capitalistic rite. A few

chairs out of three hundred were vacant, but Nikolai chose to stand at the rear of the room and follow the sale with a catalogue. Colored photographic slides of the auctioned items were projected on a screen. It was all done in a hurry for some reason, perhaps, Nikolai thought, to help spur impetuous extravagance. As for those in attendance, from Nikolai's point of view they were just the backs of so many heads. The auctioneer behind the raised lectern recited the litany of money, while a split second later than his voice the electronic calculator above displayed the pounds sterling of each bid converted into dollars, marks, francs, and yen. A silver-gilt-and-shaded-enamel desk set by Maria Semyenova, circa 1910, was fought over and finally won for six thousand pounds by someone identified only as paddle number fifty-three.

Next came the Fabergé items.

A night-table clock of gold and silver enameled rose pink over a guilloché ground attributed to Fabergé workmaster Michael Perchin, St. Petersburg, 1900. It sold for twenty thousand pounds.

A nephrite-and-diamond imperial presentation box bearing the monogram of Czar Nicholas II, made by Fabergé workmaster Henrik Wigstrom, St. Petersburg, 1900. It went for forty thousand pounds.

A jeweled gold photograph frame surmounted by the Russian imperial eagle, enameled powder blue over a guilloché ground, containing a photo of Empress Alexandra Feodorovna, made by Fabergé workmaster Johan Victor Aarne, St. Petersburg, 1911. It brought twenty-three thousand pounds.

Where he had been perturbed before, Nikolai was now fascinated. He felt affiliated to all these precious things: the card cases, snuffboxes, tiny enameled Easter eggs, stickpins, and other items born out of the old Fabergé workshop.

Lot number 152 was next, the auctioneer announced.

It was the reason Nikolai was there.

The mouse.

The photographic slide of it was projected. A tiny white mouse in a crouching position, perfectly carved out of chalcedony. Its eyes cabochon rubies, its silver ears and tail set with diamonds. The bidding on it began at ten thousand and went rapidly up. "Twelve thousand, thirteen thousand, fourteen thousand," said the auctioneer, his eyes and hand as well as his voice acknowledging the raised paddles, the bidders, left, right, and center. Nikolai was proud. The room felt changed to him now, brighter; the very air of it seemed to contain a familiar old glee. At twenty-five thousand the bidding slowed. Nikolai noticed that down near the front the paddle in the hand on the end of an arm sleeved in lively blue was held insistently, dominantly aloft. Until it was no longer challenged and the auctioneer said, ". . . fair warning . . . thirty-four thousand . . . down it goes at thirty-four thousand," and conclusive as an exclamation point the little block of hardwood that served in place of a mallet in the auctioneer's hand was smacked down sharply.

The woman in blue got up from her chair, sidled out the row, and came down the center aisle. Nikolai immediately saw she was beautiful, and as she came closer he felt even that was an understatement. The way she touched him off, heightened his senses, he was, in only a moment, able to appreciate much of her. Her straight brown hair of a length that just cleared her shoulders was healthily heavy, and moved with her. Her hair parenthesized her strongly structured face and fine features, her complexion of pale olive, her wide-set eyes with an oriental hint to them. She was tall and not embarrassed by it, not at all hunchy.

Nikolai took her to be a wealthy British woman, the thoroughbred sort, most likely the occupant of a certain branch of a branch in the genealogy of some noble tree, Lady somebody. He told himself that it wasn't her beauty that compelled him to follow her out to the corridor. He did have another reason, which had just occurred to him.

He waited for her to finish at the cashier's counter. She would have passed right by him if he hadn't politely intercepted her. He didn't beg her pardon or anything trite as that. "You bought the mouse" were his first words to her.

"Yes," she said warily.

"Would you allow me to see it?"

"It was on exhibition here for three days," she said coolly.

"I missed the exhibitions."

An almost imperceptible lift of her chin told him that was his tough luck, but then, as though suddenly realizing a different path, she warmed a notch to ask: "Are you interested in purchasing it?"

"Might I please have a look at it?"

"Are you by chance a dealer?"

"No."

"A private collector, then."

He smiled at that, and she took it as a positive reply. She removed from her handbag the little hinged maple box that bore the Fabergé stamp on its lid. She opened the box to reveal the carved white chalcedony mouse resting in the creamy silk bed of its exact indented impression. She offered it along with another question. "Are you perhaps a Fabergé expert?"

"Somewhat," Nikolai replied with polite modesty. He very carefully removed the mouse from its box. It was truly tiny, only about an inch and a quarter from nose to tail. He placed the mouse on the flat of his palm and held it at eye level, as though allowing the mouse with its rubies to get a better look at him.

"Possibly," she said, "you'll be kind enough to give me your opinion on its authenticity. You know how it is with Fabergé—so much has been faked, and so nicely faked I might add, that one can't help but be leery."

"What's your opinion?"

"Well, I just put out thirty-four thousand for it, so what I think ought to be evident." She was not quite successful in concealing that she was on unsure ground.

Nikolai took out his ten-power magnifying loupe and examined the mouse. On the underside of its tail, precisely where it should be, he found the Fabergé hallmark, the

Cyrillic initials КФ(KF), and next to that the stamped mark showing the head of a girl in profile wearing the Russian headdress called a *kokoshnik*, which conveyed that the piece was made in St. Petersburg, then the numerals 88 that stood for its silver content of 88 *zolotniki*, close to pure. Last were the Cyrillic letters МБ(MB), the initials identifying the Fabergé workmaster.

"Around three hundred rubles," Nikolai said.

Her breath caught.

"That was how much it sold for originally in 1910," he added.

She exhaled her relief.

"Today it's priceless."

"Well, hardly priceless," she contended. "I just bought it."

Nikolai was glad to tell her: "There is only one other similar Fabergé mouse. A blue one. It's in the private collection of the Queen, in Buckingham Palace."

Later she would tell him that at that point she almost said, "No shit." "Did you bid on it?" she asked.

"No."

"Why not?"

"The way you were bidding I wouldn't have had a chance."

"That's how I am when I want something."

"It's the way most people would like to be. However, it requires the means."

"You really think I bullied the bidding?" she asked with a slight smug grin.

"Entirely."

"Well, in truth I'm more of a sport than a bully. To prove it, tell you what—I'll let you have the mouse right now for forty thousand."

He pretended to be giving that consideration. Actually, he was thinking how long they'd been standing there. She had time to squander, maybe, but not to waste.

"I've been trying to place your accent," she said, "and I hope you don't mind my saying it, but the best I can

come up with is that you're an American with an affecta-
tion."

He told her his name.

She didn't reciprocate with hers. She said his name
aloud as though to test the ring of it. "Borodin? The same
as the composer?"

"He was my great-great-uncle."

"Then you're Russian. I must say I never would have
guessed." And then without hesitation, running right along
as though it were a continuation of the sentence, she asked:
"What do you say to forty thousand?"

He was tempted to tell her that her margin of six
thousand was not appropriate to the swiftness of the turn-
over. But before he could say anything she wanted to know
the time and he was sure next she would say she was late
for an appointment and hurry off, leaving him completely
at a loss. He wouldn't let that happen, he told himself.
He'd stalk after her, watch where she went, follow her all
the way into the night, act the absolute fool. "Five minutes
to four," he told her.

"I thought so," she said. "I've got the growls."

They had tea at Brown's, which was close by. "Brown's
serves a nice not stratospheric but rather high tea," she
said. Nikolai doubted that he'd ever get used to English
tea. For one thing it was drunk from a cup or mug rather
than a glass, and some people diluted it with milk or cream
and further ruined it with sugar. Like most Russians he
preferred straight, strong tea. Nevertheless, there he sat
with her in a cozy banquette at Brown's, traitor to his palate,
having what he believed was the finest tea he'd ever tasted.

It wasn't until she requested the waiter to bring another
hot, fresh pot and more cakes that she gave up trying to
sell Nikolai the mouse. And it wasn't until she'd returned
from her only trip to the powder room (later she would
tell him she'd gone in only for the mirror, to take measure
of the libido in her eyes) that she confided it was necessary
for her to sell it. By then, she had Nikolai so entranced
he couldn't think it ridiculous or even odd that she'd given
Sotheby's a check that far exceeded the amount she had in

her account at her branch of Barclays. He wondered why Sotheby's would so readily accept so large a check from her. He asked her about that.

"They always do," she said, and from that Nikolai gathered this was not a unique predicament for her.

"Not to be concerned," she told him. "I know someone who, in a breath, will buy it for forty."

"So you were speculating—saw the chance to make a profit and jumped at it."

She indicated the tip of her little finger. "Only about this much of my motive was profit. I simply wanted it, had to have it if only for a short while. The other Fabergé things were lovely, but this mouse just won me."

Perfect words. They called for Nikolai to tell her: "It was made by my grandfather."

"He was a Fabergé?"

"He was Maksim Bemechev, a workmaster *for* Fabergé in St. Petersburg during the early nineteen hundreds."

"What is a workmaster? I can imagine, but tell me."

"Someone highly accomplished, an expert, a maestro. Fabergé had hundreds of workers and specialists, many fine goldsmiths, silversmiths, and other craftsmen, but only a few workmasters. The designation was not easy to come by." Nikolai enjoyed explaining it to her. "I remember my Grandfather Maksim telling me about this mouse, how making it was such a pleasure for him."

Her eyes had gone shinier, Nikolai noticed. Even in the subdued light of the room they had wet glints. (Later she would tell him that knowing he'd taken time to go to Sotheby's to pay homage to his grandfather had greatly moved her.)

"Today at Sotheby's," he went on, "while you and the others were bidding I could almost sense my grandfather's presence. I suppose you think that's strange."

"Quite the contrary."

"I had the feeling that he was flying and hovering around."

"He probably was." She smiled knowingly and forked up to her mouth much more than a morsel of walnut spice cake. While she chewed and after she swallowed her eyes kept on him. She was guessing his age at thirty-six, which turned out to be a year short, and allowing herself to feel the effectiveness of his dark, thickly lashed eyes, black-outlined pupils. (Later she would tell him that was what she was doing and how also it was then that she'd realized how much boy there was still left in him, in appealing contrast to his maturity.)

He didn't spoil the moment with words.

Finally she broke it, asked: "Are you a Russian emigré?"

"No. My home is Leningrad."

"It's just that you seem so Western. At least you're not my idea of a Russian. Where did you learn to speak such excellent English?"

"I started studying English when I was seven."

"Are you terribly political?" Hoping not.

"No, but I am a Communist."

"I suppose in a way that's like belonging to a club."

He nodded. "It's also as much of a requirement as being able to speak English."

"Nosy me, but how do you earn your living?"

"I'm with a Soviet trade mission here in London."

"Trading what?"

Normally Nikolai avoided answering that question or answered it vaguely. This time, however, he thought it might be to his credit and he was hoping to impress her as much as he could. "Diamonds," he said casually.

She wasn't impressed, told him: "I much prefer rubies and sapphires."

The earclips she had on were sapphires, cabochons of about ten carats each. Nikolai had gotten glimpses of them whenever her hair swished back enough. He commented on their fine quality.

She wasn't in the mood for fibbing. "They're synthetics," she said.

"Safer to wear fakes these days."

'She disagreed. "A mugger wouldn't know they were fakes. He'd knock you on the head and be disappointed after." Then again, in that way she had of changing subjects in the same breath, she asked: "Do you travel back and forth from Russia?"

"Most of the time I'm here in London. I keep a place here."

"Whereabouts here?"

"South Kensington off Cromwell Road."

"No doubt you've got it decorated with old Catherine the Great hand-me-downs."

"It's a furnished studio flat, a walk-up on the seventh floor."

"How aerobic."

"An unsuccessful artist lived there until he died."

"Of exhaustion, no doubt. I suppose by the time a person climbs up to your digs she's all the more eager to lie down."

"A few have made it to the fifth."

"And those most promising you gallantly carried up the rest of the way."

"*That* has yet to happen."

"I'd rather believe it has, and I don't want to hear about it." She burlesqued jealousy.

He wished she honestly felt it. How quickly his outlook had shifted, he thought. It was now impossible for him to see beyond her.

"Anyway," she went on, "one would think Mother Russia would do better by you than a seventh-floor cubbyhole." She said it as though if Mother Russia had been there she would have vehemently denounced the slight. She paused and appraised Nikolai's appearance, down and up. "I must say from your appearance I would have thought a roomy maisonette in Mayfair or at the very least something airy in Knightsbridge . . . with a lift, of course. It's quite misleading, you know. Are you by chance a showcase Russian?"

"To some extent."

"Well, I daresay they made an excellent choice."

A somewhat backhanded compliment; nevertheless, it was precious fuel. He cautioned himself to take care— everything he said would be crucial. "It's now mandatory that we make a better impression," he told her. "No more lifelong suits or ten-year shoes, if you know what I mean."

"I like your tie," she said. "A man's tie says a lot about him."

"Oh?"

"And even more revealing is the way he knots it."

Nikolai was thinking ahead, so he only half-heard her. As well he was caught up with watching her lips in motion, enjoying glimpses of her tongue, flashes of her perfect teeth when she said certain words and with each smile.

"For instance," she confided seriously, "a loose sloppy knot gives away a man who lacks conviction. A knot too tight exposes a self-strangler, someone afraid of letting his inside out." Her fingers reached over and assessed the knot of Nikolai's tie with a couple of squeezes. "A firm four-in-hand," she declared.

"What does that tell you about me?"

"Plenty," she evaded archly.

"Actually, I prefer no tie."

"Or socks? Are you one of those? Did you know the Duke of Windsor disliked having to wear socks? I understand he embarrassed Wally countless times. There he'd be dressed to the nines with his bony ankles showing."

"You seem to be all wrapped up in clothes."

"Not always," she said with precise wickedness.

A short while after that she became less talkative, not withdrawn but just allowing her near-silence to draw him out. She seemed earnestly interested, didn't hang on his every word but most of the while kept eye contact. She also crossed and recrossed her legs quite a lot. (Two months later she told him that was a phrase of her body language which communicated, both to herself and to anyone who knew, erotic arousal.)

Nikolai wanted her to know him. If it had been possible he would have opened his head and his heart and poured himself into her all at once. He told her about his Leningrad, told her the closest relatives he had were some distant cousins in Tallin, told her about his longtime friend Lev, told her about his position with the trade mission and how if he somehow avoided all the many ways of committing vocational suicide he stood a chance of getting to be a deputy minister of trade, told her some of the privileges that went along with that level—not money, privileges. He touched upon cross-country skiing, which he missed being able to do, and also on gathering mushrooms. And she was the first ever that he told about the time he'd spent in his secret room in the palace of Prince Menshikov.

All that he learned about her during that long tea at Brown's was her name, her divorced status, and a few light opinions.

However, the following evening during and after dinner at an unpredictable but reasonably priced northern Italian restaurant on Sloane Street, which she considerately insisted was her favorite, she let him really meet her. For instance:

"Years ago I had a shop on Fulham Road," she said, "a small, sort of squeezed-between place that I fixed up and made appear inviting. I put quite a bit of hope into it, properly crowded it with nice old things: consoles, pairs of chairs, some ancestral portraits that weren't all that unattractive, an armoire or two. No clutter, though—no china figurines with kissy-kissy lips and vulnerable fingers, no preserved ostrich eggs or little bare-assed bronzes. And perhaps that was my mistake. I guess people like things they can pick up and therefore feel instantly attached to.

"Not that the shop was drab. I always had an enormous bouquet of cut flowers, and there were some good leather bindings placed about. Anyway, there I sat imagining big spenders on their way, about to arrive any moment. It was a different kind of loneliness, hour after hour of anonymous rejection. When people finally did come in to browse I think what most irritated me was their asking, 'What's the best you can do on this?'—as though my price wasn't fair in the first place. It's a question I've never asked in my entire life, never shall. I tried not to, but at times I got somewhat snippy about it."

"Then one miserable raining November afternoon I was at the shop sorting and folding some antique bed linens that I'd managed to practically steal at an estate sale in

Sussex. Very fine sheets and shams with intricately embroidered monograms and handworked hems. They were the kind much in demand and I was delighted with having gotten them, stood to make a bundle. Well . . ."

The memory deserved a pause and a resigned sigh. "I got to thinking about all the loving that had been done on those sheets and things, and for a while there I enjoyed some quite vivid fancies, I must say. But then, all at once, the damn things turned on me. I couldn't help but imagine the arguments and the pains and the deaths they had known, and quick as that down on me came a terrible funk, a veritable deluge of depression. Possibly it might not have been the sheets and shams that caused it, but at the least they opened the floodgates. Within minutes I was out of there. I left in such a hurry I forgot to lock up, had to go back to do that."

"What happened to the shop?" Nikolai asked.

"A swift, sacrificial sale. I sold everything but the paint on the walls, allowed myself to be financially raped by some of the scroungiest dealers in town. And that was that." Vivian smiled the sort of smile that stopped Nikolai from expressing sympathy.

With prompting single words, grunts and mmms, he kept her talking about herself. He was infatuated with the quality of her voice. It suited her, unique her, had a natural huskiness, was a bit gravelly, especially on some words.

"One ought to do what one is best at," she said. "After the Fulham Road shop debacle I asked myself what it was I excelled at, and quite obviously the answer was *spending*. So, I took up that for a living. Arranged with the Connaught and the Berkeley and a couple of the other better hotels to show any of their guests where and how to spend. Most of my clients were bored wives far more interested in the offerings of New Bond Street than those of the British Museum. It never went as well as I thought it would. Simply because *I* wasn't doing the spending. To be perfectly honest, it was rather excruciating for me."

To go with a sweet, some vintage port. The restaurant tried to pawn off some that was much too young, representing it as a 1968. Nikolai didn't let them get away with it, asked for the bottle it had been poured from, which was true enough, but had been filled and refilled dozens of times. Nikolai made the waiter bring a fresh bottle and open it at the table, a W & J Graham Finest Reserve 1969. "Port has to be at least seventeen years old," Nikolai said. (Vivian commented after several other such occasions that his restaurant deportment was a surprising plus. She doubted there was a maître d' or headwaiter alive who could out-savoir-faire him.)

"Then there was Christie's, the auction house," Vivian went on. I worked there for a while, even took several of their training courses in recognizing the finer things, as though I weren't already marvelous at that. During the important auctions, I was one of those assigned to a telephone. Certain people make all their bids by phone."

"Why?" Just to keep her going.

"Oh, perhaps they're laid up with something or someone or think their face is too famous to be in public. Whatever. Anyway, picture, if you can, me with a phone to my ear having to do someone's bidding. It was rather hectic and not at all fulfilling. I found out how much it wasn't for me soon enough. During an auction of important Chinese ceramics I became so caught up in the spirit of the bidding on a Tang Dynasty female figure that I completely forgot about the person I had on my line. Went bidding on my own above the hundred-thousand level. I swear, I was only vaguely aware of the person's voice cursing and shouting at me to stop. Fortunately, I came to my senses just short of the one hundred twenty-five thousand the piece went for. A complaint must have been registered, because the following day I was given notice." She laughed at the recollection and took a sip of the port.

Nikolai watched her tongue. Just the perfect pink tip of it emerged and licked taste from her lips. (Later, at an appropriate moment, she told him she was aware of how much of his attention was focused on her mouth.)

She let him know many things that night. She let him know she was an incurable gambler and said that even if someone came up with a remedy she'd refuse to take it. She didn't keep written records, just a running account in her head, and she figured she was as much of a winner as she was a loser. She claimed that whenever she lost she did so with quiet grace. (Nikolai later learned how untrue that was. She always had a supply of ugly vases and odd plates that she could smash to vent her loser's spleen.)

She let him know that she owned two houses. One there in London, a flat, really, with a seventy-five-year crown lease that she herself had bought, and one down in Devon that had been left to her. Both, she admitted insouciantly, were mortgaged up to their chimneys, but the men who counted at the bank evidently liked the looks of her, were understanding, didn't press, just politely reminded her when she got a few mortgage installments in arrears. She'd perish, she said, if ever she lost her place in Devon. The mere thought of that possibility gave her the willies. Her place in Devon was her soul.

"I wish I could pay off all your mortgages," Nikolai said.

"Do you?"

"Yes."

"Can you?"

"No."

"Don't fret. I'd just mortgage them again," she said, not having to do any inner appraising to know that was exactly what would happen. "But it's comforting to know your nice thought." She laced her fingers with Nikolai's for the first time.

Suspended from a long, delicate chain around her neck was a platinum-framed monocle about an inch and a half in diameter. Nikolai had noticed it the day before, and here she was wearing it again. He asked about it.

"It's a magnifier, not a monocle, but I call it a monocle," she said. "It magnifies ten times."

Like a loupe, Nikolai surmised. "For looking at jewelry?"

"Eyes," she said, just the one word to see how that would strike him.

He was appropriately puzzled.

"Iridology is something I became interested in years ago, and now I'm really good at it," she said.

"Iridology," he repeated with a knowing nod. He'd never heard of it.

She assumed he hadn't. "By looking closely at the irises of a person's eyes I can determine his well-being, or, if you will, his ill-being. I can tell the state of his liver as well as his libido. Are you open-minded?"

"I'd say yes."

"Because with me you're going to have to be."

Nikolai liked the future that promised.

"Let me have a look at you," she said, bringing the monocle up to her right eye. She moved in with it to his left eye. She was so close he could feel her breath against his cheek and distinguish the personal fragrance of her skin from that of her perfume. She examined the irises of his eyes a full minute before telling him: "You're bothered by one of your knees—the right one."

That was true. When he was fifteen he'd seriously injured the ligaments of his right knee while cross-country skiing with Lev. He would never have made it back to the dacha if Lev hadn't practically carried him. Even now if he happened to step off a curb wrong that knee gave way.

"Keep looking straight ahead," Vivian instructed. "Focus on one spot." After another long moment she told him: "You've got the beginnings of a sodium ring. Too much salt intake. You'll have to watch the salt." She continued examining. "You're also a bit of a kink sexually." She sat back and allowed the monocle to dangle.

Nikolai admitted to having a salt habit and a problem right knee. He told her she was uncanny.

"I could have told you much more about you, and perhaps I shall another time. People can't take too much of themselves in one dose. You know, I'm always leery when irises have dark browns. It's a sure sign of madness or inner destruction of some sort. However, your iris pigment is genetic brown, isn't it?"

"You're questioning my sanity?"

"What color were Grigori Yefimovich Novykh's irises, I wonder?"

Nikolai was astounded. Not one out of a million non-Russians would know Rasputin's real name. As for Rasputin's eyes, Nikolai had no idea what color they had been.

"I'll wager they were brown," Vivian said. "Many brown-eyed people, particularly those who aren't swarthy, aren't brown eyed at all but are suffering internally from the accumulated sins of their forefathers."

"You believe that?"

"No. I think it's just rot." Then, without a beat: *"Are you kinky?"*

Nikolai thought it best not to reply, certainly not to deny. He let a sidelong gaze, which he hoped came across as enigmatic, speak for him. (Later on in their relationship Vivian mentioned to him that during his gaze she was not only trying to read his mind but also sorting through a myriad of marvelous possibilities, and some that were a bit scary.)

Nikolai, being Russian, didn't consider the idea of iridology all that farfetched. It was his nature to put a certain amount of stock in anything mystical, or at least not to close his mind so tight that it couldn't admit possibility. Neither he nor anyone else knew anything absolute, he reasoned. Hadn't they once burned people at the stake for believing the earth went around the sun? So what if Vivian claimed she could tell about a person by looking at his eyes? That didn't make her crazy. If anything, it made her more interesting.

She explained, as though fed up with having to explain it, the fundamental premise of iridology. "Certain areas of the iris correlate with certain parts and organs of a person's body, as well as to his psychological condition. Discolorations are the clues." She wasn't in the mood for more iridology, so before Nikolai could get out a question about it she changed the subject, letting him know how much of a mystical maze he was getting himself into. Divining, magic mirrors, the casting of spells, numerology, phrenology, the throwing of rune stones, and Reiki healing were but a few of the practices in her repertoire. She believed in astral excursions, walk-in souls, specialized angels. She believed in all sorts of life: life after death, life before conception, and something she called life scheduling, which, as Nikolai understood it, was a kind of timetable that everything went by. Their meeting, for example, had been pre-intended, she said.

"Karmic," he put in.

She was brightly surprised that he knew the term. It was reassuring, it inspired her to open another level. She was on her own, she told him, had no family other than a father somewhere in France whom she didn't think of as family. She'd never seen her father, not even a photograph, although she had composed a mental picture of him from the few comments her mother had made. She had been a wanted child in the truest sense, wanted without having to endure all the intolerances, personal invasions, and other drawbacks of marriage. Vivian had never thought of that as cynical; rather, the way she saw it her mother had just been way ahead of her time. Her mother had selected, according to certain criteria, a man to have a child by. She'd entered into an arrangement with him. As soon as that had been accomplished, *adieu*—no *tout à l'heure* or *à bientôt*.

"What kind of arrangement?"

"Not a venal one," Vivian was quick to say. "I can't be sure, but I don't want to think it was for mere money. More likely it was done purely for the pleasure of it. Must have been," she said, grinning, sitting up and presenting herself, "considering the product."

"Where is your mother now?"

"On the other side," Vivian replied matter-of-factly, as though she meant nothing more than the other side of town. She went on to tell him that come September it would be five years since her mother had drowned. While swimming in a lake in Scotland. Far out in the lake. Wide, deep lake. It was September. The water cold. One moment Mother's bright green bathing cap was out there bobbing like a child's playball, the next it was gone. "Drowning isn't supposed to be a painful experience. They say it's one of the better ways to pass over." Vivian smiled, but it was not her completely genuine smile, and Nikolai knew the recollection had come from a private, hurt place in her, and he felt privileged. "Mother and I have chats," she said. "We discuss everything from poker to peignoirs. You think I'm daft?"

"No."

"That's good, because last night you were our topic."

"What did she have to say?"

"Not to tell you what she said." Vivian playfully overworked her eyelashes. "But of course that was only to make sure I would."

"Well?"

"Mother's word was that you're one of the last of the credible romantics and that if I placed any value on my independence I should take the nearest escape route. Now, is that just spiritual gossip, mother worry, or God's truth?"

"Probably all three."

They didn't make love that night. From the restaurant they walked up to Kensington High Street and Kensington Gardens and on across Hyde Park. Slow, lovers-type walking. They didn't mind it was somewhat chilly. That only pressed them together, allied them all the more. At Stanhope Gate they stopped as though the spot were marked and had their first kiss. A good long discovering one. They kissed again several times along the way, were both adequately stirred but talked themselves sleepy.

The next night, however, for four of their hours together in her bed they hardly said a word.

"Oh, by the way," Vivian mumbled while under the influence of thorough contentment. "I sold the mouse today. For forty-five thousand."

Vivian and Nikolai.

That was the start of them.

Now here they were on the M4 with London ninety-two miles behind them. And Archer too. Archer's driver had closed the gap so the Rolls was almost touching their bumper. Vivian held the Bentley steady at fifty. She was in no hurry. She raised her hand and acknowledged Archer by wiggling her fingers, which must have pleased him, because the lights of the Rolls clicked on bright three times in rapid succession.

Ninja was now in Vivian's lap, his place of honor. Dead weight, head tucked down, he was purring loudly in case anyone doubted his comfort. Nikolai appreciated Vivian's profile in the low light coming from the instrument panel. The upward, greenish cast of it made her look like a lovely witch, he thought. He'd been having a "Russian conversation," that is, silently talking to himself. He randomly selected another compact disk and inserted it into the player. Then he resumed his gentle fondling of the back of Vivian's neck and kneading of that area her neck and shoulders shared. Such attention could be his full-time responsibility, as she never got enough.

"You can touch me," she said, shooing Ninja to the rear seat.

Nikolai understood. To eliminate any suggestion of service rendered on demand he continued on her neck. He hoped she would get impatient, and perhaps she did, because she shook her head, two brisk snaps that caused her straight heavy hair to swing and whip the back of his hand. Obediently, his hand went to her left ear, fingered lightly the little crescent-shaped alcove where it was attached. The skin on the back of her ear was sensitive when correctly touched, so he gave ample attention to it, and to the lobe. The lobe was warm, engorged, and became warmer when he rolled it between his thumb and first finger and surprised it with one sharp pinch. He gave, altogether, five of their miles to her ear, tracing the distinctive convolutions of it, threatening at any moment to invade its tiny cave wherein her thoughts would lie, treasures.

The next five miles he gave to her throat, stroking it ever so slowly, lightly, from her chin down to the indent between her collarbones, then up to her chin again. When she thought he would stop, he continued. His fingers felt her swallow, and as they followed a swallow down, Nikolai's imagination took it as a promise, and he, the stirrer, was himself stirred.

Her arm. With the sleeve of her dress pushed up to her elbow, only her forearm was exposed. She helped. She unbuttoned the front of her dress four down, which allowed her to pull her arm out of the sleeve so her shoulder and entire arm was bare and one breast accessible. She continued to drive with both hands on the steering wheel while he loved her arm. Ran the length of it from shoulder to wrist with his touch. He knew her, had learned her, knew the exceptional sensitivity of the flesh over her pulse and inner forearm. Those places were pleased most by delicate touchings. The fold of her arm also called for that, as did the underside of her upper arm. He did not slight an inch.

His touch. The quality of it astounded her, had from the first, still did. His hands seemed to know instinctively the requirements of her various parts, even when her parts changed their desires. There was never any fumbling or hesitancy. When, for instance, she wanted feathery, he, without being asked, provided feathery. More pressure wanted, more pressure given. It seemed that she merely had to think the rhythm of a stroke slower to have him do slower.

Where, Vivian wondered, was the usual guesswork of it—in fact, both the guessing and the work? Shouldn't she suspect his experience? How many were the many girls and women who must have preceded her? Had they taught him? It was a bit much to accept that it was just his nature or the way he affected her.

One possible explanation that came to Vivian was that Nikolai had been she in a past life. That would account for his knowing her body and sexual psyche as though it were his own, his ability to anticipate her wants. It would also explain why often when they were making love she felt as though it were she who was doing the penetrating, their roles reversed by sensation. Whatever, be it chemistry, the spiritual residue of past lives, or what, her Nickie was a more accomplished, veritable all-round lover than she'd ever imagined would come her way. She was surely indebted to the angels responsible for that.

Nikolai gave seven miles of attention to her arm and at least four to her hand, its ticklish palm skin and crotches. Seven more to her breast, which his fingertips ran circles around, causing the areola to swell, the nipple to come out and beg.

By then the multilaned monotony of the M4 had brought them to its exit outside Bristol. Vivian executed the minor complications of the roundabout and put the Bentley on the M5 headed south.

Archer's Rolls had fallen back some at the roundabout but immediately made up. Nikolai thought how glad he was that Vivian had declined Archer's offer to have a phone installed in the Bentley. What if she hadn't? Would she be in transmission with Archer every mile of the way, chatting on about anything, indulging the distraction? She wouldn't, Nikolai told himself.

The compact disk that was now playing was the group Berlin's rendition of "Take My Breath Away." Not new but still one of Vivian's favorites. There had been other playings of it when it had been just as apropos as now with Nikolai's touch on the underside of Vivian's knee. His touch defined her tendons and the tension of them caused by her foot's pressure on the accelerator pedal. His touch became a fluttering which became light scratching along the top of her thigh, traveling up her thigh so slowly its progress was nearly imperceptible. He gave fifteen of their miles to her thigh, and again she helped. Her other foot took over the accelerator pedal, so the first foot was free to be placed up on the carpeted hump that housed the driveshaft. That leg was arched now and relaxed to the side, and she was that much spread.

The tips of his fingers ran down her inner thigh like some tiny, soft-pawed creature reveling, advancing just a fraction short of the elasticized hem of her cotton panties, pausing as though indecisive about direction, then retreating up and over her knee and on down to the curve of her calf. Again and again. Every so often he removed his touch.

Every so often he firmly stroked the finer flesh of her inner thigh. And every so often he burrowed a finger in under the elasticized hem to hide it, perfectly still, in her dark floss.

Take my breath away.
Take my breath away.

From behind Ninja gave them each an indifferent stare, blinked as though to dematerialize them, and turned away.

Vivian lowered the raised leg on the pretense of stretching it but really to express her prerogative. She soon arched it up again and Nikolai resumed with little finger nips, which were lovingly chastizing and what she had expected. Helping again, her hand captured his and led it to the mound of her, forced his hand to cup. Her hand pressed upon the back of his, her fingers matched and pressed his instructively. The cotton fabric at her crotch was moist, slicked through. She left his hand on its own to perform its touching tricks, its nibblings, rotations, strokings, and perfectly placed tattooings. She had to force her eyes to remain open. When she glanced at the speedometer she was surprised to see the indicator at eighty.

Exit 27 was the Tiverton turnoff.

Thirteen miles to go.

The arousal point of irreality had been reached, and it was not because the road under them now was much less of a road that Vivian now felt the wheels of the Bentley were gliding along rather than turning and the nighttime Devon countryside seemed to be being pulled past in the opposite direction. Urgency was in her now. And in Nikolai. They sped through the town of Tiverton and seven miles farther on turned with a skid onto a lesser road for the village of Pennymoor. There, at a fork, Archer's Rolls double-honked a good night and went its lonely way. A few minutes later Vivian turned in at her drive, where a familiar forsythia hedge welcomed them with the brush of its branch tips.

A light was on in the attached caretaker's quarters.

Tigley, the caretaker, had heard the crunch of the gravel on the drive and was already on his way out. "Evening, miss. Will there be any baggage?"

"No, Tigley, thank you, no baggage."

"Anything you'll be wanting?" Tigley asked.

Vivian's no came out feeling like a lie. "Good night, Tigley," she dismissed him politely and entered the house with Nikolai following. No need to turn on a light. They both knew the house well enough. In the entrance hall she told Nikolai, "You go on up." She went through to the kitchen. Her mouth was extremely dry from so many caught and held breaths. The little light of the stove showed her a bowl of oranges on the kitchen table. She grabbed one up and bit a chunk from the stem end of it. She disposed of that and held the orange to her mouth, squeezed it and sucked juice from it on her way up to the second-floor landing and on to her bedroom. Nikolai had known better than to turn on a light there. She held the orange clamped between her teeth while she undressed, removed her clothes as though they were despicable impairments, toed her shoes off and sent them flying anywhere, dropped her dress into a rumple that circled her bare feet, peeled off and kicked away her panties.

Nikolai, meanwhile, had only removed his sweater. His delay served her, gave her time to convey to him what her preference was this night. She remained standing, waiting beside the bed, and he believed he knew.

He tortured her nicely with dallying, took his time getting out of his clothes, folded them and hung them and even tucked his socks neatly into his loafers, which he paired and placed just so beside a chair. He was excited hard, which, of course, was a very visible contradiction to his unhurried disrobing. For him there was always a degree of self-consciousness, rather than the macho pride that might be imagined, in being hard and fully extended while standing, in having his arousal be so obvious. He assumed there were men who would strut around the room with their hardness sticking out and up, but that was not him. It wasn't a matter of shame for him, merely a feeling of awkwardness, and that would leave him as soon as she came over and pressed herself against it or took it in her hand or into her mouth. But she wouldn't this night. Nikolai hadn't expected her to. He followed his erotic intuition, went to her large bed, and situated himself face up in the middle of it. He lay with his arms angled out from his body, his legs well spread.

She knelt up beside him on the bed. Nikolai could not see her eyes, silhouetted as she was against the ceiling, but he imagined them. She was determining her desire, he thought. Several other similar times she had been unable to put off the utmost sensation of his mouth and had gone right to it. Not tonight.

She began with his leg. Swung a leg over to straddle it without yet touching. After a moment she lowered her self exactly to his skin. She was distended, puffed apart, split and sopping from prolonged arousal. She moved slightly side to side to fit as entirely as possible on him. She rocked back and forth and then ran herself the length of his leg several times, lightly, slickly, never giving up contact, and then his other leg, and then, in the same manner, his arms one after another from his biceps to his fingers.

Nikolai had difficulty keeping his fingers still, they wanted so to grasp, invade, not merely allow. For control he tried to project his imaginary point of view to a reasonable vantage above the bed from where, like a nonparticipant, he might merely observe.

Vivian's first coming was almost immediate. Nikolai knew by the quickening of her stroke on his leg and her crushing press. Her face descended suddenly, as though falling from a great height, upon his, unable to miss his mouth. There was the flavor and burn of the oil from the skin of the orange on her lips. When she was able, when she had convulsed every twinge of sensation from that coming, she knelt again, straddled, and continued.

She was like a cat distributing its pheromones, claiming her territory, which was all of him. The atmosphere of the bedroom became layered with her natural, personal fragrance. Nikolai luxuriated in it, breathed it deep, thought of it as particles of love that would remain in him forever.

Vivian helped herself to her fourth that night with her knees like a vise left and right of his head. What joy to be so used by her, Nikolai thought. What pleasure to comply! He became lost in it, as did she, and for them there was no longer a world or country or house or room. Only the environment of their sensations.

"Ya tebya lyublyu!" she gasped. It was the first time she'd said it in Russian. Saying it in Russian felt the same. She'd picked it up from the many times Nikolai had said it to her.

"Ya tebya lyublyu." I love you.

CHAPTER
◆·◆·◆ ◆·◆·◆
5

The killer placed his hand on the shoulder of the empty chair. He'd been sitting alone in the Café de l'Europa for almost an hour. He seemed to be waiting for someone, but he was being sure and patient about it. His back was to the entrance, and not once had he turned to look that way.

From his appearance he would most likely be taken for a farmer. Come into the city for a Friday night. He had the chest, shoulders, and neck of a farmer, thick from hauling and heaving. A grower of hops from Duba or Trsice? That would have been a close guess. The identification he was carrying this time, made to look old, gave his address as a rural one in Ustek, which was a town sixty kilometers to the north in the hops-growing region. Consistent with the impression was the way he had decided to dress. In a farmer's Sunday wear, an only suit, not recently bought. A believable jacket that might have fit years ago but was now at least a size tight. The dark gray fabric strained to contain him and bit into his underarms. It wasn't possible for him to have on a holster and gun beneath that jacket. Even the flattest small-caliber automatic would have shown.

The killer was drinking slivovitz and drafts of Prazdroj lager, limiting the potent slivovitz to one regular pour every quarter hour, taking gulps of the excellent lager in the time between. Nothing would be off-register tonight; every edge would be reality, distinct. The lager was for the belly. The slivovitz was for the heart. He'd have the belly for the killing and the necessary condition of heart, hard and pushed. But what for the head? Nothing for the head. Much earlier in his life he had learned that what made the human brain most distinctive was its capacity to reflect upon itself. It could think about what it had thought, what it was thinking, what it might think. Prior to each killing this conjugation of the brain came up. As it did now. He went over it and it went over him. Defiantly, he tried to promise himself that he would piss in the eye of his conscience, blind it before, during, and after.

Not knowing the victim was a help. On the opposite, weightier end of the seesaw was the fact that he, although hired, had the responsibility of choosing the victim. This time, as usual, there were certain stipulations; however, the most important aspect of it was left up to him. He didn't understand how that could be. It had perplexed him from the first, but he'd given up trying to figure it out and knew better than to ask.

He had arrived in Prague Tuesday night and registered at a modest hotel in the Radlice district close by the Konvarka railway station. He wanted to do what he was being well paid to do and get out of Prague as soon as possible. He'd never liked the city. He saw it as grimy, its buildings coated with soot from the burning of so much coal. Carapaces of scaffoldings were everywhere to facilitate the cleaning of the buildings, but, the killer noticed, there were seldom any workers on them. He thought the scaffolds probably only stood for intent.

It had taken him four days to make his choice. He'd spent most of the time in and around the better hotels, their lobbies and bars. The Jalta Hotel on Vaclavske Square had been a source twice before. The arrangement of its lobby was right. It provided him with a sofa chair from which he could hear what went on at both the registration desk and the concierge's counter. There he sat, not really reading the Czech newspaper with such interest nor so intent on composing postcard messages on the reverse side of views of Prague, but listening. Listening for the speaking of French. Merely that. By Thursday he had his prospects. All were undoubtedly visitors from France, as stipulated. Two were women, and if they had been the only two he would have been forced to choose between them. Fortunately among the prospects there were three men. By Friday he had settled on one and decided he would wait another night. Most of the people of Prague escaped from the city on weekends, and that might be to his advantage.

Now, seated at a table in the Café de l'Europa, the killer looked aside to his left, apparently admiring something of the Art Nouveau decor. Then he let his eyes drift to the right, phlegmatically scanning those persons standing at the bar. At just past midpoint he made his eyes almost indiscernibly catch the gaze of the man, the victim, in the navy-blue flannel suit. Simultaneously with that eye-catch his fingers drummed the shoulder of the empty chair.

Less than a minute later the victim, whiskey sour in hand, came to the killer's table. He was sure of the situation, sat as if the chair had been kept empty for him, and started the conversation as though it had been in progress. "I visited Franz Kafka's studio today," he said in rapid French. "I was the only one there. Why should a genius such as Kafka go so unadmired? It's ridiculous."

The killer looked puzzled, although he spoke fluent French and had understood every word. With stumbling grammar and an impeding middle European accent he asked in French if the victim spoke Czech.

The victim said he didn't.

The killer did an indifferent shrug and said they could try talking in French, but the other should please speak slowly.

The victim was used to making spontaneous assessments. In fact, they were an important part of his pleasure. He was excited by his quick decision that he was very much attracted to this Czech with the hard, chunky body. He liked the boyish shag of the Czech's light brown hair, the way his nose appeared to have been broken and never properly put straight, probably broken in a village brawl. What luck, the victim thought, that he'd taken the concierge's advice and come here to the Europa rather than to the Three Ostriches as he'd planned. Such sideroad instincts had frequently led him to good things. From the bar he had spotted and considered this Czech right off and concluded there was no chance. That he'd misjudged multiplied the stir in him. He felt his entire sexual apparatus spasm once, as though separately it were signaling its approval. He smiled at the Czech, the insinuating smile that he'd perfected years ago and had rehearsed briefly in his hotel-room mirror when he was getting ready for this night. Within that smile he told the Czech that of course he would speak slowly in French, but they wouldn't have to talk much. Talk was not the essential thing, was it?

The killer nodded and did the sort of responsive smile that he knew was wanted from him, confirming the mutuality.

Now they got to names. The victim said his first was François and his last did not matter.

The killer lied his entire name and extended his hand.

François pretended not to notice. He wanted to put off the pleasure of touching the Czech, and when he did touch him it would certainly not be his hand. He had long ago found that social niceties and drawn-out buildups were diluting. More could be felt from sudden physical candor. François summoned the waiter and asked for the check.

The killer wanted another slivovitz and told the waiter so. While it was being brought, he took in this François seated diagonally opposite and saw again why him rather than one of the others. The man's sexual preference had not entered into it. His homosexuality was obvious in his gestures and walk and speech, but to have chosen him for that reason would have been narrow-minded and unfair, the killer believed. No, the decisive thing, that which had swayed the choice, was the way this François presented himself. His immaculateness. He seemed to be asking to be chosen, standing out. The perfectly pinched Cardin suit, the pointed-toed, lightweight shoes that looked as though they would shriek at a scuff, and, above the fresh white shirt collar, a complexion pampered and lotioned and shaved at least twice a day. Both amusing and annoying to the killer was the possibility that François also shaved his legs, chest, and underarms, and probably tweezered his ass the same as he plucked his brows.

The slivovitz arrived. François gave the killer hardly time to swallow it. They left the cafe at forty minutes past nine. Outside on the wide major street called Wenceslas, François said, "I'm staying at the Intercontinental," assuming that would be their immediate destination.

Before François could hail a taxi, the killer said, "I want to see the clock. When I come to Prague I always see the clock."

"Tomorrow," François said dismissively, not knowing or caring what clock the Czech had in mind.

"It is better at night," the killer said, and without another word he made off up Wenceslas Street in the direction of the river. François mentally stomped his foot but wasn't going to be left standing there. He caught up with the Czech at the corner. They crossed and entered Melantrichova Street. At once the quality of the atmosphere was changed. This was Old Town Prague with its mazed chasms of narrow, barely lighted passageways. The Gothic structures on each side loomed so close above the illusion was that they were precarious, about to tumble and crash with their stony tops.

"You know where you're going, I hope," François said, irritated. He loathed the feel of the cobblestones through his thin-soled shoes. Normally he avoided adventures such as this.

Soon they arrived at a square and a large fourteenth-century building. It was Prague's Old Town Hall. The killer stood before it, gazing up at its illuminated clock. François paced impatiently around him. A number of other persons, evidently tourists, were there to see the striking of the hour. From out of the ornate fretwork above the clock came the carved life-sized figures of Christ and his disciples. In procession they made their forever-fixed appearances. Following along was the figure of death—robed, bony-faced, toothy death, with his inevitable scythe in hand. Death came rather jerkily to center position, bowed once, and made his exit.

"Macabre," remarked François, scringing up his nose.

"This is your first time in Prague?" the killer asked.

François said it was.

Prague because it was in these times sexually less dangerous than, for example, Rome or Paris, the killer concluded. Otherwise this François wouldn't have given the place a second thought. "You will enjoy Prague," the killer promised.

"I'm sure," François said. "Now, which way is the hotel?"

There were no taxis. The square had quickly emptied. The killer led the way back into the confusion of medieval passageways. François reacted to the press of the darkness, the black angles, the sparse and transient geometrics of lights. It pushed talk out of him. In rapid French he told the killer that he was a hair stylist for a well-known salon on rue du Faubourg Saint-Honoré in Paris. He'd done many famous heads. They requested him, demanded him. The price the salon was now charging its clients for his services was outrageous. Photographs of some of his coiffures had been featured in the last collection issue of *Paris Vogue*, he said.

All lies. François worked for a travel agency located on rue Tronchet near the Madeleine. He spent most of his salary on his wardrobe. This trip to Prague was, for promotional reasons, free.

The killer stopped on the pretense of retying his shoelace. A glance in both directions told him the dark passageway was deserted. He reached down and removed the knife from the sheath strapped to his left ankle. Both edges of the knife's six-inch blade were finely honed. An inch from its sharp point was a series of alternately angled serations. It was a military night fighter's knife.

François never saw it. As the killer straightened up, François stepped to him. He couldn't have been more accommodating. As a woman might do, he placed his forearms on the killer's shoulders, left and right, twined his fingers, and drew the killer's head to his own for a kiss, an aggressive tonguing kiss that might also help offset his nervousness. His lips were open and anticipating the soft strength of the killer's mouth when the knife went into him. With a powerful upward thrust it penetrated just below the rib cage. The blade was so sharp and its entry so right that any resistance was barely felt as it went in to its hilt. The killer worked the blade from side to side, trying for the heart. Somehow it didn't find the heart; however, it easily sliced through numerous blood vessels, including the left pulmonary artery. The killer, making sure, withdrew two-thirds of the blade and shoved it in again at a different angle, severing the inferior vena cava.

There had been no struggle or sound. With the entry of the blade François had gone up on his toes, stiffly. He hadn't screamed, although he probably felt he had. His head snapped back and his eyes opened wide, as though his eyes realized that the sliver of sky between the rooftops above would be their final sight.

The killer removed the knife and let François drop. He quickly wiped the blade and his hand on François's jacket and walked away at a normal pace. When he reached Dvorakova Street he went into a bar. Not for a drink. He didn't need a drink. He used the telephone, dialed the number he had memorized, the same number as before. The same anonymous voice answered. The killer did not know what was meant when he said only what he had been told to say: "It is now up to you."

Milan Sikma was the supervising medical examiner for the city of Prague. It was an appointed position which Sikma had held for nineteen years. At age seventy-two he was a bureaucratic fixture who only considered retiring each winter when the weather turned bad and another year was in its throes. Winter, of course, was symbolic to him and psychologically affecting. Each year, despite his dislike for having to wrap himself up and waterproof his feet whenever he went out, Sikma pushed through the days, and spring eventually came to his rescue.

He was a short, portly man with a wheeze and did not

move about quickly. Once, a few years ago, his reflexes had surprised him when, while trying to cross slushy, busy Husitska Street, he'd darted back to the curb to keep from being struck by a van. The incident caused him to wonder if there wasn't a whole other repressed self within him, a self quite agile, able to scurry and bound about. The possibility was entertaining, but it did not motivate him. He continued on at his usual velocity. Accept it, he was a type, he thought, an old type so solidified by repetition and habitual perspective that even the most radical chopping away wouldn't bring about a change. What could he do about all those folds of chin that made it so difficult to shave each morning? What could he do about the red and yellow in the whites of his eyes? His nose and ears that had become larger? His white hair that was distributed around his skull skin like some ancient awarded wreath? He no longer went to the dentist to have his teeth looked at. When his wife reminded him that he should, he mumbled affirmatively and remained faithful to the belief that his teeth would outlast him. Who should know the human body and all its parts better than he, especially his own very human body?

Sikma was a qualified doctor, a graduate of the University of Prague Medical School. During his training days he'd wanted to be at various times a cardiologist, a radiologist, a dermatologist, and a surgeon. He knew that to make the most of his career he should specialize, but, try as he did, he couldn't keep his mind made up. He'd set his aim only to be distracted by a different direction. As a result he got a rather scattered medical education and ended up as what he deprecatingly considered a catch-all doctor, one who merely examined and examined and referred and referred. Sikma was too disappointed in himself to start a private practice. The municipal job as one of the assistants to the medical examiner was as much dividend as he deserved, he felt. That he had always excelled at anatomy would help. When in 1969 the supervising medical examiner died of alcoholism and barbiturates, it was Sikma who had the seniority, who got the appointment, who got the raise that went along with it, and the authority.

It was also Sikma who, that Saturday night shortly after ten, got the telephone call from the killer. He understood the killer's cryptic message. He'd been expecting the call all week. Each time the phone had rung he'd answered it before his wife could get to it. That was the only thing about it that bothered him, having to be so obligated to the phone. Last November he'd had to wait ten days for the call. The time before that, though, it had surprisingly been only one day. What could he expect—killings precisely scheduled? Oh well, now that he'd received the call he could relax and let the thing run its predictable course.

He went into the kitchen for some slices of his favorite Cesnekovy salami, chunks of dark bread, and some sour pickles. He uncapped a cold bottle of strong Urguell Pilsner and poured it fast so it got a three-inch head. Urguell had been his beer for fifty years. Other beers didn't even taste like beer to him. He took his Urguell and food into the living room and situated himself comfortably on the sofa. A replay of a Heinz football game was on the television. Simka wasn't interested and the reception was worse than usual, but he watched anyway.

The body of François Jean Doulard was found twice.

First by a cello teacher on his way home from an excruciating lesson. While kneeling to feel for the beat of François's heart, the teacher happened to feel François's wallet. He would let someone else notify the police.

Such as a restaurant hostess who lived in the building right there. The contorted sprawl of François blocked her way. She thought she was being inconvenienced by a drunk, and when she got no response from her demands that the son of a bitch move, she warily jabbed hard at him with the high heel of her shoe, then added some jabs too vicious for any living person to endure. She gingerly stepped over the dead man and went up to her apartment.

The police, in excess number, arrived in a needless rush. They performed their measuring. They photographed.

They took a statement from the hostess. They searched the area for the murder weapon and found the victim's emptied wallet. An air of bustle and excitement prevailed for nearly two hours. Then, with the removal of the victim's body, everyone departed, the narrow passageway was again dark, and, except for the considerable blood that had jelled in the concavities between the cobbles, it was as though nothing had occurred.

Investigation of the Doulard murder was under the charge of Inspector Mikhal Vodácký. He personally would not be out trying to assemble some sense of it, but all information would come to him and he would make the conclusions.

Vodácký's conscientiousness was thickly crusted over. He no longer saw murder as a challenge or a professional insult. No matter how cold- or hot-blooded or gruesome, when it came to those whose breathing had been unlawfully stopped, Vodácký put them into one scurfy lot. His mental picture of them was an accumulated spherical shape, their identities lost in coagulation, just legs, arms, entrails, and sexual parts protruding. This sphere of his was often added to, as it was now by the Doulard case. However, it never seemed to get larger, just more dense. It was, Vodácký realized, a Kafkaesque concept, and he had never confided it to anyone. He was now in his mid-fifties and planned to retire from the police and Prague when he was exactly sixty, while he still had an adequate number of uncudgeled brain cells.

Monday morning when Vodácký received a phone call from the French consul, inquiring about the Doulard murder, he was glad he was able to say what the consul wanted to hear—that this murder did not fit the pattern of the five other murders of French nationals that had occurred in Prague over the past two years. What set this murder apart from the others was its robbery motive, the victim's emptied wallet found less than a block away. It made the thing as clichéd as the traditional demand "Your money or your life!" In this instance both were taken.

Vodácký knew how convenient it was for him that

there'd been a robbery involved. To emphasize that motive, he told himself, was his prerogative. That someone out there in Prague disliked the French enough to do away with five or six of them, so far, had understandably aroused concern from official France and the Czech Ministry of Tourism. The Sûreté had dug hard and deep in every thinkable direction, hoping to prove out its belief that the victims shared some denominator. Nationality, gender, and Prague were the only meaningful things in common. The Sûreté had pressed at a rather high level for permission to send some of its experts to Prague to assist in the investigation. Was the Sûreté questioning Czech competence? Permission was denied. The last thing Vodácký wanted was a pack of pompous Sûreté sleuths all over him. Truth be known, he'd experienced a number of obnoxious French sorts whom he, himself, wouldn't have minded adding to his secret sphere.

The Doulard murder could not be just offhandedly dismissed, of course. Doulard's room at the Intercontinental was thoroughly searched, all his personal possessions gone through. Found among them were thirty-four color photographs graphically depicting various male homosexual sadomasochistic, anal, and oral acts, which added another facet to the possible murder motive. Some of Doulard's movements in Prague were determined, including, most importantly, his visit to the Café de l'Europa. Questioning revealed that he'd left the café with another man around nine-thirty. Waiters and bartenders, when asked to describe the other man, said he had wavy red hair, straight gray hair, a mustache, no mustache. He was wearing a brown suit. He had on a black suit. He was in his twenties, in his forties, slim, heavyset, fair-skinned, swarthy. One waiter said he was certain the man was carrying a cane and he definitely remembered a black hat.

Thus Vodácký had no evidence and only contradictions to go on, and the robbery motive actually did seem most plausible. On Monday afternoon as Vodácký was passing by the office of Medical Examiner Sikma, he felt like going in and imploring Sikma not to find anything that would entangle this neat, explicable French murder. Ironically, what Sikma could have given Vodácký was absolute assurance that he wouldn't.

Sikma himself would perform the autopsy that night. He had told his first assistant, Zelený, just to get everything ready for him and then go home. This wasn't unusual, and besides, Sikma was thought to be somewhat eccentric.

At seven o'clock Sikma called his wife and told her not to concern herself with either him or his supper. He left his office in the main police building on Konvitska Street and walked the usual two blocks to his usual restaurant on Borsov, where, at his usual table, he had his usual roast goose and potato dumplings. When he returned to his office that section of the building was deserted. He took up his thirty-five-year-old fat brown briefcase and went down to the subterranean level to the morgue.

That lifeless room with its floor of tight little gray tiles and wall of stainless-steel individual refrigerator compartments was very clean; it was scrubbed and wiped daily. It had a distinct smell which was only complicated by disinfectants. Sikma entered the adjacent, smaller procedure room and bolted the door from the inside. He covered the single glass pane that was built into the door by taping up a paper towel upon which he printed AUTOPSY IN PROGRESS, along with his scrawly signature. He changed from his regular clothes, put on baggy blue surgeon's trousers and smock and cap and canvas sneakers. From a white metal cabinet that was known as his personal cabinet he got his combination cassette player/radio. He plugged it in and placed it on the chair next to his briefcase. Also from the cabinet he got an atomizer of Princess Dior eau de toilette. He spritzed a cotton face mask with it, then tied the mask over his mouth and nose. He put on a pair of surgical gloves and punched in the play button of his radio. He was inhaling Dior and hearing Dvořák's Symphony No. 3 in F Major performed by the Czech Philharmonic Orchestra conducted by Vaclay Talich as he started to work.

As instructed, Zelený had prepared everything so that Sikma would be able to do the autopsy unassisted. The stainless-steel table upon which the corpse lay had been adjusted to accommodate Sikma's shorter-than-average height, and the table was tilted just enough so the corpse would remain in place while any body fluids would run down and flow out through the opening in its raised edge. Surgical instruments were arranged neatly on a tray stand. Sikma briefly contemplated the rigored Frenchman. He didn't think "Unfortunate fellow," didn't question justice. It wasn't that he lacked natural compassion. The inert, ready-to-rot substance stretched before him had never been a personality as far as he was concerned. Besides, he thought, people had given their lives to much lesser causes. He examined the stab wound but did not have to bother with measuring it or noting its exact location. That had already been done. He was mildly amused at how hirsute the Frenchman was. An overabundance of black, wiry hair on his shoulders and chest and legs. Such a thick bush at his crotch that his penis was barely visible and his testicles were entirely hidden. The Frenchman's skin had an abnormal pallor, the color of the scum of spoiled cream.

Sikma took up a scalpel and made a continuous, deep incision down the middle, from breastbone to pelvis. The skin and fatty tissue rolled open like a split cushion. He then incised the muscles, the superficial ones such as the obliquus and transversalis. He made two other similar deep cuts, one across the lower abdomen and another from just above the navel to above the rib cage. These allowed the skin and fascia to be flapped open.

The Czech Philharmonic was giving Dvořák the excited strings he had asked for, and palpitations from the percussion.

The Miss Dior sweetly scalded the membranes of Sikma's nostrils. He'd overdone it again.

Sikma gutted the corpse almost as he would a fish. Merely as a matter of form he took several fecal samples and samples of stomach and intestinal content. He wasn't nearly as methodical or thorough as he would have been with an authentic autopsy. He carelessly yanked the viscera out of the corpse, scooped out its various substances, ripped out its arteries and veins and nerves as though they were just so much useless circuitry. When he'd disposed of the entire mess he used a pressure-nozzled hose to lavage the gaping cavity with a disinfectant.

He rinsed off his gloves and went to the chair. From his briefcase he removed a package about six inches square by an inch thick. It was tightly wrapped with brilliant blue plastic that had been heat-sealed. The package had been delivered to his office a week ago.

Sikma believed he knew what this blue package and all the previous blue packages contained. Not specifically what was in them, but for him they contained meaning, personal meaning. Never in his life had he been a patriot beyond incorrectly singing the words to the Czech national anthem at public events and mindlessly waving a tiny flag when it was called for. When the Soviet tanks rumbled into Prague in 1968 he hadn't shed a tear or gotten angry for Czechoslovakia. He'd only griped about the diesel fumes they caused and exaggerated a cough and was glad to see them roll out of the city for that reason. The year before last when he'd been approached to do this important patriotic thing he'd surprised himself by the way he jumped at the chance. Perhaps it was his age and his knowledge of how bad his general health was—perhaps it was knowing he didn't have much to lose. Any night after goose and dumplings he could clog up and be done. No matter—doing his part with these blue packages of Soviet secrets was a tonic for him. He always felt better afterward. He wished there were a blue package every week, which, of course, wasn't feasible; it would require too many French corpses.

Naturally, Sikma was curious about what kind of secrets were in the blue packages. He imagined diagrams of various nuclear weapons, maps indicating well-hidden missile sites, military and political strategies. Everyone enjoys knowing a secret, but he told himself to be satisfied with just imagining, and to do what he'd been told. What a privilege it was to be a conspirator, or, in fact, a spy. That self-designation was valuable to him and he didn't want to spoil it.

He inserted the blue plastic-wrapped package well up into the vacant chest cavity of the corpse and sutured the chest and stomach closed with large, loose stitches. Tomorrow afternoon the corpse would be on Czech State Airlines Flight 37 bound for Paris. Sikma correctly presumed that someone there in France, someone in the CSA cargo division, would be on the lookout for the corpse. That someone, with easy access, would remove the package and then see that the stitches were tightened and tied off properly.

What Sikma did not know, would never know, was that the blue packages contained diamonds. Russian diamonds skimmed from Aikhal.

This time, eighteen hundred D-flawless one-carat stones. Investment-quality.

At eighteen thousand dollars a carat, this batch was worth thirty-two million, four hundred thousand.

CHAPTER
♦•♦•♦ ♦•♦•♦
6

NIKOLAI'S EYES OPENED SUNDAY MORNING ON THE ABSENCE of Vivian. There, deserted and lumped out of shape by all her usual nightly hugging and burrowing, were her goose-down pillows. And beyond on the fabric-covered nightstand on her side of the bed was her little silver Art Deco clock. The clock had only one hand, its smaller hand. Vivian refused to have it repaired. She rather liked having a hand-icapped clock to sleep by, she said. Not being able to know the exact hour to the minute suited being in the country.

Judging from the position of that one hand, Nikolai estimated the time as something to eight rather than some-thing after seven. Where was she? Using the bathroom? No light on in there. Perhaps, he thought, she was down in the kitchen fixing a huge surprise breakfast, an inspiration that came to her every couple of months. Nikolai swung his legs over the side of the bed. His slippers were on the floor awaiting his feet. He pictured her thoughtfully placing them there. A show of affection for all the pleasure of the night before.

Nikolai blinked vigorously, clenched and stretched his eyelids. Then he opened his mouth as wide as possible and twisted it to the left and right, and his nose. Vivian had taught him that this was a good way to wake up. Get the face going first thing—that was her theory. It seemed to work. Anyway, Nikolai had gotten into the habit of doing it every morning. Most mornings he and Vivian did it together and laughed at each other's facial contortions. At the very least who could refute the merit of starting the day with a laugh?

Nikolai sniffed, rather hoping for the smell of bacon being cooked. What he smelled was something fruity and sweet. He used the bathroom and put on a floor-length white terry robe that Vivian claimed had been not exactly stolen from the Paris Ritz considering the price charged for the suite it had come from. He went downstairs. Vivian wasn't in the kitchen, nor was any part of a breakfast, not even coffee. Simmering on the stove was a copper saucepan containing water and a sachet of herbs. Hand printing on the paper bag on the counter said the sachet was a mixture called brandied peach. Vivian's doing. On other occasions it had been a stew of lavender or stock or hyacinth, and once honeysuckle had permeated the air with such a cloying odor that even Vivian was caused to gag and they'd had to throw open every door and window in the house. She had a thing for dead flowers. To Nikolai a flower that was faded and all shriveled up was through. She felt otherwise. If at all possible she'd save any kind of petal from making its drop to the ground. Huge Waterford crystal bowls of pot-pourri were in every room, sprigs of dried heather and tiny roses and baby's breath were bunched and tied by silk ribbons and hung on doorjambs, incorporated into wreaths, arranged in old baskets. Nikolai's unstated opinion was that she'd carried a nice thing too far. She would never admit she overdid it.

Also on the counter was what appeared at first sight to be a gathering of a dozen or so large brown gnats. Trout flies. Nikolai realized where she was. How early had she gotten up to go fishing? Why hadn't she instead remained in bed, fitted against him, and slept late? Where did she get all the stamina? Considering the amount of loving they'd done it would seem this morning she'd be unable to move or at least limited to slow motion. Women, Nikolai thought, and went out the back door to the garden terrace.

The day was what Vivian called a sometimes sunny day. Blue-as-possible sky with formidable puffs of white clouds scattered about. Nikolai walked along the wide brick terrace. At the far end he turned and gazed back at the house.

Her beloved house.

It was Queen Anne, not in period but surely in style. Two and a half brick stories. Six ample rooms on the ground floor, six more on the second, and in the upper half-story beneath a steep-pitched hipped roof, four smaller rooms and attic space. Built in 1875, it was the work of the architect George Gilbert Scott, Jr., which in itself added value to it. Like most well-done Queen Anne houses it had a sense of feminine balance and repose. The primness of its brick exterior and crisp white trim was offset just enough by the curves of its Dutch-flavored gables and the patterns formed by its nine-over-nine sash windows. The easy impression was that of a confident beauty of an age past at rest on a lawn. The informal gardens were her various-colored petticoats flounced and scalloped about her, and for her parasol there was the high spread of a huge sycamore.

Nikolai understood why Vivian cared so much for this house. He almost believed her when she claimed she could spend the rest of this life comfortably satisfied in it.

Several purple finches animated a nearby linden. A small, fat cloud momentarily got in the sun's way. Ninja the cat played the oriental thug, sprang out from behind a purple azalea. Up on his hind legs with his front paws poised in karate fashion, he went for any part of Nikolai. And missed. He landed on his side in an awkward twist, recovered quickly, and shot Nikolai a defiant glare to save face before darting away.

Ninja was forever doing that—pouncing out at people from behind ceramic planters and the corners of things and, more often than not, missing. Vivian defended Ninja's disposition. She said he didn't really intend to hurt, just wanted to see if he could. After all, the most he'd ever done was ruin a few pairs of pantyhose. Perhaps Ninja was myopic or had faulty depth perception and actually wasn't as clumsy as he seemed. Whatever, he was the only cat Nikolai had ever known that tripped a lot. Vivian made all sorts of excuses for Ninja's lack of feline agility. While stroking his back or belly she'd sometimes cooingly declare that it made no difference to her that dear Ninja would never be a mouser. Nikolai thought that was somewhat rubbing it in.

Nikolai went around the side of the house and saw a brand-new Lotus parked in the drive, so new the tiny rubber extruding nipples weren't worn from its tires. Archer's, no doubt. What he called one of his personal cars. At least, Nikolai rationalized, there was no need to be concerned about Vivian fishing alone and out of help's range should she slip and crack her head on a rock or something. Meanwhile, what he'd do, Nikolai decided, was have breakfast. He was famished. He'd have five or six rashers of bacon, three or four scrambled eggs, a stack of buttered toast with some of that lime marmalade he liked, and coffee, American-style coffee. He wouldn't mind fixing it himself. He'd take his time, make sure the bacon was crisp but not overdone, the eggs fluffy rather than watery. He would use the better china and a proper napkin and silver utensils instead of the everyday stainless. He'd arrange it on a tray and eat outside in the sometimes sun, eat slowly and read the *Times* if it had come, or if not he'd get into one of those fatuous American novels of intrigue in which the Russians were always so treacherous and omitted the articles from their sentences. "Is good idea," Nikolai mocked aloud. "Have pleasant peaceful breakfast."

He hurried inside and up to the bedroom. Splashed his face, brushed his teeth and hair. He put on jeans, a pair of sneakers, and a faded Miami Dolphins sweatshirt. Went down the stairs so swiftly his feet hardly touched them. As he passed through the kitchen, he opened the bread box and grabbed up a sweet bun that was left over from the previous weekend.

The field adjacent to the maintained grounds of the house was made up mainly of ryegrass and purple clover. A great many bees were working in it. It was also plentifully scattered with dandelions. Beautiful commoners, Vivian called them. Nikolai, to avoid the argument with himself that he was acting foolish, concentrated on not trampling dandelion heads. Thus his course was a zigzagging one all the way to an old stone wall. There was a gate a short way off to the left, but Nikolai just climbed up and over. And came down on what he knew was Archer land. The stream was a quarter mile farther on, but it was easy going over undulating, rockless meadow that had been cleared several centuries ago.

When Nikolai came within sight of the stream he checked his pace and attitude to a casual stroll. The stream at its normal level, which it was now, averaged about twenty feet wide and ran from two to seven feet deep. Its advantage for fly fishing was that much of it wound through open land, allowing uninhibited backcasts. Nikolai had numerous times overheard Vivian and Archer discussing the merits of this stream—how it offered a variety of challenges such as bends, deep holes, runs, and falls, and how it wasn't stocked, and every trout in it was native. Prince Charles had fished it a few times and been delighted, it was said.

The camaraderie of fly fishing was something Nikolai didn't try to share with Vivian and Archer. He refused even to give it a try, declined Archer's offer to show him how to go about it. They were, Nikolai reasoned, too far ahead of him in this. Together they had fished the Test and the Itchen. They had fished for salmon in Scotland along some of the most desirable private beats of the Tay, the Spey, the Dee, and the Tweed, and in Ireland along the Erriff and the Bullynahinch. The only trout fishing Nikolai had ever done was back home with Lev. They'd used worms and grasshoppers for bait, which were anathema to Vivian and Archer. So to hell with it, Nikolai concluded, *let* them have it.

Where were they?

Upstream or down?

From the grassy bank Nikolai spotted bootprints in the mud at water's edge. They were pointed downstream, so he made off in that direction. He passed by a tree which had an enameled metal sign nailed to its trunk, POACHERS BEWARE in discreet black and white. Archer's warning.

Around a bend he caught sight of what resembled a long single strand of golden hair against the sky, horizontally lengthening, increasing out of itself. It looped with light

grace and reversed its course, rode upon the air with buoyant ease, and disappeared. It was Vivian's fly and line being
cast. Nikolai walked along the edge of the bank to the spot.

"Get the hell back from the bank!" she snapped at him,
hardly breaking her concentration on the swirling pool fifty
feet away that was her target.

Nikolai jumped back from the edge and knelt. Now he
couldn't see either her or the stream. He crawled to the
edge. She was out in the stream, standing on a submerged
gravel bed, the water fast around her knees. Her figure was
lost in chest-high waterproofed nylon waders and a beige
tackle vest over a blue chambray shirt. Her hair was entirely
concealed within the crown of a black beaked cap. With
the outfit she was wearing, her hair tucked out of sight and
not a dab of makeup on, she looked both beautiful and
handsome, Nikolai thought, like one of those sexually am-
biguous young creatures who were the dears and darlings
of the sophisticated milieu of London, Rome, and especially
Paris.

She began another cast. Her eight-and-a-half-foot graph-
ite rod was like a whip; it whistled as it cut the air. Her
yellow-ocher line of woven silk flew close above Nikolai's
head, causing him to duck. He lay on his back and watched
her line with sharp barbed hook and deceitful fly on the
end of its leader sail back and forth above him. Finally he
felt sure enough that it wouldn't cost him an eye to peer
over the bank. Vivian was reeling in her line, giving up on
that pool. She sloshed across the stream to the near edge
of it, she got down on her knees, and dipped her entire
face in the running water for a drink. She climbed the
bank and respectfully laid her rod on the grass. She let
out a noisy sigh of relief as she dropped beside Nikolai.
"You spooked him," she said. "He was right there about
to go for it, but you spooked him."

Contrite silence from Nikolai.

Her forgiveness was a kiss on his cheek followed by a
quick on-and-off smile.

He really needed that kiss. Actually, he needed a better
one. Why should he be feeling so emotionally scuffed this

morning? he wondered. Wasn't it the woman who was supposed to have that kind of hangover? The worst thing would be for him to let her know how he felt, to ask for it. "Where's Archie?" he inquired with friendly concern.

"Christ, I'm roasting," she said. She removed her cap, only slightly disturbing her pinned-up hair. Her face was wet from the stream, but her throat and the back of her neck were beaded with perspiration and her shirt was soaked darker at the underarms.

"Catch anything?"

"Two right off. I let them go because it was so easy and promising and I didn't want to shorten the fun by making my catch too fast. However, since then, I can't get a rise. Seems the word has been spread." Once in a trout talk with Archer she'd insisted that trout had a way of warning one another, of saying in trout talk: "Hey, watch what you eat, the enemy is around."

"You were dead to the world this morning," she said.

She should have been, Nikolai thought.

"Did you have breakfast?" she asked and looked to make sure there'd be no bees beneath her when she lay back.

Nikolai decided to fib. "I had breakfast."

"I didn't," she complained.

He wished he'd thought to bring her something, a pear and cheese or something.

She seemed to read his mind, told him without looking at him: *"Ya tebya lyublyu."* Then, without a pause: "That's my kind of sky. Clouds such as those shape themselves into all sorts of things if one has patience with them."

"I love you too," Nikolai told her. Then it became clear to him what was chafing him. Not the feeling of having been used, as he had suspected. At that moment, there in the English grass by the English stream with Vivian riding the world on her back, he was stabbed by the limitations of their love. He had over their months been pricked now and then by this practical problem, but never so deep or so sharply. Each time he'd been able to avoid confronting it with distraction and enjoyment or by placing faith in procrastination, by saying inside that the circumstances would change for the better, that Vivian could be unpredictable, that he must wait and see, wait and see. Temporizing was no longer possible, however. He had to face up to the fact that the love that was now theirs was as much as they would ever have. It was remarkable, yes, but it would not, barring some miraculous radical turn, be allowed to grow as good loves normally do. There'd be no marriage and children and all such events of fused lifetimes.

He gazed at her. Her eyes were shut, what was she thinking? His throat felt crowded. To lift the moment he said: "We ought to go see if Archer has bought the catch of some poacher."

A genuine smile from Vivian.

They walked downstream and found Archer as he was about to descend to stream level to challenge a stretch of slower, deeper, jade-colored water. He was entirely caught up in it, his eyes a bit glazed and darty. "Some good ones along here," he said. "Always are. In fact this is where Charlie had at it with a monster, so he said."

Nikolai assumed Charlie to Archer was Prince Charles.

Vivian joined Archer in slipping down the bank and wading out into the stream. Before they'd gone a third of the way out, the water was up to their waists. The banks there were overhung, eaten away underneath from when the stream had been higher and rushing. Those overhung places were cool, dark sanctuaries that suited the antisocial nature of trout. They lurked in under there, and Vivian and Archer hoped to lure them out.

They did. With the help of a timely hatch of nymphs that formed a thick, playful cloud above the water's surface. First Vivian, then Archer executed perfect casts, placed hook-bearing imitations of nymphs among the hatch and fooled two trout each. They were the best eating size: large enough not to inspire unbearable pity, small enough for the skillet.

Vivian tossed one of her catches up onto the bank for Nick to see. He took in the trout's beauty, the bright specks that peppered its flanks. He held the trout high and recited Shakespeare.

> *"The pleasant'st angling is to see*
> *The fish cut with her golden oars the silver stream*
> *And greedily devour the treacherous bait."*

Archer threw Nikolai a congenial, approving look.

A trout shot downstream. It brushed against Vivian's leg. A trout so huge it caused a bow wake on the water and so fast it was only a brownish blur. It caused Vivian's heart rate to jump. She appealed to Archer. It was his turn to cast. However, being a British gentleman, with Etonian regard for manners and all that, surely he would defer to Vivian, allow her first chance at that huge fish.

Archer didn't think twice about it. Vivian might as well not have been there. He put his mind to his cast and, while Vivian glowered, he dropped the fly forty feet away, where he believed the trout would be. He barraged that spot with casts before giving up. "Gone," he said. "By now he's half a mile downstream."

"You're finished with him, then?" Vivian asked, cocking her head.

"He never stopped," Archer contended.

Vivian put on sunglasses, the wraparound type with thick black frames and plenty of lens. They were polarized to eliminate reflections and glare from the surface of the water. She craned upstream and scanned downstream. She spotted the trout at a curved area of the right bank about thirty feet away. She pointed it out to Archer. It was where blackberry canes arched out and down, a thick, madly woven net of thorny red and green canes. Evidently the trout had chosen the spot not only because it was comfortably shady but also because it was so inaccessible. Any food that came that way would have to be authentic.

"I'll wager anything I can seduce him," Archer said, readying his line.

Vivian grabbed at his reel. "You've had your try!" she contended adamantly.

Archer gritted and growled at her. For a moment Nikolai thought the man capable of adolescently thrashing the water and scaring the fish away for spite. "That's probably Charlie's monster," he said petulantly, reeling in his line and biting the fly off his leader.

Vivian poor-Archered him once, then surveyed the big trout-blackberry problem. She removed a plastic fly case from one of the many pockets of her vest. It contained an assortment of dries and wets. She knew them by name: Sooty Olive Sedge, Welshman's Button, Blue Winged Hare's Ear, Little Cinnamon Ant, Female Snowbug, and a favorite with which she'd never caught anything, the White Winged Curse. After a long moment of indecision she dismissed all those engagingly named, colorfully tied buggers for one she called her Hairy Black Winker. She'd tied this fly herself on a No. 23 hook. It consisted of four pairs of dark false eyelashes, well curled, and a little tuft of silver fox fur that she'd plucked from a fat foxtail stole she'd since contributed to a benefit shop, the proceeds of which were supposed to go to London's more beset unwed mothers.

"He'll never go for that," Archer scoffed.

His scorn didn't faze her. The only reason she didn't use the Hairy Black Winker more often, she'd always claimed, was her sense of fair play. She tied it onto the leader and was about to cast when she decided the trout was already leery from the many casts Archer had dropped and would be suspicious of anything presented to him in that manner. Wading to the bank, she found a dry twig. She broke off a three-inch section of it and discarded the rest. She stuck the mere point of the fly's hook into the bark of the twig. Just barely enough to hold. She placed the twig with fly attached on the surface of the water and let the current take it. She steered the course of the twig as best she could with her rod. It floated in under the blackberry brambles.

"No fair," Archer whined.

"All's fair," Vivian maintained. She waited until the twig and its passenger were in place before giving the line an ever-so-slight jerk. The Hairy Black Winker came free of the twig, was now afloat on its own.

The trout simultaneously lunged and opened its wide jaws. It must have struck at the Hairy Black Winker more out of anger than hunger. Of course, it was, no doubt, much angrier when it felt the hook that thing had hidden.

Vivian set the hook. Now if only the trout would come out and make a run for it, tire himself out crisscrossing, fighting her line and the current. But the big trout hadn't gotten so big by being stupid. He stayed in under the brambles, making use of them. He thrashed, riled the water, boiled it, came up out of it and got a swift but good look upstream at his adversary. He'd seen her kind before. They were always trouble.

The fight lasted thirty seconds.

Vivian's line went slack.

She reeled it in, *sans* her Hairy Black Winker. "The fucker got away!" she exclaimed bitterly. She sloshed out of the stream, clambered up the bank, strode past Nikolai as though he were a post. He felt radiated by her fury.

She made for home, straight and hard, the heels of her wading brogues indenting the turf of the field, stream water squishing from their insteps. A scarlet tanager flashed by for appreciation. Although it was reddest of all red birds and her favorite, Vivian didn't give it a glance.

Nikolai and Archer followed after her.

But didn't catch up.

CHAPTER
❖•❖•❖ 7 ❖•❖•❖

BY MIDAFTERNOON VIVIAN HAD ABSORBED MOST OF HER soreheadedness over having lost the monster trout. She was working in the garden, figuring bills on the terrace, reading in the hammock. It was like her to undertake two or three things at the same time. That way she seldom had to give much to either boredom or perseverance. As might be supposed, it wasn't unusual for her not to complete any of the things she set out to do. When that happened she blamed time, accused it of having run out on her.

Today she was adding to her "simples," her garden patch of plants with ancient reputations for medicinal or mystical value. There was eyebright for tired eyes, gentian to ease fever, hawthorn to stop palpitations. There was borage to chase depression, and mandrake, a surefire aphrodisiac. Vivian's purpose in having such a "simple" patch was just having it. To her it was a collection more than anything. At least, so far, whenever she'd felt out of sorts she hadn't rushed out and snipped herself a prescription.

She firmed the soil around the stems of three new deadly nightshades, which brought to mind how Italian women had once taken measures of this poison to give their eyes a suggestive, languorous look. She wondered how many had overdosed. She also thought she should have a horse or two going today. Yesterday's win on Eyesore had been only momentarily satisfying. More fulfilling would be to stretch that win into a streak. She'd gone over the race entries in the morning paper but hadn't seen any standouts. However, as certain as the sun would set there would be a winner in every race. Probably one was crossing the finish line that very instant, she thought. Wasn't it maddening to know that and not have a wager? Phone Gareth again, she suggested to herself. She had earlier, hoping that he and his racing angels were inclined today. When Gareth's answering machine came on she'd waited until the beep but hadn't left a message. Gareth had made it plain to her that he rarely went into a trance two days in succession. Too much of a strain, he'd said, and Vivian had been sympathetic. But, damn it all, she needed a winner today. A long shot would really show that trout. She had a mind to stick a pin into the listings for the sixth or seventh race and bet sizably on come what might. Selecting a winner in such a fashion might also revive her belief in pure chance.

She stood, arched her back to stretch it, and removed her soiled suede gardening gloves. She had on an oversized underwear T-shirt that fell off one shoulder or the other, cotton panties, and a pair of therapeutic clogs, the kind with hard red rubber nipples all over their insoles. She'd bought Nikolai a similar pair and he'd tried them, but every step he took in them was torture. She, on the contrary, could go around in them for hours with nary a wince.

"Want to drive over to Tiverton tonight for a film?" she asked.

"No." Nikolai was across the terrace, where she had him shoveling, turning over a sunny part of the garden where she wanted to put in some new lilacs.

"Neither do I. But if we stay home you know what sort of mischief we'll get into, and I'm already sore."

He was both sorry for her and pleased with himself. "What film are they showing in Tiverton?"

"I could call," she said, not even halfheartedly. She flopped down in the hammock and situated herself in it, evidently there to stay awhile. She took up the book she'd been reading, *In Search of the Miraculous*, by P. D. Ouspensky. A blue jay's feather marked her place. She read for five or so minutes and then without taking her eyes from the page she said: "I'd like to throw a tantrum."

"Go ahead. No one's around."

"That's just it. It would be a waste."

"Don't I count?"

"Inestimably, but not when it comes to tantrums. Now that I think of it, I've never behaved badly with you, never gotten raving vulgar jealous or anything like that, have I?"

"Only a couple of times."

"I can't recall even once. Perhaps we're talking about different degrees of rave. You *are* exceptionally sensitive to me."

The truth of it was she had the accommodating ability to tuck whatever she found mentally uncomfortable way back in a corner of her brain's forget file. She couldn't blank things entirely, but she could, through some personal trick she'd learned, dilute them to such vagueness that they weren't easily summoned.

Nikolai's memory was not so obliging. He clearly remembered, for instance, a night when he and Vivian had gone to a play at the Shaftesbury and during intermission at the bar he'd gotten into a conversation with a lovely Russian émigrée, who slipped him her telephone number when she thought Vivian wouldn't notice. Vivian maimed the lady with a look and accused him of duplicity so loudly every head turned. They didn't stay for the final act, hurried from the theater, Vivian four steps ahead. She tore her lamé skirt getting into the car, flung her evening purse at the backseat, drove maniacally, screaming hurts and blames so rapidly he couldn't get in even a sliver of appeal. She became abruptly silent and fixed as a statue when she stopped in front of his flat, which was her way of ordering him out. The keys to his place had been left on the dresser at her place, but he decided not to mention it. With an insolent screech of tires she left him standing there. He went to one of the embassy's spare rooms, giving the excuse that his plumbing had broken. Weeks later, when it was psychologically less costly, Vivian revealed to him that by the time she'd arrived home alone she had cooled a hundred degrees, and when she'd put herself to bed alone she was shivering inside. She had rung him up and let it ring so long it was a wonder his wires hadn't shorted and caught fire. She had imagined an entire revue of tragic and lurid things happening to him, most of them involving the lovely émigrée, whose phone number he had probably only pretended to have thrown out the car window. She'd acted ridiculous, she'd said. Nikolai by then saw no exorbitant psychological price in confessing that he hadn't slept that night and all he could find to read in that embassy room were stale *Pravdas*. He'd tried to phone her every five minutes for two hours but her line had been constantly busy and he took that to mean she had angrily taken it off the hook.

They had made up so ardently the next morning that Nikolai had been late for an appointment with Churcher.

No, Nikolai thought, Vivian hadn't ever thrown a jealous tantrum—that she recalled.

She resumed reading Ouspensky. With one bare leg extended to create swing for the hammock. Her knees were grubby from gardening. Nikolai paused from his shoveling to appreciate her. He enjoyed observing her when she was unaware. He especially liked to watch her sleep.

With her attention only apparently on the page, she grinned her know-it-all grin. "Stop spying," she told him.

"I wasn't spying."

"What then?"

"I was thinking."

"About what were you thinking when you were spying?"

He went back to work, stomped the blade of the shovel into the ground, struck a rock.

"I'm going to make supper tonight," she announced as though it were an event. "Escalloped potatoes and something. Does that water your mouth?" Escalloped potatoes deserved italics in her limited culinary repertoire.

"I'll peel," Nikolai gladly volunteered.

"No."

"Why not?"

"I prefer you wild rather than domesticated. In fact, I don't want to ever find you peeling a potato. A champagne cork but never a potato."

"What about dishes? I usually help with the dishes."

"Well, that's not enough to even be considered a concession. Tell me, darling Nickie, are Russian men as a rule really such dreadful husbands?"

"Where did you get that impression?"

"From an American journalist who spent six years in Moscow."

"He should know," Nikolai remarked sarcastically.

"I didn't hear it firsthand; I read it in his book."

"They all spend six years in Moscow and they all write books."

"Don't get miffed about it."

"I'm not."

"You had the beginnings of a miff. Anyway, in his book this fellow went on about how Russian men beat their wives. It's not a question of whether or not the wives deserve it, mind, it's just traditional. He even quoted an old Russian saying: "The more you beat a woman the thicker the soup.""

"Is way to go," Nikolai mocked, deepening his voice.

"So are monthly cramps," Vivian retorted, and then in the same breath: "Have you ever done any sailing?"

"What kind of sailing?"

"I don't know. It's just something I was told to ask. It popped into my head so I popped it out."

Nikolai had come to recognize such metaphysical traps and go silently around them. "As a boy I used to sail now and then with Lev. Neither of us was very good at it. We'd rent a boat at the yacht club on Petrovskaya and go out into the bay."

"A yacht club in Leningrad?"

"Of sorts. Anyway, it's called a yacht club."

"What bay?"

"The Bay of Finland. When the wind was right we'd go way out, farther than was safe in such a small boat."

"Because it was exciting, the danger?"

"Because it made it easier for us to pretend we were on our way to Tahiti. We'd bring books along to help us decide what we'd do when we got there."

"Why Tahiti?"

"Lev's choice. He had a fascination for Gauguin. He'd sit for hours in the Hermitage with the Gauguin paintings.

Not merely looking but rather staring spellbound at them, as though he'd entered the atmosphere of the canvases, was lost among the tropical colors and Tahitian women."

"Perhaps he was Gauguin in a previous life."

"I doubt that."

"Why not?" Defensively.

"Gauguin wouldn't choose the Leningrad climate."

"Might, for a change. What does Lev do to keep body and soul together?"

"He works for Soyuzchimexport."

"Again, slowly."

Nikolai repeated it syllable by syllable and explained that it was the Soviet trade branch responsible for the importing and exporting of chemicals.

"So Lev's a chemist."

"No. He doesn't have to be. It's just a job, somewhat similar to mine, a niche that he somehow angled himself into a few years back. He doesn't talk much about it. I suspect it's dull. Probably the only reason he sticks with it is that he gets to travel out of the country."

"Lev sounds to me like a bit of a hustler."

Nikolai agreed but thought she didn't really understand about Lev, and he didn't want to get into trying to explain how and why in the Soviet Union ambition was most often better served surreptitiously. He told her: "Lev was a hockey player. One of the best. Fast, tough, and tricky. For quite a while the highest-scoring wingman on the Soviet army team. As such he was a national hero. Practically every influential office and, of course, a great many bedrooms were open to him."

"A star," Vivian categorized.

"He enjoyed all sorts of advantages. Until the 1980 Olympics in Lake Placid when the Soviet team got beat out of a gold medal by a bunch of American kids playing over their heads."

"I remember. The Americans were such underdogs. Actually, there was no way they could lose, you know. It was just meant."

"Lev said after that loss it was a wonder he and the

rest of the team weren't made to swim home. It was never officially called a disgrace, but the consequences said as much. Lev's privileges were cut back to practically nil. He was reassigned to a much smaller apartment on the basis that he was exceeding the nine square meters per person which was the legal allotment of space. The new car he had taken for granted would not be forthcoming. His right to buy in the special shops where plenty is available was revoked. I doubt that you can imagine what a comedown it was for him."

"Poor Lev," Vivian commiserated.

"Normally when a player the caliber of Lev is done with his playing days he's well provided for all his life, given a coaching assignment at a generous salary with one of the top Soviet teams. Lev was offered the job of coaching a minor factory team in Novosibirsk. Lev turned it down, as they must have known he would. I don't believe he's had a hockey stick in his hands since."

"What does one who is out of work do in Russia?"

"It's against the law to be out of work in Russia."

"So, what did Lev do?"

"He became bitter, drank more than too much, sidestepped and ducked various authorities, falsified entries in his workbook. I'm almost certain he was working the black market, but he didn't implicate me by letting me know. Anyway, he got along without turning *gebeshnik.*"

"Translate."

"KGB."

"What does KGB stand for? I've never thought to ask."

Nikolai gave it the full-out, most menacing Russian pronunciation: *"Komitet Gosuidarstvennoy Bezopasnosti,* Committee of State Security."

"Brrrr," went Vivian.

Nikolai continued on Lev. "He's recovered considerably since he's been with the chemical export branch. He's not the good-natured Lev he once was, but at least he's not headed down the pipe."

"The drain, darling." Vivian corrected, and after a moment of introspection, "Wonder what it's like to have a friend the way you have Lev. I don't have one friend, not a one. I mean a faithful female chum."

"Beautiful women seldom do."

"Everything you say is true." Vivian smiled and made her lips into a kiss and threw it at him.

From around the front of the house came the sound of gravel crunching under tires on the drive. A car pulled up and stopped. Nikolai and Vivian were on the rear terrace, so they couldn't see who it was. They assumed it was Archer. Vivian had given the caretaker, Tigley, Saturday off, ostensibly to visit his brother but actually to play Lady Chatterley's lover to a well-off but simmering married woman in Exeter. So it had to be Archer, not Tigley. Archer, however, wouldn't be knocking at the front door. Probably someone needing directions. Nikolai slipped on his sweatshirt and went around front.

Vivian in the hammock scrunched up and closed her eyes. The tantrum cycle had passed. Contentment was left in its place. She would drift off into a nap. But she caught a fragment of greeting by voices she didn't recognize. Whoever could it be? Surely Nikolai wouldn't bring them around back. Or might he? She struggled out of the sling of the hammock, dashed into the house, and ran up the stairs.

Ten minutes later she came down and out, dressed in fresh clothes and with knees scrubbed. Concealing her uncertainty, she welcomed the older man and the young woman who were seated on the terrace with Nikolai. Introductions revealed that the young woman was as French as she appeared. Her name was Valérie de Varignon, which sounded contrived but was a pleasure to pronounce. She had an atypical Gallic disposition, an honest, lively smile. The man was Grigori Savich, and the "Minister" that Nikolai put before his name transmitted respect as would the British "Lord" or "Sir." Vivian had heard Nikolai speak of this man, so she knew his importance.

Savich charmed from his first words, even though they were the predictable apology for the intrusion. "We were out for a weekend drive and happened to be nearby," he explained. "When we phoned earlier no one answered, so we came just on the chance. Hope you don't mind."

"Not at all," Vivian charmed back. "In fact, we were in the mood for visitors, weren't we, Nickie?"

"Yes," Nikolai replied too quickly. He was still off-balance from Savich's having shown up like this. No doubt Savich in his high position could easily find out Vivian's unlisted number and the location of her house in Devon. But why was Savich there? Ministers didn't just drop in. Had Savich been in his Claridge's suite and let loneliness get the best of him? That was difficult to imagine. Savich was the sort who would battle such a mood, not give in to it. Even if Savich had craved company, why would he choose them, Nikolai and Vivian? No matter—Nikolai was delighted that Savich was there.

"Not to entirely impose we brought a little something," Savich said.

The little something was a 1.8-kilo container of caviar, Royal Beluga. It was in a blue-and-black disk-shaped tin packed in shaved ice which was kept from melting by dry ice. It had been shipped via Aeroflot just the day before from Astrakhan on the Caspian Sea. Savich had also brought a half-dozen bottles of Noskovskaya vodka, as if one or two wouldn't have been sufficient.

Vivian put the vodka into the crammed freezer compartment of her refrigerator, sacrificing several packages of frozen entrées to make room. As they waited for the vodka to chill, Vivian maneuvered the attention onto Mademoiselle de Varignon.

"Please call me Valérie," the young Frenchwoman said. She had an enviable accent. It gave color to even the most mundane things. Vivian found that Valérie needed little drawing out, was very open about herself, even her personal self. She confided amusingly that she had assumed the "de" of her name in order not to sound like a Victor Hugo character. "I am a dancer and an actress," she said as though that were evident. Then she admitted that the dancing and acting she did was hardly demanding as such. "I work at Le Crazy Horse," she said, assuming they would know she meant the Paris nightclub. She related brightly how in one Crazy Horse sketch her pubic hair (she called it her "poos-ie hair") had to be heart-shaped. "It was *très mignon* but such a bother to keep clipped just so. I shaved and got a merkin."

"A what?"

"*Comprenez* 'merkin'? A *perruque*, a wig for the pelvis." As though they were in every shop window.

Vivian decided she liked Valérie and her candor. Hers was the sort of ingenuous sophistication that especially a young Frenchwoman could get away with. She was very pretty and physical. Slender, slight in the hips but nicely waisted, she had a somewhat boyish figure, except for her rounded bottom and her breasts. All things considered, Valérie gave the impression that she would be unconditionally selfish in bed.

As for Valérie and bed and Savich, Vivian intuitively gathered that this day of countrying was a respite between sexual encounters—the one of last night, which, judging from the languor of Valérie's eyes, had been very successful, and the one of the night to come, which accounted for the nervous lower torso she also detected in Valérie. This Savich must be quite a well-practiced fellow, Vivian surmised. She turned her appraisal to him. His air said that he believed his years of experience were in his favor. And he wasn't fooling himself, Vivian felt. He must have been torrid when he was younger, was likely even more so now. Where was it she'd read that certain men naturally gave off extra huge whiffs of an arousing chemical, a kind of inverse estrus? Now what had brought that to mind? Mainly for her own fortification she gave Nikolai a part-kiss, part-bite on the nape of his neck on her way in to check on the vodka.

The bottle was frosted. The warmth of Savich's hand melted a print on it as he filled four small glass tumblers. He left the opening of the caviar to Nikolai, who removed the inch-wide rubber band that had acted as a seal for the disk-shaped tin. The large gray caviar grains were revealed, mounded up, packed snugly but not damaged. Shining fresh, not at all watery, this was Royal Beluga at its finest. A clump of grains fell from the edge into the ice, but what matter when there was four pounds?

"*Quelle décadence!*" Valérie exclaimed.

Nikolai assumed the caviar was from the embassy's supply. The vodka as well. Still, it was thoughtful of Savich.

They scooped it onto Waterford luncheon plates, huge portions, properly accompanied by just *crème fraiche* and decrusted, lightly buttered toast. Savich raised his tumbler to Nikolai, but his words were: "To your Vivian." They all tossed down to that, Vivian too.

Crunching on a triangle of toast piled with beluga, Savich asked Vivian: "Do you know how to make blinis?"

"No, but I've vowed to learn."

That was the first Nikolai had heard of it.

"Learn to make good blinis and I'll see that you receive a tin of beluga like this every week," Savich promised.

"Only if you'll come and share," Vivian told him.

"But of course." Savich laughed, pleased. "How else would I be able to judge your blinis?"

Valérie's elevated eyebrow and off-color smirk were an explicit reply.

Nikolai wasn't feeling the vodka for some reason, and he had just drunk his fourth. He warned himself that this might be one of those times when it hit him all at once. He merely sipped at his next tumblerful. He was in a listening and loving mood, would listen to Savich and watch Vivian and enjoy being proud of her.

"The czars preferred an altogether different variety of caviar," Savich was saying. "Much smaller roe and golden yellow in color. It's very rare now. Personally, I don't care all that much for it."

Savich touched on other caviar trivia, such as how Louis XV spat out his first taste, cursed, and called it *confiture de poisson*—fish jam—and how Picasso prepaid for his caviar by sending cash wrapped in one of his drawings.

"Really?"

"Truly."

During the next hour Savich complimented Vivian seven times. Nikolai counted.

The telephone rang. Vivian answered on the terrace extension. It was Archer wondering what Vivian and Nikolai were doing about dinner. He'd take pot luck, he said. Vivian informed him of her guests.

"Delightful!" Archer said. "We can all have dinner here."

Vivian told him: "We're not up to one of your stodgy gluts."

"I'll serve *nouvelle*," he promised.

"Besides, you'll insist on black tie and all that."

"Like hell. You can come bare-arsed for all I care. Be here anytime from seven on. Ta." He clicked off.

Nikolai had passed by the paved private road that led to Archer's house numerous times. He'd never taken it. Whenever Archer invited him, Nikolai declined with an excuse. It happened so often that Nikolai felt his avoidance had to be transparent. To ease embarrassment he stockpiled excuses so that he could have one ready. Even when Vivian announced that she was going over to Archer's and did he want to come, Nikolai had remained home and tried not to keep looking at his watch.

Tonight, however, he was going along. The Daimler limousine had just turned in on Archer's road, and while Vivian, Savich, and Valérie indulged in a glib, lighthearted exchange, Nikolai gazed ahead. Archer's house could not be seen from there, the outer reaches of his land, nor was it visible when the Daimler finally came to a high double gate with imposing piers. The gate was hospitably open. Beyond it the grounds were more cared for, Nikolai noticed. Trees were trimmed of all but their higher, healthier branches, and there was no underbrush to compete with their handsome trunks. Vast grassy meadows were kept mown just enough to appear at their best. In the distance off to the right a dozen or so black cows were grazing as though in a pastoral painting.

Not until the Daimler passed through a grove of oaks and over a rise did Archer's place come into view. Nikolai realized at once that it couldn't be called a house. It was a mansion, nobler and more extensive than he'd expected. Vivian should have prepared him for this. He should have asked her. The structure was of smooth-worked beige stone. It was only three tall stories, but, in typical Palladian fashion, it went on and on. The stark monotony of its facade was relieved by a centered portico with four slender columns and Ionic capitals. Wide steps curved down.

The Daimler pulled up to the steps, where two white-gloved footmen and Archer were waiting. Archer was beaming, overjoyed that they'd come. It was as though their arrival would dispel something unbearable. Savich and Valérie were introduced and warmly received, and from the vigor with which Archer shook Nikolai's hand one would never have guessed they'd been together just that morning. The footmen stood by should anyone happen to slip on the steps.

Archer led the way into a spacious entrance hall with a crystal chandelier so immense that Nikolai was uneasy standing beneath it. There were huge identical bouquets on the left and the right. Nikolai wondered if they'd been hurriedly arranged and put in place. He decided they were routine. The scent of pale yellow lilies and white-bearded irises streamed into his nostrils. The click of Vivian's and Valérie's heels on the geometrically patterned marble floor sounded overly loud. All of Nikolai's senses were turned up. Suddenly it seemed imperative that he touch something, be it the carved edge of the Régence console against the wall or the richly ornamented doorcase that he passed through, as, following along after the others, he entered a reception room. He shoved his hands except for his thumbs in the pockets of his jacket and attempted nonchalance.

Vodka martinis were concocted and poured by Archer personally. He hoped aloud they met with everyone's approval. Savich took a testing sip and after a moment of earnest deliberation during which his dark bushed-up brows animated and his tongue worked around within his closed mouth, he pronounced Archer's martini superb. He was playing the minister. Covertly, he half-winked at Nikolai to let him know none of this was to be taken seriously.

Dinner was not a matter of sitting down in one place and having it. From martinis in that reception room they went into another adjoining reception room for the starters: smoked Norwegian wild salmon, iced lobster soufflé, Galway oysters on the half shell. They then proceeded to the dining room and a table easily large enough for forty. Their seating was at one end, arranged so Nikolai was next to Valérie with Vivian opposite. Archer graciously relinquished the host's place at the head to Savich, making him focal.

The main courses consisted of roast partridge with young cabbage and wild mushrooms, and best end of English lamb with horseradish purée. The wines were a '67 Chǎteau Pétrus Pomeral and a '72 Montrachet Romanée-Conti. The servants placed the entrées on the table and then backed off to discreetly stand by, in keeping with Archer's orders. He believed the family-style casualness of passing around the food and wine would be to Vivian's present liking.

From the dining hall they adjourned, as Archer put it, to a small ground-floor salon for cheeses, including some of Dorset's legendary blue vinney. And sweets from a trolley. Lemon cheesecake, cherry cake with fresh double cream, *tarte de poivre provençal*, iced Grand Marnier parfait, and a trifle according to a recipe dated 1823. Then it was upstairs to the more relaxed atmosphere of a leathery study for coffee, nibbles, and whatever digestives they might desire. Vivian was for a bit of port, as was Valérie. The gentlemen had twenty-five-year-old Glenfiddich.

During the circuitous course of the meal the conversation ranged from banal to the esoteric, from the most recent royal dallyings to the efficacy of the casting of spells. Vivian couldn't have been less interested in who of the royal string had been lately seen in full drag or gone public with an odd erogenous zone. However, as might be expected, she was an opinionated authority when it came to spells.

Most ancient spells were pure nonsense, she said. Such as the one that was supposed to guarantee loving fidelity, a potion made up of desiccated swallow wombs and sparrow livers. But she did put solemn stock in certain voodoo spells, and she advised everyone there to do the same. She bloody well didn't want anyone sticking pins in a doll effigy of her, she said in a half-whisper, as though to prevent transmitting that possibility to someone anywhere in the world.

Savich was having a marvelous time, making the most of the luxurious surroundings, the delicious offerings, and the lovely company. Without slighting Valérie he allowed himself to be more diverted by Vivian. He hung on her words, was caught by the mere turn of her head, flash of her eyes. He leaned across the corner of the table not to miss a nuance or inflection from her. Several times to underscore a conversational point or to emphatically concur he patted the back of her hand.

"I should love to gamble in Macao," Vivian said.

"Why especially Macao?"

"It would be so unlike playing in our clubs. Much faster, and furious and loud."

"Wouldn't that be distracting?"

"How would you possibly concentrate?"

"I don't know," she replied. "Perhaps one doesn't do so much concentrating in Macao, and that's the attraction. When it comes to gambling the Chinese are anything but inscrutable, you know. They make a din of it."

"They're reputed to be excellent gamblers."

"They're not really," Vivian said. "They wager wildly without the slightest regard for the realities of chance. Every so often luck feels sorry for them and lets them win an unlikely bet, and that's what everyone oohs and aahs about and remembers." She sighed longingly. "Someday, just wait, I'll be right in the thick of it in Macao."

"I'm sure you will," Savich encouraged.

"We could leave tomorrow," Archer offered, not altogether lightly.

Didn't that cause Vivian to pause? She might be mentally making that voyage, Nikolai believed. He thought she looked particularly beautiful tonight and it wasn't that he was seeing her through his insecurity. She'd altered her makeup, he noticed. A stronger mouth and softer eyes. She had exaggerated the oriental aspect of her eyes. Thus the penchant for Macao. The cause had been the effect. The romantic notion occurred to Nikolai that time would be kind if it halted then and there, so he would forever have her just as she was in his sight.

When they were seated in the upper study Archer suggested a game of cards. They could learn whist as it had been played originally in the eighteenth century, he said. He'd just acquired a booklet of instructions that had been printed back then for members of the court. Wouldn't that be amusing?

Apparently no one thought so.

Valérie was feeling the dominance of a huge portrait that hung on the wall near her armchair. It was a full-length study of one of Archer's eighteenth-century female forebears, well done, when the lady was in her prime. "Lovely," Valérie said, "but she'd be even lovelier if she didn't have such a stern look about her."

"In those days they were invariably portrayed with their mouths set like that," Archer told her.

"Why not a smile?" Valérie smiled.

"They had rotten teeth," Vivian explained. She was seated in an armchair upholstered in a leather so soft it would have been suitable for fine gloves. She was discreetly observing Savich, who was seated on the sofa across from her. How was it, Vivian wondered, that a Russian bureaucrat, a political descendant of that man in the accountant's suit who had called himself Lenin, could be so completely at ease in these prodigal circumstances? Where was his Communist conscience? He seemed to take for granted a lap of luxury such as this, as though he had it coming. Vivian was most eager to find out what the irises of his eyes would reveal. She had brought along her magnifying monocle for that express purpose.

"I've decided to learn how to cook both *sheke* and *borshch urankii,*" she said out of the blue.

Nikolai, who couldn't recall having seen her delving into a Russian cookbook, wondered if she was serious.

Savich smiled and patted the sofa cushion next to him, and within a few minutes she had her monocle magnifying his eyes. As she examined and simultaneously discoursed on the fundamentals of iridology, Nikolai stepped out of the study unnoticed.

He needed to be alone for a while, thought that might help his perspective. All evening he had tried to shake the feeling that his being there at Archer's verified the inevitability of the emotional hurt that lay ahead for him. His smiles had been merely the pulling up of the corners of his mouth, and he hadn't been able to compete nearly as deftly as usual in the repartée. Stop being the melancholy Russian, he told himself. Or, as Vivian would put it, get centered.

He wandered Archer's place. Down the long, wide upper hallway, in and out of various rooms, appreciating precious things while trying not to be affected by them. It was of no personal consequence, he thought, that the carpet he was standing on was a perfect eighteenth-century Aubusson, or that the boulle marquetry writing table that had its place in one of the less significant guest bedrooms was Louis XIV and was worth well over a hundred thousand. He was on the landing immediately above the main staircase, feeling the pricelessness of a perfectly lighted Tintoretto, when he realized someone was beside him.

"What's wrong, Nikolai?" Savich asked.

"Nothing."

"Tell me."

"I felt like moving around. I stuffed myself with dinner." Savich persisted with eye-to-eye silence.

Nikolai stated the fact. "Vivian was married to him."

"I know."

"She was married to all this."

"And from what I gather she could be again."

"Yes."

"If she so chose." Savich made the point.

"Eventually it may not be a matter of choice."

"Very little in life is inevitable," Savich said and gave Nikolai an encouraging pat on the shoulder. "From what I see, you have nothing to worry about."

CHAPTER
✦✦✦✦ ✦✦✦✦
8

MONDAY MORNING IN GENEVA.

Arthur Newfeld believed the deal was surely sweet enough to suffer some for. But he had such awful jet lag. Worse than ever. All the hinges and other articulations of his seventy-year-old body seemed to be refusing, and his head felt mushy and lopsided.

How was it, he wondered, that so many people could fly away without a qualm and fall into any bed anyplace in the world and wake up bright and ready to do business? Not he. He was a prisoner of his time zone. Like a finely tuned, hypersensitive clock, his vital intricacies got out of whack when moved. And, as irony would have it, for the greater part of his life there'd been so much moving demanded of him. Ten times a year for thirty years he'd had to make the flight from New York to London to New York. Three hundred round trips altogether. One would have thought that after a while he'd have become conditioned to it. No one ever knew how much he dreaded those trips, all those times he'd sat in one boarding area or another at Kennedy International and debated with the reason why it was imperative that he get on the plane. He was always the last to get on, reluctantly committing himself to the torture he knew lay ahead. Whenever he arrived in London and went at his appointed hour to 11 Harrowhouse Street for his "sight" he was always at more of a disadvantage than any of the other diamond dealers and brokers. There on the table would be his parcel of rough, the small box wrapped just so with immaculate white paper, inviolably sealed by blobs of bright red wax impressed with the System's official stamp. Because of his jet lag, it never seemed to Newfeld that those were his fingers that opened the parcel, never his eyes that looked over the lot of rough diamonds the System was allowing him to buy. What strain it had been each time to appear interested, to take out his monogrammed gold loupe and bring it up to his left eye and pretend to be examining the stones. It was only ritual, of course, but it was expected of him. Truth be known, he couldn't really appraise the quality of the goods the System had chosen to dole out to him until he got them back to New York and his head was cleared.

What intensified it all the more was his having to keep his suffering to himself. He'd never spoken of his jet lag, not even lightly, to any of his fellow dealers, and certainly not to anyone at the System. He couldn't afford to have them knowing such *inside* information. They would have rated him a pushover in business, and, as well, it would have been exposing what Newfeld regarded as a personal weakness, unmanly. Thus, as the excuse to catch the very next flight home to the comfort of his own timing there'd always been pressing business back in New York or crucial family matters. In all those years there'd been no socializing or camaraderie in London, no leisurely dinners at the Savoy, weekends in Surrey, or any of that. He'd missed so much.

What relief for Newfeld when five years ago his son Theodor had finally been approved by the System and permitted to take over the responsibility of attending the sights on behalf of the family firm. The rather retired Newfeld had, at first, let out many relieved breaths. However, after a while, his guilt made him think about how much more he could have accomplished had he been a good traveler. Jet lag, now that it was no longer a monthly inevitability, seemed a surmountable, minor thing. He'd allowed it to stunt the firm of Newfeld & Son. If he had it to do over again, he'd fight it with more resolve, he thought. He might not beat it but at least he'd give it a better battle.

And now here he was in Geneva, doing just that. Standing in the lobby of the Président Hotel feeling painfully out of sync with the time and the place and the activity around him and yet determined to persevere. Not just to see the deal through but to force himself to stay on for a day or two after it was concluded, to see Geneva, stroll around the lake, do whatever.

But first the deal. What a sweet one it was. Nearly too good to be true. He stood to make four million, nearly five, without putting out a dime except for expenses. Theodor knew nothing about it. He hadn't mentioned it to Theodor because he wanted—needed, actually—to pull this off on his own. He hadn't even told Theodor about the Russian fellow who'd come into the office on 47th Street a short while back. Without appointment. An extremely fair-haired Russian who'd introduced himself as Dmitri Tarasov. He'd shown Newfeld a sample lot of goods and made the proposition to him as though aware of the private circumstances that would obviate refusal.

Newfeld wasn't naive. He immediately recognized the sample lot as Aikhal goods. All one-caraters, perfect. He assumed the deal was an underbelly sort, the kind that disappeared the moment too many questions were asked about it, the kind one just got into or didn't. "You provide the investment-type customer, we supply the goods at enough below the going market price for you to make a nice margin of profit," Tarasov had told him.

Newfeld, as instructed, had taken a particular flight to Paris and laid over for an hour at De Gaulle. At a certain airport bistro counter he'd put down his business case while he ordered and drank a *café américain*. He was surprised when, a quarter hour later, the business case he picked up was still his. He'd expected a switch. Evidently it had been taken away for a moment and returned. He didn't open it, waited until he was in Geneva and in his room at the Président to look at the diamonds. Three packets of them. Eight hundred to each packet. Each stone an exact carat. Such perfect little beauties.

It had gone so smoothly, Newfeld thought. In another hour the bank would be open and the deal would be a done deal. He still had time to go up to his room and shave. That was another thing about making long-distance latitudinal journeys. They threw one's shaving schedule off. Right now at the beginning of the day he only half-needed a shave. To hell with it. He didn't want to look in a mirror. He'd be made to feel worse if he saw his gaunt old face with its four creases so prominent across his forehead and double bags beneath each of his eyes and the aging spots on his bald skull as if he'd been splattered with sepia paint. Better that he proceed toward the deal and keep his mind on how pleased with himself he was going to feel when it was done.

He went across the hotel lobby to the cashier's cage and told the woman there he wanted to get into his strongbox. The woman buzzed him in through a door off to the left and accompanied him to the room where the strongboxes were built into the wall. He produced his key and the woman opened the correspondingly numbered little hinged door and drew the black steel box out and handed it to him, and he went into the adjacent smaller room and closed the door. He'd decided to carry his business case, but the diamonds wouldn't be in it. He rolled up his left trouser leg. He was wearing a wraparound pouch just above the calf, had put it on earlier to get used to it. He peeled apart its Velcro straps and took it off. From the strongbox he removed the three packets of diamonds. Placed them evenly in the compartment of the pouch. He put the pouch back on and rolled down his trousers.

Over forty million dollars' worth of diamonds on his leg. He *humphed* at the fact. This was good for him, he thought. Just the thing to counter his jet lag.

He strode across the lobby and used some of his strength to revolve the very polished brass door that deposited him outside on the Quai Woodrow Wilson. Directly across the way on the opposite side of the traffic was Lake Geneva. He paused for a moment to take in its gray-blue surface, pointillistically textured, the morning sun like a spill across it.

"*Taxi, monsieur?*" the doorman asked.

"Merci, non." Going against inclination, challenging the fatigue in his legs. He'd walk to the bank, which was located on rue des Alpes, ten blocks away.

Newfeld had gone only twenty-some steps when they confronted him, stopped him by saying his name. Because it was so unexpected to hear it and was said without question he responded to it instinctively. His thought right off was that the two of them might be an escort provided by the Russian to see that he got to the bank safely, but then they showed him plastic-laminated credentials that identified them as functionaries of the Security Section of the Central Selling System. They were young men, British, well dressed in vested suits, fresh white shirts, and ties. A proper appearance and a pleasant, polite manner about them. One was sandy-haired and wearing round-lensed eyeglasses with thin frames of dark wire. He was Fred. The other, Horace, had the same sandy hair but was somewhat taller and stoop-shouldered.

"Mr. Newfeld, sir," Fred said amiably, "we'd appreciate your coming with us."

"I've business to attend to," Newfeld told him.

"We won't keep you," Horace promised.

"Please, sir." Fred smiled.

Newfeld knew the rules of the System, the unwritten and officially unstated but steadfast rules regarding dealing in contraband diamonds. "Outside goods," as they were called. Over the years he'd often heard of offenders and how unsparingly and severely the System punished them. He'd always believed most of it had been mere scare talk meant to put fear into the trade. Surely these two young fellows from the Security Section intended him no harm. They were being particularly gentle. Possibly this was only a routine check. They did them randomly. They'd ask a few questions and look into his business case and that was all there'd be to it. Anyway, Newfeld thought, he had no choice but to cooperate.

They walked him down the Quai Woodrow Wilson to where it became the Quai du Mont-Blanc. Along the way they conversed with him about such things as how clean and breathable was the air of Geneva. They also recommended a couple of the city's better restaurants. At the corner of rue de Monthoux they crossed him over to the lake side and went down the grassy incline to a public jetty.

That was where things began to feel odder to Newfeld. There was the proximity of the huge lake and the lapping sounds of it, the bows of tied-up boats bobbing, the creaks and croaks of various frictions. Newfeld had never been one for water. He and boats were absolute strangers. He didn't know how to swim and hadn't given that a thought in a half century.

Fred climbed aboard a speedboat, a slick Riva. He extended his hand to assist Newfeld.

"Where are we going?" Newfeld asked.

"Just down the lake a way."

"Why?"

Fred didn't reply, just put compassion in his eyes and kept his hand out, and finally Newfeld took it, placed his foot on the nonslip patch on the gunwale, and allowed himself to be helped aboard. Horace undid the mooring lines and got in behind the steering wheel. Fred sat with Newfeld in the passenger seats behind. Horace started up the Riva. Its exhaust gurgled at the waterline for a few moments and then the Riva drew slowly away from the jetty. Newfeld managed to subdue a panic in him. He hugged his business case.

Once clear of all other boats the Riva was given some throttle, and after going about four hundred meters it passed by the Jetée des Paquins. Then it was in open water and Horace brought it up to full speed. The roar of the engine and the hit of the wind made speech impossible, so Newfeld couldn't inquire, had to presume their destination was some lakeside villa or town more easily accesible by boat. What other reason?

Horace kept the Riva on a straight course for thirty kilometers. He abruptly cut the throttle, all the way to idle. At that point the lake was at its widest, the shore six kilometers off in each direction.

"Mr. Newfeld, sir, may I please see inside your business case?"

Newfeld handed it over, and Fred searched through its contents and examined it for a concealed compartment. Satisfied, he took time to make it neat, closed it, and placed it on the vacant front seat. "Will you be so kind as to stand, sir?" Fred requested.

Newfeld complied.

Horace felt Newfeld's pockets and then frisked him up and down, thoroughly but not roughly.

Newfeld thought Horace would certainly detect the pouch he had around his calf, but then it seemed Horace had missed it, because he didn't say anything, just gazed blankly at Fred. They'd take him back to Geneva now, Newfeld thought. They'd done their duty. They'd put him ashore and he'd go on to the bank and do the deal.

Horace brought out a knife. A small, ivory-sided pocketknife with a single short blade. He opened it with his thumbnail. He reached down and inserted the blade in under the cuff of Newfeld's left trouser leg. He slit the trouser leg up to the knee, revealing the pouch.

"You could have asked me for it," Newfeld said.

"We didn't want to trouble you," Fred explained. He removed the pouch from Newfeld's leg, went into it for its contents, unfolded each of three packets. The diamonds seemed to go insane in the sunlight. They scintillated even more when Fred stirred them with the tip of a finger. "Where did you get these?" he asked as though only mildly inquisitive.

"I'm middling them for someone," Newfeld replied.

"For whom?"

"A man named Tarasov."

"A Russian."

"Yes."

"Is that his actual name?"

"I have no idea."

"Where might we get in touch with this Tarasov?"

"I don't know that either."

"Seems unlikely."

"Really, I don't," Newfeld said. He considered the circumstances and wondered why he wasn't more frightened. His age, perhaps.

"We're supposed to confiscate these goods," Fred told him. "That's the System's normal procedure in a situation of this sort. But how would you like to have them back and just go on and do your business?"

"That would be agreeable."

"All you need do is tell us how we can locate this Tarasov person."

"I honestly don't know," Newfeld said. It was the truth. The deal had been kept that one-sided. He glanced down. "You've ruined my trousers," he said, "and I didn't bring along another pair. What will people think?"

It took little more than a nudge from Fred to topple Newfeld overboard. It could have been taken as an accident. Newfeld went into the water awkwardly, sideways. He plunged right under and didn't know enough to try not to breathe, so he took water up his nostrils and down his throat. Panic made him grab at the water as though it were substantial. At once, his clothing was soaked heavy and his shoes were like weights with the purpose to sink him. Which way was air?

Then suddenly there was a blue that had to be sky. And he caught a glimpse of the speedboat. It wasn't right there. It had moved out of reach. Newfeld floundered. In his flailing to keep afloat, his arm struck upon something graspable. A life preserver. He managed to hook his arm through it. The life preserver had a line attached. Fred drew the preserver and Newfeld to the boat. He helped Newfeld climb up onto the gunwale, not quite aboard.

Newfeld heard through the water in his ears Fred asking that same question concerning the whereabouts of Tarasov. Newfeld shook his head that he didn't know. Fred let go of him. Newfeld fell back into the water. This time ass-first. He went under deeper.

Three times Fred and Horace threw the life preserver

to Newfeld, helped him partway aboard, and put that same question to him. He kept on telling them the truth, and they kept dropping him back in.

The fourth time they believed him.

And let him drown.

CHAPTER

✦✦✦✦ 9 ✦✦✦✦

AT FOUR-THIRTY, TUESDAY AFTERNOON, ALMOST PRECISELY to the second in keeping with its schedule, Aeroflot Flight SU-244 touched down at Sheremetyevo Airport in Moscow.

Nikolai ignored the lighted seat-belt sign overhead. He was already unbuckled when the Ilyushin-62 jet reversed its engines, ran out its speed, and taxied back to the main terminal. He also disregarded the flight attendant's demand that he remain in his seat. She told him twice curtly and then, miffed at being so flagrantly disobeyed, shot at him something to the effect that he and his foolish ass that he was intent on breaking would go to hell. Nikolai responded with a good-natured wink, and she tried hard to hold back her smile.

It seemed to Nikolai to take forever for the docking ramp to be brought into place and the hatch opened. He was the first passenger off. His sprint up the enclosed ramp sounded like muffled beats on a metal drum, and as he dashed down the corridor in the direction of customs, people got out of his way and looked warily at him as though he were a culprit being chased. At customs he searched for any familiar official face, saw no one he recognized, and committed himself to the routine. A prematurely gray-haired customs officer with bad vodka eyes nodded once at Nikolai as though to save his valuable voice. Nikolai handed over his passport. Its red cover told the customs officer it was a permanent external passport, good for unlimited foreign travel. It also told him that with this one he should be a degree more efficient and, no matter what, less strict. He would not ask to see inside the man's carry-on bag. He matched the photograph in the passport with Nikolai's face and thumbed quickly through the pages, noticing the Moscow, Leningrad, and London stamped entries. He decided Nikolai Petrovich Borodin surely deserved an unusual "sir" along with the usual questions that were asked like a rapid litany with no pauses for replies. The passport was stamped hard and neatly initialed and returned to Nikolai, who knew he'd been treated with swift preference but considered it a wasted four minutes. He hurried through the terminal proper and out to a taxi, a tiny Zaporzhet. The driver had a heavy foot and excellent reflexes, used the car as though it were a well-trained frightened insect, and just moments later it was out on the straight of Leningradsky Prospekt headed for central Moscow.

Nikolai, cramped in the backseat, knees knifed up to the level of his chest, didn't look out at the mainly gray, uninteresting hem of Moscow. He glanced at his watch, which told him it was quarter to five and that he couldn't possibly make the five-o'clock meeting. He'd be lucky to be only a half hour late. Now he knew he shouldn't have cut it so thin. First of all, he shouldn't have let himself be persuaded to spend Sunday night in the country. No matter that his intention had been good, and he and Vivian had left Pennymoor yesterday morning with an hour to spare for him to make the eleven-thirty Aeroflot flight from Heathrow, the last flight of the day. Three miles north of the Trenton turn-off the Bent had started coughing, and within another mile it died. It was trying for attention, Vivian claimed, either that or resentfully getting back for all the concern she'd withheld. She chided the Bent, promised it lifelong care, threatened it with some dreadful carrion junkpile. After each approach she expectantly turned the ignition key. However, the Bent merely sniffled and coughed and again died. Nikolai got out and raised the hood in the hope that what was wrong might be as obvious as something visibly disconnected. He'd never been one for engines. He hitched a ride back to Trenton for the help of a greasy-handed teenaged mechanic who diagnosed right off as though he were clairvoyant that the Bent's fuel line was clogged.

Translated into Vivian's terms, the poor Bent had suffered an embolism. She and Nikolai sat in the car and impotently watched the minutes go by while the mechanic did the special mysterious things he had to do. By the time the Bent was back on the M4 and again running without complaint, Aeroflot Flight SU-242 was twenty-five-thousand feet above Belgium and climbing.

Vivian told Nikolai not to despair, there was a bright side on the other side of every contretemps, if only one would flip it over. Why not look at this as their being given a bonus night? Time that they would have spent apart had been transformed into time they could be together. With that frame of mind they had a splendid dinner at Blades and the night took on the temper of an event.

Now, however, in the cooler light of the Russian late afternoon, Nikolai was alone and being swiftly carried to the payment of a professional price, which, at the least, would be a severe chastening. He had only himself and the Bent to blame. Was it too much to ask of him that he be on time for a general trade meeting in Moscow every other month? It didn't matter that the meetings were always dull and little more than reunions barraged with statistics on tractors, wheat, fish, and such—he should have shown up early, coated his apathy with interest, made an impression of conscientiousness on a deputy minister or two. That was what most of the other trade mission representatives would do, trying to italicize, underline, redden their names on the old *nomenklatura* so someday, with luck soon, they might be called home and elevated to assistant deputy minister. Nikolai, however, had no such ambitions. Besides, the assistant deputy minister job and Moscow were already his if he wanted it, he believed. Savich had said as much last week after the Churcher meeting. From that Nikolai gathered Savich had him already on the *asnovrior*, the *Bone* list of candidates for such higher positions whenever they were voluntarily or otherwise vacated. What Nikolai wanted was to keep things just as they were—his job, London, Devon, and Vivian. Now that he gave it a second thought, perhaps being tardy for this meeting was to his advantage. The lapse would be noted, of course, might someday be the deciding factor in keeping him from being promoted. Vivian was right again, he thought, there *is* always a brighter side. He relaxed. His mind stopped considering the credibility of various excuses. He would just say vaguely that his lateness was unavoidable, which was true, and if they asked for more of an explanation he'd give them another truth, that he'd missed his plane. That should do it.

He arrived at the ministry at five-thirty and went directly to the regular meeting room. It was empty. They couldn't have adjourned so quickly. He inquired and was told that the larger, more important room at the far end of the corridor was being used. That didn't bode well. A Foreign Ministry man who Nikolai assumed was also a *gebeshnik* was sentried at the closed door to that meeting room. Nikolai had to identify himself to be allowed in. As unobtrusively as possible he sat in a folding metal chair along the wall just to the right of the entrance and immediately appeared attentive. Ludvik Stolar, the senior deputy minister, was speaking. There were about a hundred trade mission representatives in the room, twice as many as usual. They were being allowed to smoke, and the air was thick with it. There were frequent coughs and clearings of throats. It was evident to Nikolai that this was no routine meeting. He spotted Savich seated near the speaker's lectern, and noticed he was dressed in his Moscow clothes: a neat but rather nondescript gray suit and subdued tie.

Stolar was a terrible speaker. He tried so hard to be emphatic that just about every word came out stressed and shrill. He was approximately Savich's age, had been next in line under Savich for twenty years. It was no secret that he coveted Savich's job, Savich's position on the Central Committee Secretariat and all the privileges that went with it, but the pervasive opinion was that Stolar really couldn't stand in Savich's shadow and it was only Savich's cunning that allowed the proximity. What was smarter than having a cripple chasing you? it was said. Very privately, Savich referred to Stolar as *nyekulturnyi*. This most stinging of all disparagement had in typical Russian mouth-to-ear fashion gotten back to Stolar, who was so irate that he summoned up nerve enough to obliquely confront Savich with it. Savich told him, yes, *nyekulturnyi* was what he'd said and meant. Then Stolar took refuge in refusing to believe it.

The gist of what Stolar was saying now to the meeting was that radical changes in the area of foreign trade were expected. The term "expected" was synonymous with "ordered" in such context. Everyone, all the way down the line, would have to be more and more aggressive. The push was on, the new push, different from all the old ones. There would soon be noticeable improvements in the quality of Soviet-produced goods, making them competitive with any others on the world market. Profits would be huge. This was, admittedly, a capitalistic attitude; however, ideology had no bearing on it. Anyone so purist that he felt squeamish about it should sit aside now and watch.

Savich's nod confirmed that as the official standpoint.

A woman seated near Nikolai grunted dubiously and lighted another Gauloise from the one she'd smoked down to nearly a finger-burning stub. Nikolai didn't grunt but he thought that even if by some miracle the Soviets became as economically dominant as, say, Japan it wouldn't help his own financial predicament. How many lifetimes such as his would it take for someone like him to become wealthy in Russia? He was looking at the year 2300, and even then only maybe. Anyway, all this pep-talking about wheeling and dealing didn't apply to him. His domain of diamonds was already outdoing the West.

Savich didn't talk, merely attended. At the end of the meeting he stood up and acknowledged the spirited but brief applause with a single sweeping wave of his right hand. Taken differently it could have been Savich wiping away everything that had been said and everyone there. In keeping with form he and Stolar left the room while all remained in place. Nikolai hurried out of the meeting room and saw the gray back of Savich going for the elevator. He felt the debt of an explanation and the need to pay it now; however, at the elevator Savich paused, turned, and stopped Nikolai with his most reproachful look. The impact of it on Nikolai was more than if it had been an hour-long dressing-down.

Nikolai had planned to stay overnight in Moscow. The Hotel Kosmos was holding a room for him. However, now he considered going right on to Leningrad. He wasn't due at his Almazjuvelirexport office in Leningrad at any particular time, just expected. That single censuring look from Savich had really set him off. He tried to shake it by walking along busy Kuibyshevsky Prospekt and trying to feel Russian, but no matter what attracted his eyes that Savich look remained in the front of his mind. It kept saying that Nikolai was irresponsible, soft, selfish, spoiled by the West, an ingrate who had betrayed Savich's personal interest in him. Nikolai fought those accusations with the reasoning that his tardiness had been such a minor infraction, surely outweighed by the countless loyalties he had shown in the past. What about all the times he *had* been conscientious? They stood for him, didn't they? Hadn't he been absolutely dependable, Communistically steadfast, hadn't he demonstrated a sense of allegiance? What about all the tedious hours he'd spent sparring with Churcher and others like him at the System?

His anywhere walk took him to Pushkin Square and the park there. He sat on a bench and continued his "Russian argument." Perhaps, he told himself, that Savich look hadn't even been meant for him, and it was also entirely possible that he'd misread it, projected his own sense of guilt into Savich's eyes. How could he know unless he stayed in Moscow on the chance of seeing Savich tomorrow at the ministry? That was what he would do. He would check in at the Kosmos, get a good night's sleep, and be at the Ministry early to catch Savich before he began his day. He would apologize. Savich would understand. It would be forgotten.

At that moment a young woman sat on the bench little more than an arm's length away from Nikolai. She had been sitting on the bench directly across the wide walkway, but he'd been so caught up in his thoughts that he'd only vaguely noticed her. She was dark-haired, round-faced, and plump. Typical. No doubt she'd once been a country girl, had come to Moscow for a better, more eventful life. She sat aloof for fifteen seconds, then suddenly smiled her entire smile as she turned only her head to Nikolai and asked in terrible English if he was enjoying Moscow.

Nikolai nodded, but not in reply to her question.

She propositioned him with sympathy for his loneliness and his being so far from home.

Nikolai knew, of course, that he was being mistaken for a visitor from the West, and, what's more, by an expert at making such identifications. He thought about that for a long moment and then told the young woman, "No, thank you," in flawless English. He got up and walked out to Gorky Prospekt, where he found a taxi to take him to the airport and the next flight to Leningrad.

CHAPTER
•••• **10** ••••

THREE HOURS LATER ANOTHER TAXI WAS CARRYING HIM down Moskovsky Prospekt. Just being in Leningrad made him feel better. This was his rodina, he thought, his truly native place. The very air that he occupied seemed a more comfortable fit, the mauve of the late-night sky a reminder to his eyes that it was something lovely he'd been missing. It had been six months, a half of one of his years, since he'd been here, home. After the last two general meetings in Moscow he'd hurried right back to London and Vivian, and prior to that there had been the required field trip to the mine and cutting factory at Aikhal. So the pastels, the gentle greens, blues, and pinks of the structures that were so Leningrad and that he had held but lost somewhat in mind, now reverified themselves, and when the taxi was on the Kirovsky Bridge, to Nikolai that was not just a river he was crossing over, it was the beloved Neva.

His apartment in the Petrogradskaya district was on Scovsa Prospekt. It was situated on the sixth, the top floor of a cutstone building that predated the Revolution. The building's entrance was wide, as was the stairway up. The granite steps were worn concave, and the slight gritty sounds of them were familiar to Nikolai as he made the climb, up and around, up and around. It caused him to recall a fragment of another kind of friction: a long, loud argument between his father and mother over whether to move to a new twelve-story elevator-serviced apartment building in the outlying Lakhtinsky area or to stay put. Nikolai was now, again, glad that his mother had won out.

He unlocked and entered the space of his infancy,

• *129* •

boyhood, young manhood. The apartment was three rooms, originally four. Eight years ago Nikolai had removed a wall and combined the living room and what had been his parents' bedroom. A high ceiling and three tall double windows along one side made that area appear more spacious. The foot of Nikolai's bed was butted against the window wall, fit nicely beneath the sills. That allowed him to lie facing out with his only view the sky, because the buildings across the way were three stories shorter. The sky, Nikolai thought, was a wondrous thing to see last before sleep and, no matter what its mood, remarkable to wake up to. From the end of his bed he had the Malaya Neva and its ship and boat traffic to see, and if there was no haze he had a view all the way out past Vol'nyj Island to the Bay of Finland, with the distance miniaturizing huge ships and making them seem hardly under way. Nikolai's bed had a substantial brass headboard with knobs on its posts. Formerly he'd kept the knobs and the brass rings of it gleaming, but now they were corroded and actually seemed more comfortable with neglect. The bed by its position and size dominated his other furnishings: the chest of drawers and the gilt but plainly framed mirror above it, the sizable desk and its chronically sticking drawers, the pair of easy chairs that were low-seated and difficult to get up out of. The floors were varnished dark and quick to show dust. There were several area rugs. Here a small Verkneh Kilim that refused to stay in place, there a machine-woven brown-and-yellow Bokhara never intended for prayer use. The largest rug and that which provided anchor for everything was a Turkestanian, a cross between an Uzbek and a Tadzhik, which made it neither. Nikolai had bought it at the official secondhand store on Bolshoi Prospekt. It was, for its type, a rather large knotted rug, somewhat carelessly done, perhaps for practice by the younger children of a Turkestan family or possibly by the oldest of old hands that no longer cared to weave well or just couldn't. The rug's mainly blue and red shades were unevenly faded, had been victimized by the sun.

Nikolai put down his bag and parcel and switched on

the desk lamp. There was a stack of mail on the desk. He went quickly through it. As he expected, most of it was political and to him unimportant. Bulletins and newsletters from the microdistrict, and the oblast party committees, from his trade union and the local branch of the Young Communist League, the Komsomol. There was one personal letter, from a once-removed younger cousin on the musically famous Borodin side who lived in Kalinin. Nikolai could not remember ever having met her, but for some reason she had taken it upon herself to regularly write him long, trivia-laden letters. Apparently her good intention was to alleviate the loneliness she assumed he suffered. Nikolai thought she might be projecting her own or satisfying some other need, so rather than disillusion her he always made sure his brief notes in reply contained a tinge of melancholy or a hint of brave cheer.

He dropped all the political mail unopened into the wastebasket and propped Cousin Katya's letter against the base of the desk lamp where he was least likely to forget it. He got out of his business suit, undressed completely, and sat on the edge of the bed while he placed a call to Vivian in London. When he heard the call being put through he easily pictured her in her flat, most likely as nude as he was. He had promised he would call from Moscow. He hoped she would pick up on the first ring, giving him a measure of her waiting. He heard the chirplike ringing, and after the third he imagined her having to interrupt some messy personal beauty ritual or some such thing, hurrying to the phone. There would be a click and then her voice with its distinctive slight gravel. She would know it was he calling, might not begin with a hello. Once when she'd expected a long-distance call from him she'd started with "I love you," because, as she said, the truly important things deserve preference. He let her phone ring fifteen times before he hung up. It was eleven o'clock London time. Where might she be? Eleven wasn't late, he told himself, not late enough to be either worried for her or for himself.

He got the parcel he'd brought and went into the other bedroom. For many years he'd shared that room with his grandfather, Maksim. It was now used by Lev. It wasn't officially Lev's, but, like the rest of the apartment, it was there for him and he used it freely. Lev's bed was made, but, Nikolai noticed, its spread was rumpled as it would be if two people had lain on it. He also noticed in the adjoining bathroom a fragment of tissue with the blotted pink imprint of lips floating in the otherwise clear water of the toilet bowl, and in the green glass dish on Lev's dresser, among quite a few various foreign coins, was a single iridescent plastic earclip. When had Lev last been there? Nikolai wondered. When would Lev be back? He saw that another Gauguin print had been added to the wall to the left of the bed. That wall was practically all Gauguin now.

He put the parcel on the bed and then changed his mind about just leaving it there. He picked loose the knot of the cord it was tied with and tore open its wrapper. The shearling jacket seemed glad to be released, immediately expanded. Nikolai held it up and shook it and thought how much Lev was going to like its cowboy style. He'd bought it at a shop on Kensington High at a reduced price during an off-season sale. Still, it hadn't been cheap. It was a really good jacket of its type, the inside fleece of Scottish origin, soft and thick, the outside leather pliant and pleasant to the touch, and it had buttons made from the tips of stag's antlers. Nikolai would just hang it in Lev's closet, not mention it, let Lev discover it. He found a wire hanger in the closet and pushed some of Lev's shirts and other things aside to make room. As he was putting the hook of the hanger over the closet pole the wire hanger gave way and the shearling jacket fell to the closet floor and toppled over Lev's best pair of cowboy boots. Nikolai retrieved the jacket and hung it on a more substantial wooden hanger, then he knelt to set the boots straight. He noticed something protruding from the neck of one of the boots. A French passport. Nikolai opened it and saw that it was issued to one Jean-Christian Toucel of Lyon but the photograph in it was of Lev. The passport was validly dated, appeared unquestionably official. Nikolai inverted the boot. Five other passports fell out: British, Swiss, Czech, United States, and West

German. Why would Lev risk having all these illegal passports? Being caught with them would bring a long hard-
labor prison sentence, unless, of course, Lev was KGB.
Nikolai at once dismissed altogether the possibility of Lev's
being KGB. Not Lev. More likely he was still involved with
spekulyatsiya, dealing black-market foreign currency, somehow using his job with Soyuzchimexport and these passports
to do so. That was it, Nikolai decided. He was disappointed
that Lev still chose to be mixed up in such things. However,
he would, as he had in the past, stay removed from them
and thus innocent. Best he shouldn't mention to Lev that
he'd seen the passports. He put them back into the boot
and paired the boots as he thought they had been.

He returned to his room and again put in a call to
Vivian. This time for some reason it took nearly half an
hour just to get through to London. Nikolai let her number
ring longer than before. Was something wrong with her
phone? Could it sound on this end as though it were ringing
while on her end it remained silent? He tried to blame the
possibility of such an electronic failure, to put Vivian right
there by her phone futilely awaiting his call.

He knew he was reaching.

She'd complained to him a bit about the many things
she had on her agenda that day. First she was to go to a
dealer on Brook Street and unload the ugly authentic Louis
XIV side table that Archer had given her. She expected to
get no less than thirty-five thousand pounds for it, would
haggle hard to get forty. With that money in hand she'd
pay a visit to her bank to not only wipe out all the past-
due mortgage payments on both her London and Devon
places but make several mortgage payments in advance,
giving herself a nice period of easy-mindedness. Then she
would make the rounds to her various bookmakers and
settle up with them. (The amount she'd won on her last
bet with Gareth hadn't been nearly enough to bring her
even.) She'd also personally pay off Michaeljohn, her hair-
dresser, and Harrods and Hermès too, and she'd settle some
really long, long overdue accounts at Smythson's, Penhal-
igon, Hardy Brothers, and a few others. She especially

would be delighted to pay in full her sizable bill at Partridge's, the food specialty shop on Sloane Street. What a relief to no longer feel self-conscious when she went in for a little wedge of double Gloucester or something or asked to have a few things brought around. While she was at Partridge's, she'd stock up on some delicacies for their cupboard in London and for the coming country weekend, during which she planned to very actively welcome him back, she had said. With all that much to accomplish, possibly she'd arrived home exhausted and fallen deep asleep, was now unconscious to the ring of the phone.

Not Vivian, Nikolai knew.

Hoping to round off some of his edginess, he roamed the apartment, into the kitchen, down the hallway, and around, his eyes grazing over such things as the second hinge of a door that he had used every Monday morning for a while as a boy to gauge the increase of his height. That hinge had been a confidant. Now it was merely the functional device that it was. Everything, even the mother and father and grandfather snapshots framed and placed with care on his dresser top, seemed to have shifted in meaning, receded from him. Six months ago, when he was last here, he hadn't taken any special notice of them; they also just happened to be there. Now he saw them as just flat pieces of chemically treated paper bearing likenesses. He tried to shake off that literal perspective, told himself it was a temporary outlook, would pass, had probably been brought on by his disappointment at not being able to reach Vivian. He studied the photographs. They were color prints, a bit grainy. His eyes went first to his mother, Irina Litinova, who had been beautiful to him through all his ages. She was tall, and blessed with a metabolic rate that kept her aristocratically slender. Her dark hair was middle-parted and worn straight and long, reaching down to her collarbones, allowing a vertical rectangle for her pleasing features. She refused to wear her hair up in a bun. Buns, she contended, were for babushkas or farm wives or women of the Party who believed in severity more than humanity. In the snapshot she was smiling just a hint, as though inwardly

amused more than outwardly pleased. Her arms were relaxed at her thighs, showing the back of her hands. Nikolai
had, from a very early age, associated her hands with those
of a dancer he'd seen up close when he and Lev had snuck
into a Kirov rehearsal. Such length and taper and the
exceptional grace with which she utilized and rested them.
His mother's hands were those that had led him to the elite
Yasli day nursery and to Detsky Jad, kindergarten for the
well-connected. Although there were no marshals or gen-
erals or Politburo members conveniently leafed on the family tree, it was his mother who had somehow gotten him
into the "special school" on Chernyshov Street. That he'd
been accepted because he was a Borodin, related by blood
to the musical-medical Borodin, was the explanation she
stuck to, and what other was there? Nikolai was seven when
he entered the special school and began to seriously learn
English. In the second grade he and his classmates were
required to speak only English at all times, even when they
were at play or having lunch. To lapse into Russian was a
punishable infraction. Nikolai brought home gold stars and
5s, the highest grades, and it was always his mother's marvelous hands that cupped his face and gave his mouth its
reward.

She had also seen to his political conformity, taken him
by the hand into the Young Pioneers, and from then on no
one ever questioned whether he would be of the Party. He
was the only child of loyal Party members, and it was
assumed his path was already defined. His mother, however,
did not mold him at home with the usual ideological con-
ditioning. In fact, she herself was what she considered an
"ostensible Communist with practical zealotry," and she
made sure that no one, be it peer, instructor, or political
leader, exceeded her influence over the mental shape of
her Nikolai. Whenever someone planted a Marxist absolute
in the fresh soil of Nikolai's mind, Irina discerned it and
weeded it out. She was clever about it, cautious and careful,
was well aware that she was casting the die for his values.
She did not want to do so at the sacrifice of his sense of
loyalty. Theirs was a fine line, but they balanced along it

together, and Nikolai soon enough reached the point where his understanding was indelible. He was a Communist not out of any sense of cause or fervent belief in system, not out of any feeling of debt to Marx or Lenin or past heroes, but simply because being a Communist was what was best for him to be, best for his place and time. He was, for example, his own man first and then a member of the Komsomol. Naturally, he didn't go around exposing that personal order of importance. He attended meetings but he never made a speech. He could be counted upon, counted in. Four years in a row he went to the Ukraine to help with the harvest.

Upon his graduation from the "special school" at age seventeen, Irina guided him into Leningrad State University. She seemed to know exactly what his direction should be, and was insistent about which subjects he should take. Languages and business, especially English and marketing. He did extremely well, was encouraged by her and her conviction that he was extraordinary and all he needed to do to be successful was exploit himself. He graduated with honors. Then came six months of uncertainty, during which he needed Irina's reassurance more than ever. Shouldn't he do his two years of compulsory military service now? Nikolai wanted to, just for the change from studying the army would be, and because he was restless. Irina felt all that button-polishing ridiculous; the stiff-legged marching would be a waste of him. He'd hate it, she advised; he'd want out within a week. They flared at one another over it, had their most vehement argument ever the day Nikolai happened upon an official letter that announced his deferment. Although he'd never been examined the letter said he had extreme myopia and premature ventricular contractions: nearsightedness and a sometimes abnormal heartbeat. Nikolai was furious, shouted that he was going to get bifocals and have a pacemaker put in. He hurried off to the army recruiting headquarters, filled out the enlistment forms, and took a physical examination. That same week he received a letter from the army rejecting him for medical reasons—bad eyes and erratic heart. This army-or-not matter was settled two days later by another letter, saying that he had been accepted by the Institute of Foreign Languages in Moscow, more commonly referred to throughout the Soviet Union with no less reverence as INYAZ. The notification came as a total surprise to Nikolai. He hadn't even applied to INYAZ, had thought it beyond his reach. It was almost impossible for anyone without a lot of *blat* to be accepted. It was reserved for the *nachalstvo*, the peak of the social hierarchy. It was where the diplomats and translators and foreign trade officials were trained. How was it that he qualified for that league? Was it possible that it was fairness at work, that his excellent grades at Leningrad State University and the advanced courses he'd taken at the Institute of Economics and Commerce had been noticed? Or didn't that complacent, rather victorious expression on Irina's face tell him that *she'd* somehow had something to do with it. She was happy about his acceptance by INYAZ, but considering the importance of it she took it rather calmly, as though it was something she'd been anticipating all along. Nikolai put it to her. She admitted that she'd submitted an application on his behalf, but there was nothing more he could get out of her. Nikolai pressed to know what strings she'd been able to pull. She evaded with the nicest silent reply, like old times, cupped his face and gave him a kiss. They celebrated with a huge, indulgent dinner at the Astoria.

Irina.

Now there she was in the most two-dimensional form, photographed on a day of some past summer in a loose-fitting, delicately figured cotton dress with the arm of the father, Pyotr Borodin, around her, as though it had been coaxed there by the taker, his hand defining the slenderness of her waist. The father appeared annoyed, which was his normal expression, the only one that Nikolai could recall without having to search his memory. The father laughed when he was drunk but even then it was a laugh flavored with bitterness. The father never took more than a dutiful interest in Nikolai. For some reason he was incapable of showing sincere pride in the boy, and when quite young

Nikolai stopped bringing his accomplishments home in his heart to the father. Only to the mother. Actually, these were not rare circumstances. In many Russian families the active caring was traditionally left to the mother. Nikolai learned early to be cautious of the father's disposition. It was always simmering, ready to boil. The slightest thing could get him grumbling or ignite him into an argument with the mother, and many times it developed into shoving and wrist-capturing and arm-twisting, the sort of unequal and therefore awkward violence of man against woman. Why had the mother endured the abuse, the constant sour atmosphere? Why not a divorce? Was it her Slavic fatalism to accept her lot? There always seemed to be some never-mentioned secret that kept the marriage together while it kept it apart. That was even apparent in this photograph Nikolai had chosen to have in sight.

He moved his attention six inches to the right for memories of a different quality, for Maksim Bemechev, the grandfather on the mother's side, the former Fabergé work-master, teller of czarist experiences who in the dark of the bedroom he shared with Nikolai put so much of his life into Nikolai's ears, always the romantic facets, such as how during the revolution the Winter Palace had been defended by the *Peterburzhenkas*, a battalion made up of the elegant young ladies from the best-blooded St. Petersburg families. Imagine.

Mere photographs, Nikolai thought.

The mother, the father, the grandfather.

Tomorrow he would pay them a visit. Now, however, he continued moving about the apartment, testing this sense of detachment on various things, things that belonged to him and that he belonged to. What had happened? Was this the price of absence? Had time, with its sharp ticking teeth, chewed away at his affiliation? If this wasn't home, where was? London? Anywhere in the presence of Vivian seemed to be the true answer.

He tried phoning her again and this time did not invent any excuses for her. She knew he would be calling. She knew damn well he would be worried if she wasn't there to receive his call. She was out somewhere with Archer, Nikolai presumed.

He lay on the bed, switched on the lamp that was clamped to the bedpost. A large woven basket beside the bed contained numerous past issues of magazines and newspapers. The *Pravdas*, the *Octobers*, and the *Literaturnayas* were on top. The London *Times*, France *Soirs* and *Playboys* were concealed beneath. Nikolai reached into the basket without looking. What he wanted was tucked down along the side of the basket. It was reassuring that his hand knew precisely where it would be. He brought up *Custine's Eternal Russia: The Marquis de Custine's Accounts of Royal Times*. An edition in original French that he'd had since he was eleven. He'd found it at the Prince Alexander Menshikov summer palace in Gatchina, in that sealed-off, slighted room which became his secret place. The book had been among a mildewed pile of hundred-year-old silk damask draperies. Nikolai thought it might be the sort of book that was forbidden, so he'd left it there, and the next time he came he brought what he needed to clean it. Its covers were warped, its pages dotted with acidity, and some pages were so stuck together they had to be carefully peeled apart, but it was a fine book. There was gold leaf on its edges, and the scarred leather of its covers healed beautifully when rubbed with mink oil. At first Nikolai valued this book mainly because it was something he'd found, but soon he came to cherish it for its contents, the inquisitive count's observations of the self-indulgent life in Russia during the 1800s. Nikolai read and reread it so many times he knew most of it by heart.

Now, however, it was hard in his hands and, it seemed, not nearly as precious as when he'd last picked it up. An old priceless possession had turned into a mere book. He opened it randomly: the description of a court ball to celebrate the nameday of Empress Alexandra Feodorovna on July 23, 1839. He went through a few paragraphs to see if the words were still his dear acquaintances. They refused to speak to him. He was, he thought, getting what he deserved. He placed the book down, clicked off the lamp, and lay there thinking about how long he should wait before he again tried to reach Vivian. After half an hour he got up, put on some jeans and a light sweater, and went out to get away from the phone.

He went a block over to Bolshoi Prospekt and headed south, walking briskly as though he had a destination. At two-thirty in the morning the streets were empty, except for an occasional car. It was that time when not movement or people but the structures and surfaces alone were the city. Nikolai was glad he'd decided to go out. Leningrad was his, would always be. Halfway across the Tutskow Bridge he paused, leaned on the rail, and looked down at flickers on the flow of the Neva. The river was high, he saw. There must have been a lot of rain recently, and even though it was May there would still be melting upstream. He could remember May floodings. He fixed upon a spot about fifty yards upstream and a bit off to the right and believed he wasn't more than a couple of yards off from where he and Lev used to ice-fish, always with success. They'd yank the rather small, wet silvery fish up through the hole and watch them freeze stiff as crystal within a minute. He had read somewhere, and always thought of those fish when he wondered if it was true, that freezing was a warm way to die. When other ice-fishermen who weren't even getting a nibble asked Nikolai and Lev how it was they were always so lucky, Lev would claim it wasn't luck, it was romance, and Nikolai would explain that the Neva had promised them her love. Now, here he was wondering if he'd ever ice-fish the Neva again. What would Vivian think of ice-fishing? Archer would probably liken it to taking meat out of a freezer. That might also be Vivian's opinion, he grunted.

He continued on across the river and along the quay, and as he passed close to Nicholas I, larger in bronze than he'd ever been in life, it seemed that his legs were telling him that he *did* have a destination. He went through the Gorky Gardens and after another two blocks turned onto Gevtsena Street, which before the 1917 Revolution and all the renaming that occurred with it had been Bolshaya Movskaya Street. Nikolai stopped and stood across from number 24. A four-story granite-and-limestone building of considerable size, a hundred and fifty years old. Its blue-gray slate roof was interrupted by three sharp eaves of Gothic flavor. On the ground floor there were wide entrances on the extreme left and right with four large arched store windows in between. On the floors above there were altogether thirty-three windows of identical size. The building was unlighted inside, deserted, making it all the easier for Nikolai to visualize it again as it had been in the early 1900s. Grandfather Maksim's descriptions came back to him almost verbatim:

There had been no garish sign. No need for one. The place was what it was, and those who should know it knew. Affixed to the wall immediately outside the entrance on the far left was a discreet brass plaque. Engraved upon it in Cyrillic was the name K. Fabergé, and above, also engraved, was the imperial double-headed eagle, the great warrant mark of the royal family. Two attendants served at the entrance. Their manners were as impeccable as their white jackets and gloves. They were swift to assist, to hold a bridle, assure the step down from carriage to curb for, in this instance, the Dowager Empress Maria Feodorovna and her granddaughter, Grand Duchess Olga. The mother of the Czar accompanying the daughter of the Czar. Their well-being watched over by two formidable cossack escorts. The Empress, a woman proud of the kindness with which her years had treated her, is dressed in a most recent pale green linen ensemble by Worth. The seventeen-year-old Grand Duchess wears all white, as she is required to do throughout each summer. A modest ankle-length dress of layered lawn, as simple as possible. Her white straw hat has its wide brim pinned up in front, and it is decorated there by a pale pink silk rose. The cossacks wait within hearing range as their two royal responsibilities enter the realm of Fabergé. The Dowager Empress is the epitome of confidence, amiably haute, as though bettering the air she moves through. After all, she was for many years the very Empress of wherever her steps fell. For the young Grand Duchess this visit to Fabergé is an occasion, an adventure. Although it is her first time here, she feels that she knows it well from all she has heard said about it. Only rarely is she allowed outside the confines of the Winter Palace, and, of course, never alone.

The room they enter is large, about fifty feet long and half that wide. The high ceiling is painted the softest possible blue, the walls are beige, and the angle where the walls and ceiling meet is tempered all around by a rather frivolous repetitive floral border done in pastel orange and pink and gilt. The floor is a dark hardwood laid so precisely in a herringbone pattern that hardly a crack is discernible between the boards. It is so waxed and buffed that it veritably reflects.

"Bonjour, messieurs," the Dowager Empress greets everyone in the room at once, letting it be known that this time she prefers all conversation to be in French. The sales staff in chorus return her greeting. Out from behind the showcase at the far end of the room comes Karl Fabergé himself. He has just the week before turned seventy-six, but he is still quick and bright. He is bald from forehead to nape. His full beard is white, as is the hair that flows back from his temples. He hurries forward but he is not obsequious.

The Dowager Empress expresses her fondness by addressing him with his patronym, Carl Gustanovich. They have known and liked each other for many years. Fabergé is also acquainted with the Grand Duchess Olga from her having happened to be present numerous times when he personally brought items to the Winter Palace for her father's, the Czar's, choice or approval.

And how is the Czar?

It seems he has a cold, only a slight cold, caught no doubt from overheating himself during one of his strenuous hikes.

The Czarina?

Very much concerned as usual about Czarevich Alexis but otherwise well. She has sent her regards and her appreciation for that year's Imperial Easter Egg. She is intending to write a personal note.

Will the family be staying in Tsarkoye Selo for the summer?

Anywhere else has not been mentioned, the Dowager Empress says, so she assumes they will. She herself will spend July and perhaps even August at Pavlosk, which she has always enjoyed more. Besides, her privacy is still important to her.

There is a little more of such obligatory conversation. It is brought to a close by a deep inhalation not quite a sigh, by the Dowager Empress. Fabergé does not ask if there is something special he might show them for he believes that might sound a bit pushy. He simply gestures to his right, then to his left, and questions with his eyes, in this most discreet manner asking what of his merchandise they would prefer to view, jewelry or articles of fantasy?

The Dowager Empress decides and steps to the showcase on her left. She hangs her parasol by its mother-of-pearl crook on the gleaming brass rail that is fixed to the upper front of the glass-topped case. Grand Duchess Olga does the same with her less elaborate parasol. Now their hands are free to indicate whatever of these lovely objects catches their eyes. Grand Duchess Olga is granted her grandmother's permission to remove her white gloves so that she might better know the shape and texture of those things which strike her fancy. The first she asks to see is a bonbonnière, *a sweetmeat box, circular, less than two inches in diameter. It is gold enameled with a guilloché surface, translucent pale blue and white with diamonds around the edge of its lid and a sapphire at its thumbpiece. She has come to choose a name-day present for her younger sister the Grand Duchess Marie, who is thirteen. However, she fears this tiny box may be too expensive. For three months she has been saving her seventeen-ruble-a-month allowance, which is determined at the rate of one ruble for each of her years. She tucks an errant wisp of her blond hair back in under the band of her straw. Her blue-gray eyes are livelier than usual as they scan the selection of beautiful objects in the case. Numerous guilloché enameled clocks, frames, bell pushers, perpetual calendars, all sorts of things from precious hatpins to jeweled* tcharki, *vodka cups. The moment that Fabergé senses even her slightest special interest in an item he quickly brings it out. Not in eagerness to make the sale, rather to share the appreciation, for there is nothing offered here that is not finely, tastefully made and that he is not proud of. Grand Duchess Olga examines a gold case meant to contain ball programs, and she is especially fascinated by an elaborate fan. The fan is about twenty inches long, its handle a combination of etched rock crystal and pale yellow and white guilloché enamel over gold finished off with rose diamonds and pearls. Three silk tassels dangle from the handle, and the fan part is a voluptuous gathering of white ostrich feathers. She slowly wafts the air with the fan, does quick fluttering movements with it. Its ostrich feathers respond with quivering. They bend and flow. She is amused, and so is her grandmother, who nods and forecasts that soon, darling Olga will be of an age to forsake the plain and enjoy the grand.*

The Dowager Empress is not along merely as chaperon. Even when she was Empress she always enjoyed a visit to Fabergé. She examines several objects, including a miniature frame of green and rose gold done in a moiré pattern of white enamel. It might do, she says, for a snapshot she has of the Czarevich taken aboard the imperial yacht, the Standart, *last fall. Yes, she believes the frame is exactly the correct size. She asks who it is by and is told workmaster Maksim Bemechev.*

"Lovely" is the word that conveys to Fabergé that it has been chosen. He places it aside.

Finally, there is the gift which was their purpose for coming. What shall it be for Bow Wow?—as Grand Duchess Olga calls her sister. Maria loves tiny lemon drops, places them one at a time to melt beneath her tongue. All right then, Grand Duchess Olga settles on the yellow bonbonnière *that she first looked at. No matter that it means having to sacrifice several future monthly allowances.*

Meanwhile, in other areas of that building at 24 Bolshaya Movskaya Street, more new Fabergé things are being thought up and made to come true. On the second floor, seventy-

five craftsmen are busy at their work benches, and on the third floor, a hundred more. The high benches they sit at are oddly shaped, constructed with individual recesses which permit each worker's arms to rest on the bench surface without his having to hunch. Steady hands are necessary to do such fine work, steady hands, concentration, and constant pride. There is minimal talk. The goldsmiths are heating and shaping the precious metal, chasing it with various intricate motifs. One slip of a chisel will ruin a piece they have been working on for days, and they know there is no way to get by with even a slight mistake. Every bit of their work will be closely inspected. They hold the piece they are working on up level with their eyes. For the time being, the piece is all there is, each detail a challenge, an opportunity to excel. Without breaking concentration they feel into the slinglike pouches that are nailed to the edge of the bench to find the particular tool they need. Many of these goldsmiths are less than twenty years old, outstanding apprentices. This same scrupulous attitude prevails with the setters, the finishers, the assemblers, from the most experienced professional to the youngster who for the past year has been an artelchik, *a general cleaner, and this is his very first day in his own assigned seat at a bench.*

On the fourth floor next to the design studio are the private cubicles of the workmasters. The largest cubicle is that of senior workmaster Henrik Immanuel Wigstrom, and adjacent to it are the cubicles of workmasters August Hollming and Karl Armfeldt. To be in the proximity of such respected men is an honor for Maksim Bemechev, and he is quite satisfied with the smaller cubicle that is his. Maksim at age thirty-one is the youngest workmaster now affiliated with Fabergé. He began as an apprentice in 1897 and in 1904 was promoted to a full-fledged artisan, and now it is 1912 and he has been a workmaster for little over a year. He has Wigstrom to thank for the recognition of his talents, his ability to learn excellence. Wigstrom always believed in him, encouraged him, took time to personally instruct him. Naturally being the protégé of the famous Wigstrom instantly helped his reputation, so now his own name, his own workmaster's mark, MB, appears on pieces and is rapidly becoming desirable.

At this moment Maksim is concerned with a group of twenty presentation boxes that he has been in charge of making for the Czar. They are each different except for the way they bear the Czar's monogram or portrait in miniature. Some are a combination of various-colored golds, others combine guilloché enamel and gold. They all appear splendid. However, as Maksim inspects them one at a time he places four apart from the others. Those four are not perfect. The hinges of one, for example, do not articulate with absolute ease. The diamond-set border of another is ever so slightly out of line. Unnoticeable perhaps by just anyone, but nevertheless to Maksim's eyes out of line. These boxes are intended to be added to the stock of Fabergé items that is kept on hand in a special room at the Winter Palace. Czar Nicholas II draws from them whenever he must demonstrate his largess to a visiting dignitary or someone who has done some service deserving of a special expression of gratitude. No other jeweler, not Cartier nor Boucheron nor anyone, is shown such confidence, and the arrangement is an important source of automatic profit to Fabergé. Tomorrow, Maksim will personally take the boxes to the palace and the imperial chamberlain will add them to the account. By means of a silver push bell Maxim summons one of the clerks to have the sixteen approved boxes packed and ready for transport.

That done, Maksim must go down to the ground floor to the kiln where the enamel work is fired. He will check on the progress of some knitting needles that he is making for Consuela, Duchess of Marlborough. No ordinary knitting needles these, with their ten-inch-long shafts of shaved ebony and their caps an intricate arrangement of gold, white enamel, and rubies. To the stairway down, Maksim detours so his way takes him through the design studio. He intends only to have Alma in his sight for a passing moment. However, when he sees her and when she looks up and they are eyes to eyes, he is compelled to pause at her drawing table. She is twenty-four, the daughter of the late workmaster, Knut Pihl. In Maksim's estimation Alma Terisia Pihl possesses all *the attributes of a Finnish beauty. Large blue candid eyes, a sensuous full-lipped mouth, and a complexion so exquisitely pale that it seems to have never been punished a single moment by the sun. And that is not all. Alma has proved herself a talented designer. At the moment her project is the most important one in the shop: the Imperial Winter Egg for 1913. Several ideas she has sketched for it are scattered about her table.*

Maksim is not merely attracted to her, he is aflame with her.

Headlights.

On high beam.

A black Chaika sedan approached slowly, running close to the curb so that the two men in it could get a good look at whoever it was standing in a doorway of Bolshaya Movskaya Street at this hour. Even had Nikolai not noticed the radio antenna in the center of the Chaika's roof he would have known the men were police. It occurred to him that he had no identification on him. How stupid of him to come out without at least his internal passport. How Western of him, he also thought. It was another example of the foreigner he had become. The Chaika went by and then speeded up. Nikolai knew it would circle back and stop. The policemen would ask who he was and where he lived, and when he told them they would want to see his internal passport with the *propiska*, the official stamp, that allowed him to live here in Leningrad. It would end up all right but be a hassle. Nikolai hurried down the street, took the long way around the back of Saint Isaac's Cathedral, and returned to the apartment.

It was past three o'clock.

He was reluctant to try phoning Vivian again, because if she wasn't there he'd feel worse. He lay on the bed in the dark and fought his anger and futility with imaginary visits to what he thought would be pleasant places. Such as alone in the noon sun perched on a rock on the coast of Maine with the brightness making him keep his eyes closed. He drifted off.

CHAPTER
✦✦✦ 11 ✦✦✦

AFTER ONLY THREE HOURS NIKOLAI CAME ALL AT ONCE awake.

His very first thought, as though it had been crouched there on the front of his mind awaiting the instant of his consciousness, was that he should get back to London. He would not go into the Almazjuvelirexport office and see Valkov, not even let Valkov know he'd been in Leningrad. He would just get on the first plane out any way possible. He could use his trade-mission *blat* for one of those seats Aeroflot always holds aside for the *nachalstvo*, the big shots. Hell, he *was* one of the *nachalstvo*, just not so highly favored. He would bribe, promise to bring back next trip to whomever he had to twenty pairs of Porsche-type sunglasses, and just as many Japanese digital talking wristwatches. It wouldn't matter to him that someone might have to be bumped off the flight. He would go the long way, change planes or even lay over in Helsinki. He would . . .

When he was on his feet and moving around his emotional balance was better. And by the time he was done in the bathroom and had drunk a couple of glasses of hot tea he'd recovered to the extent that he chose from his closet an average Soviet suit and unmistakably Soviet accessories, which was his way of telling himself that he'd decided to go about this day in Leningrad as originally planned.

When he was outside on Bolshoi Prospekt he didn't see an available taxi, so he started walking and kept on in the direction of his mother, father, and grandfather. The day was abnormally clear for early morning, colors were intensified, the edges of everything sharp. It was not the sort of

light that contributed best to the beauty of this city. Along
his way Nikolai went in at a shop for a round loaf of that
blackest bread called *chorny* and a wedge of strong yellow
cheese. From a street vendor he bought a bouquet of pink
carnations that were on the verge of wilt but the best of
the bunches. He crossed over the Neva again for about the
twenty thousandth time in his life and continued on down
Maly Prospekt to Smolenskoye Cemetery.

He couldn't be sure of the hours, because they were
always being changed, but when he saw the first gate was
open he knew the others would be. He went in at the
fourth gate and walked down the wide graveled lane, feeling
the press of the countless stone crosses and stars on each
side. A *dyedushka* came from the opposite direction. Nikolai noticed the old man's trousers were soiled by fresh
dirt at the knees.

To the end of that lane and up a short way of another
and on the left was the seven-foot-high symmetrically carved
and smoothed hunk of blue-black rock with his last name
cut into it. It stood for the whole Borodin plot, which was
rectangular, its perimeter defined to the inch by a black
wrought-iron fence topped by forbidding spears. Similar to
the fences for privacy in the Belgravia sections of London,
Nikolai thought. He entered the plot and stood above the
polished horizontal slab that marked the place of his mother.
He wondered what he should think. Was he feeling what
he should feel? It was difficult for the living to know what
the dead might expect of them when the living know the
dead should not be able to expect. Whatever, one thing he
felt for certain: he had been remiss in his visits here. It
had been two years. He placed the carnations across the
etched word IRINA and mentally apologized for their limp-
ness. Wasn't it for his own sake that he wished now he'd
brought a plentiful bouquet of yellow day lilies, the pale
lemon, freckled-throated ones that he wouldn't ever forget
had been her favorite? Also, he should have brought more
food, better food, and, despite the early hour, at least a
demi of vodka. It wasn't really an insult that he hadn't, he
told himself. He took an old front page of *Izvestia* from

his business case and spread it on his mother's slab. He placed the bread and the cheese on the paper and then sat on the end of her slab. The morning sun was getting through the leaves of the overhead maple branches in irregular splashes, bright helpful countermeasures. He gazed at the five-pointed Soviet star that was etched above her name and believed that it rather than a cross was what she would have wanted etched there, given the choice. Her apparent Communism would be, to her way of thinking, the most valuable thing she could leave him. Nikolai couldn't picture her in the packed ground beneath him down there in a box. The way she must look by now was beyond his acceptance. Bones and clothes and hair. He glanced to the next grave, the slab of his father, and that triggered a reenactment as the facts and his imagination had it assembled, condensed by reiteration and time gone by.

An argument, probably no more vehement than any of their others. After the argument (she always recovered from them quickly) the mother at her desk about to write him, Nikolai, a letter. Only the three words "My dearest Nikolai" got out of her pen before the revolver point-blank in the father's hand sent the bullet into the back of her head. Then on that same piece of paper the father wrote, "I have just killed my wife," just that, no reason, nothing else before putting the muzzle to his right eye and firing.

Going through the reenactment was for Nikolai prerequisite to being there, but he no longer dwelled on it. Besides, he was not there to hurt or hate but to celebrate his ancestors, to make up for the past two Easters when it had been impossible for him to observe tradition.

He tore a piece of bread from the loaf and broke off a chunk of the cheese. It was the less-expensive, strong sort of cheese that rats and mice are particularly attracted to. Nikolai liked it. He hadn't realized how hungry he was. He ate almost half the loaf and a good part of the cheese. Dropped some of each on the slabs of his mother and father. He did not forget his Grandfather Maksim, never would. He moved to the far corner of the plot, where his grandfather's slab was located, although he was not a Borodin.

All of his grandfather's people, including Grandmother Lilya, were among the half million World War II dead buried in the mass graves of Piskaryov Memorial Cemetery. They had died in the Nazi siege.

Nikolai paid tribute to Grandfather Maksim with one of countless recollections: an afternoon at the dacha in Komarovo, lying naked in the grass, ants making them squirm and slap while the sun warmed them and Grandfather with eyes closed, reliving, recounted some of the pleasant times he'd had during those years right after the Revolution when he had tried to live in Paris. He had worked for Cartier for a while. He had almost married an American, but he missed the boat, literally—got to Le Havre three hours after the *Ile de France* had sailed. No matter, the woman was shrewish and evidently had no patience. But Maksim thought he would have made a splendid American.

Nikolai smiled as he reheard Grandfather Maksim saying that. He went back to his mother's slab to decide on what he would sing. Instead of a song he hummed a theme from Stravinsky's *Petrouchka*. It was, he felt, perfect for now, especially the first Shrovetide Fair part, so gay and sprightly. His mother used to hum fragments of it unconsciously. So that was how he did it now as a finale to his respects. He hummed quietly and then louder, and then feeling the spirit he la-dadada'd and otherwise imitated the instruments full out, even the drum part.

The melody was still in Nikolai's head when a half hour later he arrived at his office at the headquarters of Almazjuvelirexport. Originally this branch of foreign trade had been situated in Moscow, and like all other Soviet involvement with diamonds it was kept at the lowest possible profile. However, twelve years ago, the Politburo had felt it would be more comfortable if Almazjuvelirexport was removed from the immediate political neighborhood. It seemed there were still some old Party fundamentalists around the Kremlin who were rubbed the wrong way by anything so historically capitalistic. Whenever they wanted to exemplify progress being made in the wrong direction they got going loudly on diamonds, associating them with the likes of Catherine the Great, whom they always referred to with emphatic delight as Catherine the Whore. To illustrate their contention regarding diamonds they used such decadent magazines as *Town and Country* and *Vogue Française*, paperclipping those pages which displayed photographs of wealthy Western women so weighted down by diamond necklaces, earrings, and often even tiaras that they could hardly hold their heads up. Also in those photographs were the men of money, the exploiters themselves. Were they not wearing their women and therefore the diamonds? Never mind that the selling of this commodity to the West was substantially beneficial to Soviet economy. Social purity was more important than profit, the Party dinosaurs said.

Few agreed. Nevertheless it was an embarrassing bother having always to put up with this outdated and impractical point of view. So Almazjuvelirexport was relocated in Leningrad, where it ran just as smoothly and that much more unobtrusively. It occupied the entire extensive wing of a mansion that had always been painted a peach shade. The mansion, built in the baroque style of Rastrelli in the 1800s, had been a gift from a Romanov prince to his ballerina mistress, in appreciation, no doubt, for her outstanding performances.

Almazjuvelirexport had sixty-four employees there, although it could easily have done as well with half that number. Ostensibly it was set up to operate as would any corporate entity, with a corporatelike management hierarchy and the right to make or break deals on its own. There was, of course, no issuing of stock or dividing up of profits. In effect, the only shareholder and profit-taker was the Soviet state through its Ministry of Foreign Trade. Thus the Minister of Foreign Trade, Grigori Savich, was ultimately responsible for determining how Almazjuvelirexport went about its business. If anyone had a measure of autonomy it was Savich, and although Almazjuvelirexport was but one of the sixty-some export-import organizations in his charge, he seemed to take a special interest in it.

The head of Almazjuvelirexport functioned like a chief executive officer. He had the final say-so on all day-to-day matters and he reported to no one but Savich. He was Feliks Valkov, a forty-five-year-old Party man. Although aggressively ambitious, Valkov had a lot more push than pull, and that would limit him. He wasn't even remotely related to anyone on the upper power level, nor did he have that rare and almost priceless circumstance of a "close friend up there." His best high connection was the one he had with Savich, but it wasn't the sort that would ever take him up. In fact, his tie with Savich seemed only to serve for business; apparently no tight personal knot had developed over the years of their association.

Valkov's educational background was only adequate. There was no "special school" or Institute of Foreign Languages in it. He had qualified for Moscow State University, where his major studies were geology and marketing. He got the most he could from the extra English courses that he took, and he was otherwise conscientious in learning to speak that language well. But he had no way of getting out of serving his two years in the army. His first professional job was as a geologist, one of many with the task of locating deposits of strategic minerals. He brought early attention to himself by helping to find much-needed cobalt deposits in the Urals and in Krasnoyarsk Territory. His knowledge of geology naturally embraced gemology. He was assigned a supervisory position at the diamond-mining installation in Aikhal. Never once was he heard to gripe about the Siberian remoteness, the extreme winter cold, or the merciless summer mosquitoes. After nearly three years he was advanced to an administrative spot at Aikhal. Then he was instrumental in vastly improving the quality and output of Aikhal's diamonds by insistently advocating changing over to electronic cutting and polishing machines. To make sure he was right he spent a lot of time learning firsthand all he could about the cutting and polishing process, and he got to be very chummy with several of the more experienced cutters. In 1975 he was put in charge of the Aikhal installation. The state couldn't have done better. During Valkov's six years Aikhal didn't have a single major setback, in fact it had hardly any problems at all. Valkov was as strict as he had to be with the personnel, got rid of the chronic bitchers while he scratched the backs of the essential skilled workers, particularly the cutters.

His outstanding account of himself at Aikhal got him the Almazjuvelirexport appointment. It was a huge step up. Valkov relished the recognition, but what delighted him more and what anyone in his place would have considered the real reward was the privileges. The spacious apartment and chauffeured Zil limousine. The dacha on the Bay of Finland, the permanent passport and unrestricted foreign travel. At last, the quality life he deserved, he thought. What it also meant was a happier and, therefore, a more sexually cooperative wife. He had married Yelena while he was in charge of the Aikhal installation. She had detested the place, likened it to Siberian exile. Numerous times she threatened to flee. Valkov was constantly having to placate her. She wasn't the sort of woman who would tolerate mistreatment. Untypically, she didn't have the fatalistic attitude that made most Slav women accept their poor lot. The majority of Slav women resented it, perhaps, but not outwardly or actively, when a Russian male spewed such things as "Women are more useful than equal" or "A woman has no soul, only vapor." Yelena Valkova was not the sort to take that, would never be. She was different. For one thing, she was beautiful. Not hefty from a too starchy diet as most Soviet women, but tall and slender. No doubt her beauty had a lot to do with shaping her outlook. Beauty had the right to demand, she believed, and she wasn't at all modest about how important it was to her that she *have* things. Yelena was driven with wants. What she certainly *didn't* want, however, was a child. Nor did Valkov. During their eight years of marriage she'd had six abortions. She didn't bother Valkov with them. They were her problem. She just went and had them. Having six abortions wasn't that unusual but it did put her just slightly ahead of the average number for Soviet women of child-bearing age.

Yelena was more than happy to trade Aikhal and Siberia for Almazjuvelirexport and Leningrad. She dreaded the thought of ever being considered *nyekulturnyi*, and there was no longer any chance of that. She had many things others didn't. She was able to travel with Valkov to Paris and even New York, where she could be as fashionable as she wanted. She even had diamonds, a secret little horde of thirty choice stones ranging in size from half a carat to two carats and one treasured stone of ten carats. Valkov, exercising the prerogative of his position, merely picked one up now and then as a sample of production and surprised her with it. For the time being she could only play with her diamonds. They weren't even set. But perhaps someday . . .

By the end of Valkov's fourth year in Leningrad he and his Yelena were taking their privileges for granted. Their satisfaction with what they had and could have went flat. Advantages that had been of utmost importance now seemed petty. So what if they could have calves' liver whenever they wanted, when they had dined at Maxim's and Taillevent? Where was the joy, really, in impressing people who were always so easily impressed? Yelena had been devastated by comparison during a September-afternoon stroll in Paris along Faubourg Saint-Honoré. She'd been there before, but that time, for some reason, the force of fashionable possessions struck her differently and she came away feeling diminished. Valkov had a somewhat similar experience in Paris on the same trip, when, just for the sake of curiosity, he'd gone into a real estate agent's office and inquired about the price of a villa on the Costa del Sol. Neither Yelena nor Valkov discussed having these feelings, but they made them known with irritated moods, episodes of ennui, frequent dissatisfaction with each other. Separately they began thinking upward, looking upward, and at about the same time both came to the realization that in the Soviet system this would be their eternal plateau, as high as Valkov would ever go. His foreground had reached the limit of his background. If only he had been one of the so-called *zolotaya molodyozh*, the golden youth, with a father on the Central Committee or of high rank in the military. If only his education had been at the Institute of Foreign Languages or the Moscow Institute for International Relations. If only he had come up to where he was the softer way.

Almazjuvelirexport.

Feliks Valkov.

Nikolai dialed Valkov's interoffice number and asked the secretary when Valkov might be available to see him. He was told Valkov had just gotten in and had a very full day; however, in about ten minutes he could give Nikolai the next ten.

That suited Nikolai. There was nothing specific that he wanted to get into with Valkov. This touching base with him was merely a courtesy, and overdue inasmuch as their only contact in three months had been by telephone.

Nikolai sat back in his desk chair. Its swiveling mechanism complained with a creak. He noticed how dusty the fake-leather-covered arm of it was. It occurred to him that he'd sat down on a layer of dust. In fact, his mere presence in the office had stirred up a lot of it. The shaft of morning sun coming through the only window had millions of frantic motes in it. That, he thought, was what he was breathing. He wondered if when he inhaled those motes stayed in him. Every surface of his office was coated with dust. The desk, the small table overburdened with several years of unimportant memorandums and copies of the *Bulletin of Foreign Commercial Information*, the metal four-drawer file cabinet, everything. He hadn't been here. No one had been here. Even the three ball-point pens that he took from the trough in his desk drawer had gone dry. It was depressing. However, this wasn't really his office but just a space in which to sit for the few days a year he was in Leningrad, a place to keep things that he didn't take the time to sort and throw out. That was why it was so small, had terrible light, was located way back here within hearing range of the flush of the employees' toilet and farther than everything else from Valkov's office. Nikolai thought about complaining that his office wasn't being vacuumed and dusted but then he decided he didn't really mind having it the way it was, actually would prefer to think of it that way rather than well tended and waiting for him when he was in London. He caused another minor dust storm when he got up and went out.

The door to Valkov's office was shut. The secretary's indifferent glance was Nikolai's permission to enter. Valkov was standing before the bank of tall french windows at the far end of the room, faced away, gazing out as though he were mulling over a difficult decision. Nikolai believed it was a pose, because Valkov took his cue too abruptly, turned, and came at him with the assumed small smile that he had ready and his right hand extended like a weapon. Their handshake matched firm for firm. They greeted each other in Russian but then spoke only in English. Unlike Nikolai, Valkov had a tinge of Russian accent. It was like a bit too much salt in soup; the flavor could never be removed. It pointed out the disparity between his and Nikolai's educational background, and therefore other differences as well.

"When did you get in?" Valkov asked for small talk.

"This morning," Nikolai fibbed for the hell of it.

"I have to be in Moscow tonight," Valkov said as though that wasn't ordinary. He spent considerable time in Moscow, prided himself in being an absolute Muscovite. Once, in this regard, when having a drink with Nikolai he had toasted, *"Pervyi srednii ravnykh!"*—First among equals! Valkov's physical appearance made Nikolai wonder how much truth there was in the man's claim to the many pure Russian generations his family went back to before the keeping of family records. Valkov's coloring wasn't just fair, he was so fair he seemed to come only a fraction of a gene from being albino. His hair was blond but the sort of white blond that tow-headed youngsters begin with. His brows were that same shade and so were his lashes, which were, unfortunately in his case, thick and unusually long. He had angular features that would have been strong if he'd been dark, but they lost much to his pasty complexion. His lips were pale, his eyes light green and heavy-lidded into slits. The impression he gave was physical weakness, perhaps susceptibility to disease. The opposite was true. He was in excellent condition and quite athletic. He belonged to what Leningraders called the Walrus Club, a group who chopped swimming holes in the ice of the Neva.

"I understand you had a very successful go with Churcher," he said, referring to the 5 percent price increase.

"So it appears."

"Congratulations. Minister Savich phoned this morning and told me how it went. I wish I could have been there."

"That would have made it absolutely merciless." Nikolai flattered the man because the opportunity was so obvious.

Valkov gestured for Nikolai to be seated. As Valkov's chair received his weight, Nikolai noticed it didn't complain, rather the real-leather-covered seat cushion let out a sort of grateful sigh. The surface of Valkov's spacious desk had nothing on it other than a telephone. His phone didn't ring. It lighted up, as it did now. Without apology he took the call.

Valkov spoke low. Nikolai didn't try to hear. He looked about the room and remembered how it was said that this had once been the ballerina's boudoir, where she had done her horizontal *pas de deux*. Now prominent and well lighted on the wall was the predictable portrait of Lenin, the one of him seated at a table preoccupied with writing with a pencil. Nikolai had all his life tried to care for Lenin. Several years ago in the main reading room of the British Museum he'd seen a reproduction of the actual official bulletin which was drawn up to announce to the world what had taken place in Ekaterinburg in 1918. On it all references to having executed the Empress and the children were crossed out and the words "Publication prohibited" written over them. What could be more graphic evidence of shame? Even the signature on the bulletin was, probably out of shame, illegible. The Bolshevik leaders were in favor of executing the Czar, but only him. They wanted to exile the others. It was Lenin who was adamant, insisted that Empress Alexandra, Grand Duchesses Olga, Tatiana, Maria and Anastasia and little Grand Duke Alexis also be shot and bayoneted to death in that cellar of the Ipatiev house. Nikolai thought Lenin's motive had been as much personal as political, and he was often reminded of that when he saw a picture of the man.

"Would you care for a glass of tea?" Valkov asked, a formality.

"No, thank you."

"You return to London when?"

"In a few days."

"The next field trip to Aikhal is scheduled for sometime in September, you know."

"I know." Did they now think that he had to be reminded of times? Had Savich said anything to Valkov about his being late for the meeting yesterday? Whether Savich had or not wasn't crucial. Nikolai's professional stance was split, with one foot in Almazjuvelirexport and the other in the Ministry of Foreign Trade; however, his weight was in the Ministry. Valkov realized that and was chafed by it. He would have liked nothing better than to do away with all this artificial civility and put his knee hard and heavy on Nikolai's neck.

"The reason I mention Aikhal," Valkov said, "is that the trip will more than likely be postponed."

"Oh?" That was good news. To Nikolai the required annual field trips to Aikhal were a waste of time. They were supposed to give Almazjuvelirexport executives a thorough understanding of the methods of recovering, processing, and finishing diamonds, but they were little more than superficial tours.

"Instead," Valkov went on, "you and I and a couple of others may go elsewhere." He unlocked his center desk drawer and from it brought out a heavy manila envelope that was bulging with whatever it contained. He undid the envelope's flap and, with care, slid something wrapped in black tissue onto his desk. Slowly, relishing the moment, anticipating Nikolai's reaction, he unfolded the tissue.

Revealed were emeralds. Uncut emerald crystals of various sizes. Altogether about a thousand carats of them. Some were no larger than kernels of corn. A few were as long as a pencil and twice a pencil's thickness. All were perfectly formed, six-sided, and not just bright green but a pure, deep, lively green that shot out to the eyes. Nikolai's thought was they looked like solidified crème de menthe.

"Emeralds," Valkov enunciated.

Nikolai came close to saying aloud, "No shit." Even if he'd tried to be blasé those emeralds would have made it impossible. He thought he'd like to have one for Vivian, one of the large ones.

Valkov pushed the emerald-bearing black tissue paper eight inches closer to Nikolai. "I'd like your opinion of them."

Nikolai, aware of Valkov's gemological expertise, knew the man was taking advantage. He cooperated, humbled himself. "I know zero about emeralds."

"Being in the gem business, you should never admit that," Valkov advised him somewhat censoriously. "An experienced gem man such as myself can ascertain the quality of any colored stone in a matter of seconds. In fact, with my bare eye I can even tell what part of the world an emerald came from. Take these, for example. Where would *you* say these were dug up?"

"That's not fair." Nikolai grinned. "You got a look at the postmark."

Valkov had a stunted sense of humor. "At least you could take a guess," he said snidely.

"Okay." Nikolai shrugged and after some thought said, "Maybe they're from Uzbekiskaya."

Valkov looked like someone who had just smacked full-speed into an invisible wall. "Savich told you," he said.

Uzbekiskaya had been a wild guess, but Nikolai knew he'd never convince Valkov of that. So he said nothing, just looked well informed. He'd been honest about his knowledge of emeralds. They were green, rare, and expensive, he knew, but he'd never had reason to learn about them. Actually he wasn't all that fascinated with gems of any sort, not even diamonds, despite the technical information he'd assimilated over the years. He could tell a really good diamond from a bad one, but to him they were not a passion, only a commodity.

"How much did Savich tell you?" Valkov asked.

"Just a mention."

That put Valkov back on track. "Several months ago these emeralds were found on a captured Uzbek guerrilla who was bound for Afghanistan to trade them for weapons. Our military people there have since learned the location of the principal mines and more or less gained control of them. Moscow wants us to have a look, evaluate the yield, and say whether or not it would be worth the bother of pushing our way into the emerald market. So, come September, we'll be flying to Dusanbe rather than Aikhal."

You go, Nikolai thought. The last thing he wanted was to be in an interdicted zone and get blown away while picking up little green stones. Coward he wasn't, but well . . . why was it that the idea of dying in the desolate mountains of Uzbekiskaya was so much worse than the idea of dying elsewhere—worse, for instance, than being run down by a ten-ton truck while dodging across Piccadilly? Besides, if he went to Uzbekiskaya it wouldn't be mere misfortune that he was killed. His impression of the guerrilla fighters of that area, gathered from BBC newscasts and documentaries and various articles, was that they were practically born with rifles in their hands and were all vying to prove who was the sharpest shooter. Fuck that.

"I suggest between now and then you learn as much as you can about emeralds," Valkov said and put a period on the conversation by standing abruptly and glancing at the way out.

Now *that* to worry about, Nikolai thought as he left Valkov's office and walked down the hall. He had two months, but already excuses to get him out of the emerald field trip were being presented by what he believed was his will to survive.

He arrived back in his dustbin of an office and closed the door. Sat and contemplated the telephone call that had been imminently there between his consciousness and his actions for the past eight hours. What should his opening words be? Certainly he shouldn't begin with "Where the hell were you all night?"—even if that was his emotional inclination. Did he have enough control to be casual?

Telling himself the best way to sound relaxed was to be relaxed, he leaned back, put his legs up on the desk, and crossed them. Took a half-dozen slow breaths so deeply filling they made his stomach hump. With the phone balanced on his crotch he placed the call, and within a minute her number was ringing.

She picked up. Her hello was sleepy, but he believed it had a lot of hoping-it-was-him in it. "Where are you?" she asked.

"Leningrad."

"You were supposed to go to Moscow."

"I did but I didn't stay over."

"I tried reaching you at the hotel, the one where you said you'd be, the Kosmos. I had a devil of a time making them understand. They told me you were registered. They paged you and everything. Why would they tell me that unless it was true?"

"I didn't even go to the hotel. I came on to Leningrad instead."

"How was I to know? Honestly, I must have tried to get you at least twenty times. It ruined my concentration."

"I thought you were going to be home last night," Nikolai told her calmly.

"I intended to be."

An interval of silence asked why she hadn't been.

"I went with Archer to his club."

"For dinner?"

"For poker. You know, my regular game at Brooks's."

"He sneaked you into it again?"

"I wish he hadn't," she thought aloud.

Nikolai jumped right on that. "Why?"

She diverted him brightly with: "How's the old hometown?"

"No different."

"I miss you enormously. You know how mumpish I get even when we're apart in the same city, so think what I'm like when you're far away in another country." Then, in her unhalting manner: "Where did you spend the night?"

"My apartment."

"I also called there twice."

"Must have been when I was out."

"With whom?"

"Leningrad. A long walk."

More silence while she accepted that.

"It's your fault, you know," she said. "If you weren't so fucking special maybe I wouldn't be so fucking jealous."

He laughed. God, he loved her. "Did you get all your errands run yesterday?"

"That dumb dealer gave me forty-two thousand for the table. That ugly thing. Imagine!"

"Cash?"

"Good as. A cashier's check."

"And?"

"I went straight to my bank with it. The sweet, understanding man in mortgages who usually tends to me wasn't there. Seems he was transferred or something. Anyway, there was a dreadful fellow in his place. Dried up old priss never even glanced at my knees. He kept harping about how often and how much I'd been in arrears. He was a mess, couldn't talk without spraying spittle."

"You put him in his place."

"You bet I did. I iced him with a look, threw him a high shoulder, and left."

"Without making the mortgage payments?"

"I had to get out of there. Either that or suffocate. Banks do me that way. I think I react negatively to the presence of so much cash."

"What bills did you pay?"

"I had a nice late lunch at the Berkeley. I rather enjoy observing married female boredom, but not so much when they don't have the pluck to do anything about it. There they sit, libidos squirming, while they put polite tiny bites into their tight tiny mouths."

Nikolai only half-heard her words, because he was mentally assembling her yesterday. He believed he had it. "How much did you lose?" he asked.

"I got phenomenal cards," she said, "for a while. Then it leveled off to just my winning my share of pots. We were playing stud and I'd get aces or kings but always open and everyone would fold on me, so few of the pots I won were large. It was maddening." She sighed as though to erase that part of it and brought her mood up a notch. "I was a sport, though," she said. "I didn't bitch at all about the cigar smoking, nor did I even pretend to be shocked at the obscenities."

The five men she played poker with owned much of London. They were older, the sort who very likely had once put down their Pimm's Cup No. whatever just long enough to shoot an ambling tiger from a well-appointed tree blind.

"It was a bloody strange night," Vivian went on. "What with my having to get up from the table to try to phone you every twenty minutes and all the good but second-best hands I was dealt."

"Did you lose it all? All forty-two thousand?"

"And a bit more," she said blithely, "counting the markers I signed."

"Shit!"

"A description of me or just my luck?"

Nikolai didn't reply.

Vivian took that as his answer. "You're angry."

He sure as hell was. Perhaps someday, he thought, someone would invent a device that would allow the person on one end of a phone conversation to press a button and deliver an electric jolt to the person on the other end.

"Don't be angry," she advised pointedly. "You've got no right to be angry. I blew the money, but it's my affair."

She was annoyed. It would be painful for him, worse than anything, to have her miffed at him. He wouldn't let it get to that. Softly, he explained, "It's only that I hoped your making the mortgage payments and paying off all your other bills would get you out from under so much stress."

"What stress?" she said satirically. "Really, Nickie darling, don't be upset. Don't fret for a minute."

"Not me."

"And don't be disappointed in old Viv, either. Are you?"

"No."

"Good. Believe me, something will come up. As a matter of fact, I think it already has."

"What?"

"Well, Archer came by a short while ago to commiserate and to make sure I hadn't taken strychnine. Only stayed for a minute. It seems he left something on the hall table."

"*Seems* that he did?"

"He did. At first, seeing that it was an envelope, I thought it might be one of his huge, timely checks, in which case, bless his heart, I would have torn it to shreds or scribbled 'canceled' across the face of it and returned it immediately, believe me. As you know, I've done both any number of times. However . . . are you still there, Nickie?"

"Yes, go on."

"For a moment I thought we'd been cut off. Is this call being monitored?"

"Possibly."

"For heaven's sake, why? It's so innocent. Anyway, the envelope is addressed by a German someone in Hamburg to a German someone in New York and sent by way of the *Hindenburg* on its last trip. It has the special *Hindenburg* stamp on it, and the paper is even a bit singed. It might be one of the few pieces of mail that wasn't destroyed. Worth a bundle, wouldn't you think?"

"I'd think."

"But hell, Nickie, I'm not a collector of such things. I haven't the slightest interest. More than likely I'd forget what it was and end up sharpening the point of an eyeliner pencil on it. Right?"

Archer, gigantic-hearted Archer, Nikolai thought. True, he liked Archer well enough, close to well enough to consider him a friend, but wasn't it evident that Archer encouraged Vivian's squandering at every opportunity? Wasn't Archer a veritable conspirator to it, often supplying the means *and* the ways? That being the case, Archer's motive was also obvious: provide now and, through habit and necessity, become the legal provider later. Ironic as it might be, Nikolai told himself, he was being killed by friend Archer's kindness. What steps might he take to avoid that?

One thing came immediately to mind. It was something Nikolai had considered doing for the past year, but until now he hadn't been in the right place at the right time. It was something that could substantially interrupt the cycle of dependency Archer had going, or at least take some of the momentum out of it. Never mind the logical reasons against, Nikolai thought, he'd heard them from himself before and now refused to listen.

Vivian was saying: "I'm going to call Archer and urge him to take back this *Hindenburg* letter. But I doubt he will. You know how he is. That, of course, will leave me no recourse but to quibble over a price for it with some scroungy stamp dealer. Come to think of it, I know of one on New Bond."

"I'll tell you what to do with it," Nikolai said.

"What?" Surprised he had a suggestion.

"Get into a taxi, go to Archer's flat, don't say a word, just leave it on *his* hall table."

"Don't be daft! I've accounts to pay. There are the mortgage loans. I owe four bookmakers."

"Trust me, do it."

A skeptical grunt from her, and some hums and sibilant mumbles as she carried on her inner argument. Finally, she asked: "Are you absolutely sure?"

"I'll be there tomorrow."

"Hurry, lover." She hung up before she could change her mind and he picked up his business case and left his office before she could call back.

CHAPTER
◆·◆·◆ 12 ◆·◆·◆

HE WAS COMMITTED.

He went down the stairs and out the main door of the talented ballerina's mansion. He glanced down the wide gravel walk to the gate that gave to Fontanka Quay. A car was stopped in front of the gate, a bright red car, a convertible with top down. As he proceeded down the walk, Nikolai realized that it was a Mercedes-Benz 450SL. It had to be the car of someone of the *nachalstvo*, someone who was above giving a damn about being obvious with such a privilege. Nikolai saw the back of a blond female head on the passenger side and then, from beyond her, like a jack-in-the-box, up came Lev. Too anxious to bother with the door, Lev vaulted up over the side of the car with Nikolai's name coming so joyously from him it was like a victory cry. He charged at Nikolai and caught him in a two-armed hug that squeezed out Nikolai's breath. Nikolai returned the hug and the elation. They kissed on the lips, a brief man-to-man kiss.

"I haven't seen you for a hundred years," Lev said, grinning.

Nikolai came right back with: "I see you at least every day." Then he stemmed the mood by indicating the red Mercedes at the curb in an absolutely forbidden zone. "But tell me, why did you choose a car such as this? If you had to steal a car, why not a nice invisible gray Zhiguli?"

"You like this car?"

"No," Nikolai kidded.

"If you want this car you can have it. I can give it to you legally."

"Don't shit me."

"I bought it yesterday from a Georgian who drove it up from Tbilisi loaded with oranges. He fucked me on the price, but money is shit to a good Communist, right? Isn't it beautiful?" They were beside the car now, and Lev ran his hand over the perfect finish of the rear fender. It was as though he'd touched the girl, for at that moment she turned bright-faced to him, her eyes pleading for attention. Her name was Kecia, and when during the introduction Lev said her name she swished her heavy blond hair back from her cheeks as though proud of her looks, wanting to present them entirely. She was Finnish and could not have been more honestly pretty. Her clean face glowed as if just washed in a cold stream. She spoke no English and very little Russian, but, Lev explained, she had ways of making herself perfectly understood.

"Get in, we'll go for a ride," Lev said, opening the passenger door.

"What do you have to do today?" Nikolai asked.

"Nothing disagreeable."

"Can you run me out to the dacha?"

"Sure."

Nikolai thought that Kecia would climb into the narrow space behind the seats. She was slender enough to make it only a tight squeeze. She surrendered the passenger seat to Nikolai, but then got in on top of him. He spread his legs and she sat on the merest edge of the seat with her buttocks fitted tight into his crotch.

Lev started the car, gave the accelerator pedal a couple of pumps to make the tachometer needle jump all the way around into the red and to cause two appropriate roars. He dropped the gearshift into first and made the cobbles scream as he pulled away, did an immediate U-turn, and sped alongside Fontanki Canal. At the first major intersection, Nikolai expected they would continue straight on, which was the correct way to go, but Lev took a right. That put them on Nevsky Prospekt, Leningrad's main thoroughfare. Traffic was sparse in all eight lanes, with about as many buses as cars. The gray elephantine buses lumbered along, possessive of their own side trail, while the cars moved tentatively, as though fearful of making a mistake. In their muted colors the cars seemed embarrassed to be cars, and, indeed, to Lev's red Mercedes they were merely easy obstacles that might as well have been standing still as he darted past and swerved around and squeezed between them. In the distance where Nevsky Prospekt ended, the lancelike gold spire of the Admiralty was reflecting the sun. Although in years past Nikolai had seen it so often that he no longer noticed it, he appreciated it now and was proud of it. Lev braked suddenly at a pedestrian crossing, not more than six feet from a gray-uniformed *militsioner* in his assigned spot in the middle of the thoroughfare. He was a young policeman but experienced enough to know that when he saw such a car he should pretend he didn't. His eyes raked across the red Mercedes and its passengers without showing the slightest interest, and even when Lev chose that moment to put a cassette in the player with the volume loud, the policeman pretended not to notice. The pedestrians were a different matter. Many stopped and stood to take in the car, to let its happy bright red splash into their day. It caused them to nod and smile, privately confirming secret convictions. There were, of course, the envious too, visibly angered by the sight of it. For both sorts Lev spun the volume of the speakers even louder, and Nikolai knew it was not coincidence that the music being played was from *Cabaret:*

> *"Money makes the world go round,*
> *The world go round*
> *The world go round.*
> *Money makes the world go round . . ."*

Part of Nikolai wanted to scrunch down and be unseen, but even if that had been the greater part of him, it was impossible, prevented by Kecia's occupation of the space he would need for scrunching. She understood none of the words being sung, and so, innocent of their significance, was just enjoying the sound of them, letting their spirit get to her shoulders and her head.

The Mercedes went on being a scarlet dervish among the slow, drab traffic along Nevsky Prospekt. At Gogola Street Lev swung an illegal left with no protest from the *militsioner* stationed there. Two blocks over and a half block up Mayorova Prospekt they turned into an alley and came to a stop within the range of several sour-smelling garbage cans. Lev reached down and dug in under the edge of the car's floor mat. Not at all circumspect about it, he separated several U.S. twenty-dollar bills from a sheaf of foreign currency. He folded the twenties and slid them into his shirt pocket, then got out and went up the wide concrete steps that served the rear kitchen and delivery entrance of the Hotel Astoria. Seated to one side on the top step was a middle-aged man badly in need of either more beard or a shave. His eyes were sunken and sleepless-looking. The jacket and trousers he was wearing were from two different cheap suits and were baggy, badly soiled, buttonless. Nikolai scrutinized the man and took him at once for a *stukach*, a snitch, an informer for one of the government police forces. What gave the man away was his shoes. The *stukachi* never completed their disguise by wearing bad shoes.

Lev passed right by the *stukach* and entered the hotel's kitchen. Nikolai decided if the man already had something to tell his benefactors there was nothing that could be done about it. Might as well ignore him. He thought to while away the time he'd tell Kecia about this hotel, the Astoria, how it was Leningrad's best and was where Hitler had planned to stay when the city surrendered. But then Nikolai remembered Kecia didn't speak his language, and he didn't speak enough of hers to relate such things. Kecia stood up to stretch and give Nikolai's lap a rest. She leaned forward against the frame of the windshield. That put her tight, shapely buttocks level with Nikolai's eyes and well within range of his bite. He amused himself by debating with himself whether it should be her left or her right. Very tempted, he clicked his front teeth together, mentally delivering a nice little erotic snap. His imagination enjoyed the playful *ouch* that would undoubtedly have evoked.

Lev came out of the hotel, followed by two kitchen

workers in white carrying sizable cartons, which they put in the car's trunk.

"Picnic," Lev explained as he got in and started up.

It was a two-hour drive to the dacha, most of it over a shoulderless black-topped highway that passed through Kronstadt. The final five miles was a country road heaved up and deeply rutted in many places by the previous winter's severe cold and melt. Familiar landmarks told Nikolai the distance yet to go, and when they passed through a grove of tall white birches grown so naturally straight and evenly spaced they appeared to have been planted to measure and carefully tended, he knew the next thing that would please his sight would be the dacha.

Situated on a slight grade, it was rather bashfully set back beneath two enormous pines. A house of wood, reminiscent of those built in Russia as far back as the sixteenth century. The wood of its siding, shingles, eaves, and framing was left entirely bare to defy the elements for as long as it could. By now it was weathered to a golden color with streaks of black. Only the knots had remained immune. As though in an attempt to make up for its plain vulnerability, every inch of every surface and angle was repetitively embellished with carvings and cutouts, geometrics and scrolls. A two-story gingerbread house.

It wasn't locked. The dachas located in the more fashionable Komarovo area were frequently broken into, but such a thing was unlikely here. Nikolai hadn't been to the dacha since the first week of the previous September, and it was exactly as he'd left it. They went around and opened most of the windows and shutters, gave both floors of the house an airing. Kecia swept without raising a lot of dust. Lev took the cushions outside and beat them vigorously against one another, brought them back in all plumped and ready to give comfort. Nikolai turned down the beds, theirs and his. He'd spent a lot of his younger years enjoying this house but not nearly so much of his maturity, and over the past six years, since assignment to London, he'd hardly been there at all except to check on it. He felt the same change in his attachment here as he'd felt in the Leningrad apartment. It was as though the dacha had become impatient with him, lonely, angry, and he'd had a falling out with it, and only an extended time together might repair the schism. It was only a house, he told himself, but as he went down the stairs the creak of a tread that he couldn't remember ever having not creaked took exception.

He and Lev sat on the porch with a bottle of raspberry brandy. They drank from inexpensive stemmed glasses. The sun was still above the trees that edged the clearing. Kecia had removed her clothes and was now down at the stream leaping from the smooth gray exposed belly of one rock to another. She appeared entirely caught up in her ballet *au naturel*, but every so often she paused, put a hand to her brow like a visor, and squinted up to the porch to verify that she wasn't being ignored.

Lev and Nikolai raised their glasses to her and drank some of the *eau-de-vie*. Like a vaporous specter lurking within the delicate raspberry personality of the clear liquid was a potency that transformed their stomachs into little hells and immediately ran molten through all the tributaries of their bloodstreams. Nikolai blew out a long whistling breath, like a safety valve letting off excess heat. Not being able to hold his alcohol well was another change. Back in the days when he and Lev had been on the run together a half-dozen of these brandies would have been nothing, but not now. He wouldn't even try to keep up drink for drink with Lev.

"Remember when you were into Finns?" Lev said.

Nikolai remembered.

"How superstitious most of them were? Well, this one believes the most enjoyable love is made when her head is to the north."

"Does she carry a compass?"

"No, but she has an amazing sense of direction." Lev grinned. He remained pleasant when he said, "She will go home next week, or surely the week after. She hasn't even mentioned it yet but I can feel it with her."

"Perhaps this one will come back."

"No, she won't come back, but neither will she forget."

Lev said it as though he considered it an even trade. "Are you still with that English lady?"

"Vivian."

"I know her name. I wanted to hear it from you. The way a man says a woman's name when he's far from her is as much as a confession."

"And what did I just divulge?"

"That most of your heart isn't here." Lev tilted his face to the sun, which was still too bright for his eyes to remain open. "Why is it the same sunlight feels so different here in Russia? It seems to contain more benevolence. Has it ever struck you that way?"

"Yes." Nikolai thought of the illegal passports he'd come across in Lev's cowboy boot. "Have you been traveling a lot lately?"

"To Milan a couple of times. And Paris." A single sardonic scoff. "They've had me calling on perfume makers, taking orders for ambergris." Lev kept his eyes closed while he spoke.

Nikolai took stock of his friend's face. The ridge of his brows exaggerated by scar tissue, the left cheekbone asymmetrical from having been fractured, the broken and re-broken nose. Nikolai's memory superimposed the unmarred face that had been Lev's as a boy, before all the injuries from hockey sticks and pucks and punches. Nikolai also noticed the way Lev's face was pulling at itself, the mouth and eyes and forehead not in accord about what they should feel. It was the sort of thing that only a person who cared would see. Nikolai had noticed it before, but it was even more pronounced to him now. What he felt came out. "You shouldn't take such chances," he said.

No comment from Lev. He stood, unbuttoned his shirt halfway, and then impatiently yanked the tails out of his trousers. Pulled his shirt over his head and off, then sat and resumed his sunning, eyes shut. Lev was ignoring the remark he'd just made, Nikolai thought. But after a moment Lev told him: "You think I didn't see that *stukach* on the Astoria steps? I spotted that scum before you did."

"That's what I mean. You saw him for what he was but you still flashed all that hard currency."

"What I really wanted to do was shove a bunch of dollars down his throat."

The flaunting of the red Mercedes down Nevsky Prospekt, the deliberate indiscretion with the *stukach*, the rather careless hiding of the passports—Lev seemed to be asking for the worst kind of trouble. Black-market profiteering with hard currency, any kind of foreign money, was *spekulyatsiya*, a crime considered as serious as murder in the Soviet Union, punishable by a life sentence in a labor camp or by death. Judges didn't fool around with it, just dropped the hammer hard. Lev surely knew that. What could be done to help his friend give up this self-destructive course?

Lev opened one eye to see Nikolai's concern. "Don't worry," he said, lightly brushing it off. "Any worry will just be a waste of time. I know what I'm doing." He smoothed his light-brown hair with both hands, harshly cupping his scalp from forehead to nape. He raised his legs, extended them straight out stiffly, and flexed his feet. Nikolai heard the soft snap of Lev's ankle joint. Even that brought Vivian to center stage in his mind. Almost every night she lovingly removed the unrealized tension from his hands by yanking his fingers one at a time, making the hingings of them snap like that.

Lev had two quick drinks, tossed them into himself as though they were needed. Then he said quietly: "A new spaceman came around last month."

"Oh?" "Spaceman" was their term for the government flunky who made rounds checking that the legal maximum of 12.1 square meters of living space per person was not being exceeded.

"He wanted to measure and go through his routine, but I'd just gotten in from a trip and was tired so I gave him a plastic shopping bag from Printemps, some stationery from the Hotel Plaza Athenée, and a promise that next time he came I'd have a good, solid Italian toilet seat for him. He insisted that I watch while he changed the number of occupants on his form from two to twelve by putting a one before the two that was already there. For good measure, pardon the pun, I gave him fifty rubles on his way out."

"You spoiled him."

"I suppose, but I wanted him out. I'll say this for him— he didn't bow and scrape."

"Not even a thank-you?"

"He recited a justification."

"Which one?"

Lev imitated with a monotone in a lower register: "We pretend to work, the government pretends to pay us."

They laughed. It seemed to Nikolai that their laughter met midair, combined, and, together, was brighter.

The sun dropped itself behind the trees and the air was at once colder. Bearable but no longer comfortable.

Kecia scurried up the steps to the porch, her skin beaded wet and goose-bumped. She grabbed up the bottle of *eau-de-vie* for three large consecutive swallows. Nikolai watched them go like lumps down her throat and thought it was an advertisement for Finnish women when she didn't wince afterward.

They went inside and had an early dinner at a rectangular wooden table that ran along the wall beneath a window. They shared a bench with nude Kecia in the middle dispensing equal attention left and right. It was a long indulgent meal made up of the delicacies Lev had obtained *na levo*, on the side, as they say, from the kitchen help of the Astoria. There were crab claws and the little meat dumplings called *pelmeni* stuffed with the best lean meat and various types of the most desirable mushrooms prepared in different wonderful ways and a fresh-baked loaf of *borodinskii*, the dark sweet bread crusted with caraway seeds that Nikolai's taste buds now told him how much they'd been yearning for. They finished with sticky-flaky slabs of baklava and glasses of tea and off-color jokes that Kecia laughed at only because she believed they must be funny.

It was a spring day, one of the longer days when time was not as much in the sky as in the body. Lev and Kecia got up from the table and headed up to their bedroom. Partway up the stairs they turned to Nikolai, and he understood they were wordlessly inviting him to join them. He declined by remaining as he was and smiling softly, and they continued on up.

Moments later Nikolai heard one of Lev's shoes hit the floor above, then the other. He heard the bed. He heard the silence that would be kissings and touchings. A spill of giggle from Kecia curtained his visualizing. He reminded himself that he'd be in London tomorrow and thought how good it was that by choice he was now alone.

He went to the spare room off the kitchen where infrequently used tools were kept. He found a stone-cutting chisel and a small steel-headed mallet. He checked a flashlight. It was weak but, he decided, working well enough. He put all three items into a net string bag and went out the back way and across the clearing to a grassy bank that had a summer cellar built into it. The rusted hinges of the cellar's door resisted and gritted stridently. Two creatures ran across Nikolai's feet. His first thought was that they were rats, but he saw they were chipmunks. He clicked on the flashlight, ducked down, and went in to spiderwebs and the jumps of frightened crickets. The cellar was about ten feet deep by six wide. The board shelves all around had become as gray and dry as its walls. On one shelf were several forsaken corked bottles of dandelion wine and on another some jars of apricots his mother had put up that probably by now contained enough botulin to kill everyone in the world. He cleared away the jars on two of the shelves in the rear. Using the mallet, he banged the shelves free. He stood them aside and stepped out of the cellar to let the dust settle. He couldn't wait long enough, went back in.

He knew the exact spot on the rear wall, realized now as he kneeled and looked at it how firmly he'd held it in mind all this while. Twenty-five years ago this coming August he and Grandfather Maksim had been together there in the summer cellar, the idealistic, czarist-hearted old man only a year before his death, the boy Nikolai a year before adolescence. The two had knelt as if in prayer next to one another on this bare, dry-parched ground and created their secret.

"I am here, Maksim Maksimevich," Nikolai said aloud, because it seemed to him there was a question in the air of this enclosed space that deserved an answer. But he did not believe he needed to say more than that. The rest, why he was there, was known, he felt, had been witnessed all along and was approved of. He placed the sharp edge of the chisel on the seam of cement grouting that outlined the flat face of a certain rock in the wall. He struck the chisel with the mallet and the aged cement gave way easily. Within five minutes most of the grout was cut away. He used the chisel to pry at the rock, and it came out enough for him to get a grip. He worked the rock back and forth and at the same time applied pull and, as though knowing it eventually must, the rock surrendered suddenly and tumbled to the ground. Nikolai directed the flashlight into the small cavern that was now exposed.

There they were.

He reached in and got them one by one and placed them in the string net bag, counted them as he took them out. That there were seventeen was another thing that had been etched in his memory. When he had all seventeen in the bag he shone the flashlight in through the hole just to double-check. The light hit upon something else, the only thing that remained. He reached in and brought it out. A photograph, professionally taken. A photograph of a lovely woman, but not just a lovely woman—one who looked straight at whoever might look at her, ambiguously offering and challenging. Who was she? Nikolai had never seen this photograph before, and it didn't seem to him that Grandfather Maksim had withheld much from him. Grandfather Maksim must have put it in the wall along with the other things when he wasn't looking. Why? Was it another secret? Or had Grandfather Maksim foreseen this day and its circumstances and wanted to make known his opinion of the matter? Nikolai was convinced that was it when he turned the photograph over and saw handwritten with care and a special flourish on the back of it the date and name:

1912, Alma Pihl.

CHAPTER
•••13•••

AN ATTENTIVELY POSTURED KITTEN.

From paws to ears two inches tall.

It was carved of gray chalcedony with glistening green eyes that were cabochon demantoids.

"Precious!" Vivian exclaimed, holding it at eye level on the flat of her palm and examining it all around. "Perfectly precious, isn't it, Archie?"

"I'd say," Archer concurred with momentary enthusiasm, although seated where he was across the room he was too far away to judge the tiny figure.

Nikolai had assumed Archer would be around sooner or later, but not right off. While impatiently aiming himself all the way from Leningrad to Vivian he'd imagined these moments would be special and theirs alone, the sharing of a happy salvation followed by an intense celebration. However, when he arrived at Vivian's apartment the first touch he got was Archer's welcoming handshake, and then he had to settle for a proper kiss from Vivian rather than an appropriate one. He couldn't blame Vivian. He hadn't specified privacy. Nor could he blame Archer, really. How was Archer to know he wouldn't just be crowding, but crushing? Besides, Nikolai felt, Archer was genuinely amiable, glad to have him back, had missed him, said so, and punctuated his words with a couple of brisk pats on the shoulder. That was mainly why Nikolai hadn't taken Vivian aside and told her to get rid of Archer on any pretext. It would be offensively obvious, Nikolai thought. Worse, it might hurt. An alternative for Nikolai was to put off until later the surprise he'd brought, but it was impossible for him to be that composed about them. His satchel practically opened itself. The gray chalcedony kitten practically sprang out to Vivian's hand. What a pleasure it was to watch her unwrap it, to see her wonder turn to fascination, then to aesthetic respect.

She carefully placed the kitten on the long linen-runnered table that backed up the sofa, positioned it so it was in good light beneath the lamp. Its eyes gleamed mischievously. She hesitated, glanced from Nikolai to the satchel and back. It pleased Nikolai that she wasn't being presumptuous about it, was excited but not grabby. He gestured that she should help herself. She reached into the bag without looking, let her fingers feel and choose. What she brought out this time was considerably larger, wrapped as the kitten had been: wound like a mummy with strips of cotton cloth (an old sheet Grandfather Maksim and Nikolai had torn) and beneath those protectively cushioned with newspaper.

An oblong maple box, about seven inches by four inches. Vivian undid its hinged catch, opened its lid, and there, nestled in creamy velour and an exact indentation of its shape, was a bouquet of cornflowers and buttercups in a clear vase.

The lining of the lid was imprinted К ФАБЕРЖЕ, K. Fabergé, and centered above that was the double-headed Russian eagle, the imperial emblem. With extreme care Vivian lifted the bouquet from its place. The vase and water part of it was carved of a single piece of clear rock crystal in such a way that the vase appeared to be two-thirds full. The stems of the flowers were set down in the "water," touching bottom as they would had they been real. The blossoms were flawlessly enameled and had pistils of diamonds.

Vivian knew she was holding something rare and valuable. Her eyes savored it but her hands seemed relieved to be responsible for it no longer when she returned it to its box and placed the open box on the table alongside the chalcedony kitten.

"My Gawd!" Vivian gasped, reaching again into the satchel. "Nickie, love, how many such things have you brought?"

Nikolai shrugged, acted blasé. It was going well, he thought, and, as it turned out, it was good that Archer was on hand. The spontaneous impact might be more effective. He'd kept an eye on Archer for a reaction, but, so far, nothing. That didn't mean Archer wasn't worked up inside. Archer would probably keep on sitting there with a crossed knee pretending to be unmoved, but Vivian's delight was obvious, impossible to ignore.

One after another Vivian removed and unwrapped the contents of the satchel. She lined them up categorically on the table.

Three carved stone animals, counting the kitten. Three vases of flowers. Three carved stone figures, each about five inches tall: a soldier of the Imperial Escort, a dancing Muzhik, a traditional English John Bull. Two *bonbonnières* enameled sky blue over a sunburst-patterned guilloché ground, chased with gold and bordered with diamonds. A tiny desk clock of translucent strawberry red. A pair of miniature frames, enameled pale pink, studded with rubies.

Vivian knelt upon the sofa, her front to the back of it, her elbows on its crest. Her eyes scanned the seventeen objects. Impressed and perplexed, she asked: "Where in ever did you get them?"

"From an old friend," Nikolai told her.

"He had them stashed away?"

"For years." Which was, of course, true. The various workmasters at Fabergé, in the spirit of professional camaraderie and pride, often presented one another with pieces of their work. These had been given to Grandfather Maksim by Hollming and Aarne and Nevalainen and Armfeldt and by his mentor, Wigstrom. In 1917, after the Revolution and the formation of the Committee of the Employees of the Company of Karl Fabergé, or, to put it more accurately, when Fabergé quality came to an end, Grandfather Maksim had left the firm with these objects in his possession. He thought of them as valuable to his heart. The Bolshevik government would have considered them merely valuable, just so much gold or silver that could be melted down. Thus, Grandfather Maksim had to keep his owning of them a secret. Somehow, throughout all the years and changes, he'd managed always to have a good enough hiding place for them. Nikolai didn't know whether or not even Irina knew they existed. He believed she probably did, but he never mentioned it to her in case she didn't. Looking back upon it, Nikolai thought there was something wryly amusing in the possibility that both he and his mother had been conspirators without ever knowing it. As for his father, Nikolai had always felt that withholding this information from his father was the same as keeping it from that abstract menace called "the authorities."

Vivian spun around, animated with her surmise. "You smuggled them out!" she whispered as though there were risk of being overheard. "How about that, Archie? Nickie smuggled them out."

Nikolai had never heard the word "smuggled" said so sibilantly and with such drama.

"Clever fellow," Archer said.

"Damn right!" Vivian seconded possessively.

Nikolai soaked it up without showing it. Vivian was right, though, about the smuggling. The Soviet government now considered Fabergé items to be works of art and wanted them in its museums, or at least on the mantels and desks of its most privileged officials. To be caught taking anything Fabergé out of the country was a serious offense, a form of profiteering, *spekulyatsiya*, the very thing Nikolai had warned Lev about. So going out through customs at Pulkovo Airport in Leningrad had been more than an incidental squeeze for Nikolai. Before getting in line he'd gone into the men's restroom, appraised his image in the mirror, and decided nothing about him looked suspicious. Fortified with that assurance, he attempted to neutralize his mental state, to trick himself into believing that the satchelful of contraband, which really was a swift trial and the rest of his life at hard labor, wasn't on the end of his arm and that the trip ahead was just routine. Waiting on line he'd slouched, yawned a couple of times, blinked sleepily. When it came his turn the customs official just matched his face flesh with the photograph face in his permanent passport, smacked a page with his red stamp, and motioned him on. Concern for naught, Nikolai thought; his casual manner had worked. He would never know that his satchel would have been looked into had the usual second customs official not been summoned to take an emergency phone call from his wife of a week, who needed to tell him how much she was waiting.

"Your old friend . . ." Vivian said.

"What about him?"

"I take it he wants you to sell these Fabergé things for him."

"No," Nikolai told her. "He doesn't need money."

"What then?"

"He gave them to me."

"Outright just gave them to you?"

"Yes."

"Incredible. Don't you find that incredible, Archie?"

"Phenomenally generous," Archer replied.

Vivian studied Nikolai. He felt transparent. She seemed to be reaching a whole string of conclusions. "Are you being truthful?" she asked.

"Entirely." Nikolai immediately regretted his choice of word. Only a fine line separated honesty and omission. He just didn't want to go into the details of Grandfather Maksim and expose all those feelings, at least not now. They would give the situation a different emotional color, be obstacles for Vivian.

"Your old friend must have made some stipulations," Vivian said.

That brought to Nikolai's mind the photograph of Alma Pihl that Grandfather Maksim had included in the cellar cache. Alma Pihl, Fabergé designer and Grandfather Maksim's grand passion. It wasn't until Nikolai had become an adult and himself ignited that he was able to translate the erotic qualities of Grandfather Maksim's tone whenever he'd spoken of Alma Pihl. The hesitations to review pleasures, the throaty grunts of reminiscence—all such things were, retrospectively, obvious clues. So now it seemed to Nikolai that by the Alma Pihl photograph Grandfather Maksim was communicating his presentiment that when the time came for Nikolai to put this precious trove to use, a passionate love would be involved and Nikolai shouldn't hesitate. Was that not a stipulation? He told Vivian: "The only condition was that I do with them whatever I want."

"And what," Vivian asked, "do you intend?" She felt she knew but needed to hear.

"For you to have them."

Her reaction was important to Nikolai. It would be telling, he thought. Worse would be if she went through the charade she used when Archer gave her expensive ugly things, refused and reluctantly gave in to having no recourse other than to suffer accepting and selling. If that was what she did she'd be putting him no higher than Archer's level, Nikolai reasoned. He'd be disappointed and would kick himself for having overrated his standing with her. On the other hand, if she just accepted, plainly, happily accepted, it would be a positive admission.

Vivian remained silent. She seemed to be equivocating. Actually, she was prolonging her sense of occasion, the sweet fragility of the moment. She extended an imaginary line between her eyes and Nikolai's eyes and told him seriously: "I'll sell them, you know."

"That's the idea—solvency."

"Fair warning."

"Consider me warned."

She rose from the sofa. "Archer," she said without looking at him, "either put your hands over your eyes or at least try to refrain from playing with yourself." She went to Nikolai as though magnetized, her mouth right to his mouth, her body clamped against his and struggling to get closer. A long kiss of the sort that feeds and gathers on its lack of shame. When they broke from it they had to step back abruptly, betraying their bodies.

"No one has ever given me anything so valuable," she declared ambiguously. She began pacing to the far edge of the rug and back, symptomatic of her happiness. Her cat, Ninja, appeared and began paralleling her moves. Nikolai sat. His legs had been kissed out from under him and his arousal was showing. Simultaneously, like a mass out-weighed, Archer got up and went to the table that held the Fabergé objects. He looked them over. "If they're authentic Fabergé they're worth a small fortune," he said.

Nikolai took silent exception to the word "small," al-though he realized that coming from Archer it was relatively true.

"Of course they're authentic Fabergé," Vivian con-tended without missing a step, and then, hardly missing a syllable, "How much would you say they're worth?"

Archer made an uncertain face.

"Venture a guess."

Nikolai didn't want to.

Archer guessed their neighborhood was somewhere around three hundred thousand.

"Lovely neighborhood," quipped Vivian.

"That's assuming, of course, that they're right," Archer said. "Do they have provenance?"

"Oh, fuck it, Archer, you sound like a flitty French antique dealer. What better provenance than Nick? His grandfather was with Fabergé."

News to Archer.

Nikolai was almost sure now that Vivian had the pieces together, knew that his "old friend" and Grandfather Maksim were one and the same. Still, this wasn't the time to bring it up. There were enough emotions ricocheting around.

"The most expert eyes have been fooled at one time or another," Archer said. "Forging Fabergé has been a popular and profitable pursuit for the past thirty years. Have you a loupe?" he asked Nikolai.

Vivian told him there was one in the top drawer of her secretaire. Archer found it there and began examining the objects, judging the quality of the work, the punches of the Fabergé imprints, the initials of the various workmasters, the symbols indicating seventy-two-*zolotnik* (eighteen-karat) gold.

Meanwhile, Vivian went partially through a stack of Christie's and Sotheby's auction catalogues and pulled out the recent ones of sales at which some Fabergé objects had been featured. Paging through the catalogues, she noticed how few items of this importance had been offered and when they were how impressive had been their prices. *"At least* three hundred thousand," she happily reported. Among her papers she found a calendar of forthcoming auctions. Neither Christie's nor Sotheby's had a Russian one scheduled until late October. She needed to make a sale sooner, like tomorrow. That meant she would have to throw herself on the mercies of a dealer.

"Even many of Fabergé's contemporaries imitated him," Archer said while squinting through the loupe at one of the *bonbonnières.* "Hahn did, for example, and so did Kochli and Britzen. Much of their work was fine enough to pass and needed only to have the Fabergé mark and one of the workmasters' initials punched onto it to increase its value."

"I wasn't aware you were so up on Fabergé," Nikolai said.

"I've owned quite a few pieces," Archer said, and admitted lightly, "Also got taken a number of times. Nothing like stumbles to make one cautious of steps."

"I can't *wait* until October," Vivian put in, which indicated where her thoughts were. She had resumed her pacing.

Archer was doing his best to dampen things, Nikolai decided. But then . . .

"Without a doubt these are right," Archer said, tossing the loupe in the air and snappily catching it as though celebrating the fact. "And if my opinion holds, I know a fellow who will take the lot off your hands and pay as much as or more than you'd ever get at auction."

"A dealer?" Vivian asked, not keen on that.

"Private collector," Archer replied. "Absolutely bonkers about Fabergé but knows his stuff. I'll ring him up."

CHAPTER
••••14••••

THE NEXT MORNING AT NINE.

Nikolai arrived at his office on Kensington Church Street to find that since Tuesday there had been eight calls from Churcher, who evidently refused to accept that Nikolai was away on business. It was typical enough of Churcher to disbelieve, Nikolai thought, but eight calls in three days was odd. Something important must have come up, or anyway something Churcher considered important.

Nikolai contemplated his telephone. This did not feel as if it wanted to be one of his Churcher days, he decided. There was too much of the good of last night in him, and Churcher would surely spoil it. Nikolai couldn't keep his eyes from covering over, from refusing to register *now*, preferring instead to review fresh memory. It was as if his eyes wanted to roll back in their sockets. Had he died? Why did people have such a thought when living was at its best? He blinked to force his eyes to acknowledge *now* in the form of the telephone. Conscientiousness and Churcher were only a sequence of seven tones away. Perhaps if he had a glass of hot tea first—

As though responding to the suggestion, the phone chirped. Nikolai was certain it would be Churcher. It was Churcher's snooty secretary asking if Nikolai would pop around as soon as it was convenient. Nikolai was tempted to tell her to hang on while he consulted his agenda, and then tell her his first open hour was next Tuesday late afternoon, say around four. "I'll be there in a half hour," he said.

"Fine," she said and clicked off.

Nikolai had counted on a half hour being too soon for Churcher. The only reason he'd said a half hour was to sound cooperative. Now no time for a tea. No time for a call to Vivian to enjoy hearing her sleepiness, her natural throaty voice even throatier. And taxis would be at a premium at this hour. Nikolai took in two deep breaths and adjusted the knot of his tie to help get himself in a Churcher state.

When he stepped out onto the street an available taxi was coming along as if ordered for him. He thought how Vivian wouldn't admit it was a coincidence, but rather claim she'd called upon the taxi angels for help, and had been heard. She had angels for everything. They were specialists who might or might not come to her aid, depending on something as vague as whether or not they happened to be paying attention. Nikolai remembered Vivian once even attributing to angels the location of a convenient loo when she'd been caught having to go badly while out shopping New Bond. Some woman, Nikolai thought, smiling to himself as the taxi made business London whiz by. The reasons he loved her kept multiplying.

He arrived at 11 Harrowhouse and was announced to Churcher a minute early. The receptionist on the main floor said, "You may go up," as though granting permission to heaven. She gave Nikolai an initialed slip of paper that allowed him to get off the elevator on four. There, Churcher's secretary had her thinnest-lipped expression waiting for him. "Mr. Churcher will receive you in his office."

"Now?"

"Immediately."

Nikolai went down the hall and in. *"Privyet!"* he said amicably. Usually, Churcher would come right back at him with *"Privyet!"*—Greetings!—but not today. He just nodded once. He was seated behind his desk, painfully solemn, like a man with a bone stuck in his throat trying not to cough. "Sit," he said.

Nikolai wondered if he should also bark.

"You know Pulver."

"Yes."

George Pulver was standing slightly behind Churcher's high-backed chair with the staunch, opinionated air of an aide-de-camp. Pulver was head of the System's Security Section, a position he'd held for eleven years. He wasn't a figurehead—that is, he wasn't an old school type who had been handed the job. Before joining the System he'd been Interpol and before that with the Yard. He was in his early fifties, too stout for tennis, not the type for golf, too impatient for bridge. Out of his gray, wrinkle-prone suit he might be taken for something like a crane operator. He had hyperthyroid eyes, a cleft so deep in his chin it looked like an old wound, and very apparent upper *and* lower cheap bridgework. Nikolai didn't underestimate Pulver, believed the bottom line on him would be smart and mean.

"I've been trying to reach you all week," Churcher said sternly.

"So I understand."

"Doesn't your office keep in touch with you or you with it?"

"When it's essential."

"Everything I say to you is essential, Borodin. Every word."

Whatever was eating at Churcher had already corroded him quite a bit, Nikolai thought. He'd endured many of Churcher's sour spells over the years but he'd never seen him this rankled.

"What were you doing in Moscow? Discussing another increase?" Churcher asked snidely.

Say nothing, Nikolai advised himself.

"You people are bloodsuckers. Enough is never enough."

"How are the next sights shaping up?" Nikolai asked just to say something. He wished Churcher would offer tea as he usually did. He also wished Churcher would get to the point instead of bitching.

"Almazjuvelirexport," Churcher said, badly mispronouncing it and letting it hang there for effect. "When you were last here with Minister Savich you will recall I brought to your attention that we believe Almaz . . . uh . . . fuck it all . . . your firm has for some while now been exceeding the agreed-upon limit of finished carats that it would market."

"We assured you that was unfounded."

"And I assured you we would not tolerate any more of it."

"Whatever you say," Nikolai shammed capitulation.

"Don't get cheeky with me, Borodin," Churcher snapped. He jabbed his index finger at Nikolai. "I can have your cushy London pillow yanked out from under your arse in a second."

Nikolai doubted that. He took the threat impassively, sat there meeting Churcher's hard fixed gaze. What the hell, Nikolai thought, why didn't Churcher go for a smile, just let out a big broad one? When he reached Churcher's age he'd be trying to get in as many smiles as he could. Why didn't Churcher fart if he had to, loosen up, pull down his tie that was like a noose, yell out at his secretary to get off her behind and fetch tea? What was worth all this grimness?

Pulver showed Nikolai what.

From his jacket pocket he took out what is known in the diamond trade as a briefke: a special type of paper folded five times in such a manner that it serves as a packet for containing diamonds. This particular briefke was one of the larger, more substantial kinds, about five inches by three inches, lined with a slick, slightly blue paper. Pulver's fleshy fingers were surprisingly agile in unfolding it. He placed it open on Churcher's desk. Nikolai had to stand to see what was in it.

Churcher narrated: "Monday last, Pulver's people intercepted an underhanded transaction in Geneva. I'm ashamed to say a dealer who had been a sightholder with us for some thirty years was on the receiving end. What you see here is some of the goods." Churcher used the point of a letter opener to stir the mound of diamonds that lay within the briefke. "Identical stones, investment-quality, D-color, flawless one-caraters. Do you need to examine them to know they're Aikhal goods?"

Nikolai didn't. Only Aikhal diamonds had such frozen purity. "How much is here?" he asked.

"Eight hundred pieces. There were two other packets like this. Twenty-four hundred pieces altogether."

Nikolai went for a blank expression.

"Our dealer," Churcher continued, "probably paid cut-rate for them. Say sixteen a carat. Not for himself; he was middling it for an investor. No doubt the money was destined for a Swiss account. Doesn't matter. What we're interested in knowing is from whom our dealer bought these goods. The source."

"Ask your dealer."

"He died of a stroke. Anyway, lack of one. Went overboard and drowned in Lake Geneva."

"Unfortunate."

Churcher paused and took another tack. "Damn, Borodin," he appealed, "why don't you people just own up to having taken advantage and from now on live up to your bargain? It wouldn't be mentioned again, I promise."

"I have no knowledge that Almazjuvelirexport is involved," Nikolai said.

Churcher put on his tortoise-rimmed glasses as if hoping the world would look improved through them. His hands were shaking.

"We're on to you," Pulver warned Nikolai.

Nikolai wasn't fazed. He was innocent, so why should he worry? He'd taken Savich's stand on this matter. Savich would feel the same about it now as he had when Churcher had brought it up only a week ago. As for the dealer in Geneva, he was most likely a figment. The true thing, though, was the goods. There was no denying they were Aikhal. A lovely lot. Nikolai ran the tip of his finger through the pile of them. He appeared seriously thoughtful, about to make a revelation. "May I take a couple of these with me?" he asked. His tone implied they might be evidential.

"Surely," Churcher replied.

What Nikolai had in mind was ear studs for Vivian. Her lobes deserved eighteen-thousand-dollar glints. Possibly

Churcher would, in the literal course of everyday business, forget Nikolai had taken them, just two.

Churcher separated a random pair from the lot. He instructed Pulver: "Have him sign for them."

An hour later Nikolai was waiting on the street outside 46 Bruton, a typical older private residence that had gone commercial. He'd left the taxi at Regent Street and walked the rest of the way because he was early and wanted to find a luncheonette for anything that might do for breakfast. Now he felt he would have been better off if he'd stayed hungry. The two frosting-topped crullers he'd bolted down at a standup counter were a balking lump refusing to be processed. They stuck around the lower exit of his esophagus as though angry at having been eaten and letting that be known by squirting up acid.

Had he time to find someplace to buy a roll of antacid tablets or possibly a few gurgles of Perrier? His watch told him he might, but when he looked up and down that short street and didn't see a store of any kind, he decided to stay there and persevere. What mental distraction would help? Offered up was that lot of diamonds Churcher and Pulver had been so peeved about. Nikolai had misgivings about the attitude he'd displayed in that morning's meeting. He'd been a bit cavalier toward Churcher's concern. Better he should have come off as the solicitous Russian partner and just let Churcher huff and thrash all he wanted. Truth be known, he felt a bit sorry for Churcher, Churcher's having to maintain face while kissing ass. His need to hit out every so often was understandable.

What about those diamonds? There had to be something to them the way Churcher was again pressing the issue and Pulver with his police mentality was hovering like a hawk ready to swoop. There was no questioning that the diamonds were Aikhal goods. Their distinctive, fine colorlessness and perfect, identical cuts identified them. Then what of Churcher's accusation that Almazjuvelirexport was selling more finish than it was supposed to? Nikolai always knew within a week the firm's sales figures. The records were kept clear and tight with no chinks to slip amounts through, and if the firm had a secondary, covert policy going, certainly he'd be in on it. That left only the possibility that the diamonds were coming to market in some way other than the normal channels. How about directly from Aikhal? It would mean someone assigned to Aikhal was skimming from the yield and the production of finished goods without its being noticed. Hardly likely. Someone would have to be putting aside that batch of stones and to know a way of getting them through all of Aikhal's complex security measures. It would mean having to steal out sizable batches at a time. Aikhal, remote as it was, prevented any steady flow of thievery. There just wasn't enough coming and going. A stone or even a few were pilfered now and then, but nowhere near the amount needed for the accumulation of diamonds Pulver was supposed to have confiscated from a dealer in good standing, who, Nikolai gathered, had taken the long drink in Lake Geneva rather than face up to whatever charges and punishment the System believed suitable. It was an accepted fact in the trade that the System never called on the police, dealt with its own in its own ways. Nikolai imagined the errant dealer being pushed overboard, but then that wouldn't have been done by any of Pulver's people, he realized, at least not until they'd gotten the source of the diamonds out of him. Who, then, would have done the pushing? Perhaps, Nikolai thought, Savich was right about Churcher's having invented this matter only to provide himself with a bitching point for future negotiations. As much as Nikolai respected Savich's judgment, now that he was giving the thing a second thought, Savich's assessment didn't settle it for him. It just didn't want to slip by the way it had last week and earlier that morning. Savich's assessment seemed altogether too convenient, too palpable. There was accommodation to the way it fit. How could he tactfully bring that to Savich's attention? He couldn't come right out and tell the Minister of Foreign Trade that he'd misread a man, glossed over something that warranted being looked into. Nikolai believed that after six years he knew his Churcher. The man hadn't been dramatizing today: He'd been honestly upset, and not without a reason more serious than the contrivance of a negotiating ploy. Also, something else about it was bothering Nikolai, something he couldn't quite bring clear, something that was nudging at him from inside as if trying to remind him there was more to it that he should be conscious of. The link to it all. What was it?

Belch.

Archer's Rolls limousine rounded the corner and pulled to the curb. Vivian opened the rear door for herself before the chauffeur had a chance to get to it. She extended one leg, like a lovely overture, and then bounded out of the car. She was in high spirits, finishing off some laughter caused evidently by a remark Archer had made a moment before. Archer got out on the other side. Vivian, from ten feet away, brought the aim of her eyes around to Nikolai. It was as though he'd been misplaced when playfully, with exaggerated British arch and enunciation, she exclaimed: "Oh, there you are, Nickie darling!" She came to him hand first as though her wrist were a favor, but at the last second she dropped it and proceeded with her mouth. A careful kiss, the merest peck, the kind that wouldn't disturb her lipstick. "Hi, lover," she said, reverting, and that put the place and the time and everything back into perspective for Nikolai.

He told her: "You look fetching."

"Don't I always," she said.

"Don't you," he agreed, smiling his best smile. However, it was obvious to Nikolai that Vivian had spent time and attention on her appearance. Perhaps because he'd made this day special for her, he thought. She'd given the ends of her straight-to-the-shoulder hair a buoyant flip and done quite a bit more than usual with her makeup, helped her large eyes look huge and decorated their lids with precise smudges of a brilliant blue. She'd also blended on just the right extra amount and shade of pink exactly where high on her cheeks a healthier-than-average flush would show. Her dress was of pale gray silk jersey with a V neckline that showed what she had without showing it.

"Nick," was Archer's friendly greeting instead of a plain hello.

"Archer," Nikolai acknowledged nicely.

The chauffeur got the satchel from the trunk, and Nikolai took it from him. Archer didn't offer to carry it. It was his belief that the better-bred gentleman never carried anything in public except in an extreme emergency. Whatever he purchased was always sent around or else he had his man with him to do the toting. It was one of the stuffy rules he'd learned very early and felt was worth keeping.

He led the way into number 46 and up one long flight of stairs so plushly runnered they were dangerous. No doubt Archer had been there before, knew the place well. Vivian and Nikolai followed along down an impeccably maintained hallway that ran right and then right again to end up before a varnished oak door that, like all the others they'd passed, bore no name. They entered a reception area where a desk was situated for intercepting but there was no one behind it.

"Beckhurst!" Archer called out.

A vigorous clearing of throat was heard from the adjacent inner office, followed by: "Come in, come in."

Beckhurst was seated at a George III inlaid mahogany writing table. Archer told him not to get up, and he didn't try, just offered his limp handshake across the desk when Vivian and Nikolai were introduced. "Sit down, sit down," Beckhurst said.

Nikolai recalled that when Archer had mentioned this person the night before, this compulsive Fabergé buyer, he'd referred to him as a school chum. Well, either Archer was sipping from the miraculous waters of youth or this fellow Beckhurst was living the fastest, most degenerating life of all time. Beckhurst was eighty-some if he was a day. It was exercise for him to speak. The lids of his ginny eyes glistened wet, and his sallow complexion was camouflaged by the alcoholic bursts of thousands of capillaries. Still in all he yet had most of his hair, combed straight back, and it was not entirely gray. He was also dapperly dressed. Nikolai glanced at Vivian. She was gracefully settled in her armchair and didn't appear to be concerned a degree by this being Beckhurst. Possibly Archer had told her what to expect. Nikolai looked to Archer, who reassured him with a slight shift of eyes and an almost imperceptible nod.

"Let's see, yes, let's see," Beckhurst said.

Archer opened the satchel and removed the Fabergé objects and placed them one at a time in front of Beckhurst, who had to lean back to get his bare vision focused on them. He put a loupe into the socket of his right eye, sort of tucked it into the folds of the loose skin. When he clenched that eye to hold the loupe the entire right side of his face went ugly, the corner of his mouth became a lopsided hole exposing upper molars and gum, his left nostril closed and his right one was awry and dilated. He hunched over to examine under ten-power magnification the imprints on each of the objects. He seemed particularly appreciative of the Fabergé flower creations, although he didn't remark. In fact, throughout his appraisal Beckhurst didn't utter a single word, and when he was done he didn't declare whether he was satisfied or not. His only punctuation was a deep breath so wheezy that it was harmonic. He took out a gold pocket watch and looked at its face as though it were an old enemy.

Archer reached across the desk, closed the lid on one of the Fabergé maple boxes, and asked: "Genuine, do you think?"

"Genuine, indeed genuine," Beckhurst nodded jerkily.

"Then you might be interested in purchasing them?"

Beckhurst dug around in the center drawer of the writing table for a small electronic calculator. The well-manicured tips of his rather transparent fingers seemed to randomly massage the calculator's digits. Nikolai didn't see how when the device was used like that it could possibly present an accurate total. Beckhurst finally stopped fiddling with it. He raised his eyes and fixed them on Vivian's plunge and for a long moment was gone from the business on hand.

"Well?" Archer pressed politely.

"Two hundred thousand," Beckhurst let out.

"How much?" Vivian asked.

"Three hundred thousand," Beckhurst grumbled as though he resented having to repeat himself.

Vivian thought she should again ask how much on the chance Beckhurst might unmindfully up his offer another hundred, but then she didn't want to risk jarring him back to two hundred. "Done at three hundred," she said.

"Done, done," Beckhurst agreed with absolutely no enthusiasm.

"How would you prefer payment?" Archer asked Vivian.

"Cashier's check and immediately," she replied.

Beckhurst couldn't have been more accommodating nor more immediate. From his shirt pocket he produced a once-folded check, which he handed to Vivian. Vivian glanced at it and showed it to Nikolai. It was a cashier's check made out to cash to the amount of three hundred thousand pounds. Nikolai believed that Beckhurst's having the check all made out and ready was too much of a coincidence. He was about to mention that when his voice box felt as though it had just become wrapped, tied, and knotted, and now wasn't that Grandfather Maksim gesticulating in protest and bobbing back and forth across the front of his mind? Nikolai watched the check disappear into Vivian's gray suede clutch.

Perfunctory thanks and goodbyes. The Fabergé objects were left behind. Nikolai, Archer, and Vivian were again out on Bruton Street. "What a nice older gentleman," Vivian said. "I'd much rather do business with his sort than with some bleeding dealer."

"Where to now?" Archer asked. The curbside passenger door of his Rolls was open.

"First to the bank, then let's pay bills," Vivian said and ducked in to take her middle position on the plush. Nikolai and Archer flanked her. When the Rolls got under way she hooked an arm left and right, beamed a grateful smile Archer's way, then sent an equal to Nikolai, but his with a bit of lascivious eyework in it. Nikolai was still suffering his cruller affliction. He asked if Archer had any kind of fizzy water in the car. Archer surpassed that. He opened a compartment to reveal a magnum of champagne bedded in shaved ice, its neck already peeled and its cork just popped. Archer's man had timed those preparations exactly. All Archer had to do was give the cork a finesseful twist to have a barely visible vapor wisp up out of the bottle like some at-long-last-released specter. Archer distributed the glasses, filled them, then proposed: "To solvency!"

"To solvency!" they toasted conspiratorially and gulped down about half of that pouring.

"May I belch?" Nikolai asked.

"May I join you?" Vivian asked and did. Her belch didn't match the explosiveness of Nikolai's but was a sort of liberated empty stomach growl that had a bit of melody to it.

Archer pretended to find them both in bad form. "Gawd!" he exclaimed.

"You should talk," Vivian chided. "You, the Western Hemisphere's all-time champion belcher, and, I might add, wind-breaker."

"Shall I let one go?" Archer asked.

"No!" Vivian laughed and went suddenly straight-faced as she turned to Nikolai, "Quick, down with the windows before he shatters them!"

The Rolls pulled up and double-parked in front of Vivian's bank. She was happy to go in. Her deposit was instantly honored. She wrote two checks against it that zeroed out the first and second and third mortgages owed on her London flat and her house in Devon. While seated at the bank officer's desk awaiting the details of those arrangements she decided to use more than her knees. A gleaming cylinder of lipstick seemed to accidentally drop from her purse. She bent over to retrieve it, thus fully utilizing her plunge. The bank officer's eyes went for it. His Adam's apple disappeared twice below his shirt collar. He was the one who'd had no sympathy and been unaffected by her earlier that week. Vivian gave him an indignant *humph* and communicated hard-eyed that in another breath she was of a mind to register a complaint to his most superior superior. His efficiency was a plea, she thought. He swiftly supplied her with a sheaf of blank checks, suggested an interest-bearing account, reassured her she would never have any hitches, he'd personally see to it.

"You've personally *seen to it*, all right," Vivian told him and on that made her exit to another flute of Taittinger. She noticed from the level in the bottle that Nikolai and Archer had been at it. Nikolai was grinning as if he'd just come from the dentist and been shot with novocaine on both sides. Archer's ears were almost a flamingo shade headed for cerise, a giveaway. They were chatting on about weapons, Archer extolling the merits of a certain over-and-under twelve-gauge that Purdy had made for him a dozen or so years ago. Next time they were in the country Archer would show it to him, even promised to let him have a try with it. Nikolai said his experience had been mainly with rifles and pistols. Had Archer ever shot a Makarov SL? Archer admitted he didn't believe he had, said he'd never been much for handguns but Vivian was, Vivian was an excellent shot, a natural, watch out for her.

Vivian reached to Nikolai's inside jacket pocket for his pen. It was a ballpoint. She detested ballpoints; they wouldn't write when there was even the slightest amount of oil on the paper, such as when she'd put some lotion on her hands. She helped herself to Archer's inside jacket pocket for his fountain pen, a black-lacquered eighteen-karat-gold Dupont. Archer ordered them by the dozen, was constantly losing them, leaving them on someone's desk. Vivian used the back of one of her new checks to jot a list of her debtors. Not to remind herself—she knew them well—but just to determine what would be the most convenient order of payment. She numbered them. While Archer and Nikolai continued on about guns across her face she instructed the chauffeur.

The traffic was dreadful, as usual, but the Rolls kept its dignity as it made its way from one of Vivian's creditors to another, from bookmaker to Asprey's, from Forthum's to Culpepper's, from another bookmaker to Hatchard's to the White House to Smythson's, from the upper half of a run-down house in Maida Vale, where she paid Gareth, the medium tout, what she owed him for the past month's few

winners, to a garage in Pimlico that had worked on her
Bent two and a half years ago and had given up on her.
She paid her accounts at Harrods and a really old, old one
for a great many flowers she'd ordered from Pulbrook &
Gould on a day when she'd felt only bouquets would lift
her. She'd almost forgotten that one. It was pre-Nikolai,
seemed like another age. Her final payoff was at Brooks's,
Archer's club, where she left in separate envelopes checks
to cover the markers she'd given for her poker losses three
nights previous. Couldn't say she was a welcher. Then she
copped Archer's Dupont, clipped it into Nikolai's inside
jacket pocket, and announced: "I'm famished."

They lunched at the Connaught. Although they had no
reservations and arrived past the time when serving was
over, Archer's presence was like a credential that got them
pleasantly welcomed and shown down the narrow oak-
paneled hallway to the dining room. Archer, now in his
element, indicated a freshly linened table by a window, and
as they were being seated he palmed a twenty to the maître
d'hôtel.

Nikolai felt several degrees more important than usual.
He'd lunched here a few times with Churcher at the expense
of the Soviet government but had always been made to
wait. He casually surveyed the room. Vacant set tables,
fewer guests than waiters, those mostly middle-aged women,
menopaused well-offs, diffidently dressed, small-talking over
tea and allowing nibbles of butter cookies to dissolve in
their mouths. Nikolai, influenced by a morning and noon
of too much champagne, thought how it might be fun to
be a snob for a while, one who wouldn't admit to liking
anything much and nothing anyone else did, who suffered
ennui to such an extent he seemed to float around, whose
wit was amusingly pessimistic and something to be wary
of, the possessor of a vast, piercing vocabulary. That sort.
Nikolai checked the edges of his shirt cuffs to make sure
they weren't soiled. He heard himself say, "Nothing, thank
you," in response to the question of a drink before lunch.

They ordered. Vivian ordered too much. Throughout
the meal she seemed edgy and often removed. She hardly

touched her food. The waiter took notice and inquired if there was anything wrong. She replied vaguely, as though she saw no reason why he should ask. Several times she went off on a side road of thought, then returned and talked a lot, strung her sentences and subjects together like a train made up of different types and shades of cars. She went from mentioning that in her opinion it was morbid for someone to pay over fifty thousand pounds for the death mask of John Keats to saying that she believed there had been numerous incidents of human parthenogenesis, times when women became pregnant with no male involvement, and thus quite possibly the immaculate conception had been an electrical occurrence. What did they think Napoleon really died of? Before either Nikolai or Archer could reply Vivian was off on the fact that Picasso's father, Ruiz, had been a worker in a factory that turned out forgeries of Spanish art, Goyas and things, she supposed. Then, after a pause so brief it couldn't have accommodated more than half a thought, she stated that Vita Sackville-West and Lady Elsie Mendl were two of her all-time favorite women, although Vita might have been happier had she come out for her sexual preferences a bit more and spent less time in gardens, Vivian said.

For dessert she chose three different cakes, a lemon tart, and a huge blob of trifle from the trolley and ignored them all. She was again off on one of her pensive journeys, far away this time. She came back very abruptly. "I don't owe a soul," she blurted. Her hodgepodge of thoughts had coalesced into that one. It wasn't a painful realization, but neither was it comfortable for her. "I don't owe a bloody soul," she said, apparently disconsolate. Quickly, self-consciously, she dispelled the evidence, pulled up the corners of her mouth to make a nice smile for Nikolai, and told him: "Thanks to you, Nickie dear." To dilute her insincerity she reached over and gave the back of his neck a few loving kneads. Her gold bangles collided on her arm. The ring of them seemed excessively loud. She began eating the trifle, an excuse that allowed her to mull.

The changes Vivian had just gone through hadn't been

missed by Nikolai. He didn't quite understand them but was not entirely off the mark. She was, he thought, suffering the shock of solvency. It was an unfamiliar condition for her, but she'd get used to it and be happier. The woman I love, he thought as he studied her. Today she had a tinge of darkness half-mooned below her eyes. Without makeup it would have been more discernible. A penalty for last night's indulgences that a deep uninterrupted sleep tonight could erase. If that was possible. She didn't seem to know her limitations. Nor, for that matter, did he. What was it about their chemistries combined that enabled them to pull through the tiny openings of their vulnerabilities such swollen knots of pleasure, insatiably, time and time again? It wasn't lack of fulfillment that drove them. It was quality of feeling, perhaps the disbelief of it. Nikolai wanted so much to please her, to continue pleasing her with such intensity. Not that it made him feel like more of a man. Actually, it caused him to identify more closely with what it was like to be a woman.

"What shall it be, to the country tonight or tomorrow?" Archer asked, pushing the mood up a notch.

Nikolai looked to Vivian, who remained blank.

Archer waited. "I detect at least a temporary disdain for the bucolic. What is it, a symptom of *nouvelle richesse?*"

Vivian smiled weakly.

Archer finished off his nearly cold tea. Nikolai would let this resolve itself. Whether it would be the country or London didn't matter. What mattered was his proximity to Vivian.

Indecision hung there. Finally, Archer said: "I know what we need. Just the ticket. A holiday."

"A weekend somewhere different," Vivian said thoughtfully.

"Why not a full-fledged holiday? A good long one," Archer said.

Vivian brightened, then dimmed. "Nick couldn't get away on such short notice. He has his diamond business to look after." She shrugged and smiled. "I'll settle without sacrifice for a weekend."

Nikolai waited a beat, then enjoyed telling her: "I might be able to take some time!"

"Really, darling? That would be wonderful!"

"The Algarve," Archer suggested. "I believe you once mentioned you'd never been to Portugal."

Vivian didn't respond to the Algarve. "Perhaps Biarritz," she said.

"Glitzy," Archer warned, "especially this time of year. But Saint-Jean-de-Luz is delightful and only minutes from Biarritz."

After a brief second thought Vivian for some reason vetoed Biarritz.

"Wherever," Archer said. "Let me look after everything. We could fly tomorrow, or even tonight. What do we think of that?"

Nikolai wondered if it was what Vivian wanted. His getting away wouldn't be a problem. He had his annual six weeks' vacation coming. Vysotsky could take over for him, service Churcher. He'd have to call Leningrad, of course, let Valkov know. The only thing about this vacation idea that bothered him was that pronoun "we" that Archer had used. Was it the inclusive or that strange British objective "we"?

CHAPTER
◆◆◆15◆◆◆

THE FOLLOWING TUESDAY THEY WERE IN MADRID. STAYING at the Hotel Ritz in a huge corner suite on the fifth floor. Archer, true to his word, had arranged everything, put his Westwind jet at their disposal, hired a limousine, and through some sleight of influence managed to get them quartered on such short notice in that great white palace of a hotel. The Ritz Madrid was so selective that it had at one time or another turned away the cream of Hollywood and the milk of Europe's nobility.

On Sunday Archer had phoned. "All comfy?" he'd asked. "Very," Nikolai told him. "Just checking," Archer said and clicked off.

Now they had been at the Ritz for three days. The sun over Madrid was up and unchallenged as usual. A waiter in a tuxedo that actually fit him well and wasn't yet shiny at the seat or elbows had brought a breakfast of plump, light rolls and coffee and tea and blackberry preserves in a silver bowl. The waiter's appearance caused Nikolai to think how much he would dislike having a job that required the wearing of a tuxedo and patent-leather shoes all day. He expressed that to Vivian and she chalked it up to his socialist conscience using reverse psychology on him. She wondered if when Nikolai was old would he seek solace in Communism as most people did in religion? God, she hoped not.

She didn't have a stitch on, was in the sitting room, scrunched down on the sofa with her feet up and crossed on the low table. She slathered butter on a hunk of a roll, then blackberry preserves. A dollop of the preserves fell off and landed an inch or so below her navel. She left it there long enough for Nikolai to consider licking it off. She scooped it off with a finger and consumed it. With a chew of roll in her mouth out of nowhere she asked: "Do you like it here?"

"You're here," was Nikolai's reply.

"I mean, don't you find this place more than a bit self-impressed?"

Nikolai shrugged impassively. "I know of millions who would say it's decadent."

"I felt it the moment I stepped into that velvet-lined lift."

That hadn't been apparent to Nikolai. She had seemed excited to be there. Might it be that she was blaming the hotel for her actually being bored with him? He asked her.

She told him his question didn't deserve an answer. She threw him two kisses and then examined the underside of her coffee cup, where as she'd suspected it said Limoges.

Hell, Vivian thought, Edith Wharton had believed that an hour of anything was enough. She stood up, brushed the crumbs from her breasts, and said: "Let's get out of here."

Nikolai began packing. Vivian notified the two pilots, who were standing by. And at twelve minutes to two the wheels of Archer's Westwind jet gave up their contact with the runway of the Barajas de Madrid Airport, climbed to twenty thousand feet, and was put on a northerly course. When Vivian had notified the chief pilot he had wanted to know where they'd be going. Vivian wasn't sure and said so. The chief pilot explained he was required to file a flight plan. She told him, "Righto, make it Deauville."

But now that they were in the air she wasn't really keen on Deauville. She gave both Nice and Monte Carlo consideration.

Nikolai, meanwhile, appeared to be gazing out at the variegated patches of Europe below. Really he was trying to quell the disturbance he'd felt ever since he'd gone to check out at the Ritz. The cashier had informed him that everything was already taken care of. Nikolai didn't need to ask by whom. He insisted there was a mistake, wanted to see the bill. The cashier obliged. Nikolai saw the itemized bill stamped *pagado*. He was furious. He explained why to Vivian, who was waiting there in the lobby. "Let it be," she had said, her mind elsewhere. Nikolai's upset was taking a long time to subside. Hell, he thought, he might as well have Archer adopt him.

Vivian snapped apart her seat belt and walked forward to the control cabin. She informed the pilot of a change in destination and had the copilot place a call to Archer. Rather than arrive without accommodations.

Two hours later the Westwind touched down at Echterdingen Airport in Stuttgart. Awaiting was a Mercedez-Benz limousine. Nikolai had decided he wouldn't let these Archer things get to him and spoil their holiday. He knew he was no freeloader, and besides, wasn't the bottom line the fact that Vivian was with *him*? He climbed into the Mercedes and just accepted the sixty-mile trip to Baden-Baden.

At the reception desk of Brenner's Park Hotel they were greeted with importance. The manager himself, a French sort of German very accomplished in suavity, showed them up to their fourth-floor suite. He waited with them until their baggage was brought, then, before departing, politely refused a gratuity.

Vivian kicked off her shoes and unbuttoned her blouse all the way down. "Up Madrid," she said brightly. "This is better, isn't it, lover?" She went out on the balcony for a moment.

Nikolai had the feeling that they had usurped someone's resting place.

"Dostoyevski used to stay here a lot," Vivian said, returning, "So did all those horny Russian grand dukes." As though those facts had influenced her decision to come there.

"You've been here before?"

"No, only claimed that I have." She went into the bedroom and approved of the bed, its expansiveness, two double beds pushed together. All in all the suite was luxurious, with its high ceilings, crystal chandeliers, silk-covered walls, and elegant nineteenth-century German furnishings of dark teak.

Nikolai wondered if a grand duke had ever really occupied these rooms and done grand things. The possibility did make being there more interesting for him. He took off his jacket and tie and shoes and stretched out on the sofa. He'd known about Dostoyevski. The great writer had also been a loser. His novel *The Gambler* had been set here in Baden-Baden. He'd knocked it out swiftly to pay off his roulette debts.

"Looks like you're for a nap," Vivian said, dropping into the deep armchair opposite the sofa.

"Just close my eyes for a while."

"I'll see to the unpacking."

Nikolai grunted his gratitude, took a deep, releasing breath, and began enjoying his nap.

Vivian took a tangerine from the silver salver on the table. She peeled it and broke it into its sections before putting one in her mouth. She accidentally swallowed a seed and wondered if it might get stuck someplace within her. It was certainly more benign than other sorts of seed she'd swallowed, she wryly told herself. Her private world, she thought, giving a shape to her aggregate experiences. She was, she realized, in a self-appraising mood. Should she indulge it, question her personal ledger, or skip all of that and go directly to the inevitable conclusion that she did not know how right or wrong, good or bad she was because there was no way for her to make a bed-rock comparison? She could only measure, by imagination, herself against others. Any meaningful chastising or, for that matter, praising of her had to come from her. She was, she thought, like a sun basking in its own heat. What seemed best to her, seemed to fit the configuration of *her* soul, was to allow her spirit to have its way. Otherwise she was merely a performer, and there certainly was little honesty in that.

Nikolai shifted onto his side, put his back to the room. Apparently he was going for more than a mere nap. Vivian could hear the air going in and out of him. Sleep breaths.

Her Nikolai, she thought. She was sure she loved him. There had been for her nothing consequential before him, she felt. He, him, his had been the true start of her. An igniting. Was that how it was, right in the momentum of one life or another the entrance of a mate for eternity? Was it a reward earned from past lives, a plateau reached, perhaps? She didn't feel all that evolved. She did feel there were now heavens in her.

She did the unpacking, then quietly went out and down to the lobby to make some credit arrangements. When she returned, Nikolai was still asleep on the sofa. She sat at the desk with her checkbook. It was a mess, scribbles and blank stubs. She had no respect for any level of book-keeping, even as simple as hers. Usually, the mere sight of her checkbook repelled her, and she never bothered to open her monthly bank statements when they arrived in the mail, just tossed them into a cardboard box in the back of her hall closet or threw them out with the trash.

Using hotel stationery, she listed the amounts she'd paid out to her creditors, added them up, and subtracted the total from three hundred thousand pounds. She still had over two hundred and ten thousand pounds. That is my balance, she thought, staring at the figure. Why was it called a balance? Was it because without it one would fall? Not her, she assured herself, she had her angels.

She chose an evening dress, a simple figure-hugging silvery Donna Karan, bare on top, dependent on little more than a thread of a strap. Then the accessories, including open sandals with high slender heels, practically weightless. She laid her things out neatly on the bed, and, beside them, Nikolai's evening suit and shirt and black tie and all. She wouldn't awaken him until she'd done herself. She intended to stun tonight, be a killer.

They had a leisurely dinner in the hotel dining room, then walked out into the fresh Black Forest night. A stroll at lovers' pace down Lichtentaler Allee and up Friedrich-strasse brought them to the casino, an imposing white struc-ture fronted by a row of eight columns thirty feet high and a wide portico that accommodated more than two hundred yellow-cushioned chairs. People of the evening were seated there in groups and pairs, chatting around their smoke, laughing into their cognacs. Both Vivian and Nikolai caused halted sentences, turned heads, as they passed by and entered the casino. They showed their passports and went into the main salon. "We'll only watch," Vivian said, leading the way deep into the large room. It was early. The roulette tables were not yet crowded. Nikolai and Vivian were drawn to the table that appeared to be the most active. They observed the play and the players for nearly half an hour, became acclimated to the subdued lighting, the elegant iniquity of the atmosphere.

"Darling, play a little," Vivian suggested.

"I'd just as soon watch," Nikolai whispered. He found fascinating the losings and winnings of such large amounts, the almost disrespectful lack of regard for money. For instance, the German gentleman seated nearest the wheel. He probably would have raised screaming hell had he found a four-mark error on his dinner bill an hour ago, and here on that last turn of the wheel he'd impassively lost a thousand.

"My roulette angels seem to be telling me you'd be lucky," Vivian said.

"You play if you want," Nikolai told her.

She understood his reluctance. "Set a limit on yourself and see how it goes. Come on," she urged good-naturedly, "we're in Baden-Baden."

Nikolai didn't want to be a killjoy. He purchased fifty chips worth a pound each.

"What number should we play?"

"Don't think, just play the number that you seem told to play."

"What about your roulette angels?" He was amused.

"What about them?"

"They're yours, aren't they, not mine?"

"We're soul mates," she said. "They'll talk to you. But of course you have to listen."

He waited a moment, as though listening, then placed five chips on the place on the layout of the table that was designated ODD, thus betting at even money that the winning number would be odd. The spin was in progress. The wheel slowed. The white ball seemed to have a mind of its own. It fell into number 18 and as though dissatisfied there hopped out and went into the adjacent slot, number 29. Nikolai had won. The croupier paid him five chips.

"Let the ten ride," Vivian said. "That is, if you feel *told* that you should."

He did and won on odd again. He picked up his original bet and his winnings of fifteen pounds.

"See?" Vivian said and gave his ear a fast celebratory kiss that sounded to him like a minor explosion.

Nikolai hadn't done much gambling in his lifetime. For most of his years there hadn't been either the opportunity or the time for it. In his youth he'd played cards with Lev and some fellows once in a while, but that was for the comradeship of it and the vodka they drank more than the few kopeks that were wagered. Soon after he was assigned to the trade mission in London he went alone to the races on three occasions, spring Saturdays when he had nothing better to do than satisfy his curiosity about what it was like. He went to Beverly and Salisbury and one night to Kingfield. Watched, altogether, nineteen races run, made four small bets, and lost all four, but seeing such handsome horses run was worth it. Since Vivian, he'd gone with her twice to her private gaming club, the Clermont, and spent more time at the bar than at the table with her. In fact, the second time he'd gone to the Clermont with her, while she was caught up in play he'd gone out and sat on a bench in Berkeley Square Park across the way for nearly an hour and hadn't been missed. She came away claiming she'd broken even. He thought she was white-lying about that and he did the same by letting her think he believed her. On several nights during the past year he had lain in the dark feeling paired by touch with Vivian in her bed while she explained the rudiments of blackjack and baccarat, roulette and craps, wanting to share her interest with him. Every so often she'd stop and ask if he was listening and he'd umm-hmm for her and sometimes would even ask a question for her sake.

Now he was fifteen pounds ahead at Baden-Baden and discovering how entirely different was the feeling of knowing the next bet he made would be his trying to win their money while betting their money. He sat out a spin and then placed ten pounds on the space designated *1st 12*. The slot that the ball finally took rest in was number 6, making Nikolai a winner three times in succession, and this last time at two-to-one odds.

He played on. At the end of an hour he had learned the game fairly well and was two thousand and some pounds ahead. Possibly, he thought, there *was* something to Vivian's roulette angels, because never once during his hour of play had he allowed logic to influence him. Rather, it was as if he'd put himself completely at the command (or was it whim?) of a determining force that sort of poked hunches into his head whenever it was pleased to do so. Those times when he lost it seemed that some force also determined that he should, for contrast, to keep the reaction to winning at its proper intensity. Vivian was with him all the way, pulling for him, encouraging after a loss, squeezing him one place or another after a nice win. Once during a relatively critical wager, Nikolai felt himself getting an erection and could only partly attribute that to Vivian. Strange, he thought, and wondered what other such recesses were in him that he'd never been aware of.

The wheel was again spun.

Nikolai was suddenly indecisive about which play he should make and how much. The force that had been providing him with guidance seemed to have deserted him, or at least was no longer paying attention. He believed in the number 6 but the number 14 was more of a possibility but 23 was perhaps better. He hadn't known such ambivalence until now. He took it as an indication that he should quit while he was ahead. He skipped three turns and then told Vivian, "You play."

"You're doing fine."

"No, please, you take over."

"Why?"

"That's what I feel." Also he felt selfish. Vivian had shown marvelous patience, especially for someone who so enjoyed wagering. He relinquished to her his two thousand in chips and plaques and stood behind her chair. By how much his neck and shoulders and arms now relaxed he realized how tense he'd become.

Vivian's play was swifter, more decisive. Her wagers were spread out over the layout of numbers, and seldom did she stop placing chips on various lines and intersections of lines until the croupier announced there could be no more bets. Nikolai told himself he wouldn't mind if she lost the entire two thousand that had required so much emotional energy for him to win.

However, she didn't lose. The plaques on the table in front of her piled up. At one o'clock Nikolai was happy to have her back with him when she turned to him, looked up, and said, "Let's make it an early night." An attendant was summoned to accompany her to the cashier, who exchanged the hard pieces of plastic for banknotes, a thick sheaf. Twenty thousand pounds.

They were marvelous winners, Nikolai and Vivian. Their arms-around walk back to the hotel was practically a strut that was practically a dance. They'd beaten the house, the Omniscient favored them; they were cleverer than fate, the angels were hovering, circling, doing loop-the-loops above their heads.

That emotional climate carried over into their lovemaking.

The next afternoon they went exploring around the small town and ended up climbing one of the surrounding hillsides, a steep open slope with grass so tall and thick it made the going strenuous. Vivian called it "hiding grass," because when they lay down in it they were out of sight, except for whatever was in the sky. They kissed a lot. After that romantic laziness they had an excellent light dinner at Katzenberger's Adler in the nearby village of Rastatt. They were at the casino by ten.

It had been decided that Vivian would do the playing.

♦ 211 ♦

She saw no reason why they both shouldn't, but Nikolai really didn't want to. His previous night's play had been a short high-feverish sort of positive experience that he felt would be better left singular. Even winning again would dilute it.

Vivian had the twenty thousand they were ahead to play with.

The angels weren't around. By midnight it was lost.

"Sixteen!" she muttered on the way back to the hotel. "Fucking sixteen." Several times during her play she had bet heavily on number 16, but, perversely, it wouldn't come up except when she wasn't on it. It was as though the number disliked her. When they arrived at the suite they went straight to bed. Vivian didn't even remove her makeup, which was not like her. There was no mention of the casino, but Nikolai doubted that it was very far back in her mind. She got right into her current reading, a book entitled *Angels and Man*, skipping pages to get to that part headed "Angelic Responsibility." Nikolai dozed off. Gambling was surprisingly enervating.

He awoke around four. Vivian wasn't there. He called out to her but didn't really expect a response. He knew immediately where she was, and for a while considered getting up and going there. However, he reasoned it would be worse if he did. He remained in bed, waited in the dark. He couldn't recall having felt lonelier. At close to five he heard her come in quietly. There was the stealthy sound of her barefoot steps on the rug, the rustle of her undressing, the puff of the pillow as it received her head, the frictional whistle of the sheet on her skin as she pulled it up over her. Nikolai sensed her condition, the hurt. She was like a wounded creature torn by a trap. He reached for her, brought her to him, silently soothed her, cupped and stroked her head. The tempo of her heart against him gradually slowed. She was drained.

He was certain she had lost, but actually it made no difference whether she had or not.

When she was deep asleep, Nikolai got up, careful not to disturb her. Noiselessly as possible, and automatically, as though having no choice, he removed his things from the wardrobe and its drawers and from the bathroom. He packed in the sitting room and then dressed. He didn't inflict upon himself the pain of a look in on her before he went out. He hired a car to take him to Stuttgart, where he caught the first available flight to Frankfurt. From there Aeroflot would take him home to Leningrad.

Vivian's eyes opened at ten-thirty that morning. Consciousness came to her with the dubious tidings that she was once again broke, fresh out except for a leftover thousand or two. There'd be mortgages in her immediate future. *Merde*, part of her said. *Tant pis*, said the other part. She would tell Nikolai over breakfast, she decided. She'd grin and admit to having been defeated. Would she have to say how sorry she was? She called out, and when there was no reply thought he might be out for a walk, perhaps gone up on the slope again. She imagined him sitting up there, his gaze fixed on the windows of the suite, waiting to see the drapes drawn, telling him she was awake and to hurry to her.

She didn't realize the extent of his absence until she was in the bathroom peeing and noticed his razor and brush and other such essentials were gone from the marble shelf above his sink. She went to the other room and saw the empty wardrobe, his luggage not in the foyer closet.

She couldn't remain standing, lowered herself to the edge of the sofa, hunched tightly, elbows on knees, fists jammed to cheekbones. She was beyond crying. The air seemed anesthetic. She was numb all over. Her mind tried to come to her rescue. It's only a tiff, it said. Nikolai was probably hurrying back to her this instant.

Finally, she presented something to herself that she could put stock in: *Self-preservation, Viv, is an antidote for panic.*

CHAPTER
•••16•••

ARCHER BELIEVED HE KNEW HIS VIVIAN, IF NOT PHYSICALLY at least psychologically, better than anyone. What he was for her now would be extremely important in nourishing what he hoped she would be for him in the near future. Don't be too hasty or clumsy in picking up her pieces and putting them in your pocket, he cautioned himself.

He gauged the depth of Vivian's hurt and took a position on the edge of it, a vantage from which he would surely know when it reached the stage of healing over. He filled it as much as possible with listening. In her unhalting manner, as though to drain a wound, she related to him the entire episode in detail, from Madrid to desertion. In fact, she went over it twice, as though searching for anything she might have left out. Throughout, Archer soaked up her words with concern, understanding frowns, sympathetic well-timed nods. Now and then, trying to splash a little laughter up out of her, he threw in one of his most arid or cynical quips. He also suggested distractions on the chance that she might grab hold of one and pull herself more quickly up out of this emotional mire. For instance, would she care to go trout fishing in Nova Scotia? Nothing salvages certain sunken hearts more readily than the taking of a couple of ten-pound browns. Or would she want to go somewhere and shoot something? What better way to separate the wrath from the woes?

The farthest Archer succeeded in getting her to go was to dinner at La Tante Claire. He had to wangle a reservation from a club crony who'd booked that scarcity a month ago, promised the fellow a stack of expensive favors in return.

As it turned out, Archer might as well have taken Vivian to a fish-and-chips place. She didn't care what he ordered for her, just anything, she told him, and sat there sucking on the slice of lime that came in her Perrier without making a sour face. She didn't want to talk about her Nikolai dilemma anymore. She didn't want to talk about anything. Nothing was worth words.

Thus, Archer had to fuel the conversation, hardly a pleasure for him. He could see everything he said passing right through her as though she were incorporeal. Hearing so much of only himself and coming up against the blanks of so many mute moments made him realize how tiresomely dull he'd probably been all along. Anyway, not nearly as amusing as he'd thought.

Another revelation for Archer was his own reaction to Nikolai's absence and the prospect that it might be permanent. The departure of Nikolai was not surprising to him. He'd anticipated that eventuality. However, now that it had come to pass, Archer felt part of himself was missing; a fresh, fairly potent hollow had taken a place within him where all his longtime most personal hollows dwelled. Of course, Archer thought, Vivian could alleviate that if only she were able to sustain a genuine smile in response to him and indulge in some of her normal wry rapport. Well, couldn't she? In the course of his one-sided conversations Archer steered around the mention of Nikolai as though it were a perilous obstacle. Several times he forgot and came within a syllable of collision. His public-school mentality suggested that now that his rival was down he should kick him, but for some reason, he could not bring himself to denigrate Nikolai. Besides, his better judgment advised that that would be an unwise and ineffective strategy.

What then might he do for her, and therefore do for himself, that would at least assuage if not cure?

Had Vivian not been Vivian but an ordinary sort, a visit to the jewelers, to Collingwood or Garrard, would have been regenerating. A Burma-ruby-and-diamond necklace would have been just the ticket to getting her down the road in the direction of being cheery. And quite possibly a sable from Fendi to knock around in might have been the what else needed to get her within one good carry-me-up-the-stairs drunk of destination.

But not Vivian.

She wouldn't even allow Archer to buy her something ugly that she could sell. He showed up at her door with a pair of Louis XIV marine barometers. Worth fifty thousand if a penny. Vivian didn't answer her bell, poked her head out her second-story window, saw him and the hideous valuables his chauffeur was carrying, and refused to let them in. No amount of pleading by Archer could persuade her. He left the two barometers on her doorstep. So did she. They weren't there the next morning, and she phlegmatically assumed that someone, most likely the trash collector, had lugged them off.

Vivian wasn't being intentionally perverse. She just wasn't the same Vivian without Nikolai, and for the time being she didn't feel like trying to be. Life was punishing her and she was struggling with the issue of whether or not she deserved it. How much easier, much better, it would have been if Nikolai had stuck around and confronted her. They could have had a good healthy relationship-cleansing fight, thrown a lot of verbal punches and counterpunches, accusing hooks, jealous jabs, threatening lefts and demanding rights. Perhaps they might even have carried it a bit further than a shouting match, really wrestled and clawed it out and dealt with it and not been deprived of the making-up enjoyments.

Instead of this miserable frustration.

She had phoned Nikolai's Leningrad apartment, which was where she believed he would most likely be. The Russian operator told her that Nikolai's instrument was out of order. I hope so, because mine surely is, Vivian thought. His office in Leningrad had refused to be helpful, recited a string of Russian that made her feel more helpless. When she had phoned his London office her calls were relayed to the embassy, where a human answering machine told her: "Mr. Borodin is not in. Do you wish to leave a message?" Again and again. Vivian phoned there so many times one day that she felt a nuisance and resorted to placing a tissue over the mouthpiece and disguising her voice. Grasping, she had also tried to reach Savich in Moscow. He was a delightful worldly man, she thought, he would be helpful, he was Nikolai's boss and would know his whereabouts. She got through three secretaries but not all the way through. She left her number.

Having hit all those dead ends, she went to the Soviet consulate and applied for a visa. All the red tape, filling out an application form, supplying three signed photographs of a specific size, the brief, personal interview, even the booking of a flight at the Aeroflot office on Piccadilly was unduly difficult for her; the effort seemed to be across the grain of her mettle. Her approved visa came by post. That same afternoon she went to Hyde Park, helped herself to a folding chair from the Park Department shed, and chose a spot way out on the lawn, as removed as possible from everyone. She was there only a few minutes before a vagrant approached her and begged a shilling, and two young boys with string wound around their fists ran to her and wanted to know if she'd seen where their kite had fallen to. She pointed in any direction to have them gone.

She bent over and lowered her head. Her heavy, straight hair fell forward. She swished it freely back and forth so that when she sat up it completely covered her face. Now she had her public privacy, the insularity she was entitled to. She imagined a succession of irrelevant things before coming to the fantasy of a high-flying-bird's-eye view of herself—a speck of a person treading to keep afloat in a lake of green—and that brought out from one of the most frequently used gates of her memory that fragment of time when she had last seen her mother alive far out alone in that cold lake in Scotland.

I'm not going under, Vivian vowed, no matter what. She would have her mourning, a period of awful, aching missing. She was already in it, but she wouldn't wallow any more than she would flounder. Nor would she resist it all that much. This was a debt. Unlike the sort she so habitually incurred. This was a karmic debt, a trial she owed her existence from a previous lifetime. It was entirely up to her whether or not she paid it, and in what coin.

With her frame of mind a notch improved, she went home. She canceled her chase to Leningrad, dropped her passport and visa into an everything drawer, undressed, and lay nude on the sofa with one leg up on the fat back of it. A shamelessly exposed, solitary position. In the gloaming of the London day with only the perpetual strains of the city for accompaniment she considered options and potentially therapeutic impulses. Such as opening another shop, a different approach this time, a place jammed madly with all sorts of worthwhile, charming junk for which she would charge outlandish prices. She would serve cheap wine to customers and act the obsessed collector so in love with every item that letting anyone purchase something was almost out of the question. (She'd soon tire of that.) Tomorrow she might benefit from being packed to the chin in warm mud like some tropical frog or having her hair cut too short. She could go platinum, had always wanted to. (Changes might be in order, but not self-destruction, not even to that extent.) She could become a female Gareth, a medium tout. Gareth didn't have a corner on being blessed by racing angels. She'd noticed in that morning's paper that in the 4:10 at Doncaster there were only five horses entered. A perfect race for angelic touting. Something must have influenced her to notice that. (Maybe she should try to chuck that way of thinking. Anyway, limit it.) She could drive down to Devon, purposely speed, and get a summons for it on the way down. Wake up early and have a big brekker, smoked kippers perhaps, surely some splits. The jam she had there, excellent raspberry she'd put up with Nikolai's help last summer, but she'd need to get the scones and the cream and everything would be closed in Pennyworth. Besides, shouldn't she go to the bank tomorrow and arrange a mortgage? (Not yet.) Shouldn't she remove Nikolai's things from her closet? (Positively not yet.) Why was it that for the second time since Baden-Baden that Irish punter she'd encountered three years ago during the March meeting at Cheltenham had come to mind? Matty "the

Boy" Flynn. Why was it she was able to picture his face so clearly, fast smile, windburned complexion, slightly crooked lower front teeth? Said he'd been a priest way back. On the boat coming over he'd won twenty-some thousand at poker. What a devil! It had been at the bar of the Cottage Lake that, simultaneously, Matty's eyes had taken her and his voice given her a twenty-to-one winner. (As her taste had then it would still find him too much the dandy.) Not so long ago she'd read somewhere and thought it just so much scientific bull the theory that love was merely the brain overdosing on dopamine and norepinephrine— she'd memorized those substances, thinking they could be put to use during table talk. Well, if there was any truth to it, perhaps they knew of something—an injection?—that worked as an antidote. (She wouldn't take it even if they did. Not yet.) If, farther down the road than she'd be able to see now even if she were standing tiptoe on the peak of Mount Everest, lonely push came to lonely shove, wouldn't she remarry Archer? (She was too fond of him to ever do that to him.)

Night had come. The lamp on the table behind the sofa was one with an old beaded pull chain. She extended her foot, felt around with it, and tried to get the pull chain between her large and second toe. After five minutes of trying she managed it. Illumination brought the room back to being the room. With only her and her moping in it.

She got up so quickly she was a bit light-headed on her way into the kitchen. She found the particular cookbook she'd bought with good intent last year at Hatchard's and split it open to the place she'd marked with an old unopened Harrods bill. She read the recipe for blinis aloud three times. It didn't seem difficult. Blinis were nothing more than a sort of pancake. If she'd realized they were this simple she would have had a go at making them long ago. Mother Russia, she thought, you're about to be exposed. She got out everything that was called for. Except for the buckwheat flour. She didn't have any but assumed regular flour would do. She would be well organized, not have to stop and search her cabinets for something as she usually did. She lined up the utensils and ingredients on the counter in the order they'd be used.

Before beginning, she went to the study for her compact disk player and powerful little speakers. Brought them into the kitchen and put them on the counter opposite. For inspiration and company she chose the "Polovtsian Dances" from *Prince Igor*, by Nikolai's great-great-uncle Alexander Borodin, performed by the London Symphony Orchestra. She turned the volume way up, so loud it seemed to claim the air and contribute to making her kitchen microcosmic.

One of the early sections of the piece, a whirl of woodwinds, was, Vivian thought, perfect accompaniment for her whisking of the egg and the milk, and as she went along the music was like a personal underscore for the various motions required of her hands, all the way to the spooning of the batter onto the hot surface of the butter-greased iron skillet.

Vivian's spirit was sailing as she watched the circles of batter cook. Blinis were one promise she could check off her past-due list. See? Their upsides were beginning to texture with little bubbles exactly as the recipe said they would. Vivian flipped the blinis over and saw that their cooked sides were burned black. How could that have happened? She'd been standing there watching them every second. She hurriedly threw the overdone blinis into the trash container beneath the sink, got them out of sight, making it easier for her to pretend that the next batch was the first. She should be allowed that much of a handicap, she thought. After all, she *wasn't* Russian.

She didn't give up. Not until around midnight. Borodin's *In the Steppes of Central Asia* and his Nocturne for String Orchestra from Quartet No. 2 were with her all the while, over and over. She blamed everything, ingredients, recipe, stove, skillet, before getting around to herself. The making of blinis was an unmerciful little trick, she decided. Someday she'd have another go at it. She turned off the stove and the Borodin and left the mess she'd made. To clean it up now would be tantamount to being beaten *and* enslaved.

She took a shower, scrubbed her skin red with a loofah, especially her breasts and belly where batter had splattered and caked. While she was drying she was pierced again with wondering what Nikolai was doing and thinking right then. She pinched off her imagination, didn't let it dilate and hurt her with detail. Nikolai wasn't laughing, wasn't touching anyone, wasn't having an easier time of it than she, she mentally recited.

Ninja came sneakily around the doorjamb. He looked up at her aloofly with his huge, mustard-colored eyes, turned his head away momentarily, then to her again. His tail lost its hook, straightened up.

Vivian knew his feline tail language. "I love you too," she told him, and at once thought what a drastic shade of difference there was between "too" and "also."

Ninja came to her, brushed her lower legs with his head, flank, and tail. Marking her as his with the humanly unsmellable scent of his pheromones. He kept on with it, slithering furrily between her ankles and around. She nearly tripped as she stepped over him and went into the bedroom to get her iridology monocle from the tray on her dresser. She looped its delicate platinum chain over her head and returned to the bathroom, where Ninja was now postured sphinxlike near the bidet, awaiting her next resort.

Attached to the wall at the edge of the main mirror was another mirror, a round one about eight inches in diameter. It was extendable in an accordion manner. It also magnified. Vivian put it to use whenever she had the patience and inclination to be more precise with her makeup or the courage to closely appraise the condition of her facial pores. More frequently she used it for self-diagnosis.

She pulled the mirror to her, adjusted it to suit the light, and with her face close to it brought her magnifying monocle to her right eye. There then was the ten-times-two-times image of her gray iris about the size of a poker chip. The first different thing she noticed about it was that it was glintless. Not even a flicker of mystery or mischief in it. And there was some blue showing through, which she could only interpret as overactivity of her unhappiness potential. She winced, then mentally shrugged and said: What the hell do you expect? She rated the density of her iris at about two and a half. Not bad, considering, although in the three-o'clock area nerve rings were quite pronounced and between nine and twelve o'clock were some squiggly fibers which indicated a borderline-to-serious malfunction in her animation and life center. Otherwise she saw no critical discolorations or signs of trauma. Her heart and lungs and bowels and downstairs department were apparently doing well. She'd be willing to wager, however, lay a thousand to one, that less than a week from now if she again examined that same iris there'd be a wispy whitish swirl at five o'clock, a sure giveaway that her libido was complaining.

She clicked off the bathroom light and got into bed. Her body was sleepy but her mind wasn't. Ninja jumped up on the bed and settled against her hip. Small comfort. Vivian combed through the fur along one of his haunches with her fingertips. He turned on his purr, so emphatic a purr that it was close to a growl. Things could be a hell of a lot worse, Vivian told herself. Nikolai could have left her for another woman instead of merely because of the way she was.

With the speed of thought she ran time and events back to that last night last week in Baden-Baden. What if she hadn't gotten up and allowed herself to be pulled to the casino? Supposing she'd lain there awake all night fighting it? Possibly, unlikely but possibly, she might have fallen asleep without realizing it and the next thing she'd have known her feet would have been reaching to find Nikolai's legs, putting skin to skin for reassurance the way she nearly always did when she was returning to realities. Nikolai would be with her now. She'd still be solvent. Nikolai mattered. But as far as the money was concerned, what difference did it make whether she blew it all in a two-hundred-thousand-pound lump or frittered it away a pittance at a time? That's what she would surely have done, bet and squandered it away. Soon enough it would have gone to zero. Admitted, she had committed a foolish romantic gaffe, but hadn't Nikolai overreacted? Loss of money, no matter what amount, wasn't reason enough to be wasting all this precious together time. She'd tell him that.

Her last vague thought before sleep was that perhaps she'd have better luck if she tried making borshch.

CHAPTER
•••• 17 ••••

AT THE VERY MOMENT WHEN SLEEP TOOK VIVIAN, LIKE THE other half of a barter three thousand miles away, it gave up Nikolai. He came awake suddenly, sharp awake with his senses fully receptive. Since he'd arrived at the dacha a week ago the nights and mornings had been like that for him. No matter how late he stayed up he awoke at about the same time, when the sky was still dark. It was as though his consciousness had to precede the dawn, not allow the day and its choices to arrive before he had a chance to summon up resistance.

He lay there by the open window of his bedroom and watched the coming sun extinguish the stars. Where now, he wondered, were all the tiny creatures that had been so vociferous in the black of night? Had they lost their courage now that they might be visible, were they cowering down among the blades, beneath leaves and logs, squeezed by fright into any available crack? He listened. The stillness of the early morning was contradicted only by the running of the stream and two caws from a distant crow. He wished he would hear someone moving about downstairs, the sound of water being drawn, the clunk of a kettle being put on the stove, the wonderful, providing smell of something being cooked, anything. He wished to hear humming from down there. Irina used to hum as she went about. Her own private orchestra in the back of her throat. Vivian had also been a hummer, especially when she was busy doing house-keeping things in Devon. Not so much in London, though.

Nikolai was able to think of Vivian now without feeling so much of a protesting ache in him. It had been the right thing for himself, his coming here to the dacha, where there was no phone, no one. He couldn't have chosen a better place to do his battle. The hard work had helped, the way he'd driven his body in spite of his mind. He'd sawn and split three stacks of logs for next winter's fires, telling himself he would be coming here more now. He'd also completed the dry stone wall that had been his father's final project. It was a more difficult task alone, Nikolai found. He'd wrestled and leveraged into position with a greenwood pole the huge rocks needed for the footing and then lugged other rocks to the site and used a ten-pound sledge to break them into the needed shapes with flat faces.

For something more to do at night he had rearranged most of the furniture. It was while moving his mother's heavy chest of drawers that he discovered the letters. They were in the shallow space between the frame and the underside of the bottom drawer, could not have just fallen there. The letters were addressed to Irina. There were ten, bound by a piece of common string. The earliest was dated 1950 and postmarked Kiev. The most recent, on better-quality stationary, was 1961, with a Moscow postmark.

Nikolai's automatic inclination was to read them, but then he reasoned that out of respect to Irina he shouldn't. They had been secretly kept by her; they should remain her secret. He returned them to their hiding space and regretted having disturbed them, because now he knew they were there, would always know. It was like some of their indelible substance, whatever it was, had come off on his hands. He silently asked Irina if she would mind his reading them. It seemed she gave permission. As Vivian would say, it was probably Irina who had led him to move the chest of drawers in the first place. He got the letters out again, could have easily broken the string, but took time to pick loose the tight little knot Irina had made. He read by the light of a kerosene lamp:

My precious—
Last night you began with
doubt that I honestly cared

*for you.   Then, influenced by
sensation, you were sure of
me.   You tried to leave me
with that impression; perhaps
even now you believe you
succeeded.   However, when
you turned your head to
exchange our parting look
I translated your eyes and
read the incertitude in them.
Again, it seems, you are
giving in to what you feel
is the insufficiency of our
arrangement.   Please measure
the passion we share and
remember it was that which
brought us to enter one another.
I beg you, do not be confounded
by my fickle nature, or, for that
matter, feel the need to exonerate
it.*

It was typewritten and unsigned, not even initialed.   Why
should it be, Nikolai thought, when only Irina needed to
know who it was from?   And how surely she must have
known!   All the letters were equally brief, little more than
notes, really.   Their content quite similar: Ardor and admission.   Apparently all were from the same well-educated
person.

Nikolai read each of the ten letters a second time, more
slowly, trying to extract from them any indication of what
his mother must have felt.   He was stunned and intrigued
and touched by this disclosure that she'd had a lover over
all those years, 1950 to 1961, and perhaps before and perhaps
after then.   Had there been other letters?   Only these kept
for some reason, possibly because they contained no mention of name or place and if found would only incriminate
her?   Nikolai wondered.   What had happened after 1961?
Had the affair been suddenly broken off, or had the heat

of it eventually cooled to the point where the cautions of infidelity became too demanding? Who had this man been? Where was he now? Would he know, would he care, that Irina was no longer alive? With only the handwriting and manner of expression to go on, Nikolai could only idealize an image, one that he kept changing, improving for his mother's sake.

Irina and passion.

As a youth Nikolai had had the commonplace blind spot that prevented him from accepting an erotic side to his mother. When he reached adulthood, his imagination, of course, was realistic, although not graphic about it. Never had he anticipated such intimate proof as these letters. They elicited fantasies that were conceivably what had occurred: Irina readying, prettying herself for an assignation, hurrying to it, stealing the time for it with one excuse or another, sharing a greeting kiss with the accumulated want in it, eagerly undressing or enjoying being undressed, stimulated by the taboo of her own afternoon nudity, relinquishing it, opening that special part of her through which Nikolai had been created and out of which he had come. The more Nikolai imagined, the more voluntarily erotic Irina became. He decided it made him happier for her. It also helped genetically explain his own passionate disposition and allowed him to credit it not so entirely to the effect Vivian had on him.

Now on the seventh morning of his self-imposed exile he got up from the bed hoping he'd left most of his loneliness in it. He put on a pair of old canvas sneakers, some khaki shorts, and a sweatshirt. Downstairs, he took a basket from its hook on a beam and went out. By the time he'd gone twenty steps down the incline, the night wet of the grass had his sneakers soaked and his feet chilled. He paused at the edge of the stream to take stock of his emotional condition and thought he felt fairly good. He had no dislike for the day. During his pause he happened to glance down to a small, shallow landlocked pool. There were, he saw, minnows in it, a dozen or so. They were startled by his looming presence and darted from side to side seeking escape. It would not take long for that pool to go dry, Nikolai thought. He knelt and dug with his hands, scooped away pebbles and sand to create a channel that connected the isolated pool to the main stream. A way out. The minnows would find it.

Feeling somewhat better, Nikolai continued on across the stream and entered the woods. It would be a while before the sun would warm there. Ghostlike wisps were around the trunks of the trees as though resting from their swirls. Nikolai saw wild boar hoofprints. A wild boar was not to be messed with. A short way farther on Nikolai found what he was searching for. Fresh up out of the rich mulched soil. They were *podberyozoviki*, brown-capped mushrooms. More than enough to fill his basket.

He took the mushrooms back to the house, carefully washed, peeled, and sliced them, and sautéed them in butter with some onions. He ate them along with the last of the dark bread and made himself admit it was a better breakfast than any English sausage and eggs no matter who cooked them. While his breakfast settled he sat on the porch and read ten pages of Turgenev's *On the Eve*. In Russian. Then, as though a time had been reached, he went inside and straightened up the kitchen, packed the few things he'd brought, and got into the rented Niva. He took a moment to thank the house before starting the car and heading for Leningrad.

When he arrived at the apartment he knew at once Lev was there. A playful female voice came from Lev's room. Nikolai didn't try to be quiet, went about normally, opened one of the windows, went through his mail. Within a few minutes Lev came out. He left his door open. His bed was in view, but Nikolai didn't look in.

"Someone pulled out the telephone," Lev informed him. "It was like that when I got here about an hour ago."

Nikolai nodded and concealed his lack of concern with a moment of attention to the telephone wire, which was a pile of loops on the floor. "Who's that with you, Kecia?" he asked, just to get onto a different subject.

"No, Kecia went home to Helsinki."

"As you predicted."

"She sent me her pretty cousin, Ula."

"That was decent of her."

"From what I understand it's a large family." Lev grinned, then asked: "How is it you're here in Leningrad again so soon?"

"Just business, a small emergency."

"How long will you be around?"

"I don't know yet."

"Must be hard on your London lady," Lev commented. He got two bottles of beer from the refrigerator and went back into his room, closed the door.

Nikolai attended to the telephone. He hadn't yanked out the wires but merely unscrewed the cover of the wall plug and disconnected them. He'd done it to protect himself from himself, to make it that much more difficult for him to dial Vivian. He believed he was in good enough shape to handle it now. He reconnected the wires. The phone, like some creature revived, rang immediately. She, Nikolai thought, surely it would be she. His insides were wrenching, there was the voltage of a quiver on the back of his neck, his earlobes felt as though they were about to catch fire. He wasn't ready to hear her, he knew, nowhere near ready.

The phone rang insistently. Nikolai sat there within reach of it, paralyzed by ambivalence. It stopped ringing, and worse then was the giving up conveyed by its abrupt silence. When, after a short while, the phone rang again, Nikolai gazed at it and thought how one simple motion on his part could span him to her. His hand seemed disobedient. It picked up the receiver and brought it to his mouth and ear. The hello that came from him was courageously crisp.

It was a call from Moscow. One of Savich's secretaries told him to remain on the line. Savich came on. "I've been trying to get in touch with you."

"I'm on holiday," Nikolai explained.

"So Valkov said."

"Is there a problem?"

"That was to be my question."

It had something to do with Churcher, Nikolai thought, probably Churcher's concern about that packet of contraband Aikhal diamonds. He should have written a meeting report, hadn't only because he'd been so distracted. Now Churcher had taken his howl to Savich and mentioned that meeting and brought attention to this gap in Nikolai's conscientiousness. There was no excuse for it and he didn't feel like trying to invent one.

"I had a call from your Vivian," Savich said.

That was it? Nikolai was twice relieved. That it didn't concern the Churcher matter and that Vivian had gone to such an extent. He had begun to feel his distress was exclusive. "What did she have to say?"

"I didn't take her call or return it yet," Savich said. "I thought I should first speak with you. What is it, Nikolai? Are you in trouble of some sort?"

"No, no trouble."

"I sense you are."

"It's only something personal."

"Of course it is. The best thing for you would be someone's ear. Whom do you have to confide in?"

"My friend Lev," Nikolai replied automatically, but then realized he didn't have Lev at the moment. At this critical moment Lev was in pleasure, oblivious to all else, way over on the opposite side of feeling.

"Come down here," Savich directed.

Why should Savich be interested in his personal life? Nikolai thought. Anyway, how could he possibly open up to Savich? There'd be the unease, the self-consciousness of imposition. And embarrassment. Still, for some reason, Nikolai felt drawn to Savich's offer. "When would be convenient for you?" he heard himself ask.

"I leave for Paris early tomorrow," Savich said. "I'll be gone for ten days."

"My situation can wait."

"No. Catch a flight down this afternoon. Take the five-o'clock."

"Really, it's not that urgent. Besides, the five-o'clock will be all booked by now."

"There'll be a seat for you."

"I'll be on it."

"You'll be met."

CHAPTER
⬩⬩⬩⬩18⬩⬩⬩⬩

THE AMBER HEADLIGHTS OF THE GOVERNMENT LIMOUSINE were on flash.

Up ahead on Moscow's Highway M10, ordinary cars cleared over so the limousine could have the outside lane to itself. At every intersection uniformed militiamen held back other traffic. The black Zil pressed its official prerogative all the way into the city proper, where the M10 became Gorky Prospekt. Its driver was blasé about doing eighty-some on congested Gorky. Its passenger was of a similar frame of mind. Any other time Nikolai would have gotten on the intercom and ordered the driver to slow, but as circumstances were, such peril felt appropriate. He just sat back, ignored his undone seat belt, and gazed out the tinted side window at the sepia blur of everything. That he could see out while no one could see in at him also seemed a suitable condition.

At Mayakovsky Square the limousine screeched left onto Sadovaya. It flashed aside the thick flow of that bustling boulevard for nearly a mile, then turned right onto Rileev Street, a much smaller way, quiet and, for the most part, fashionable. When it had gone several blocks of Rileev it swung in at the paved drive of one of the apartment buildings along there—a towerlike structure, pleasingly landscaped with arborvitae and other evergreens and situated well back from the street. Nikolai had expected Savich's Moscow residence to be in an older, conservative place. This was blackened steel and glass, and, according to Nikolai's quick count by twos just before the limousine nosed down into the subterranean garage, it was eighteen stories high. The garage was immaculate, with an impermeably coated concrete floor. The rubber heels of the driver's shoes made suffering squeaks as he accompanied Nikolai to the elevator. It was the quietest, fastest Soviet elevator Nikolai had ever ridden. At the sixteenth level it stopped and opened to offer a tastefully carpeted corridor which served several apartments. Nikolai was about to step out when the driver gestured that this wasn't the floor. In the momentary pause before the elevator doors closed Nikolai thought how he wouldn't mind having an apartment there, a modest one-bedroom or even just a studio that he could fix up. He'd get rid of most of the things he had, certainly those that were petrified with sentimentality. His great-grandmother's samovar, for instance. Never used and yet preserved like a shrine. Out with it! He'd begin anew all the way down to his everyday dishes. Never again, when he was taking a sip from a glass, would he think that his lips were touching where Irina's had, or when a fork went into his mouth would it occur to him that its tines had experienced a slip over the tongue of Grandfather Maksim.

The fantasy saddened him. He chastized the upper third of his head for having thought it up.

A key was inserted into the flush lock on the face of the control panel. As though sighing, the elevator went to seventeen. Its doors parted again to reveal a spacious private entry hall. There, standing on gleaming marble beneath a crystal chandelier of six thousand facets, was Savich.

He had saved his smile so he could break out with it now at the first sight of Nikolai, and instead of a mere handshake, he transmitted twice the amiability by extending both hands palms up in the Russian manner. Vigorous man-to-man squeezes were exchanged.

"I'm glad you came," Savich said. He said it as well with his eyes.

"It was kind of you to suggest it," Nikolai replied. He swiftly appraised his surroundings, noticed a gracefully curved ascending stairway on the left, and assumed that Savich's apartment included the entire floor above.

Savich turned and led the way down a wide center hall.

Nikolai, following along, happened to glance into one of the rooms they were passing, a large room, the sort that seemed to be awaiting an occasion with its suite of gilt Empire pieces arranged just so, its walls dressed with creamy silk. An ornate Chippendale mirror shot Nikolai back to Nikolai and helped him verify that he was actually there. At the deep end of the hall Savich slid open left and right pocket doors and stepped aside for Nikolai to precede him. They entered Savich's study, the room that was most personal to him. It was where he spent his precious time alone. A pair of matching *bergères à la reine* were situated at a conversational angle to each other. The down-filled seat cushion of one had surrendered much of its plump. Nikolai gathered that was Savich's chair and sat in the other.

"What will you drink?"

"Whiskey, thank you."

"How do you want it?"

"Neat."

"I'll have the same," Savich said as though imparting that to someone else in the room. He remained seated. The sharp-peaked bush of his black eyebrows canopied his sockets as he assessed Nikolai.

Nikolai felt that the next words were expected to come from him. He knew what they should be. "I apologize," he said, "for arriving late at the general meeting two weeks ago."

"From what I understood when I left Devon, you would be leaving shortly thereafter. In fact, I expected you to be on the flight that I took. I thought it would give us time for a chat."

"At the last minute I gave in to persuasion and stayed down there an extra night."

"By far the better option."

"Then what time there was to spare went to car trouble. Otherwise I would have made it. I'm truly sorry."

Savich didn't acquit Nikolai further. He just deserted the subject. "You look terribly uncomfortable," he said. "Why don't you take off your jacket and tie."

Nikolai had worn one of his everlasting Russian wool

suits, believing that appropriate for what he intended to say. It was now liberating to get out of the jacket and remove the tie he'd knotted too tight. He unbuttoned his shirt two down. He felt like stretching but didn't.

The drinks came. Brought by a manservant Savich introduced as Do Kien. He was oriental, typically diminutive and sinewy. He moved as though to disturb the air as little as possible and placed the silver tray on the table without making a sound. Should he pour? he asked almost imperceptibly with his head and eyes.

"I'll take care of it," Savich told Do Kien, dismissing him with his tone. As an unimportant accompaniment to the transferring of ample portions of whiskey from an antique Waterford decanter, Savich mentioned that both his servants were orientals. "Do Kien does all the cooking. His wife, Mai Lon, won't go near the stove or even chop up a vegetable. He, in turn, is above doing any cleaning, won't even empty a wastebasket. Every so often they argue about it. You've never heard such screaming volleys. Do Kien calls them discussions. Actually, I've learned it is rather difficult to tell when they're having a peaceful talk or flinging vitriol. In Vietnamese, it all sounds so emphatic."

"How long have they been with you?"

"Nearly two years. He came here to Moscow to study political philosophy at the university but found it not to his liking. Before that for ten years he was a captain in the Vietnamese army. I've seen his commission papers signed by General Van Phu himself. Do Kien is proud of what he was but for whatever reason doesn't want to return to it. At least, not yet."

"He struck me as younger," Nikolai put in. His imagination transported the stealthy Do Kien to the Vietnam jungle, pictured him with an automatic rifle at the ready, patrolling for enemy units along the Cambodian border. Nikolai found it not so simple to bring this Do Kien back to boiling potatoes for Savich.

"Na zdorovye." Savich tilted his raised glass at Nikolai.

Nikolai returned the toast.

They both took large gulps to stress their sincerity.

With his throat still warm from the excellent whiskey, Nikolai told Savich, "The morning before I left London I had a meeting with Churcher. He had the head of security in on it."

"Pulver. George Pulver."

Nikolai was mildly surprised that Savich knew of Pulver, who wasn't on the level Savich usually dealt with. But then it was in keeping with Savich's thoroughness. He went on: "Churcher and Pulver were extremely disturbed over a packet of finished Aikhal goods they managed to intercept."

"How many carats?"

"Twenty-four hundred, or so they claimed. I was shown only eight hundred. The other sixteen may or may not exist. Anyway, Churcher is again accusing us of selling beyond our quota."

"Did he happen to say from whom he took the goods?" Savich sounded mainly curious.

"Not by name, just that the man was somehow drowned in Lake Geneva."

"Seems a bit dramatic, don't you think?"

"Possibly. But knowing Churcher as well as I do I'm almost certain he wasn't inventing. Not this time."

"Did you do a meeting report?"

"No, I—"

"Good. If there is any substance to this it's best that as little as possible be made of it at the moment. You've met Gleb Kulinich, of course."

"Kulinich?"

"The Minister of Mines. He was along on your field trip to Aikhal last September."

"I don't recall anyone named Kulinich."

"He made the trip under an assumed name and not in any important official capacity, merely to snoop around. A rather short, big-bellied fellow with numerous chins and a constant scowl, always breathing loudly."

The description helped Nikolai remember the man.

"Kulinich is attempting to convince the Central Committee that Aikhal and all the other diamond mining and recovery installations would be better placed under his charge. To this point his campaign has been unsuccessful. However, there's no need to fuel it with even the rumor of a problem." Savich got Nikolai by the eyes. "Do I have your confidence?"

"Of course."

"If Churcher broaches the matter again, don't get into it with him. Or with Pulver. Tell them my instructions are that they should take it up directly with me."

"I understand."

Savich thumbed back his shirt cuff to look at his wristwatch. "Now," he said, getting up, "I must make a call."

"Shall I step out?"

"No, stay where you are. I'll only be a few moments."

Nikolai welcomed this interlude alone. It gave him time to enjoy the fact that he'd just lightened his professional conscience. He estimated that he felt about 25 percent better. It also allowed him to take in this room, which he believed probably personified Savich.

An eighteenth-century Régence bureau sat on the right, a truly substantial one and rare for not being overly embellished with ormolu. On its gilt-tooled brown leather top, correspondence lay overlapped in a line, weighted in place by a miniature bronze of Herakles nude. Herakles, so muscular, with a tiny pointed spout of a penis protruding above a lopsided sack. The surface of the desk shared by a jade letter opener, simply a sharpened lavender blade, a shagreen-covered agenda, and a fine Daum Nancy vase containing pens, ordinary ballpoints and felt-tips, some bearing the names of hotels. Stuck out among the pens, like a beauty suffering inelegance, a solid gold Dupont. It reminded him of Archer.

A pair of George III mahogany breakfront cabinets. Blue moroccan bindings squeezing spine to spine along the glassed-in shelves. Titles and authors' names patiently glinting out over the shoulders of Chinese porcelain snuff bottles and erotic netsuke figures. The eight-fold Coromandel screen, the salmon-and-gray marble pedestal supporting a fat, zealous fern, the collection of seventeenth-century falcon hoods in a mahogany case.

Nikolai, from where he was sitting, had no idea what those were, the falcon hoods. He got up and went across the room for a closer look at the little sewn leather caps with their feather-tufted crests. They were arranged in four rows, seven across, the spaces between punctuated here and there by brass bells. Where had Savich found them? Nikolai wondered. Had he gotten them all at once or one or two at a time over the years? Nikolai was fascinated. For a moment he was transported to the sensation of such a bird, its disposition temporarily subdued by blindness, as though its eyes were as lethal as its talons. The hood was slipped off, the entire sky offered, the perch of wrist tossed upward, launching. Go kill!

Nikolai moved on around the room, gave attention now to the paintings hung upon the gray velour walls, hung with little or no regard for arrangement. That, rather than exclude any one. A Boldini nude was putting on her black silk stockings next to mystically entwined bare figures by the Symbolist Lévy-Dhurmer next to a small, guileless Maillot. Here, no overcrowded Flemish bouquets or studies of waves in dash or pastorals of sheep being herded home. But women, one after another, their displaying displayed. They seemed more in alliance than in competition, each presenting the imagination with conceivably whatever had occurred before or after these caught moments. There was a voluptuous, longing one with almost geometric flesh done in 1932 by Tamara De Lempicka; another, contrastingly lithe and eerily *fatale*, depicted by Fernand Khnopff. A rather somnambulant Dante Gabriel Rossetti, 1864, was the close neighbor to a wistfully suggestive Frederick Lord Leighton which shared closely with a much smaller, charming Théodore Rousseau. The Rousseau a young woman, presumably a model, possibly his lover, if, indeed that gender was his preference, seated nude in the sling of a folding chair, intent upon the page of a magazine. Nikolai imagined the moment, the artist calling out to her and she, with total physical confidence, rising from this honest attitude to invent a pose. How sensitive and correct of Rousseau to have left her as she was, Nikolai thought before he transferred his gaze to the nearby long Louis XV parquetry table. On its *brèche d'Alep* marble top stood another collection.

Photographs.

How many? Were there not more than a hundred? And not one female face duplicated. Within their propped-up frames, their tiny silver circles, putti-crowded ovals, and classic linear rectangles, each contributed to the legion and, at the same time, set herself apart. As Nikolai went beyond his initial panoramic impression and began examining the photographs individually, he realized that here he was entering Savich's more intimate ground. He felt he was a trespasser if not a sort of thief, but then he reasoned it was evidently Savich's choice to allow such exposure. Nikolai compared the feminine energy that looked out at him now, that usually looked out to Savich. The smiling snapshot of whoever she was gone a bit brown with time. The professionally taken portrait just this side of demure, her complexion impossibly lineless. The defiant candid nearly nude with her fists on her hips holding open the oversize hotel bathrobe. The surprised one in sable on a street, most likely turned by her name and snapped before playful protest. Some were dated by their attitudes as much as by what they wore. Which were the most recent was obvious to Nikolai. Those seemed more requiring, less dependent on guile or modesty. Here and there were signed ones. The flourished or plain promises of a forever or an always did not give them an advantage, Nikolai thought. Each face was to a degree fixed with the same hopefulness, the same confidence in pleasure, the same concealment of melancholy. All those mouths kissed, all those eyelids closed, all those brains momentarily pacified. Where were they now, at this very second? Nikolai doubted that even one of them was weeping. And what of that frame conspicuously vacant? It was one of the larger upright frames, silver elaborately chased with bezel-set cabochon rubies integrated into the design. Nikolai had noticed it right off. It was centered, importantly placed and yet vacant. Was it the frame of honor, awaiting the elusive her who would excel for Savich, who would anesthetize him with her sensations? Or had there been an occupant in that frame and had she, out of jealousy, to escape the torture brought on by her own possessiveness, torn herself away? On the other hand, perhaps Savich had simply decided she no longer belonged. However, that was not as easy for Nikolai to imagine.

He went back to his chair and attempted to summarize his impression of the room. There was an eclectic harmony to it, erotic while at root romantic. Or was it the other way around? He doubted that Savich usually allowed business associates in here, not unless he wanted to allow them into his self. Then why me? Nikolai wondered. He poured another inch of whiskey into his glass. The friction and clinks of the stopper of the crystal decanter seemed loud. He heard his throat's slick swallowing mechanism. He would avoid the subject of Vivian if he could, he decided. The less he talked about her the better.

Savich returned.

"My phone call took longer than I expected," he said apologetically.

Nikolai thought Savich had probably sacrificed his engagement for that evening, disappointed someone lovely.

"And I had to make sure dinner would be right. We're having calves' liver. Does that suit you?"

"I planned to take the nine-o'clock back to Leningrad."

"It will be all booked."

"I bribed the seating agent."

"Then you've wasted money," Savich insisted wryly, ending that. He pulled a taboret closer between their chairs. An oversize book was open on it. Savich closed the book and propped it against the leg of the table. Nikolai noticed its title: *The World's Great Power Yachts.* Savich put his feet up on the taboret, and indicated that Nikolai should do the same. Having their feet so mutually supported and in such proximity was a very unexpected sharing for Nikolai. It made him feel less relaxed. He couldn't help but compare his black, mainly useful Soviet shoes with the smart brown Ferragamo loafers Savich had on. Savich's socks were cotton lisle with some silk in it, woven so a subtle embroidered dart ran up over the knub of his ankle.

"How about something to hold you until dinner?" Savich suggested.

"No, thank you."

"Are you sure? I can have Do Kien prepare something. Would you like some sterlet?"

Nikolai loved that smallest of sturgeon, and they were almost impossible to come by. "I'll save my appetite for dinner," Nikolai said.

"Good. Then we'll be gluttons." Savich took three successive small gulps from his glass. He frowned just perceptibly and tugged at the hairs on the backs of his fingers. He brought the aim of his eyes around so it was directly at Nikolai. Nikolai imagined a black beam coming from Savich's pupils, locking in on him, a ray that prompted and extracted. What had Vivian seen in Savich's irises? When Nikolai had asked her, in fact asked her twice, she'd dodged the question. If she'd answered it might have been helpful now.

"When we were in London together," Nikolai said, "you told me in your opinion I'd performed well on my job."

"You have. You've done extremely well."

"It's not much of a challenge. Mainly all I do is soak up Churcher's complaints and tremble on cue."

"You're being remarkably modest. Truth is, you've got things there on the London end running so smoothly they seem routine. I hardly ever hear even a caution from our legal department, and it used to always be stirring up problems. Our transportation people are more punctual than ever with our shipments to the System, because you've kept on top of them. All in all, Nikolai, it's no strain for me to commend you."

"Thank you."

"You know, every feather you put into your cap also goes into mine."

"You mentioned there was a place for me here in Moscow whenever I might want it."

"When did I say that?"

"We were in the car coming from the System. It was a Friday."

Gerald A. Browne

"I don't recall."

Nikolai doubted Savich ever forgot anything.

"Anyway, is such an offer possible?"

"You want to be assigned to Moscow?"

"Yes."

"Why the hell would you give up the spot you now enjoy to be in the frenzy of this bureaucratic hive?"

"It's just that I've had my fill of London, of Churcher and the System and all."

"Seems you've given this thought."

"Plenty."

"You know, of course, there are countless comrades who would sell their souls to be in your London shoes."

A nod from Nikolai, conceding that. The way he saw it, reassignment to Moscow was essential to his resolve. The protection of distance. He wouldn't even return to London to get his personal belongings if he could help it. He'd have someone from the embassy ship everything. As for the clothing and other things of his that were at Vivian's flat and down at her house in Devon, he'd just consider them lost. He pictured her throwing them in the trash bin. The middle of his chest panged as though it had caved in.

"Perhaps you're letting ambition get the best of you," Savich said.

"Would that be so terrible?"

"No, but it would be ordinary and therefore disappointing. I had you, especially you, standing out from the pack, from all those desperate climbers."

Nikolai assumed from that that he'd been on Savich's mind to a greater extent than he'd realized. He considered it a compliment.

"What is it you see ahead for yourself, Nikolai? A deputy ministership?"

"Possibly."

"Or could the destination you have in mind be my job?"

Nikolai laughed tensely.

"You wouldn't care for it," Savich said, "believe me. Discount the privileges. Eventually they get taken for granted, and then what else is there?"

Nikolai thought of Lev, how the stripping of his privileges had so shattered him. He decided upon what he would say next but he paused a long moment to give it weight. He told Savich: "I've lost my sense of place."

"What do you mean?"

"I seem to no longer have a Russian perspective."

"You shouldn't admit that, not even here."

"I've been with the trade mission in London for six years. That's nearly half my adult life. The other afternoon I tabulated it and found that of my last two thousand, one hundred and ninety days I spent altogether only seventy-eight here in my own country, and thirty of those way out in forsaken Aikhal."

"I had no idea your being in London was such a hardship. Quite the contrary—my impression was that if we ever wanted you back you might not come."

"Defection has never entered my mind."

"Of course it has. Anyone in your circumstances would be seriously attracted to that option."

"So, isn't that all the more reason to bring me home?"

"Or perhaps," Savich said, matter-of-fact, "it's good reason to have you there."

Nikolai didn't know how to take that. Was it an oblique suggestion that he defect? Surely not. Savich meant leaving him in London would be a good test of the strength of his loyalty. That had to be it. "It's just that I have this feeling of being neither-nor."

"It will pass."

"I've had the symptoms, so to speak, for quite some time. A year, a year and a half."

"Why haven't you mentioned it until now?"

"I've been putting it off. A couple of weeks ago in Pushkin Park a whore mistook me for a Western visitor."

Savich was amused. "What an insult."

A slight shrug from Nikolai.

"You've had a falling-out with Vivian."

"Not really."

"To cause such a crisis you must have quarreled over something important."

"We *did not* quarrel."

"And I suppose she didn't phone me four times."

"Four times?" Nikolai had assumed Vivian had called Savich once and given up after that. Four was a much more gratifying number for him. It meant Vivian's pain was at a pitch equal to his own and, quite possibly, that she also wasn't getting any good sleep. It might mean she too lay in bed in the dark and suffered when, reaching with her legs, she touched nothing. She too was deadened from the waist down while short-circuited, incapable of interest or concentration, on the verge of exploding, from the neck up. It could even mean she wasn't having Archer around, wouldn't let him in, absolutely wouldn't let him in, had seen him once and not found him such a comfortable sanctuary, Nikolai thought.

Savich removed his feet from the taboret. He sat forward and pressed: "Tell me about it."

As much as Nikolai had assured himself that he wanted to avoid the subject, it came pouring out. He was like a man just released from a long solitary confinement, grateful for an ear. He related the Baden-Baden episode and all that had led up to it. He didn't just hit upon the high points but got down fairly deep into some of the emotional chasms.

Savich was the perfect listener. The little nods of his head encouraged Nikolai on. He remained rapt and silent even when Nikolai paused for comment. Finally, at the half-hour mark, Nikolai began repeating himself and Savich decided he'd absorbed enough. He sat back and returned his feet to the taboret. "You abandoned her," he said, not accusingly.

"I got out while I still could."

"You must have been furious at her."

Nikolai wouldn't admit to being furious.

"Your grandfather's Fabergé objects were so precious to you. Didn't she realize that?"

"Yes."

"Then she was aware of the sacrifice you were making."

Nikolai came close to asserting that his late grandfather

had considered Vivian a worthy cause and had urged him to sell the Fabergé things.

"Don't you believe she was insensitive?"

"No." Adamantly.

"But—"

"Vivian never vowed to change her ways," Nikolai told him. "In fact, she warned me that she was likely to run right through the money. I guess I just didn't expect that to happen as it did, all at once."

"You're defending her."

"Of course I am."

"Why should you?"

"I love her."

Savich was pleased with Nikolai's admission. He was like a lawyer who'd just inversely proved a point. Now on to another. "Was leaving her entirely your idea? Or perhaps at one time or another she suggested it."

"All mine."

"She must have at least alluded to it."

"No."

"Maybe she did but so obliquely that it went right by you. I find it difficult to believe that she had no reservations about the relationship."

"It's not like Vivian to look very far ahead."

"But *you* have a telescopic view of the future."

"Well, in this instance I could see the inevitable."

"Which was?"

"Brawling, wounding, eventually each of us retreating to our opposite elements. I have no way of satisfying her financial needs now and certainly no such future prospects. At least none of that magnitude."

"A Communist's fate, eh?"

"You might say. I'd have to have millions. Maybe not as many as Archer but nevertheless millions. You've no idea what a squanderer Vivian is." Nikolai said that more fondly than he realized.

Savich asked: "Is that honestly the only reason you're not with her this moment?"

Nikolai shrugged.

"It's not merely an excuse?"

"I'm avoiding a lot of unhappiness."

"And, I must point out, in your overly cautious, self-dispiriting Russian way, depriving both you and Vivian of all the happiness that could be enjoyed between now and your foreseen emotional Armageddon. Nikolai, you're being a damn fool."

Nikolai brightened. "You really think so?"

"I most certainly do." Savich looked off. His eyes covered. He was elsewhere, in another time. When he returned to the here and now he told Nikolai softly: "I envy you your Vivian."

That, Nikolai believed, was like a man who owned a whole hothouse of flowers envying another man's single bouquet.

"She's unique. Like most women with such beauty she uses it, but she doesn't rely on it excessively. She'd be desirable even if she wasn't so beautiful, because not a moment with her would ever be dull. Think about it. Have you ever been bored with her—socially, sexually, whatever? I don't mean have you been exasperated—of course you've been exasperated with her. She'd provoke that. But bored?"

Nikolai honestly couldn't call up one moment of boredom. He'd been entertained even when Vivian and Archer were going through all their ugly-expensive-gift-you'll-have-to-take-it-back-and-get-the-money-for-it routines.

"Your Vivian is living her life more than her life is living her. Ironically, her eccentricities, the very things that make her seem inaccessible to you in the long range, are the very things that have you so taken. Do you doubt that? Well, imagine her without them and what do you have?"

Not his Vivian, Nikolai thought.

"Anyway," Savich sighed conclusively, "no matter, it's Moscow you want."

"If possible," Nikolai said, not able to conceal his diminished conviction.

"It's possible enough. But for me it may not be the most advisable thing at the moment. For some time now I've been criticized for showing favoritism, particularly toward you, for allowing you to remain assigned to London all this while. Nothing to it, of course. I've left you there because you know Churcher so well and apparently he's satisfied with having you to deal with. Besides, there's no reason why you'd be my favorite, is there?" Savich evidently thought Nikolai's reply so obvious he didn't wait for it, went right on. "However, if I were to reassign you to Moscow now it would appear as though I were giving in to the pressure, admitting there was substance to the accusations. Don't you agree?"

Nikolai agreed. But he didn't believe it. Savich had the final say when it came to the *nomenklatura* for the Ministry of Foreign Trade. One had to be on that select list of candidates in order to get anywhere, and Savich could, with a mere word, shift a name from the top to the bottom or have it stricken completely. Furthermore, Nikolai reasoned, Savich was too confident of his standing to react to such petty maneuvering.

"What we could do, though," Savich said, "is transfer you elsewhere with the intent of eventually bringing you here. I'm sure you wouldn't mind doing a stint in Leningrad, your home ground. That should get you happily back in your motherland's arms. How do you get along with Valkov?"

Nikolai's reply of "All right, I guess" was transparent.

Savich pretended not to see through it. "A year or two with Valkov in Leningrad should do it. Then you can move into a spot here in Moscow if you still want it."

The idea of being in Leningrad with Valkov instead of in London with Vivian was almost sickening to Nikolai. He wished he hadn't gotten himself into this. It had turned into a bind.

"Is that your stomach growling?" Savich asked.

"I don't think so."

"Well, it's not mine. I had a snack just before you arrived. Are you sure you won't have a little something? Perhaps some pâté or tapinade?"

"I'd still just as soon wait for dinner."

"At least let me know if you get light-headed."

Nikolai's stomach squished and grumbled about his refusal on its behalf. He'd put nothing into it except whiskey since his mushroom-and-onion breakfast. What possible harm could there be in accepting a small slab of *fois gras*? it pleaded. What price politeness?

"Valkov," Savich said, as though titling his next topic. "Valkov is the epitome of his type. Ruthless, ego-driven, Communistically warped. His aspirations make him most useful. Do you see him like that?"

"I don't have your vantage."

"The convenient thing about him is that he doesn't require any pushing or pulling. His own exorbitance serves as his carrot, keeps him moving on track. And then, of course, there's Yelena. How well do you know Mrs. Valkova?"

"Vaguely."

"That's incredible, considering her looks and the aggressive way she presents them. I would have thought that at one time or another, prior to Vivian, Yelena might have gotten to you."

Nikolai shook his head no, and his facial expression said absolutely not. It was not a total lie. Yelena Valkova had come on to him once. It had been after regular hours at the office of Almazjuvelirexport. She was there on the pretext of meeting Valkov, who'd gone to Moscow for the day, but she must have known all flights in were canceled because of a sleet storm. Her voice on the intercom surprised Nikolai, summoned him to Valkov's office. There on the floor just inside the entrance was her full-length chinchilla coat, in a pile the insolent way she'd just let it drop. Nikolai would have to step over it. It would, he thought, be like stepping over Valkov, and that made Yelena all the more tempting. She was perched on the front edge of Valkov's desk, the heels of her shoes spiking left and right into the arms of a chair. Her skirt was gathered up, her marvelous legs apart. Her panties were bunched in her hand. She said everything by flinging her panties at Nikolai. His altered senses saw them transform from nothing into flimsy, flesh-colored material, much like silk fabric impos-

sibly appearing from a magician's fist. The beautiful Yelena
got hold of him with her eyes for a long moment before
she lay back across the desk. Nikolai remained at the
doorway, enjoyed a good long helping of the circumstances,
then glanced down at the chinchilla. He turned on it and
went back down the hall to his office. After a short while
he heard Yelena leave, which increased his misgivings. That
unconsummated opportunity was to this day italicized among
his erotic memories.

"When it comes to avidity, I believe Yelena outdoes
Valkov," Savich said, "although I'm not sure he realizes
that she's much too complex for him. Frankly, I find her
a bit more than merely interesting, don't you?"

Nikolai wanted off the subject. "Valkov mentioned a
field trip to Uzbekiskaya in September, to evaluate emerald
yield."

"First I've heard of it."

"Oh?"

"And such a thing would have to originate with me. I
think he must be just pinching your nose."

"He showed me some emeralds—in fact, quite an impressive lot."

"Nevertheless, let me assure you we have no intention
of getting into the emerald business. Valkov's September
field trip is a figment of his dislike of you. Are you certain
you haven't done something to cause him to have such ill-
feelings?"

Only breathe, Nikolai thought.

Do Kien, the Vietnamese army captain turned servant,
appeared to inform them that dinner was ready.

Savich and Nikolai went into the dining room and sat
across from one another at midpoint of the long, gleaming
mahogany table. Mai Lon did the serving. Nikolai noticed
how deft and delicate were her movements. When a plate
or glass was placed it seemed to float down in front of him.
It was as though the slightest rattle or tinkle would be
committing the sin of intrusion. Nikolai guessed that Mai
Lon, with her diminutiveness and fine oriental features and
complexion, was no older than twenty. Actually she was

forty-one and on behalf of Communism in Southeast Asia had killed six enemies in close combat and at least triple that number in various firefights. Savich did not know this much about her, had no idea that just behind Mai Lon's set little smile and marveling eyes was such lethalness.

Along with the several courses of dinner the conversation skipped and drifted from topic to topic. It had no destination or purpose other than geniality. Politics were not brought up, religion was avoided, and Vivian was a subject apparently already settled. Frequently observations of no relevance were put in, splinterlike thoughts that in other company would have gone unexpressed. Such as Savich's isolated statement that he found Venice not only more dank but, as well, more decadent in winter. From the pros and cons of existentialism they went into the pleasure of fear, then on to medieval gallantry, which they agreed had for the most part been unfairly exploited. As an example Nikolai related an account he'd read of how a lady of those times, wishing to confirm her desirability, dropped one of her gloves from the Pont-Neuf. Her knight, without hesitation, leaped into the Seine after it and could only drown under the weight of his armor. Savich was knowingly amused. They touched upon the spiritual abstractions of Kandinsky, the profound directness of Isak Dinesen, the libidinal appeal of reed-thin ballerinas. Savich claimed that serious ballet dancers were exceptionally talented at lovemaking because of certain internal muscles that were incidentally developed during their many years of rigorous training. Thus, they were able to clench so possessively they made one feel attached, causing titillating fears of castration and slavery. Nikolai did not comment. Those Kirov dancers he'd had that much to do with years ago evidently hadn't trained long enough, while conversely, Vivian had never in her life performed even a single *plié*.

Dessert was served with minor ritual. A *gâteau mille-feuille*, the flakiest possible pastry, layered four times alternately with *zabaglione*, topped by crème Chantilly dotted with whole glazed cherries. Savich oohed playfully over it when it arrived, and Nikolai had to remind himself that this was the Minister of Foreign Trade, his very important utmost superior. Savich had succeeded in making him feel right at home, like family, and Nikolai didn't hesitate to ask for a second portion of the cake before it was offered. He was emotionally improved, comfortable there, unconcerned that the last flight to Leningrad had already departed. It was understood he would stay the night.

At one o'clock he was shown up to the room that had been readied for him. A bath had been drawn; a dribble of hot from the spout was keeping it at perfect temperature. A swift dip was Nikolai's intent, but when he was in up to his chin he relaxed and thought of how on the way up he'd seen Savich's five graduated pieces of Morabito luggage standing in the entry hall. Black with brass fittings. So elegant and obviously expensive. Wasn't that a bit too blatant a flaunt? or was it part of the new approach, the attempt to impress the West with Russian taste and sophistication? How pleasant it would be, Nikolai thought, to make the trip to Paris with Savich, to be limousined everywhere, to be privy to Savich's high-level dealings, to have dinner with him at Grand Vefour. They would stroll the Place Vendôme and Avenue de l'Opera, stroll and talk women, perhaps enjoy together a choicely located table for the midnight show at Le Crazy Horse. Be satisfied with the personal rapport and contact already allowed, he told himself. If only Irina, his mother, could see him now, he thought. How proud she would be. And surprised. Even she, with all her ambitions for him, had never imagined him in Minister Savich's bathtub. If Irina, like Grandfather Maksim, was hovering around in some immaterial state, Nikolai was sure she was beaming.

He went to bed. The bed linens received him like an immaculate envelope. The pillow covering couldn't possibly have been fresher under the press of his cheek. He turned onto his side, his usual off-to-sleep position, although he didn't think he was anywhere close to going under. On the nightstand was a bronze-and-ivory figure of a woman leaping uninhibitedly, an Art Deco piece. The downcast lamplight sparkled off the tiny various jewels of her cloche headpiece. They were hypnotic.

It seemed as though he'd merely blinked, or at most closed his eyes for a moment. The jeweled cloche was still glittering. The lamp was still on. But his watch told him it was morning, nine o'clock. He hadn't slept so soundly in ages. It was a good sign. He was regenerated enough to deal with anything. He got up, shaved, dressed, and went downstairs, not expecting breakfast but glad when Do Kien directed him to a table by the window of a room flooded with undiffused morning sun. He wasn't really hungry. It was just that he didn't feel ready to leave. The table was set for one. Savich's luggage was gone from the entry hall. The apartment seemed emptier. Asked if he preferred coffee or tea, Nikolai said he'd have both. He sat in the quiet brightness, and while he gazed out and down at the mainly dun-colored shoulders of shorter Moscow buildings, he considered the alternatives.

His circumstances, he realized, were unchanged, although they seemed to have a different shape and shade. Savich hadn't given him any straightforward advice, hadn't said he ought to do this or that, hadn't imposed his greater experience. But it seemed he had. One thing for certain, Nikolai thought: he wasn't voluntarily going to suffer one or two years of Valkov. Nor, for that matter, could he remain in London and keep away from Vivian. The alternative, and what Savich had more or less suggested, was that he leave things as they were, enjoy his arrangement with Vivian for as long as it lasted, not look ahead to the pitfalls, regardless of how obvious, deep, and maiming they might be. Could he return to London and go coasting along like that, taking the moment and telling tomorrow to fuck off? Honestly, he doubted it. In his love for Vivian there was no room for such precariousness. However, he thought, how easily he would be able to make room for security.

The dilemma had been on his mind for so long that by now it had distilled to a simple contradiction: money was essential to Vivian, and as a Soviet citizen he had no money, literally none, would never have. And that was that. Savich was right about his having thought of defecting and taking a job in the West. However, that wouldn't solve everything. On several occasions Nikolai had scanned the employment advertisements in the London *Times* and been grateful that he didn't have to contend with the roil of such competition. Outstanding as his marketing abilities might be in the Soviet Union, they were by no means exceptional in the West, where doing business for profit was the very fuel of existence. Besides, even if he landed one of the better jobs, for example that of marketing director for a leading export-import firm, the salary he could expect, the forty thousand pounds per year, wouldn't be adequate. Forty thousand was about the average value of one of Archer's ugly gifts. There was, of course, the option of going to work for the System, of giving Churcher the advantage of all he knew about the Soviet diamond operation: confidential yield figures, projections, negotiating tactics, and so on. Churcher would go for that, would secretly use him and pay him dearly. For a while, anyway.

Diamonds, Nikolai thought.

The little contraband pile he'd been shown recently by Churcher would be enough. Not even a fistful. He'd thought of diamonds as a commodity for such a long while he'd lost his personal appreciation of their cash value. Now, however, he imagined a replay of the scene in Churcher's office, only this time Churcher and Pulver went into a state of suspended animation, froze in midgesture, while he, Nikolai, casually folded up the briefke containing the eight hundred carats of D-flawless Aikhal goods, pocketed it, and sat back, giving the cue for Churcher and Pulver to reactivate but with a total lapse of memory regarding the diamonds. Churcher offered tea and small-talked that Mrs. Churcher was coming into town that evening for dinner and the theater, and Pulver stiffly but cordially excused himself, saying he had some things to tend to. And there he, Nikolai, sat, just minutes from walking away with more than fourteen million dollars' worth.

Some fantasy.

It was followed immediately by another set at the installation in Aikhal. He, Nikolai, there on a field trip, had unrestricted run of the place, so it wasn't unusual for him to be wandering around the finishing area where the electronically controlled machines were cutting and polishing stones at the rate of a dozen a minute and depositing them into a traylike receptacle. The cutters on duty were blind to him as he took a pinch or two of diamonds every now and then from each machine's output, just dropped them into his shirt pocket and felt them accumulate into a bulge. One thousand D-flawless one-caraters, unmissed, to be easily carried away because he as a ministry representative was never searched or questioned, turned into eighteen million dollars.

It could happen, he told himself as he came back to the reality of the indefectible early June sky over Moscow. It *is* happening, something else inside him contravened. Perhaps it wasn't being pulled off in the slick way he'd just imagined, but someone in Aikhal was helping himself (and, no doubt, others) to finished goods, and the ideal spot for that along the chain of diamond production was the moment they'd been cut. The skimming of a few pinches at a time from the trays on a regular basis, the accumulating of pinches until they amounted to hundreds (thousands?) of carats, and then the transporting of them through the fine sieve of security—that explained the extra lots of finished Aikhal goods that had been showing up on the market. It seemed Churcher had valid reason to complain, although he was undoubtedly off in pointing his accusations at Almazjevelirexport.

Should he inform Savich of this suspicion? Nikolai wondered. But if it proved out, wouldn't it be viewed as a blemish for Savich, proof of incompetency that his rivals could use against him? And what would he, Nikolai, get out of it other than being distrusted as a *stukach*? A medal maybe? Shove their medals, Nikolai thought.

Anyway, corruption, maybe not on this grand a scale, but nonetheless corruption, was an unmentioned additional benefit known to come with certain jobs. The fellow who worked in the slaughter house was expected to sell steaks and roasts on the side. What about the caviar packers who had for several years been putting herring labels on tins containing the best beluga so they could ship those tins to the West and pocket the substantial difference? Stealing, great and trivial, was often what made conditions bearable. It had grown into the way of life, and only those who were supposed to get caught got caught.

Thus, Nikolai found it difficult to blame whoever was skimming diamonds from Aikhal. They had to be audacious, crafty, resourceful, and, according to Churcher's numbers, greedy. To be honest, Nikolai thought, he envied them. Would that he were in a position to pull off such a thing. Just one packet of goods such as he'd seen on Churcher's desk would solve everything for him. When was he scheduled to go to Aikhal again? If the Afghanistan emerald drama was only in Valkov's mind, perhaps there'd be a field trip to Aikhal come September. But that was four months away, and even then, when he was in Aikhal, what would he do—sneak around and filch a few carats? It certainly wouldn't be as easy as he'd fantasized, helping himself to all the carats he wanted from the machines.

That thought was the hinge that swung open an obscure gate of his memory, allowing a certain recollection to emerge. It didn't come shooting out and strike him like a bolt. Rather, it swashed oozily around in his head for a moment and then surfaced. He remembered something that had occurred when he was in Aikhal last year, last September. A man, a sharp-faced, wild-eyed sort, had stopped him in the corridor, sort of cornered him and blurted out a string of whispered words so rapidly they didn't make sense. Nikolai had caught only fragments of what the man said, gathered vaguely that it had to do with someone stealing. His thought at the time was that the poor fellow was suffering from being too long in Siberia. There had also been the distraction of the man's terrible breath, a foul combination of alcohol, garlic, and dental caries. Nikolai had silently endured the man to have him sooner gone. He'd immediately forgotten the incident. He wished now that he'd hung on the man's every word, been impressed enough to have arranged to discuss the matter further with him. Why was he wishing that? Nikolai asked himself. What difference would it have made? He had the sensation that his mind was detached, on its own, out of his control, intent on constructing a nefarious recourse. To that end it presented him with another detail of that encounter in the corridor at Aikhal: the man had furtively shoved a sheet of paper in among those Nikolai was carrying. Nikolai hadn't ever bothered to look at it.

Chances were it contained the information that he now admitted he wanted very much to know.

CHAPTER
•••19•••

UPON HIS RETURN TO LENINGRAD THAT AFTERNOON, NIKOLAI went directly to the offices of Almazjuvelirexport. He arrived there just as everyone was leaving for the day. He ran into Valkov, who was on his way out.

"You are on holiday," Valkov said.

"Which means I can be wherever I want."

"I suppose." Valkov exaggerated his indifference. "Were you aware that Savich has been trying to reach you?"

"Really?"

"It appears you've gotten yourself in hot water."

"Let it boil," Nikolai quipped.

Valkov decided to smile. "We should get together some evening." He was always saying that very thing to people he never had any intention of socializing with, as though it camouflaged his dislike.

Nikolai knew that and jumped right on it. "Tomorrow night. We'll have dinner. I'll pick you up at eight."

"Tomorrow night is impossible," Valkov said automatically and walked away.

The place was deserted. Nikolai hurried down the hall to his modest office. Nothing was changed, not a speck. The late daylight glancing through the window hit upon the surface of his desk and showed where he'd disturbed the dust last time he'd been there. He went to the gray four-drawer metal filing cabinet in the corner. He knew he needn't bother to look in the top drawer, for that was where he kept, well organized, his scant cull from the thousands of memorandums and bulletins that flowed at him. If anywhere, the single sheet of paper that had now become so important for him to find would be in one of the other three drawers, which were jammed carelessly with all sorts of written and printed material. He had a vague recollection of having deposited whatever he'd brought back from Aikhal in one of those drawers. However, he also had an equally vague recollection that that was one of the times when he'd decided not to add to the accumulation and had just dumped it all into the trash basket.

He pulled open the second drawer down, removed everything from it, every scrap, piled it on his desk. He went through all that carefully and then got into the disordered contents of the next drawer. About halfway through that pile he came upon it. Hidden appropriately between printouts showing the gem quality yield from the Aikhal installation last year. It was an ordinary work report. Scrawled on the back of it was "Prague: Konviktska 16/ Potlaska 34" and "Paris: 131 rue de Paradis," apparently three addresses. Also "Kislov," which Nikolai took to be a name, perhaps the name of the fellow who had slipped this information to him.

To check on that, Nikolai went to the nearest computer in the accounting office just down the hall. He asked the computer for the listing of personnel assigned to Aikhal, and on the display screen appeared names in alphabetical order. If indeed that fellow had been Kislov, Nikolai thought, he'd phone him at the installation on some pretense and possibly get more out of him. Nikolai skipped quickly to the Ks. There was no Kislov listed. He asked the computer if it had anything ever on Kislov. It told him in a few words that Kislov, Josep, had accidentally frozen to death last January 12, New Year's Eve. (Not divulged was that Kislov's sister in Ulyanovsk, when notified, had wanted nothing to do with his remains. So the body, in a heavy plastic bag, had been placed in a wire basket and horizontally suspended from the understructure of the installation, close up and in a spot where even the highest leaping wolves couldn't get to it. There it had remained, like a side of meat frozen through, until just a week before, when the ground was believed to be sufficiently thawed. Still, the two men assigned to do the burying had to chip and hack after digging down less than a foot. They considered it a waste of energy and left Kislov's corpse shallowly covered, susceptible to sniffs even a mile away.)

Nikolai got a shiver.

Something told him not to believe the word "accidentally."

He asked the computer if it had anything on the addresses, the two in Prague and the one in Paris. They meant as much to it as they did to him. What nebulous leads they were, Nikolai thought. Not much to go on but better than nothing.

He went home. Lev and his most recent pretty Finn, Ula, weren't there, but the remnant odor of their lovemaking was distinct and not unpleasant in the air. After about forty breaths, Nikolai became acclimated to it, couldn't smell it anymore. It caused him to think differently of those times Archer had dropped by at Vivian's apartment shortly after he and Vivian had made a lot of love. Archer, amiable as ever though hurting each time he inhaled.

The light was on in the kitchen. Nikolai went in. He felt the teakettle. The burner beneath it wasn't on but the kettle was still warm. Lev and Ula must have left only a short while ago and apparently they'd be returning soon, for Ula's handbag was on the table with an exposed pink lipstick and several other messy-looking makeup items out of it. Nikolai had thought he'd discuss with Lev what he was getting into. Lev, with his black-market dealings in hard currency, knew a bit about the underside of things. No doubt he'd try to dissuade Nikolai, and that would be a turnabout after all the times Nikolai had urged Lev not to take such dangerous chances. When Lev found out how determined he was he'd do the next-best concerned thing: contribute helpful suggestions. And the more he suggested the more likely it was he'd want to take part. Sharing the risk would lighten it.

Nikolai waited an hour and a half. He changed, packed a few things, and took a flight back to Moscow. During the two-hour layover there he sat on a hard, ass-shaped plastic seat in the waiting area not really reading *On the Eve* but rather trying to adjust to the sense that he'd entered another dimension from which he was viewing everything slightly off-register. It was, he realized, a symptom of his now being committed to thievery, albeit secondhand. It was like being on the way to the front of a personal war. Better not to think of Vivian so much, he told himself. She might be an imperiling distraction. Wouldn't that be ironic—if at a crucial moment he got killed because his mind was on her.

It was ten after four in the morning when Czech State Airlines Flight 312 landed him at Ruzne Airport, Prague. First thing after coming out of passport control he exchanged some of his money for korunas. He hadn't made a hotel reservation. A tourist folder he'd read on the plane gave the Intercontinental an A-deluxe rating, so he had a taxi take him there. He walked into the lobby and to the registration counter as though he expected to be expected. The registration clerk recognized the hundred-koruna look in his eyes and cordially accepted his hundred-koruna handshake and only minutes later Nikolai was the registered occupant of a front room on the sixth floor. He hung his jacket and tie in the lonely closet, took off his shoes and paired them partly under the foot of the bed, zipped open his suitcase but did not remove anything from it. Needing, for ease, to get more acquainted with the space that now contained him, he went around opening drawers. There was no hospitality really in the blankness of the hotel stationery or down the printed laundry checklist that included every possible wearable, soilable, washable thing. The almost-used-up message pad in the bedstand drawer was accompanied by a stubby pencil, entirely pointless, worn down to its wood.

Nikolai called on a reserve of spirit to counter depression. He stood at the window and saw dawn getting underway, the sky steel-blue to mauve, rather funereal. "Prague," Nikolai said aloud disdainfully, and drew the drapes. He went to the bed and dropped himself face up across it. Perhaps, he thought, he should remain awake, take the day that was almost already here. He reached for the room-service menu, held it above him. It seemed that every other word was "dumplings." He chose sleep.

Six hours later he came awake, sharp-minded, all at once awake again. He couldn't remember if he'd dreamed or not, but from the tension in his shoulders and neck he thought he must have had a bad one. He used the bathroom, then ordered from room service. Coffee for two, sweet rolls for one. A fresh shirt and a fresh pair of socks picked him up a bit. The coffee that was brought was Turkish, boiled strong, with the grains left in the bottom of the server. Three fast cups of it went right to Nikolai's nerves and made his hands and feet have to be doing something. His tongue was still finding grains of the coffee in his mouth when he was in the elevator going down to the lobby.

He learned from the concierge that Konviktska Street was eleven blocks away. The concierge marked the way on a city map, then sold it to him. Nikolai paused outside the hotel entrance to estimate the mood of the sky. It was solidly clouded, undecided whether to rain. He set off along the Dvorakova Embankment with the Vltava River on his right. The river looked indolent, had a sour, ocher cast. At the Manesur Bridge he turned his back to the river, dodged across six lanes of malicious traffic, and entered Staré Město, the Old Town. Obeying the map, he had no problem finding Konviktska Street, and only an idiot could have missed number 16. There were five black-and-white police cars parked diagonally to the curb in front of it, and several prominent signs prohibited any other vehicle from even stopping there momentarily.

Nikolai was perplexed. Why would this Kislov fellow have given him the address of the central police station? Were all five stories of this gray stucco-and-stone building occupied by the police? Evidently so. Even the adjacent building was allied to it in a medical way, for a police ambulance van had just gone in there. It was not inconceivable, of course, that a Czech policeman or two could be mixed up with pushing along contraband diamonds from Aikhal. However, if that was the case, what was he supposed to do, walk in there and randomly pick someone out and follow him around on the hope that he'd make a revealing move? Shit, Nikolai thought, he could still be at that a year from next Christmas.

He stood across the street from the police station for quite a while, mulling over how to deal with it. He sort of half settled on the premise that Kislov had noted that address only so he'd know where to go if he needed help. That was more palatable than admitting to such an early, easy defeat. Anyway, he still had the other address. He consulted the map for Potlaska Street.

At that moment an older man came out of Konviktska 16. There was no reason why Nikolai should have especially noticed him. He was just an average-looking, slow-moving Czech burdened by seventy years of dumplings on his bones. He came across Konviktska and passed so close by Nikolai could have heard him wheeze. Even if the man had stopped and introduced himself as Chief Medical Examiner Sikma, it wouldn't have been meaningful.

The street index on the reverse side of the map told Nikolai that the coordinates for Potlaska were G and 4. Nikolai found it in District 8, the Karlin District, which from the hotel was quite a way downriver in the opposite direction. He took a taxi, and during the ride, somewhat mesmerized by the to and fro of a garish plastic Saint Somebody suspended from the rear-view mirror, it hit him that he was acting absurdly, on impulse, driven beyond logic by his need to have and keep Vivian. All that would come of this Prague escapade was the lesson that mere wanting and trying wasn't enough. He should have been born one of the naturally rich or at least the only son of a capitalist with a fortune so vast it was impossible to deplete.

He got out of the taxi. There were no street signs, but the driver assured him this was Potlaska. It was in a manufacturing area. All along there were brick and stucco structures two and three stories high. No signs on any of them, and only a few displayed a street number. About halfway down the block Nikolai made out the faded numerals 32 painted on a front and surmised that the next had to be 34. It was one of the taller buildings, unattractively sheathed in corrugated siding. Nikolai thought it best not to stand there and possibly be seen taking special notice of the place. He casually looked it over and proceeded down and around the block. How forbidding this area would be at night, he thought. It was ugly and grim enough in the daytime. The only living green things were the weeds that had straggled up from cracks and pressed so dependently against steel-mesh fences. No sidewalks here, just the raw, crumbling edge of blacktop bordered by a strip of powdery dirt. Metallic litter everywhere, fragments of tin and steel, parts of parts, broken pieces, a predominance of rusting. The narrow space between two buildings on the next street over gave access to a back alley from which Nikolai got a good look at the rear of number 34. He also reconnoitered the alley before returning to the street. He continued on around the block at a faster pace.

He entered number 34.

And found himself in a combination reception area and showroom. Rather makeshift. There was one tubular chrome chair upholstered in a poor imitation of black leather. A similar tubular-legged table was against the wall beneath a series of black-felt-covered shelves. Crystal goblets, bowls, vases, and various other items were displayed on the shelves. They were harshly illuminated from above by a rack of lights, which unfortunately also emphasized dust and finger smudges. On the left wall was a closed door and a rectangular opening for the head of a receptionist, a young woman with coarse features and a mass of incorrigible black hair.

Nikolai thought fast. He affected a British accent and a suitable elevated manner. "I'm Jeremy Mason-Hodge," he said, "here for my appointment."

That meant nothing to her, of course.

Perhaps she didn't speak English, Nikolai thought. It would seem odd now if he started spouting Czech. He kept on with it.

"I presume you received my letter stating I would be here on the third. I posted it over a month back."

"Letter?" she uttered blankly.

"Oh dear." Nikolai sighed. "I rather thought things

might not be right when I didn't get a confirming reply from you. I hope my trip hasn't been a total waste."

"This is the Zuzana Bohemian Glass Works," she informed him, as though Nikolai had lost his way.

He nodded. "*I* am the buyer of glass and crystal for Selfridge's in London. You do know of Selfridge's, don't you? The department store."

A smile improved her. "You want to buy crystal?"

"I *may* place an order, yes."

She handed out a catalogue along with an order form.

Nikolai sat in the chair and began filling out the form. He had no idea or the complete, correct address of Selfridge's, so he just put down Oxford Street, London W2. He paged through the catalogue and from the photographs in it purposely chose items he believed the Zuzana Bohemian Glass Works had little call for and therefore was overstocked with. Things they'd be happiest to sell, such as humidors, bath-salts jars, calling-card plates, cruet sets, and ink stands. He bought, so to speak, two dozen of each. He thought the receptionist thought more of him when she saw the order. "What was that total?" he asked.

She read it to him.

"As soon as I arrive back at the hotel I'll phone London and have a bank draft for the full amount sent off by post."

"That would be appreciated," the receptionist said, now noticeably dismayed.

"I wonder," Nikolai said, "would it be asking too much if I had a look around the works? I don't want to put anyone out, but you see, we'll want to print a little folder calling attention to the painstaking way Zuzana crystal is made. Naturally, we'd want that information to be as authentic as possible."

"I'll see," the receptionist said and left her cubicle, taking Nikolai's order form with her. Shortly she returned, accompanied by a tall, rawboned man with a thick mustache and hard eyes. The receptionist presented him quite formally as Mr. Kaplicka, the foreman.

"You want to see the works?" Kaplicka asked amiably, with a thick accent.

"Yes."

"Come. I myself will show you around."

During the next hour Nikolai was given a tour of the main area of the plant and at the same time an abbreviated course in glassmaking. Kaplicka, the foreman, seemed to welcome this opportunity to display some of his knowledge. To start he took Nikolai by the metal bins in which the raw materials for making crystal were kept—the silica, lime, soda ash, and oxide of lead. He explained that these were mixed in certain quantities; he was vague about how much of each was used. Zuzana, he said, had a special formula all its own, a secret that had been handed down for three centuries.

Nikolai thought to himself that the only way a secret could be kept three hundred years was for someone along the chain of generations to have forgotten it.

Kaplicka next led him to the furnaces. There were seven, identical, spaced well apart in a row. They were about chin height and not much different in appearance from the ordinary coal or wood cellar furnace. Only one was in operation at this time—and Nikolai took that as a favorable indication. Perhaps Zuzana did not really have to depend on being in the crystal business, he reasoned. It could be just a front. He stood well back to observe the glassblowing crew at its job. Kaplicka provided a nonstop commentary and interpreted special terms as he went along.

Nikolai watched one of the men thrust the end of a six-foot blowpipe into the oval opening of the oven, saw him dip the blowpipe into the intense glowing orange and withdraw a blob of molten crystal. Kaplicka said such a blob was called a gather. At once the man rolled the viscous stuff back and forth across the flat surface of an iron slab, roughly shaping the gather. He then passed it on to a second man, who held the other end of the blowpipe to his mouth, took in a deep breath through his nostrils, and gently blew the molten crystal into a more definite form. That second man, Kaplicka said, was the server. After doing his part the server passed the blowpipe to a third man, the gaffer, for him to do the final blowing and shaping. The gaffer was the master of the group. He used a paddle and a two-pronged fork of cherrywood to alter the contours of the crystal. He measured often with calipers. Quite a few times he stuck the crystal back into the furnace to keep it hot and workable.

Nikolai thought the gaffer a prima donna, the way he waited aside with a removed attitude while most of the steps of the process were done for him. As though he were above all but the precise finishing blows and touches, the final results, and, no doubt, the credit. Also what put off Nikolai was the way the gaffer performed. As he blew and spun the blowpipe he darted about, at times practically pranced, gave the impression that he was nervously creative, high-strung. Many of his movements reminded Nikolai of those a fencer would go through while practicing, his footwork especially. He was, Nikolai had to admit, amazingly light-footed and quick for a heavyset man. Was this how gaffers usually acted? Nikolai wanted to know. Kaplicka told him it was traditional.

Kaplicka guided him on to where the various crystal objects were cut and polished. Three women were hard at it, seated at a workbench that was equipped to accommodate ten. The women had on circular, tight-fitting goggles to protect their eyes from the fragments of glass flung at them by the high-speed spin of the cutting wheels. Hunched over, so round-shouldered they seemed deformed, they looked obsessed, weird. Also what added to that impression was the painful screech of the glass being cut. On a tiered movable table at the far end of the bench was the work that had been finished: tall, fat vases, lavishly faceted. Even in this poor light they were throwing glints and spectrums.

Had Nikolai been truly paying attention he would have learned more about the intricacies of crystal making. He appeared to be attentive, hmmmed and grunted and uh-huhed frequently, but more than half the time he was so intent on looking about for anything that might connect the Zuzana Bohemian Glass Works with Aikhal diamonds that he was hardly aware of Kaplicka's voice. Nevertheless, he saw nothing suspicious; this fellow Kaplicka seemed open and honest, and glass was about as opposite from diamond as anything could be. When the tour was over the only things Nikolai took away were a hunch and a mental picture of the layout of the place.

He chose to walk back to the hotel. The mile and a half would be good for his head, give it time to argue with itself. Part of his reasoning still contended that that fellow Kislov had been suffering Siberian delusions, that these Prague and Paris addresses he'd given Nikolai were pointless, that Kislov himself had nothing to do with the fact that diamonds were being skimmed from Aikhal and sold in the West. Kislov had dreamed it up and just happened to be right.

Kislov also just happened to be dead, countered the other part of Nikolai's reasoning. Don't take the next available flight to London, it urged, not while there remains even a mote of possibility. Listen to your hunch. Remember what Grandfather Maksim used to say? *The stone unturned most often hides the treasure.*

Stop grasping, the first part demanded.

Shut up, said the other part.

On Hastaska Street, a few blocks from the hotel, Nikolai went into a store that looked as though it offered for sale just about everything. He wanted a hundred-foot length of ordinary clothesline. It came only in fifty-foot lengths, so he bought two. He also bought a carpenter's hammer. Several doors down from that everything store was a restaurant, a small but serious one, the brightly lighted sort. A waitress with pink clean hands, strong-looking forearms, and a way that said she knew and sympathized with loneliness served him *svíčková na smetaně*, roast loin of beef with cream sauce, and a bottle of Budvar. On her own the waitress brought him a large slice of *jablkový koláče*, apple cake, and although he would rather have used what space remained in his stomach for another bottle of the excellent beer he had to respond to her generosity. He thanked her with his almost best smile and didn't leave her a huge tip because she might have taken that as indication of his lack of understanding.

He felt better after having eaten, stronger, more optimistic, and when he was back in his hotel room he immediately undressed and sat at the desk and used a sheet of hotel stationery to write down step by step how he thought it should go. He diagrammed what he could recall and approximated those measurements that would be vital. For an hour he lay in the dark and allowed himself to think of Vivian as intensely as he wanted. He didn't even have to touch himself to be hard.

At ten o'clock he put on a pair of jeans, a dark sweatshirt, and canvas deck sneakers. He pocketed two hundred korunas and some change and decided against taking along any identification, because he knew that as a rule these people disliked Russians, and he might stand a chance of passing as a foolhardy American or something and bluff his way out of trouble if it came to that. He also pocketed the versatile Swiss army knife Lev had given him on a birthday ten or so years ago, and the little Mag-Lite flashlight that he usually used to shine at the bedside clock in the middle of the night so he wouldn't disturb Vivian.

He took a taxi from the stand just outside the hotel entrance and had it leave him off at the intersection of Sokolovská Boulevard and Saldova Street. He remembered the way, would walk the rest of it, in the direction of the river and on into the Karlin District. He hadn't taken ten paces before it began to rain. No here-and-there warning drops, it came pouring right down. Nikolai decided not to try to get in out of it. For one thing, it looked like the sort of rain that would last. For another, he was fatalistic about it, thought perhaps rain was supposed to be a part of it. Within a couple of blocks his sweatshirt and jeans were soaked through, his sneakers squishing. Under other circumstances he might have been chilled; however, the rain had a cooling, calming effect. It offset the feverish excitement of his body, at least superficially. It didn't slow his bloodstream.

He'd been right about this district being spooky at night. The rain made it even more so, darker, everything more obscure. The blocky structures could easily be imagined into geometric beasts that with the slightest provocation would roll over and crush him. Nikolai kept to the middle of the streets. There were no cars, no people. It was as though some invisible devastating force had made the area prohibited, the very atmosphere dangerous. He was relieved to reach Potlaska Street and number 34. At least *it* felt familiar.

He reviewed the corrugated exterior of the Zuzana building. The front was sheer, not even a window. The only possibility would be in the rear. He went around to it. The building to the right was independent, separated by a wide alley. The two-story building on the left was butted right up against the Zuzana building. It had a flat roof and a loading platform that was roofed over. Exactly as Nikolai had remembered. He walked down the alley that ran between the backs of these buildings to where he'd seen some empty wooden crates stacked. He pulled out one that was about ten feet long and three feet wide. He guessed it had once contained some kind of machinery. Using the hammer, he pried off the top. He turned the top over and hammered every third board from it. What he had then was a ladder of sorts. He carried it back to the loading platform of the building that adjoined Zuzana. He propped it up and used it to climb onto the roof above the loading platform. At once he hauled up the makeshift ladder. He propped it against the wall and climbed to the second-story roof.

He paused there. So far, so good. But the rain wasn't being a help. He blinked, bent over, and shook his head rapidly to get the rain from his eyes for a moment. He straightened up. Facing him was the side of the Zuzana building, uninterrupted corrugated metal. And there was its roof. As he had estimated, to the edge of it was a good twelve feet up. The pitch of the roof was steeper than he'd thought, at least forty-five degrees. The slant of the roof was being hit by a lot of rain. Each four-inch groove in the corrugation was like a downward trough, so water gushed off the edge as though coming from dozens of spigots.

He knelt and took out the two lengths of clothesline. He tied them end to end so they made a continuous hundred feet. He arranged the line as it needed to be, in arm-length loops, coiled but free, like a lasso. The line was wet, somewhat stiff, and heavier, not so easy to handle. Perhaps that wouldn't be a problem. Most of all he had to keep it from tangling. To one of the free ends of the line he attached the hammer, looping the line over the head of the hammer, snug around the neck and the claw. He wasn't confident of his knots, but when he stood up and the hammer was dangling on the end of the line it felt there to stay. He held the coil of loops loosely in the upcurved palm of his left hand while his right grasped the line about three feet from the hammer. He twirled the hammer like a boatman taking a sounding. The line sang as he increased the speed of the twirl, and when he had it twirling as fast as possible he let it go.

The hammer sailed upward through the rainy dark on a diagonal course. The loose loops of line fed out from his left hand. He had figured the Zuzana building was forty feet wide, then an additional ten feet allowed for the pitch of the roof. The hammer had to clear that distance. He believed it had; the line still had tension on it. He let the tension take the line until it went slack, didn't want any more. He hurried down to the back alley and around to the opposite side of the Zuzana building. The hammer was there, lying in the mud. He reclaimed it and tied that end of the line to the protruding elbow of a plumbing pipe. Then he returned to his makeshift ladder and climbed back up to the second-story roof of the adjacent building. He took up the slack of the line and paused for a moment to feel good about having accomplished this initial part of it, told himself he was more clever than the average thief. Why, though, right on top of that feeling, canceling it, did he feel farther than ever from Vivian? Here he was on the rooftop of some little factory in the rain in the night in the middle of Czechoslovakia. Where was she at that moment? Nikolai again pictured her with Archer, probably in his newest Rolls, but not amused by something clever Archer had just said, not caring whether she was there or not.

Rather, miserably remote because of the presence of his absence, Nikolai hoped.

He tied that end of the line to a standpipe. Then he reached up the line, grasped it with both hands, and brought his feet to the side of the Zuzana building. Hand over hand, a vertical step at a time, he hauled himself upward. He hadn't thought this part would be difficult, but it required his entire strength, and all the while the accumulated rain streamed off the edge above and beat on him like a waterfall. At one point he tried for a deeper breath through his mouth and the water got into his windpipe and choked and burned. He hung there, coughing, but didn't relinquish an inch of what he'd gained. He managed to reach the edge, slung his right leg up onto the roof, then pulled up the rest of him. He stood on the slope, resisting the sharp angle of it with the help of the line. He climbed to the peak.

On the other side of the roof, about a third of the way down from the peak, was a metal chimney pipe which served the ovens, and about ten feet down from that was a window, one of several situated along the roof for ventilation. The window was about four feet square. Like a trapdoor, it was hinged on the high side, with a substantial raised edge all around to prevent rain from running in. Nikolai's plan had focused on that particular window. He'd noted it while foreman Kaplicka was explaining why, for flawless crystal, the ovens had to be kept heated at 2,400 degrees Fahrenheit and the gaffer was blowing and swishing about. It couldn't be just any of the windows, it had to be that particular one.

Nikolai turned his back to it. Now he needed tension on the line from the other direction. As soon as he'd taken up what slack there was he stepped backward off the peak and descended cautiously. When he got to the window he saw it was held propped open on the low side by a vertical notched rod. The rod, and therefore the window, could be raised or lowered by means of a long chain that hung inside. Nikolai peered in at the main work space thirty feet below. The mouth of one of the ovens was casting a madder-yellow reflection upon the concrete floor, and the light that was on in the front-office cubicle far off to the right was providing enough to vaguely define some edges and shapes. He had no trouble making out the steel beam that was directly below the window, one of the five crossbeams which held this structure together. It was Nikolai's only way of getting across to the caged-in area. That area measured about twenty by twenty. It was enclosed by double steel mesh, a much heavier-gauge mesh than the heaviest wire sort, like that normally used for gratings. The enclosing sides went up twenty some feet. The thing about the caged-in area that had most fed Nikolai's curiosity and nourished his hunch was the way its only entrance was triple-locked. Why, Nikolai had thought that afternoon upon noticing the three heavy-duty locks, should that area be made so inaccessible, unless at one time or another something of greater value than crystal was kept in there?

He went in feet first through the window opening. While keeping hold of the raised edge of the window he searched with his feet and found the flat surface of the beam. It was twelve inches wide. At once, Nikolai was almost knocked off balance. By the noise. The rain beating on the metal roof just above his head was a din like a thousand Kodo drummers. The percussion seemed to vibrate all the way to the center of Nikolai's brain, overwhelming his thoughts, blurring his concentration. He had the urge to escape the noise, climb back out the window. Instead, he took two steps out onto the steel beam and two more and then his will to not fall three stories prevailed. He continued on, taking it a small, sure step at a time. When he reached midpoint, about twenty feet out, he stopped abruptly. His eyes had caught movement below. It was someone off to his left emerging from where the shadows were darkest. A man. He had on dark trousers and dark shoes, and his hair and full beard were dark, so to Nikolai he appeared phantasmal, like only an inflated white shirt floating slowly along. What made the man surely real to Nikolai, however, was the straps of his shoulder holster and the holster itself with the shiny black butt of an automatic pistol sticking out of it. A watchman. What was it here that required an armed watchman? Nikolai took it as another indication that he'd come to the right place. What a waste of time the police station would have been.

The watchman was now directly below Nikolai. He stopped there and brought his hand to the back of his neck. He glanced up. Nikolai suddenly realized that his saturated sweatshirt and jeans were dripping, and there was nothing he could do to prevent it. Drips were giving him away. The watchman was now looking right up at him, squinting to make him out up there in the dark. Next the watchman would draw that pistol, aim it upward, and pick him off. Shouldn't he jump and land on the watchman while he still had the chance? That's what he'd do if this were a movie, Nikolai thought. Good was always leaping from balconies and ledges so it could land on bad, and making it look so easy. But this would be a thirty-foot jump, Nikolai reasoned, the same as jumping from the roof of a three-story building. He'd probably misjudge and land on the concrete floor and break both legs and then he'd be helpless as the watchman stood over him and took point-blank aim.

The watchman was still squinting up.

Nikolai stood absolutely still.

The moment seemed distended, as though ambivalent fate required extra room to put whatever it would into it.

The watchman went to the wall nearest the ovens. He yanked on the long dangling chain to close the window Nikolai had come in through. That apparently satisfied him. He hadn't seen Nikolai up there in the darkness; he blamed the open window for the drips. He continued on to the front of the place and disappeared into the office.

Nikolai waited until most of his previous resolve had returned. He realized now there was danger to this beyond merely being caught. Concentrate, he cautioned himself. Consider every move before you make it. No slip-ups. He proceeded slowly across the beam, and after his tenth step he'd reached the spot where it passed about seven feet above the top edge of the steel-mesh enclosure. Earlier at the hotel Nikolai had visualized his attempting this part of it. All he had to do now was be as successful at it as he'd imagined. As a boy he'd never been much good at perching on the tops of high places, a shortcoming he'd never thought would be crucial. Walking this steel beam had been one thing. Easy enough. It was a foot wide. Even Ninja wouldn't have had trouble with it. The top edge of the mesh enclosure, however, didn't offer more than three or four inches.

He sat on the beam with his legs dangling over one side. Here goes everything, he thought, and keeping hold of the seriflike shape of the lower part of the beam he slid off it, all the way down until he was hanging by his hands. He searched with his feet for the top edge of the enclosure, extending to find it, using the entire length of his body and the additional length of his arms. His sneakers brushed the edge, just brushed it. He needed another inch or two. Hell, he wasn't made of elastic. He couldn't hang on much longer. His arms and fingers were starting to burn from strain. Something told him he'd have another couple of inches if he thought himself longer; if he could relax his shoulders just enough and his arms just enough and at the same time manage to hang on. No choice but to give that a try. He didn't have the strength left to pull himself up. He closed his eyes and asked the tension of his shoulders and arms to relinquish a couple of inches. He kept feeling with his feet, and now more of the surface of that edge came in contact with the soles of his sneakers. To relieve his fingers and arms he let the edge have some of his weight, and then he became confident enough to commit entirely to standing balanced upon it. He felt close to giddy with accomplishment. Hell, he was as sure as a statue, could stand perched up there forever. How was it that purpose made up for shortcomings? The question seemed to nudge him and make him waver. He quickly crouched, grabbed hold of the edge with both hands. Like a clumsy monkey clambering on the inside of its cage he descended to the concrete floor.

He glanced about the enclosed area. The light from the ovens allowed him to make things out. Along the wall was a workbench and three high stools. To his left were heavy-duty cardboard containers of various sizes, about thirty or so. Most of those looked sealed-up, ready to be sent; a few had top flaps open, apparently were in the process of being packed with crystal objects. Also there on that side of the enclosure was a huge transparent plastic bin three-quarters full of foam packing material, the little white scallop-shaped sort.

On the right, a desk and typewriter, and next to the desk, two metal files, and beyond the files in the far corner, an upright steel cabinet. The cabinet seemed to Nikolai the most likely place. He was sure it would be locked, but when he went to it and tried its doors they swung right open as though the cabinet were eager to show him it contained nothing of serious value. Just letterhead stationery, printed order forms and invoices and such, a first-aid kit, a bottle of antacid, a half-used bar of heavily perfumed soap lying on a musty-smelling washcloth. On the bottom shelf, an umbrella and the heels-and-straps jumble of five women's shoes, two pair and an odd. Behind the shoes in the corner, a metal box, the kind usually used for keeping cash. The box would be locked, Nikolai thought, locked because it contained diamonds, a thousand carats of Aikhal goods. He'd pry the box open and there would be a fat packet, his answer to everything, worth twenty million or so at dealer's price. So easy.

The box wasn't locked.

In it were four twenty-koruna banknotes and a few fifty-haler coins.

Nikolai replaced the box, closed the cabinet, took his attention to the adjacent files. The files also were unlocked, so Nikolai wasn't very hopeful as he went through them. Nevertheless he was systematic, thorough, searched in and under and in back of the file folders in each of the four drawers. He brought out his flashlight, wrapped his fingers around the illuminating end of it in such a way that when he turned it on its beam was diminished and more directional. Randomly he examined some of the file folders, the letters and duplicate invoices they contained, hoping to hit upon the other address, the Paris one that Kislov had given him, 131 rue de Paradis. He believed that in confirming a connection between there and here he might also find a clue. He was into the bottom drawer of the file when he suddenly became aware that he could hear the papers his fingers were disturbing. The rain had stopped. Now he would have to be more cautious about making noise. The watchman was a hundred feet away in the front office, but the way this place was constructed every sound was amplified. In fact, now Nikolai could even hear the intense heat inside the ovens, the steady roaring exhale of molecules in a frenzy. The bottom drawer made a metal-against-metal screech as he pushed it closed.

He gave up on the files and began searching the desk, was going through its disorder when he happened to glance up in the direction of the front office as he had been doing every so often. This time the watchman was coming out. The watchman had heard him, Nikolai believed. That was a flashlight in the watchman's hand. The watchman's attitude was different; there was a sense of urgency and purpose to his stride. Caught in this cage, Nikolai thought. His only chance was to hide.

Keeping down, he crept across the enclosure to the cardboard shipping containers. Their arrangement of some stacked upon others offered a sort of lair. Nikolai crawled in. A narrow space between containers allowed him to see the watchman approaching. Every clack of the watchman's leather-heeled shoes on the concrete floor was a subtraction. In a moment, Nikolai thought, there would be the flashlight's beam playing in through the steel mesh. These containers wouldn't conceal him for long. They were the obvious hiding place, probably where the watchman would first look. He was sure to be found. There would be the point of that pistol, hard words, some roughing up. What ultimately would be done with him, to him? He doubted it would be anything so benign as turning him over to the police.

The watchman was no more than twenty feet from the enclosure. But now he began humming a bright Slav song. He went past the enclosure to the wall across the way. He opened a door, pulled on a bare bulb, undid and shoved down his trousers, and sat on the toilet bowl. The flashlight turned out to be a rolled-up magazine that immediately distracted one end of the watchman while his other evacuated. The toilet door was open, and although Nikolai had an unimpeded view of the man he preferred not to look. He spent the time gazing into the side of the nearest cardboard container, listening to what Irina had to say about his behavior. She wanted to know what in the world he was doing there cowering on the hard bare floor of this Czech factory with the sounds of defecation in his ears. Was this what she had so conscientiously prepared him for? She didn't mind his being in love, but couldn't he be just normally, deeply in love? How quixotic of him to believe he could sneak in and rummage around a bit and come up with a handful of diamonds. A ridiculous notion. She was ashamed of his head for containing it. He should have asked her advice. She would have made him realize how irrational and extensively optimistic his reasoning was. She would have told him, as she had so often, "Communists don't get rich, they get comfortable."

The flush of the toilet was too much for her. She was gone. Nikolai's mind became resynchronized with his eyes, registered what his eyes were fixed upon. He doubted what he saw. It was right there where he couldn't miss it, but too coincidental to be true. He waited until the watchman had returned to the front office. Then he switched on his flashlight and read clearly the Zuzana shipping label on one of the containers:

Boule de Cristal
131 rue de Paradis
Paris 10th arr. France

CHAPTER
•••20•••

THE LACK OF A SENSE OF PLACE THAT NIKOLAI HAD COM-
plained about to Savich was dispelled the moment he set
foot upon the cobbles of Loundes Close. Gone so immediately and entirely that Nikolai wasn't sure that feeling had
ever been valid or even his. Where he belonged, *rodina* or
no *rodina*, was with Vivian no matter where in the world
that might be. Stick a pin into any map for anyplace, as
long as it was with her, within touch of her. Being beyond
that range would always cause him to ache.

Now, marvelous fortune, he was only fifty familiar paces
from her door. His insides, chest, groin, and head were
overinflating with anticipation. Throughout the flight from
Prague he'd managed to keep that feeling reasonably in
check by reading snatches of a Gogol and gazing out at the
night sky a lot. Constantly imposed on his consciousness,
however, had been the happy fact that he was aimed at her
and closing at five hundred miles an hour. When he'd
allowed himself to dwell on her, which required a certain
kind of enjoyable bravery, he'd envisioned her curled up
on her sofa, emotionally distracted, unable to concentrate
on anything, not even on handicapping tomorrow's races.
It had occurred to him several times during the flight that
she, uncanny as she was, might intuit that he was on his
way and be sitting there waiting.

What hadn't occurred to Nikolai until now, this very
second, was that Vivian might have had the lock on her
front door changed. He tried the key. It slipped in nicely
enough, but would it turn? If it did this time, never again
would he doubt it. He felt the blade of the key meet the

resistance of the bolt. The bolt seemed not so friendly, stubborn, perhaps unyielding. But then it retracted with its usual crisp, admitting snap and there was her cat, Ninja, at the top of the stairs. As soon as Nikolai saw Ninja there playing patient sphinx, he knew Vivian wasn't home. Ninja phlegmatically turned his head and gave a look that said, "Well, you're back are you?" but otherwise didn't budge a hair as Nikolai stepped over him.

Where could Vivian be? Where couldn't she be? The place was filled with her and empty. Tangerine peels that weren't yet dried were in the bowl on the table that served the sofa. There also was that day's newspaper opened to the page where the racing entries were listed. Evidently she hadn't been gone long, at least hadn't taken off in a cloud of despair for some distant attraction such as Macao.

Nikolai told himself he shouldn't stay. He'd relinquished his right to stay and would need to reestablish it. He'd go to his apartment, not walk the block fifty times. He'd go to his apartment and relax and try phoning no more than once an hour. For now he'd limit himself to just a look around. He went straight into the bedroom, straight to the closet she'd designated as his. His clothes and shoes and all were still there, exactly as he'd left them. He was ashamed of having half expected they'd be carelessly stuffed into a cardboard carton with his name scribbled on it for identification. He stood by his side of the bed and decided there hadn't been any encroachments. He went to the dresser to his assigned drawer. It wasn't the same. His socks and underwear and such were all folded and rolled and more neatly organized than ever. He saw love in that order. His toothbrush still stood with hers in the silver tumbler by the bathroom sink. That was most reassuring. His toothbrush would have been the first thing to go. At what point, he wondered, would she have ridded herself of all these remnants of him? No matter. He'd returned in time. Now he'd changed his mind. He'd sit on the top step and wait with Ninja.

No sooner had he pushed Ninja over to make room than he heard the slam of a car door just outside. It sounded like the door of a taxi, not a Rolls, he thought. Next was the sound of the bolt unlocking and then there she was, inside, preoccupied with securing the night latch. That done, she turned, glanced up, and saw him. For a long moment she remained fixed, eyes to eyes with him. It was as if each thought the other an apparition that would evanesce if a word was spoken. Finally she came up the stairs, and he moved aside to let her by. He believed he understood why she didn't greet him with an embrace and kiss. A mere embrace and kiss would not suffice.

She dropped her shoulder bag to the floor, plumped a couple of pillows with vigorous slaps and jabs, and sat on the sofa close to its right arm. Nikolai cautioned himself not to do anything she might interpret as assuming. He got up from the steps, came in, and took the chair across from her, as might a visitor who'd just happened to drop by.

"I'll make some tea," she said.

Far from what he'd imagined would be their first words. "Not for me, thanks."

"Perhaps later."

At least there was going to be a later, Nikolai thought.

"How've you been?" she asked casually.

"How about you?"

"Not well," she admitted matter-of-factly. "Not at all well."

Nikolai tried a smile. "You look wonderful to me."

There was a catch in her sigh. "I've had the dumps. Ever had the dumps?"

"What are the symptoms?"

"Mopes, fidgets, droops." She touched the defining concavity between her collarbones. "A huge jam-up of woes right about here that keeps laughter from coming out. Ever had that?"

"It's been going around."

"Nothing much one can do for it, I suppose. Just let it run its course. What did you do for yours?"

"Went to the dacha."

"Oh, so that's where you were. I had most of the world

and then some trying to find you. Even my lost-persons angels were at a loss. Were you at the dacha alone?"

The outfit she had on was new, Nikolai thought. At least he couldn't recall ever having seen her in it, and surely he would have remembered, because it was such a fierce yellow and the short skirt was so raunchy. He wanted to go over and lick her knees.

"I mean, you weren't with one of Lev's libidinous Finns or anyone, were you?"

Nikolai savored her jealousy. He looked away, as though his reply wouldn't hold up under her scrutiny.

"Don't be brutal with me, Nickie," she implored. "I know I deserve it, but please don't be." She let her plea hang between them until it had expended most of its fervency. "Are you wondering where I was tonight?"

"It doesn't matter."

"Sure it does. I hope it does."

"What I meant is, it doesn't matter because you're here now."

"I went to dinner and half a concert at Albert Hall with a school chum, a she, Millicent Millington. I hadn't spoken to her in years. Thought it might be healthful for me to renew some old ties, although none were ever what one might call a meaningful knot."

"Half a concert?"

Vivian nodded. "Throughout dinner, and I mean practically every second from appetizer to demitasse, Millie Millie, as we used to call her, couldn't talk of anything other than *her* predicament. It was impossible for me to get in a word about you."

"What was bothering her?" Nikolai asked, merely to maintain verbal momentum.

"About six years ago Millie Millie married splendidly to more than ample money, and she was, so she claimed, exceedingly satisfied with her life until one afternoon last fall when she dallied with a neighbor down in Sussex."

"And, as it goes, she simultaneously fell out and into love."

"Right. However, this neighbor happens to also be a

wife. By now they're really into it. They get lost together during the hunts so they can have at it in the hedgerows. Millie Millie spared me none of the details. In fact she was so graphic it was sordid. It was like she'd found God and he has a clitoris."

"What about her irises? I assume you had a look."

Vivian had on her magnifying monocle. She fingered it, spun it by its stem. "I'd thought I might," she said, "but there was no need. Millie Millie was so excited with her switch she was practically walleyed. Anyway, I begged off at intermission, said I had excruciating cramps."

"Do you?"

"I was fibbing. Have you ever known me to have cramps? Besides, that or whatever has never stopped us." In her unhalting manner without so much as a breath she ran right into another topic. "I'm sorry about how I behaved in Baden-Baden."

"I shouldn't have run out on you."

"Considering my abysmal behavior, *I* would have run out on me." She lowered her eyes a fraction. "In fact, I more or less have."

"I apologize for leaving you high and dry."

"High and wet," she corrected. "No matter, it's my blame. You can't have it, not even a smidgen of it. You sacrificed your precious Fabergé things for me and I pissed the money away."

"Not without warning me that you probably would."

"Don't let me off the hook. I was insensitive. I had a long tête-à-tête with my conscience, which if possible is something I normally avoid, and we agree, my conscience and I. I was insensitive."

He leaned forward to emphasize his words. "Viv, I didn't take off because you got caught up in a losing streak."

"What could be worse?"

"I would have left even if you'd won a bundle."

"That's worse." She frowned.

"I was struggling with the future."

She understood what he meant. She'd also done some struggling with it, wondering what they'd do when he got called back to Russia. Would she go with him? Would he want her to? Wouldn't their love be different there? She'd have to join up, wouldn't she? Become a Communist, pretend she disliked owning things? She'd have to get used to not having money coursing through her life. It was almost unimaginable. One of her beliefs was that thoughts were energy and whatever was thought of enough would become circumstance. On that basis she'd put this personal Armageddon out of mind.

"The future, you say?"

"It was giving me a very bad time."

"Well, it's still there."

"But I believe I can handle it now," Nikolai told her.

"You think you can change me?"

"I don't want any changes."

Relief alleviated the tension in her cheeks, and her mouth softened. "You shouldn't have to suffer even my venial sinning," she said. "Hell, lover, I want to be good *for* you, not just *to* you."

Her words were his. He remembered for the impact of comparison how vacant and dispirited he'd felt when he was away from her. He thought of how possibly he'd solved all their divergences in Prague. He glanced at the newspapers on the table, her many red-ink scratchings on the lists of racing entries. "Been winning?" he asked.

"I haven't been betting, just picking. My bookmakers must think I've gone blind. Gareth has been trying desperately to get in touch with me. The other day he was at my door. I didn't answer. No use tempting myself. Strangely, I seem to do better when all I do is pick." Her expression clouded with consternation. She raised her chin to clear it away. "Actually I'm trying to wean myself out of horse-playing altogether."

"Why should you?"

"Well . . ." She seemed unsure of which reason to give. "It recently occurred to me that financially demonstrating confidence in the swiftness of a handsome beast in the flesh was one thing, but there was no reason other than greed to put such faith in mere names and statistics. Besides, I don't lose well."

"But you're big to admit it."

She laughed heartily. "My woes seem to be giving way," she said. She sprang up, went past Nikolai and on into the bedroom.

Nikolai decided he shouldn't follow her. He heard the bedcovers being turned down, pillows being piled in place, a drawer being slid open, things in the drawer being pushed aside to make room for her bedside clock, the drawer being closed. He heard her enter the bathroom. There was the squeak of the handle for the hot as she turned it, water hitting the bowl of the sink, the soap dish being slightly disturbed, a soundless interval while she dried. Nikolai imagined her seeing herself happier in the mirror. He would, he vowed, always be generous with whatever made her happy. She was humming a part of Borodin's Nocturne for String Orchestra from Quartet No. 2 when the telephone rang. She answered it in the bedroom. As sharp as Nikolai's hearing was, he couldn't make out what she was saying. A couple of trills of laughter pierced out. Nikolai told himself he shouldn't be possessive of her laughter.

She returned. "That was Archer. I told him you were back. He was happy to hear it."

"My pal Archer."

She didn't resume her place on the sofa. Rather, she half leaned, half sat on the arm of it with the forward edge of the arm supporting her just below her buttocks. Her weight was on one foot. Her other foot was crossed over, its instep gracefully elongated. She seemed unaware that her pelvis was so pronounced. "You *are* back, aren't you?"

"Yes."

"I mean for good back."

"Or whatever."

"I haven't turned you into a cynic, have I? I hope not. One of the numerous qualities I love about you is your brooding optimism."

"Has Archer been around much?"

"He calls often to check on my emotional barometer.

Archer's been sweet, really. Just now he wanted to know if my mood was up to playing poker at his club. He offered to stake me. When I told him you were here he knew it was out of the question."

"Why not enjoy yourself?"

"I fully intend to."

She went to him, parted his legs with her knees so she could stand closer. With both hands, as though his head were a crucible, she tilted his face up. The kiss was long. It made her lower abdomen feel as if it weighed a ton and took away her legs and her breath. To regain a rhythm to her breathing she finally removed her tongue and lips, straightened up. His arms were around her hips and buttocks, holding, his palms curved to match her sides. His cheek and ear were pressed against her middle, and she wondered if he could hear the arousal in her. While they remained like that, confirming reunion, she gazed around the room and admitted the difference his presence had brought to her place. There was renewed value in everything, not only the Lavery landscape above the mantel, but, as well, the mundane, such as the brass umbrella rack in the corner on the landing. There was even beauty in the spent potted primrose on the stand by the window, which last week in full flower, all blue and pink, hadn't been able to reach her appreciation. "I love you so, Nickie," she said to the top of his head, and she was pleased that he allowed her words independence, that he didn't automatically match them aloud. She thought with her want that she would like it if he carried her in, as he'd done the very first time they'd loved. As though he heard her mind, he stood and took her up. Her willingness made her seem weightless. She lost both her pumps on the way.

Their loving was greedy and generous and lasting, and afterward they both fell into a deep, good sleep. They were awakened by what sounded like a sack of potatoes being flung against the bedroom door. It took them a moment to realize it was Ninja. Neglected, yellow-eyed Ninja. They heard him get a good running start and again throw himself at the door panel.

"A cat only its mother could love," Nikolai remarked. He'd never been able to make Ninja purr.

Vivian got up and went out. Ninja went belly-up at the sight of her. She gave him a half-dozen scratchy strokes and fed him a whole eight-ounce can of mackerel. "Are you hungry?" she shouted from the kitchen to Nikolai. His reply sounded as much like yes as it did no, so she made up a tray of things and brought it in.

"What's the time?" Nikolai asked.

"I ignored the kitchen clock, but I did notice it was dark out. Do you think it's the same night or the next?" She placed the tray on the floor by the bed and climbed back in under the sheet. "I was having the most extraordinary dream," she said.

"Was I in it?"

"Off and on. But mainly it starred Millie Millie."

"Extraordinary, huh?"

"Very."

"Who knows—perhaps you'd enjoy such a sortie in Sussex."

"How can you assume I haven't already?"

"Have you?"

"Are you curious or threatened?"

"Both."

"I've had opportunities," she said playfully.

"And?"

"Not in this life, darling, nor the next, unless for some lesson we both choose to come back as women."

"Do you honestly believe that you and I are bound forever?"

"So I'm told."

"By your angels, I suppose."

"Aren't you convinced?"

"They don't talk to me."

"You don't listen."

"How many times do you think we've lived before?"

"Plenty."

"We just keep coming back?"

"Until we get it right, no mistakes."

"Then what?"

"Then we go on to some higher plane of existence."

"Together?"

"Possibly not."

"This may be the time we get it right," Nikolai said thoughtfully. "It feels right."

"Doesn't it, though."

"I'm for making a mistake."

"You!" she chided. She placed her hand on his chest, as close as she could get to his heart. She discerned his heartbeat and thought it a strong, contented thump. "I bought two handsome teak benches for the terrace down in Devon," she said.

"Used or new?"

"New. But I couldn't settle on exactly where they should go. I must have moved them around for an hour. As you know, normally I'm not so indecisive."

"Did you spend much time down there?"

"Only a day and a night. The house and everything seemed to miss you as much as I. I did manage to plant a flat of violas, and I got as far as dressed for fishing but didn't go. Sat out on the back steps with my waders on like a catatonic. Did you get like that at the dacha?"

An affirmative grunt from Nikolai.

"On the drive back from Devon I had the urge to go to Paris and look up my father."

"Could you locate him?"

"It would take some doing. Anyway, by the time I got home the urge had left me. At least it was no longer on the surface. Must have been just another acute attack. I've had them off and on since I was in my teens."

Nikolai wondered why her French father didn't look her up. He couldn't imagine anyone not wanting to know her.

"We're going to have four children," she predicted. "Three girls and a boy. We'll give them romantic Russian names like Tatiana and Lilya. Naturally the boy will be Nikolai. Nikolai Nikolaievich. Won't that please you?"

"Why not three boys and a girl?"

"Are you going to insist on three boys?"

"Perhaps."

"It won't do you any good. I've already put in for three girls."

"You submitted an application, I suppose."

"In a way. They're already waiting to be born."

"What if *I* put in a request?"

"Mothers get preference."

"That's unfair."

"Did it ever occur to you that mothering has always been, while fatherhood has only been recently realized?"

"According to whom?"

"Common sense and anthropology. Just a few thousand years ago, no one knew how women became pregnant. Fucking wasn't connected with having babies. Fucking was just fun, something that felt good. Giving birth was mystical, and, I should mention, not so much fun."

"How long are those teak benches?"

"Six feet."

"What color are the violas you planted?"

"Mixed."

"I like best the mauve ones."

"You would."

"What do you mean by that?"

"I recall your remarking at various times that you think mauve is funereal."

"Well, it is."

"I've always thought as much."

"So what you're implying is that my tastes lean to the morose."

"Lor, how you Russian blokes carry on." She rolled onto her side and threw a claiming leg over him. Her crotch pressed his hip. The small of her back was easily within his reach. His hand appreciated there for a while, then went to her buttocks. After several serious squeezes she murmured to the neck skin below his ear: "Carry on."

They didn't venture out of the apartment for two and a half days, and then when they did go out it was at three o'clock Tuesday morning. Nearly everyone else was asleep, which made London more agreeable. Arms around they strolled in step to Hyde Park Corner and along Piccadilly on the Green Park side. At St. James's they gave up Piccadilly for Jermyn Street, where, while looking shop windows, Vivian said that if she had her way all of Nikolai's shirts would be made to perfect measure for him by Hildetch & Key with his initials engraved on pearl buttons. Nikolai said that he would like to be able to buy Vivian a solid gold comb, not an excuse for a comb but a long, usable, hefty one. Vivian enjoyed that idea, imagined herself sitting somewhere in soft sunlight languorously running gold teeth through her hair.

That afternoon Archer phoned wanting to know if he could pop by. He hadn't called since Nikolai's return, and his timing seemed a bit too right. Nikolai suspected Archer had his chauffeur or someone on lookout. How else could he know almost to the hour when it would be less intrusive for him to call? Vivian gave Archer more credit. She believed that he had become spiritually attuned to them.

"Does that mean Archer feels what and when we feel?" Nikolai asked.

"To a degree, darling, to a degree."

Archer arrived empty-handed and cheerful. He welcomed back Nikolai with a shake so vigorous it was as if he hoped Nikolai would tear off his arm. Vivian saw through Archer's elation. She noticed that he kept lacing and unlacing his fingers, a phrase of his body language she interpreted as distress.

"Have you been to the theater alone?" she asked, knowing how much that usually depressed him.

"Not in weeks. Why do you ask?"

"Something's bothering you."

"You're mistaken. Anyway, it's nothing, nothing at all. I'm splendid, really."

"Archer . . ." she pressured.

"Except for my Caravaggio."

"Stolen?"

"No such luck. I was informed yesterday that my Caravaggio is *not* a Caravaggio. In fact it was painted no earlier than 1900. For the past ten years I've been hoodwinked by it. How detestable!"

"Poor Arch," Vivian commiserated.

"From what I understand it happens all the time," Nikolai put in. "Even the museums get fooled."

"Hell yes, Arch."

"It's said that Manet painted five hundred canvases, of which three thousand have been sold."

"I know, I know all that," Archer muttered.

"Must have set you back a pretty penny. Surely you have some recourse. What about the person who sold it to you?"

"A dealer in Rome. He's dead."

"Serves him right." Vivian scowled.

"The financial loss was substantial, but that doesn't matter, and, of course, being duped is uncomfortable for anyone," Archer told them. "What disturbs me most is how close I came to being thought a fraud. Supposing I'd suddenly passed on and had bequeathed that Caravaggio to someone dear—you, Viv, for example—and then it was found to be a fake? Whatever would you and everyone think of me?" Archer shook his head sharply as though dispelling evil. "What a near miss!"

Nikolai felt like giving Archer a hug.

Vivian suggested dinner at Turner's.

On Wednesday Vivian again changed the bed linens and placed a large order with Partridge's.

On Thursday they took things to read and a hamper of things to munch on and went to the grass of Regent's Park. Vivian was, as usual, into several books at the same time, reading snatches of each. Such as one titled *Craneosacral Balancing*, which, she explained to Nikolai, had to do with relieving stress caused by the blocking of the fluid that bathes the central nervous system. Her current reading also included *The Colour of Rain*, Emma Tenant's *roman à clef* about the decadence of the Chelsea crowd during the 1960s, and a biography of Hilda Doolittle, or H.D., as she was called, who Vivian said was possibly the most fascinating

woman of this century. Look who's calling the kettle shiny,
Nikolai thought. His reading that day was the latest issue
of the *Economist*. He caught up with the interminable world
affairs and finances, and scanned the classified section in
the back, grimly noticing that the highest annual salary
offered was twenty-two thousand pounds.

On Friday afternoon when they were about to leave for
the weekend in Devon, an air express van pulled into the
close and made a delivery to Vivian. A heavy-duty cardboard
container that measured about four and a half feet deep by
two feet square. Every surface of it was plastered with red,
unmissable THIS END UP and FRAGILE stickers.

"Whatever can it be?" Vivian said as she examined the
shipping label and verified that it did indeed indicate her
name and address. "The Zuzana Bohemian Glass Works,"
she read. "Prague?"

"Something I had sent," Nikolai told her.

"When were you in Prague?"

"Recently."

"You never mentioned it."

"I thought it might not be important." Which was true.
He'd lost about 90 percent of the faith he'd had in his
hunch. From this regained London vantage he'd looked
back upon the entire Prague episode and seen mostly his
foolish desperation.

"Shall we open it now or let it remain a surprise for
Monday when we get back?"

"Now." He went and got his Swiss army knife, pulled
out the proper blade for her.

"Want to tell me what's in it?" she asked playfully.

Possibility blew on the spark of his hope.

"Last chance," she teased. There was a dry slashing
sound as she slit one of the top edges.

Nikolai's mind left London. He was again in the Zuzana
building inside that steel wire enclosure, having just discovered this container with the Paris address on its shipping
label. The entire label was covered over with clear tape to
protect it during shipment. Using his knife, Nikolai carefully
picked at an edge of the clear tape until he had enough

free for his fingers to get a sure grip. He peeled the tape off. The shipping label came with it. There were several identical cartons among those packed and ready to be shipped. Nikolai chose one that seemed less favored, had numerous smaller cartons stacked around and on it. Before he moved those he took special notice of how they were arranged. He peeled the shipping label from the identical carton. On the counter he found fresh shipping labels and a roll of the clear tape. The addresses and other information on the labels had been typewritten. Nikolai went to the desk. The typewriter was an older electric. He switched it on. Its hum seemed loud, might be heard by the watchman in the front office. Through the open door of the office Nikolai could see the man's legs extended and up on a chair, just his legs. He pictured the rest of the man, particularly his pistol. He inserted a shipping label into the roller of the typewriter, adjusted it so it was correctly aligned. He couldn't just go ahead and type. That would make too much noise. The consistent clatter of it would get to the watchman's ears. But perhaps if there were adequate intervals between the typing of the characters it would be less noticeable, possibly taken as a normal noise of the building, a sound made by the ovens or the dripping of rain.

He was a hunt-and-hope sort of typist. He shielded the beam of his flashlight to find the keys and copy exactly the label with the Paris address. Twice he made errors and had to begin again with a fresh label. He'd hit a key and wait, hit another key and wait. It was nerve-racking. Each time after hitting a key he expected to see the watchman's legs brought down, see the watchman come out to investigate with pistol drawn. It took three-quarters of an hour for Nikolai to do the Paris label and about as long to do the one addressed to Vivian. He was relieved to the point of nearly sagging when he turned off the typewriter. Using the clear tape, he affixed the Vivian label to the container that had been destined for Paris. The Paris label went on the other identical container. He switched the placement of the containers and arranged the other cartons around them just so. It was essential that nothing appear disturbed. He put the tape back where he'd found it, crumpled the old labels and the mistake ones into a ball that he shoved into his pocket. After a final check that he hadn't overlooked anything and a last glance at the watchman's legs, he climbed to the top of the mesh enclosure. He knew that if he stood on the top edge of the enclosure the steel beam above would be beyond his reach by a few inches. So he planted his feet surely on that narrow edge and, from a crouch, sprang up to grab hold of the beam. After pulling himself up onto the beam, he went across it to the window. He pulled the chain and opened the window enough notches so he could crawl out. He couldn't lower the window from the outside, so he counted on the watchman's not noticing it was again open. He retreated the way he'd come, up and over the roof and down, untying the line and taking the makeshift ladder with him. He went around to the other side of the building and untied there. He returned the ladder to the pile of wood boxes and threw the clothesline into a trash bin. It began to rain again. The air smelled sour. And as he walked down the dark lifeless street in the direction of Sokolovska the first germ of doubt infected him. He'd risked everything, put out a great deal of effort and probably accomplished nothing.

Now Vivian had the container open. It was jammed with protective packing material, little white scallop shapes of foam. She dug down into them, felt around, and brought out a crystal wine goblet, intricately faceted. She held it up, admired it, and let out a downscale sigh of appreciation. "You must have noticed that just about every good glass I own has a nick or two. No matter how careful I am, every time I wash up I seem to do some damage." She took other crystal goblets from the container, placed them in rows on the table. Altogether thirty-six. "Well," she said, "you certainly didn't stint. May I gather these are a contribution to my trousseau?"

Nikolai's indifferent shrug was offset by an affirmative smile. Vivian gave him a swift smacking kiss that just did get the corner of his mouth. She returned her attention to the container. "I believe I felt something else in here," she said as she dug deeper into it. She brought out a cut-crystal bottle about five inches tall, dense, heavy crystal. Nikolai thought it a cologne bottle, until Vivian, puzzled but managing to keep up the high spirit of the moment, said: "A bitters bottle. I suppose it's something everyone should have. I've never known you to use bitters. Archer swears that a dash or two along with a raw egg will chase a hangover." She stood the bottle alongside the goblets and resumed digging in the container. When she brought out a second bitters bottle she was nice about it, didn't comment, and she continued to be considerate and silent as the container gave up twelve more.

Nikolai was embarrassed. What could he say? "For gifts," he explained.

The container also yielded a dozen cut-crystal inkwells.

"Those were thrown in for goodwill," he told her. "They were overstocked."

Vivian took up two of the wine goblets and went into the kitchen. At once Nikolai turned the container upside down, dumped all the foam scallops onto the floor, and began searching through them. They were incorrigible little things, squeaky and so light they went airborne with the slightest disturbance. Static electricity stuck them to Nikolai's sweater. Ninja, who had been a tolerant observer, jumped in and bullied them, swatted them every which way, and finally demonstrated his opinion of this strange substance by raking at it with his front paws as though it were excrement. Nikolai found nothing among the foam. Perhaps the container itself, he thought. He set about tearing that apart.

Vivian returned with a tray bearing the two wine goblets, freshly washed and sparkling, and a half bottle of '78 La Tâche from the previous night. "Whatever are you doing?"

"Just breaking down the box so its easier to throw out."

"You're making a mess."

A mess, Nikolai thought. Now without a doubt Prague had been a fizzle. All that getting soaked and climbing over rooftops had been for naught. All that ingenuity wasted.

He resented every minute of it. He even resented having made the goddam flight. That fellow Kislov had been an insane son of a bitch, that was all.

Vivian placed the tray down and brought Nikolai his wine. She touched his goblet with hers to cause a ding that said quality. "Our first drink from them," she toasted, "and may we always remember it was with leftover wine." They sipped to that. Nikolai watched the tip of Vivian's tongue slip out and gather wine from her lips. Her tongue was like an efficient little animal literally attached to its moist pink cave, he thought, reclusive and yet capable of so many sweet tricks.

"We must hurry, hon," Vivian said. "I want to be in Devon and out in the stream for the first twilight hatch."

Nikolai gulped the wine. The rim of the goblet grazed the bridge of his nose. Incidental light caught a facet of the goblet's intricately cut pattern and bounced the flash of a spectrum into Nikolai's eyes. The instant seemed parenthetical, inserted for emphasis, to ensure that Nikolai's mind transformed the flash into a possibility. He crossed the room to the fireplace, removed the folding screen and the andirons. The fireplace had been swept clean for the season. Without hesitation, he flung the goblet against the brick firewall. Fine lead crystal that it was, it shattered into powder and tiny particles.

"A romantic Russian gesture, or are you pissed at something?" Vivian asked. "Either way, you're being destructive."

"Bring a lamp," Nikolai told her. He was down on his knees on the hearth.

"You've gone daft. Too much fucking and so on will do it every time."

"The lamp," he ordered. "Over here!"

"Yes sir." She unplugged the table lamp behind the sofa. "I'll have you know I value this lamp. It's only reproduction K'ang Hsi but I don't want it broken." She set it on the floor near the hearth and plugged it in. Nikolai unscrewed its finial and removed its silk shade. He bent over and stuck his head into the fireplace. Among the minuscule shards and slivers of crystal he spotted one, defined by its shape and intactness. He picked it up and brought it around to the light of the bare bulb, held it respectfully in the basin of his palm.

A diamond.

A one-carat diamond, clear as water and as cold-looking as ice.

Vivian just stared at it. Her jaw had gone slack. With a degree of ceremony Nikolai dropped the diamond into her hand and stuck his head back into the fireplace. He found another diamond, then another, and another! He could easily make them out. Oh, bless, double bless the soul of that fellow Kislov, Nikolai thought.

Vivian fetched a mixing bowl from the kitchen to hold the diamonds. Optimistically, her largest mixing bowl. To improve the light she arranged two upright lamps with 250-watt bulbs. She knelt beside Nikolai and elbowed him to make room so she could enjoy helping with the harvest.

For the next five hours they smashed crystal and found diamonds. Their fingers got cut, but enterprise was anesthetic. When they'd thoroughly gleaned one batch of smashed crystal, Vivian sucked it up with her tank-type vacuum cleaner to give them a fresh surface for the next smashing. She had to change the bags of the vacuum frequently.

While hard at it, she told Nikolai: "You're a tricky one. You knew all along there were diamonds hidden in the crystal, didn't you?"

"More or less."

"How did you know?"

"Intuition."

"Many women but very few men have it. Do we get to keep these diamonds, or is this a smuggling scheme the Kremlin has you involved in?"

"They're ours," he replied calmly. "Yours and mine." He was hyperventilating. His head felt twice its size.

"How did they get to be ours?"

Nikolai wondered what of it he should tell her.

"I know," she said. "Now we come to the macho bullshit part where the woman is kept in the dark because what she might know might hurt her. Don't give me that."

He told her all of it, droned it out, everything from Kislov to Churcher to Prague to now.

"You stole from the stealers!" she exclaimed brightly.

Nikolai thought that a forgiving way of putting it.

"So that disqualifies you as an out-and-out thief. You must look at it that way, Nickie. I won't have you up to your chin in conscience. Guilt would taint everything. What's more, you stole for a most worthy cause."

No doubt she meant *them*.

She used tweezers to pluck a sliver of glass from her second finger and allowed two drips of blood to fall to the hearth before putting the tiny wound in her mouth. "One thing for certain," she said around her finger. "The stealers won't be happy. I suppose you have an idea who they are."

"No."

"Are they apt to suspect you?"

"Never."

"You're in the clear, neat as that?"

He believed he was.

"Clever," she praised.

"Aren't I, though?" Nikolai smiled, allowing himself this rare moment of immodesty.

They smashed the bitters bottles and the inkwells, and when they'd smashed the last articles and retrieved the diamonds they contained, Vivian swept well with the vacuum so they wouldn't be cutting their feet when they padded around barefoot. Then, seated in the kitchen, they swabbed tincture of Merthiolate on each other's wounds and applied adhesive strips. The clear glass mixing bowl was there on the table.

Two thousand, nine hundred and ninety-seven diamonds had come from the wine goblets.

The bitters bottles had yielded nine hundred and ninety-six.

The inkwells nine hundred and ninety-eight.

In all, four thousand, nine hundred and ninety-one.

The diamonds were identical. Round cuts, each precisely a carat. The finest quality, pure as water, with the stark, icy brilliance that made Aikhal goods so desirable.

Vivian gazed at them. She went off on a side road of vision for a bit of private auguring. Nikolai noticed the distance in her eyes and wondered what she was foreseeing. Was it Macao? Was it a hillside villa in Monte Carlo, situated so advantageously that it looked down upon the roof of the casino? Wouldn't they, some late nights, on the spur of the moment, dress grandly and stroll down to roulette? She'd never lose. Wouldn't they keep her winnings (until they overflowed) in a box in her closet at the foot of her many evening gowns? Wouldn't they sit in the lounge of the Ritz in Paris, accompanied only by a sweating silver bucket with the neck of a favorite fine vintage sticking up out of it, and casually observe the desperations of others? They'd know one another so well that a mere flick of an eye or closed-mouth grunt would be adequate commentary. Wouldn't he buy her a racehorse, one that would never let another horse pass, one that would start in front, stay in front, wire to wire? Gold combs, engraved pearl buttons.

Vivian gave the mixing bowl a spin. The diamonds responded with increased blaze and scintillation. "Hot stuff from such a cold place," she reflected.

Nikolai thought about the odd number of stones in the lot. He believed the lot was actually five thousand carats, an even kilo, and that they had overlooked nine pieces. Those nine were now somewhere in the used vacuum-cleaner bags. They were worth, give or take, a hundred and sixty thousand dollars.

But to hell with them.

CHAPTER
••••21••••

MANY IN THE BUSINESS OF DIAMONDS BELIEVE IT MORE than coincidence that the diamond district of Antwerp is located directly across from the zoo. Their point is made when at certain times a lull in the traffic noise allows the cries of the animals to be heard by the diamond dealers, brokers, and such who keep offices in the melancholy older buildings along Pelikaanstraat. Undeniably, just as much clawing, bleating, and screaming occurs daily on the diamond side of the street. Recent legend has it that a rather vicious and perhaps facetious laugh by a hyena heard through an open window changed the mind of a prominent dealer who was only a word away from buying a large lot of Australian rough that looked much better than it was. As it turned out that timely laugh saved the man a fortune. Now, rarely is a deal consummated that the buyer doesn't first cock an ear in anticipation of such worthy guidance.

For no apparent reason the zoo was unusually quiet that Wednesday afternoon when Nikolai and Vivian came to Pelikaanstraat. Vivian was at the wheel of the rented red BMW 735i. Nikolai watched the street address numbers descend from 212. When they got to the sixties he had Vivian pull over. She stopped where the curb was painted yellow to signify that standing was prohibited. A uniformed traffic policeman was right there. Vivian shot him such a dazzling smile it made the BMW invisible.

"How long do you think you'll be?" she asked Nikolai.

"No more than a couple of hours." Nikolai felt speeded up inside. For sure his heart was going over a hundred. "What will you do?"

"Park someplace legal and find some chocolate." The pamphlet she'd read in the hotel room had raved about Belgian chocolate and lace. Vivian had no interest in lace, hadn't since her antique-shop days when she'd learned that some Belgium women were so venal they went blind weaving it. "I'll get you some chocolate," she promised. "You still prefer that sweet, sissy kind?"

Nikolai nodded absently. Chocolate was one of the farthest things from his mind. He leaned across to Vivian, presented his face for a routine see-you-later kiss. Her lips grazed the corner of his and his cheek on the way to his ear. She gave the lobe a nip that would last awhile. He got out of the car and corrected the set and fall of his suit jacket. He was wearing his best dark blue three-piece business suit. Vivian had remarked about it earlier when he was putting it on, had said it was sincere, as warm and sincere as a pee down the leg. He tugged the points of his vest and tested the knot of his tie. Vivian thought he looked too good. "Loosen your tie a little," she told him, "just enough so you can almost see the top button of your shirt. And I think the white square in the breast pocket is a bit too sharp. You should look a telltale degree *nyekulturnyi*. As distasteful as that may be to you, it'll give you an edge. Perfect would be a pair of wire-framed glasses. I wish we'd thought of it."

Nikolai took her suggestions, loosened his tie and eliminated the pocket square. He reached in the backseat for his attaché case.

"Don't forget your hat," she said, handing it out to him, a black felt with a grosgrain band. They'd bought it yesterday in Geneva.

"I veto the hat," Nikolai said.

"I thought we'd agreed on it. Anyway, try it on."

He did to please her.

"I like you in a hat. I really do. You ought to wear it to bed sometime soon." She did her wicked grin, which she thought was the most heartening way to send him off. She slipped the gear into drive and swerved out into traffic.

Nikolai entered number 62, the Diamond Club of Antwerp. Immediately inside was a guard with a passive manner and scrutinizing eyes. The lump on his right hip was undoubtedly a pistol. Nikolai went up three steps to the landing of the spacious foyer. There was considerable coming and going, and he had to wait in line to present his credentials. His membership in the Diamond Club of London was supposed to be honored here. The attendant on duty double-checked his Soviet passport and club identification card and examined the interior of his attaché case. He signed the registry and passed through the arch of a metal detector to show he wasn't carrying a gun, bomb, or whatever.

That put him in the club's main room. It was a place to *do* business rather than escape from it. A huge, tall room about one hundred by fifty with a twenty-five-foot ceiling. One entire side was windows from the floor all the way up. Beneath the windows, at a right angle to them, were twenty identical long tables. These were situated to make the most of the natural north light. Nikolai had more than once heard it said that the daylight of Antwerp was the best in the world for viewing the truth of a diamond. It had something to do with the diffusing high haze that normally hung over the city.

Nikolai stepped aside and paused to observe the activity in the room. The five tables on the left nearest the entrance were crowded. Every chair was occupied, and there were men standing close around. Nikolai recognized those as the regulars. His London club had a similar group, a clique of small to medium-size dealers whose profits and ego satisfaction were derived mainly from outsmarting one another. Practically every day they gathered and haggled, and although diamonds and money changed hands, that was only the serious part of it. At the next several tables were not nearly so many dealers. They sat gossiping or conducting transactions head to head. They were each dressed in some sort of business suit, a good hard worsted or an ill-fitting wash-and-wear. Here and there was a garish tie, a shirt serving its third day, and on every head something, be it a second-generation black homburg, a felt fedora, or an embroidered yarmulke held in place by a bobby pin.

Nikolai took a seat at one of the vacant tables on the far right. He placed his attaché case on the chair next to him and drew it close. To occupy his eyes he studied a discarded briefke in the nearby ashtray. It had seen its day. Its edges were frayed and soiled from having been taken out, opened, and put back so many times. Nikolai read the faint penciled scribble *"5ctsMQ"* on one corner of it, and on another corner was the code "XXXBOT4." Why did dealers bother with such shorthand and codes? he thought. Why didn't they come right out and say what sort of diamond they had, what its color rating was, its faults and merits, instead of going through the ritual of making a buyer find out for himself? Which he'd no doubt do if he was any kind of buyer.

Nikolai gave the room two full minutes of indifferent gaze, then looked out the window. The view was the rear of other three- and four-story buildings and some old shrubbery that had been harshly trimmed back. At that moment a city bird, a mature sparrow, lighted on one of the upper twigs of the shrub. He cocked his head so all his left eye could take in Nikolai, and then, as though not trusting his left, he turned his head abruptly to get Nikolai with his right. Nikolai had the feeling that if the window had been open the bird would have flown in, hopped over, and chirped a few words of good advice. Probably he'd witnessed a great many diamond deals, this sparrow with the jerky head and jittery feet. The bird fanned open its wings and flew off.

Twenty minutes went by.

Nikolai pushed his hat back and drummed on the edge of the table with his fingers. He wanted to be noticed, taken as a dealer from out of town, one feeling displaced and wary. He looked the part, didn't he? Why hadn't anyone yet approached him? Was it because he was Russian? How would they know? He didn't look typical, had always been told that. However, the attendant to whom he'd shown his passport might have an ax to grind and have spread the word about his nationality. Probably very few Russians who were still Russians came here. He could have passed himself off as an American if he'd had a U.S. passport. Then he would have been immediately descended upon. Those various passports he'd accidentally discovered in Lev's cowboy boot came to mind. He now had to admit their convenience.

He'd just decided to give the place another twenty minutes when a man came over and stood at the end of his table. A middle-aged man with such a prominent paunch he had no choice but to leave his suit jacket open. His shirt front gaped from button to button and his wide, twenty-year old tie was so carelessly knotted its narrow end hung down longer by four inches. He stood there, his eyes fixed hard on Nikolai.

Nikolai acknowledged him cordially with a single nod, but the man just continued to glare. "Do we know each other?" Nikolai asked.

The man stuck out his lower lip. He had an ugly mouth, unfortunately large and dry except at the corners, where a little seepage glistened. His eyes looked chronically tired. He grumbled something.

"What?"

"You are sitting there," the man said.

"And you're standing there."

"That is *my* place."

"Yours?"

"I have been waiting almost half an hour for you to move."

"What's the difference between sitting here or there?" Nikolai indicated the next vacant table.

"It is mine, that is the difference."

Nikolai thought it too unimportant to be an issue. He started to get up.

The man gestured tolerantly for Nikolai to stay put. He half turned away to leave, then changed his mind and took the chair opposite. It was the same sort of chair as the one in which Nikolai was seated; however, the man seemed to find it uncomfortable, something he would temporarily endure. "I do business every day from that chair," he said.

"There is a certain amount of profit in people knowing where I will be, not having to search about."

Nikolai thought the man's accent was Dutch. Each word seemed to catch slightly on something viscous before coming out. Ever since his student days at the Institute of Foreign Languages Nikolai had taken pride in how correct he could be when it came to placing a man by his accent. To be more exact he guessed this fellow was from somewhere in eastern Holland along the German border, Enschede perhaps, or Winterswijk.

The man gave his name as Jacob Loodsen, and as though to prove that he took a business card from his shirt pocket and handed it across. Nikolai noticed the card was cheap, printed rather than engraved on rather soft stock. It bore no address or telephone number, just the name JACOB LOODSEN above the words FINE DIAMONDS.

Nikolai introduced himself. He didn't reciprocate with his business card because it would reveal that he was associated with Almazjuvelirexport.

"Where are you from?"

"London," Nikolai replied.

"You do not sound British."

"You don't sound Chinese."

Loodsen laughed. His eyes nearly disappeared when he laughed. "This your first time in Antwerp?"

"No," Nikolai fibbed.

"Then maybe your second time. What is your opinion of Antwerp? Is it the diamond heaven you expected?"

"Yes," Nikolai said conclusively and turned his attention once again to the activity in the room. The regulars were still at it. Two dealers four tables away were arguing emphatically, temporary enemies over what not long ago had been a mere pebble on a beach of Namibia. The atmosphere was layered with guttural grumble and chatter and the sibilance of near-whispers. Nikolai translated those into griping, bickering, conspiring. He decided he disliked this place as much as he'd ever disliked anywhere.

"Want to do some business?" Loodsen asked, as though that signified a measure of acceptance.

Loodsen was so obviously small-time, Nikolai thought. Any dealing with him would be inconsequential. But, on second thought, perhaps anything would be better than sitting here trying to look like the ideal victim.

"Do you want to sell me or me to sell you?"

"It doesn't matter," Nikolai told him.

"You sell me," Loodsen decided accommodatingly.

Nikolai went along with it. He removed a briefke from his attaché case and placed it on the table. Loodsen picked it up. There were no markings, no codes or anything on the briefke, and Loodsen thought that strange. "What is it, a mystery?" he remarked as he was unfolding it. His eyes intensified when the diamonds were revealed. Six one-carat stones. Loodsen took out his ten-power magnifying loupe and examined each of the diamonds, gave them more than a cursory look. "Nice goods," he said. "Where do you get such goods?"

"Hong Kong."

"Do you know what they are?"

"D-flawless."

"My eyes rate them F, maybe E."

"They're Ds."

"And I saw a few inclusions."

"Your loupe must have lint on it."

"Okay, to you they're D-flawless. When I asked you if you know what they are, what I meant was do you know where they were born."

"Of course."

"They are river whites. I have not seen rivers like these in many years. They must have been hiding in the dark in Hong Kong."

Nikolai knew Loodsen was referring to the type of alluvial diamonds once found in and along the Orange River in southwestern Africa, distinguished by their superior brilliance and pure colorless quality. If these Aikhal diamonds could pass for rivers, so much the better.

"How much you asking for these?"

"What are they worth?"

"Less now than a moment ago."

"Why is that?"

"Because I am trying to buy them." Loodsen grinned.

"Make an offer," Nikolai said, not seriously, just practicing for when it would be serious.

"For the lot? How many carats in the lot?"

"Each piece is a carat."

"Exactly?"

"Yes."

"Not a point or two less?"

"Precisely a carat."

The open briefke was on the table between them. Their words were like a substance passing over it. Loodsen louped the diamonds again. "Nice make," he said, commenting on how well they were cut. He jiggled the briefke ever so slightly. The diamonds danced a bit in the crease of a fold. "These all you got, six?"

"Why do you ask?"

"To be honest, I cannot afford to buy this nice. It hurts to admit, but that is the way things are for me at the moment." Loodsen did a sigh with a little wail of self-pity in it. "However," he went on, "I know somebody who could afford. Do you have others? You would have to have more than merely six."

"Who is this somebody?"

"How many more do you have?"

"I didn't say I had more."

"I hope you do. You are a pleasant young fellow. I wish you riches."

"Thanks."

"My brother-in-law, my only sister's husband, is an important broker. I do not care for him, but once in a while I use him to do myself a favor." Loodsen folded up the briefke and extended it between his fingers. "How many of these do you have?"

"A few."

"What does that mean? Another six, another ten, what?"

"Let's just say *more*."

"On you?"

"No."

"Where you can quickly put your hands on them?"

"What difference does it make?"

"My brother-in-law will ridicule me if I take you to him and all you have is a few. He thinks he is such a big shit."

"I don't think I would like your brother-in-law."

"Money is money."

Loodsen was right about that, Nikolai thought. He wondered where Vivian was at that moment. He pictured her with a jawful of bitter chocolate.

"You ever dream?" Loodsen asked out of context.

"Sometimes."

"Would that I never did. I get enough of diamonds during the day without having them in my sleep. The dream I have almost every night is not about a diamond so big I cannot get it into my pocket. It is about nice polite stones such as these. That is why I mention it. In my dream I own a few. I feel good that they are mine. Then I blink or something and I look again and the few have become twice as many and so it goes until I have a handful. I am so excited I wake up and all I really have is a handful of *putz*, which, with me," he admitted wryly, "is not much."

Nikolai wasn't genuinely amused. Something told him to look to tomorrow. He could try a different tack tomorrow, randomly choose a few brokers out of the directory and make appointments with them. They took advantage when they sensed you were aching to sell. He'd tried to avoid that. No matter; he'd be tough and get his price. Today hadn't been a total waste. He'd gotten a feel of Antwerp. In that regard Loodsen had been a bit of a help. He studied Loodsen again. The man was totally oblivious to being such a mess. Couldn't he see the hairs growing out of his ears, that spot under one of his chins where he'd missed the last three or four times he'd shaved? He was pathetic, a grub in a field of plenty.

"If you do a deal with my brother-in-law," Loodsen said, "I can middle. Nothing from you, just from him. That is why I want to know how much of these nice goods you have. The bigger the deal the more I stand to make, but if I do not know what the deal is I will not know what my cut is and my brother-in-law will be able to lie to me."

Nikolai didn't doubt that. He tried to imagine the looks of Loodsen's sister. If there was a family resemblance, how had she gotten someone to marry her? Maybe she had compensating talents. As Vivian often said, in some way everyone is blessed.

At that moment two dealers paused to confer nearby. Very well dressed, evidently successful. They stood so close to each other the brims of their black homburgs brushed. There was an air of conspiracy about them as they alternately turned ear to mouth to keep their words out of everyone's range. Nikolai observed them and thought they were probably pincering someone into selling too low or buying too high. As they turned to continue on their way, Loodsen greeted them by name. They looked right at Loodsen, but through him, didn't say a word.

A sudden empathic pang dissolved all of Nikolai's other intentions. "What's your brother-in-law's name?" he asked.

Ten minutes later Nikolai was around the block on Schupstraat with Loodsen wheezing and waddling beside him. They entered number 106, a well-maintained pre-both-wars building, and went up in a cage-type elevator to the fourth floor. Loodsen's brother-in-law's office was directly across the hall from the elevator. There was his name, DAVID NAGEL, lettered in black-outlined gold on the upper panel of the solid, highly varnished door. Nikolai and Loodsen went into a small entry, actually a cubicle about six by six. Most places of business in the diamond trade have this sort of first-line-of-security arrangement: a double entrance with two doors electrically interdependent, so that the exterior door giving to the cubicle has to be closed before the interior door can be opened. Loodsen and Nikolai stood in the cubicle. The receptionist peered out at them through a small partition of double-paned bulletproof glass. "It's me, Jacob," Loodsen said. The receptionist looked at Loodsen dubiously, but then the bolting mechanism of the inner door clicked and Loodsen went in, followed by Nikolai with hat in hand.

"Mr. Nagel is on the telephone," the receptionist informed them, as though anything was far more important than what they were there for. "And he has another call waiting," she added. She was a mature woman, severe in appearance, with dark hair pulled straight back to the point of pain from a hard, angular face. She was also noticeably pregnant.

Nikolai studied her briefly and wondered if it was possible that when she came into this life she'd been allocated just a certain small amount of pleasantness and squandered it as a child. Perhaps during an acute and rare attack of motherly instinct she'd given in to artificial insemination. He wondered what the person was like who had most recently kissed her. During the wait, he remained standing. He skimmed through a couple of the trade journals that were there on the table and was reading lies about what a high yield of sizable gem rough the System was getting out of Australia when the receptionist said: "Go in."

Nagel was behind his desk in a contemporary black leather chair too formidable for him. He was a small, slight man of fifty or so. A gray man. Not only was his hair gray but also his suit and tie and shirt. There was even a grayish cast to his complexion. The only colorful things about him were the light blue of his eyes and the pink of his tongue, the tip of which flicked out every so often as though to sneak a taste of the situation.

Loodsen made introductions. He had telephoned to let Nagel know he was bringing Nikolai by. Nagel gestured Nikolai into a chair and offered a cigar from a sleek silver Bulgari box. Evidently he expected Nikolai to refuse, was merely showing off the box, because he almost closed the lid on Nikolai's fingers. Nikolai chose a cigar and rolled it between thumb and forefinger. The dry crinkling of its tobacco-leaf wrapper told how stale it was. Without comment, Nikolai dropped the cigar back into the box, and Nagel, squirming a bit, returned the box to its exact place on his desk. Nikolai sat back as Nagel sat forward to get to business.

"I understand you have goods I might be interested in," Nagel said.

Nikolai would let the six diamonds speak for themselves. He placed the briefke containing them on the desk. Nagel opened it. His facial expression didn't change a twitch. He silently bare-eyed the diamonds for a while. Using a pair of black tweezers, he turned one over and picked it up by its girdle. His handling was swift and sure. It was something he'd done countless times. He examined that diamond with a loupe, then another, until he'd had a close look at all six. He betrayed more than mild interest. For an even closer look he swiveled his chair around to a binocular microscope. Magnified sixty-three times, the diamonds could hardly hide any secrets. Last, he weighed each diamond on a Mettler Electronic Scale, sensitive to a hundredth of a carat. The scale's green numbered readout indicated each was precisely one carat.

While Nagel was thus occupied, Nikolai glanced at Loodsen, who was edgy, like a starved man about to be assured of his next fifty meals. Loodsen made an optimistic mouth and worked his eyebrows a bit. Nikolai looked past him to the wall, where a large print was hung: one of Klimt's gaunt mistresses up to her throat in geometrics. From her, his eyes wandered to the near corner of Nagel's desk and a chunk of kimberlite rock that contained a poor diamond of about eight carats in matrix. How ironic, he thought, that everything so emotionally crucial to him should now hinge on something as unfeeling as diamonds. He straightened his leg, causing his hat to fall from his knee. He bent over to retrieve it just as Nagel swiveled around and said: "Letikahane." Nikolai thought Nagel was speaking Hawaiian.

"No," Loodsen said. "They are river whites."

"I know Botswanan material when I see it," Nagel said. "These are out of the new mine at Letikahane."

"They are *rivers*, extra extras," Loodsen insisted.

"To you every fine diamond is a river."

"They never saw Botswana."

"Go sell cubic zirconium to the tourists. You don't know shit about diamonds."

"You stink."

"I'm asking you to leave. We have business to conduct here."

Loodsen didn't budge.

"This is my office," Nagel said curtly. "Here you show respect."

Loodsen hunched his shoulders, made fists in his jacket pockets, and turned to Nikolai. "Do not let him tell you your goods are not rivers."

Nagel took a long breath through his nostrils to cool his tone. "For your information," he told Loodsen, "goods like these now coming out of Letikahane are on the average of finer quality than the best rivers ever were. So you see," he said to Nikolai, "I am not trying to depreciate your goods. In fact, if anything I have just placed myself at a negotiating disadvantage, which should indicate how straightforward I am."

A sarcastic grunt from Loodsen.

To give the impression that he was taking Nagel's words to heart, Nikolai waited a long moment before asking: "How much a carat for my goods?"

"That would depend on the size of the lot. From what I gather, you have many more than just these six."

"Anyway, more."

"Are we talking about fifty more, a hundred, or what? I must know to make a price."

"One-carat D-flawless rounds have a set price."

"Yes, but . . ."

"I realize the price varies somewhat day to day. What's it at now?"

"As of this afternoon, the going price was in the sixteen-to-eighteen-thousand range, depending on how good the make."

"And these?"

"Beautifully made, top price."

"Eighteen thousand a carat. That's in dollars?"

"We normally quote and deal in dollars."

"The dollar hasn't been at its best lately."

"If you'd rather we can convert to some other currency. French francs or pounds."

"I guess dollars are all right."

"So, how many one-carat stones are we talking about?"

"Let's start with a hundred."

"I sense, Mr. Borodin, that you feel the need to be clever with me, so to save us both that sort of energy I'll come right to the point. I have a client, a principal, an American who is disenchanted with Wall Street. He wants to make a sizable investment in diamonds."

"What would be sizable?"

"I have discretion to commit to a hundred million."

Nikolai tried to appear unfazed. He denied that his shirt collar suddenly felt a size too tight. There wasn't really something in his throat that wouldn't let a swallow go all the way down. He could have looked Nagel square in the eyes if he'd wanted to. He nonchalantly fussed with his hat, thankful now that he had it for a diverting prop. He took his time, shaped the brim and redimpled the crown, while he thought what a piece of cake this was turning out to be, a fortune falling right into his pocket. "All right, then," he said, as though conceding, "let's make it a thousand carats."

Nagel was pleased. "All of this investment-quality," he stipulated.

"Exactly. You won't be able to tell one piece from another."

"I'll pay sixteen thousand a carat."

"You just told me they were worth eighteen."

"In such a quantity I expect a discount."

Nikolai had intended to sell the diamonds five hundred carats at a time, if he could. He reasoned that in those amounts he'd be able to get the highest possible price while causing the least stir on the market. Moving five hundred carats here, five hundred there would hardly cause more than a ripple. However, the circumstances Nagel was presenting were too convenient not to take advantage of: a private buyer, someone who would salt away the stones in order to enjoy their appreciated value five or ten years from now. Nikolai doubted he could find a better fit. "I want eighteen," he said.

"But you'll take seventeen."

"Seventeen five."

"Seventeen five is fair," Loodsen chimed in.

Nagel shot Loodsen a lethal glance, then told Nikolai unequivocally: "Seventeen is my offer."

Nikolai believed Nagel would charge his client eighteen. That and then commission. "Done," Nikolai said.

"Done," Nagel agreed. "How do you want to receive payment?"

"A wire transfer to my bank in Geneva."

"Which is?" Nagel had pen ready.

"Zwensen and Company, two-eighteen rue de Rive, twelve-eleven Geneva," Nikolai replied, as though he'd been long familiar with that name and address, instead of having known it only since yesterday. He and Vivian had flown to Geneva for the sole purpose of setting up an account to receive their anticipated millions. Archer had suggested this particular private bank, and a phone call by him had smoothed the way. The director of the bank, Herr Heilig, had personally looked after them, advised on how best to do a transaction of this sort, and opened an account with the deposit of a mere fifty Swiss francs rather than the normally required ten thousand minimum.

"When would you say we might finalize the deal?" Nagel asked.

"How about tomorrow?"

"No problem. Shall we make it here at two o'clock?"

"Fine with me."

Nagel explained how the deal would go: "You bring your thousand carats. As soon as I have looked at them and found them to be of investment quality, I will notify my client so that he can instruct his bank to transfer the seventeen million to your Geneva account. We will wait here for the short while required to complete the transfer, no more than a half hour. You will phone your bank and verify the funds have been received. Everything will be done more or less simultaneously. Does that suit you?"

"I assume you will see that Jacob gets his cut."

"He'll get his," Nagel said ambiguously.

"How much? I want to know." Nikolai made it sound as though the deal depended on it.

"One-half of one percent."

Nikolai mentally moved decimal points and divided by two and realized Jacob's end would come to eighty-five thousand. Certainly adequate compensation for a walk around the block.

Jacob smiled gratefully at Nikolai.

Nikolai tried to think of any loose ends. The deal seemed simple and clean. He conveyed his satisfaction with it by standing and extending his hand to Nagel. Nagel's hand felt narrow and bony, like something that all the juice had been squeezed from.

"Where are you staying?" Nagel asked casually.

"At the Excelsior."

"Good sensible hotel. Perhaps you'd enjoy some amusing company this evening."

"No, thanks. I brought my own."

That night an early dinner.

Both Nikolai and Vivian thought they were hungry, but they just nibbled at their main courses and visually appreciated the sweets.

They were staying at the Rivierenhof, not at the Excelsior as Nikolai had told Nagel. Nikolai wondered about that fib. It hadn't been premeditated. In fact, it had surprised him when it came out, and after the meeting when he was on Shupstraat he decided the reason for it had been instinctive caution. That made him wonder all the more.

Except for the fib, Nikolai reported his afternoon to Vivian. She wouldn't settle for mere highlights, wanted to know word for word what had been said. Throughout dinner she pumped him for details and impressions. Nikolai realized it was her way of making up for not having been there, so for good measure he invented a few things that he believed might color it more for her. Such as his having detected a bugging device incorporated in the Klimt lithograph.

"For what reason would he have a bug?"

"Who knows? Perhaps he uses it to review what was said, inflections and all, giving himself that much of an edge."

"Or maybe it's his protection against renegers."

"People in the diamond business never renege. A word is as good as a written contract."

"You believe that?"

"It saves on legal fees."

"This Nagel, did you get a good look at his eyes?"

"If you mean his irises, no."

"I'll bet if you'd noticed you would have seen his irises change color every now and then. What shade were they, anyway?"

"Pale blue."

"With silver striations bunched up at six o'clock to nine o'clock, right?"

"Hell, I was never that close to him."

"His irises probably went from pale blue to gray-green whenever he lied to you."

"Irises do that?"

"Especially when they're telling giant, crucial lies. With just fibs it's hardly discernible."

Nikolai was relieved to hear that. He locked eyes with her. "I love you, Viv," he said, and after an adequate beat: "Did my irises just change color?"

"I should hope not. Anyway, I couldn't really tell. Your eyes are so dark and deceitful-looking to begin with." She smirked playfully. "Are you certain you saw Nagel's bug?"

Nikolai nodded. He wished she'd drop it. His fibs were infecting his truths.

"Well," she said, "I suppose being Russian you should know a bug when you see one."

Nikolai exaggerated a Russian glower and scratched his head in several places as though bothered by lice. He enjoyed his own sense of humor. Vivian did a stony-faced stare. The waiter came and asked if they would have coffee.

"Demitasse," Vivian ordered, affecting her longest possible *a*. In practically the same breath she told Nikolai: "Am I ever proud of you!"

"Why?" He wanted to hear it from her.

"The way you handled yourself doing business today. You amaze me."

"Are you being serious?"

"I've never been more so. Think of it, darling, and try to suppress your modesty. You come here to Antwerp, a strange city, knowing absolutely no one, without even a twice-removed reference to go on, and within mere hours you've swung a deal that's enormous. Didn't you know you weren't supposed to be such a slick capitalist?"

Nikolai was saved from having to reply by the arrival of the demitasse. The waiter showed off with his pouring of it, flourished the silver server so the brown-black stream that came from its spout was more than a foot long and stopped abruptly without a drop spilled. Nikolai imagined how many customers the waiter had scalded perfecting such technique, how many lawsuits he had caused. There was risk in just about everything.

Vivian used silver tongs to pinch two cubes of sugar into her cup. "Not to muffle any of your thunder, Nickie darling, but your success today proves something I've always believed: there's no big trick to getting filthy rich. Of course, it helps to be a bit filthy to begin with, but really all that's required is a headful of smarts."

"Or a bowlful of diamonds."

"Seventeen million dollars," Vivian mused. "And you've hardly made a dent in your hoard." She brought her tiny gold-rimmed cup to her lips and wriggled her extended pinkie at him. Between sips she asked: "Would you mind terribly if I married you for your money? Among other more important reasons, of course." Before Nikolai could reply that he was agreeable to marrying her and remaining married to her under any conditions, she was off on another sideroad, relating how that afternoon she'd found her way to a delicatessen there on Pelikaanstraat, a kosher place called Moskowitz's, where she'd sat at a counter and had potato pancakes with sour cream and cherry jelly, which were delicious. However, occupying the seat next to her had been an American woman who volunteered loudly that she was from Larchmont, New York, and was disappointed with Antwerp because she'd searched in vain all over the city for a little lizard to add to her collection. The woman had what must have been close to a dozen gold and platinum pins in the form of lizards on the lapels of her suit as well as a couple at the neckline of her blouse. She was veritably crawling with them: lizards studded with green garnets from head to tip of tail and with tiny diamonds or rubies for eyes. "Repulsive little monsters," Vivian said, and, after hardly enough time for a synapse: "You know, probably the most tragic thing is to have tons of money and not an ounce of taste. Thank the angels that shall never be our problem. We'll never have linens on our terrace tables dyed precisely to match the shade of our nearby hibiscus blossoms. It will never occur to us to have a swimming pool constructed in the shape of a heart or with mosaic mermaids on the bottom." A final sip of her demitasse. She set her cup down and held her hand over it to prevent the waiter from doing an encore of his audacious pour. "Damn, I wish you'd thought to get a close look at Nagel's irises," she said while Nikolai signed the bill.

As soon as they were up in their suite, Vivian undressed, swiped the back of her knees with Tabu, toed into a pair of high-heeled mules, and put on a full-length, pale green silk charmeuse robe. She tied its sash firmly. "Why don't you go shave again?" she suggested offhandedly.

Nikolai went into the bathroom, stripped down to nothing, and softened his twelve-hour beard with a steaming facecloth. He heard the slick friction of Vivian moving about in the sitting-room. He considered the power she held over him. Hadn't she intentionally let him stand there watching her get out of her clothes? Hadn't she purposely put on those high heels before anything else? Surely her suggestion that he shave hadn't been an afterthought. He, her man, was like an electric something that she could turn on and off. He lathered his jaws, gazed in the mirror at himself smiling at himself, and knew he wouldn't have it any other way.

When he was done and went out to her he found her seated at the desk. She'd removed the shade from the desk lamp for stronger, more direct light. Before her on the surface of the desk lay two automatic pistols, with silencers, holsters, and other accessories. Nikolai had known she'd brought them along, had tried to reason her out of it and had thought he might have until he saw her unpack them and put them in her dresser drawer beneath a layer of lingerie.

The lighter pistol was hers. A .380 Beretta. Archer had brought it for her a while back because she'd mentioned that she'd feel a bit easier having a firearm of some sort in the flat. She'd quickly learned it and come to feel possessive toward it, and on edgy occasions before sleep she'd check to make sure it was in its place, sharing the shallow drawer of her nightstand with a jar of handcream, satin eyeshades, the telly remote control, and a few pieces of chewy butterscotch toffee that had gone hard and stale. What she particularly liked about the Beretta was its grip, which felt perfect for her hand. Plus the fact that it took a thirteen-round staggered magazine. At various times she took her pistol down to Devon to get in practice; Nikolai had watched her, dead serious, plug away at tin cans set in a row on a fence. He had also come across some paper targets that she'd shot up and kept as a record of her improved accuracy. Scribbled in the upper right corners of the targets were notations such as "30 yards rapid fire Sept. 30." Several recent targets showed all her shots had torn through near the center in practically the same spot. There was no doubt in Nikolai's mind that she knew how to shoot. His only question was when, if ever, she would put that ability to use.

The other pistol was Nikolai's. He'd received it as a stocking stuffer from Vivian last Christmas. A Sig Saur P-226. The sales clerk at Purdy's, where Vivian had bought it, had first suggested a Browning .45, but Vivian had fired that type of pistol a few times with Archer and found it unmanageable. It was enough to make a mercenary soldier flinch, and its recoil was so excessive that half the time it got fired at the sky. No, she didn't deny the Browning .45 had stopping power, she told the clerk, but wasn't hitting bloody essential to stopping? The Sig P-226, however, seemed just right for Nikolai. A 9mm Parabellum, it held fifteen rounds in its magazine, had good heft to it.

The first time Nikolai fired the Sig was in the snow down in Devon. A bright afternoon with the sun glaring off everything, so that Nikolai had difficulty just seeing the quarter-pound-size caviar tin Vivian placed on a fence post for a target. About the size of a human heart, she'd re-marked. He'd never mentioned how he'd won trophies back in his Komsomol days. As he took his stance and aim he could sense her doubt that he'd come within a yard of hitting the tin. He'd show her. He was also motivated by wanting to get this shooting stuff over with. It wasn't compatible with love. Besides, his feet were cold and he hadn't yet had lunch. The first shot he squeezed off sent the tin flying. To prove that hadn't been luck his second shot made it leap and skitter across the snow. Vivian had tried not to appear impressed, praised only the merits of the pistol. He'd handed her the Sig and hurried into the house.

Now there she was with both weapons and a carton of Belgian chocolate.

"Why do that now?" Nikolai asked.

"I've been putting it off," she replied absently, with a huge hunk of extra-bitter chocolate in her mouth, making her cheek appear swollen.

Nikolai stood behind her and watched her break down and clean the Beretta. His love with a lethal thing in her hands, he thought, those same hands that . . .

Some primitive source within him sent a shiver from his tailbone to the base of his skull. It drove him to the refuge of the nearby chair. He sat across its soft lap, his legs angled over its fat stuffed arm. He shouldn't resent Vivian's concern with the pistols, he told himself. What harm in her wanting to feel more a part of what was going on? Observing her from that mental vantage was more comfortable for him. She was so engrossed in her task that she wouldn't take a moment to retie the sash of the robe. The robe slid off her left shoulder. She retrieved it. But the second time it slid off she just let it have its way.

Other parts of her had at various moments amazed Nikolai. This time it was her left shoulder. The raw light was starkly defining it. He was, of course, familiar with its external conformation, thought of it as one of a pair of perfect shoulders, and he knew well from having traveled it so often the fine texture of her skin there. However, it seemed to him unfair and frustrating to be so limited. Would that he were able to feel and know her all the way to her bones. What of the fibers and sinews, the special tissues of her, the bouquets of nerve ends and capillaries? He would, if it were possible, race about inside her with her blood. At certain times more than others it was easier for him to imagine that he was experiencing her experiences. When he was quietly within her, not moving in and out but remaining in, held in, he could sometimes transcend his self and his separateness and feel he was as much being filled as filling. But it was such a transitory sensation, usually lasting no longer than a few breaths.

"I'll bet you've never broken down your Sig," she said, returning him to a wider angle of thought. "You really should, you know. Never know when you might need to depend on such a friend. Do you want me to clean it for you?"

"No."

"I already have." She held up one of the stubby silencers and squinted into it. "I've also loaded three spare clips for you."

"Thanks." Nikolai decided he'd come down to a level as practical as the one she was on. He got up and went into the bedroom. The maid had already prepared the bed for the night. A gold-foil-wrapped Teuscher chocolate mint had been placed on each pillow. Sweet dreams might have been the intention, but wasn't the hotel aware that there was more caffeine in chocolate than in coffee? Nikolai yanked the top sheet down and off onto the floor at the foot. He lay face up on the bed. He didn't realize how his mind was racing until he closed his eyes. The image that kept recurring was the figure 17 with six zeros after it. How would he view his world then? Changed? Merely the imminence of wealth had him looking at it somewhat differently. The anticipation was sort of the same he'd felt as a boy when Grandfather Maksim was getting out the pails and Irina was packing a lunch for the next day when they would go berry picking. If Grandfather Maksim were to materialize right now in this room, Nikolai thought, he would dance around the bed. He would tug at his beard, merrily bob his head from side to side, take a deep breath as though inhaling pure joy, and dance until the perspiration was dropping from his earlobes. Not until the very last, a day or so before dying, had the spark gone from Grandfather Maksim's eyes. Chances were it had come back as soon as he'd passed over, because that was how Nikolai saw him now.

And what of Irina? Nikolai hadn't heard from her since that night in Prague in the crystal works when she'd tried to put him in his place. Was she so self-conscious of having been wrong then that she was now silent and hiding? Didn't she know he would forgive her anything? If she were alive now, Nikolai imagined, he would whisk her off to London, defect her, set her up in one of those creamy clean townhouses on Chester Terrace, and put in a standing order with Pulbrook & Gould to always have huge bouquets fresh in every room. He and she would sit in a glider in her garden and remark to one another how lovely life was. He would observe her hands and see peace in them and perhaps she would read aloud those letters from her anonymous lover and tell Nikolai about him and allow their sentimentality to spill back over the past. His father wouldn't be there, just not be there ever. Irina would have a car and driver. She would dress expensively, feel youthful, and be discriminating with her passion.

Seventeen million dollars.

Only a fifth of what the ultimate total would be. Five times seventeen was eighty-five. Eighty-five million. He would have to come up with four more buyers as cooperative as Nagel. That would take some doing. Nikolai disliked all the guile and wangling at this level of the diamond business. It seemed to him that the reputation the business had for being traditionally honest was used to cover the hustle of the dealers ever ready to outsmart one another. No matter. First this transaction with Nagel, then four others equally discreet, Nikolai thought. As long as he and Vivian were there in Antwerp, they might as well stay on and get it over with. Every day wouldn't be like today. It would take a week, more likely two. They'd be climbing the walls by then, especially Vivian. Her opinion of Antwerp had already descended. She'd chosen to mention how that afternoon when she'd passed an old man with an old dog seated in a doorway both had growled at her.

The telephone chirped.

Nikolai picked up, expecting it would be Archer. No one else knew where they were.

It was Nagel. He apologized for intruding on Nikolai's privacy.

"How did you locate me?" Nikolai asked.

"It wasn't all that difficult."

"I changed hotels," Nikolai offered.

"So the concierge at the Excelsior informed me."

Nikoali had never been near the Excelsior. He felt embarrassingly transparent.

"Anyway," Nagel told him, "there were only so many hotels where you could be, considering the requirements of your taste."

Now flattery. "What can I do for you?"

"Perhaps an important favor."

He wants out of the deal, Nikolai thought. They'd shaken on it. It was a done deal. No outs.

"After you left my office," Nagel said, "I had a telephone conversation with my client."

"And?"

"In describing the fine quality of your goods I evidently

got a bit carried away, and, well, you know how a rich American can be when he gets it into his head that he absolutely *must* own something. My client is now pressing me to obtain more than the thousand pieces for him. When I told him that might not be possible, he got upset."

"Merely upset?"

"To the extent that our transaction may be in jeopardy."

"So he walks." A shrug in his tone.

"I don't want to lose him."

Neither did Nikolai, really. If this deal fell through it would mean today was wasted. No seventeen million head start. He'd have to scratch around Antwerp tomorrow still looking for a first buyer. "What is it you want me to do?"

"Do better than a thousand pieces."

"How many better?"

"Judging from my client's frame of mind I'd say as many as you can come up with. Within reason, of course."

Here for the grabbing was the solution to what he'd been lying there concerned about, Nikolai thought. A chance to turn over the entire lot in one fell swoop. The only reason for not doing that was how visible five thousand carats of Aikhal would be hitting the open market all at once. With Nagel and his American investor it wouldn't be the open market. So in that regard a thousand carats might as well be five thousand. What was more, Nagel believed these diamonds were from Botswana. That seemed incredible. With their uniform color and cut they were so obviously Aikhal goods. Apparently Nagel had "bad eyes," which wasn't to say his vision was clinically impaired, but rather that he was one of those who couldn't tell the source of one diamond from the next. Many dealers couldn't but claimed they could, because the ability was an accepted measure of knowledge in the trade. It was true that diamonds from, say, Sierra Leone had certain characteristics which set them apart from others, and a dealer with "good eyes" could see that. In this instance, however, Nagel was about four thousand miles off. That was the convincer for Nikolai, along with the prospect of wrapping up everything tomorrow and getting out of Antwerp, getting on with the better life. He told Nagel: "Any amount above the initial thousand pieces would have to be at the full going rate."

Nagel protested.

Nikolai stood firm. Eighteen thousand a carat.

"It seems you have your knee on my neck," Nagel said, capitulating.

"Eighteen then?"

"Done."

"Done."

"But you haven't yet said how many more pieces you'll be bringing to the deal. I must let my client know tonight."

"A few short of five thousand."

"Five? That should satisfy the bastard."

CHAPTER
◆·◆·◆ **22** ◆·◆·◆

PROMPTLY AT TWO THE NEXT AFTERNOON, NIKOLAI AND
Vivian were at Nagel's office. Nagel was surprised that
Vivian had come along. He was polite, but his cordiality
was forced and it was evident he disapproved of her being
there. Nikolai chalked that up to the chauvinistic streak
which still ran wide through the diamond business, especially at the upper levels. The System, for example, had
never allowed a woman on its board of directors, and none
of its top executives was female. Typical was the sardonic
remark that women were the recipients of diamonds and
that was concession enough.

Nikolai had mentioned this attitude to Vivian, thinking
she might prefer not to be where she wasn't wanted.

She, while artfully smudging powdery brown eye shadow
on her left lid, had told him: "If you think for one second
I'm going to let you traipse around alone carrying many
millions in diamonds, think again." She let that sink in for
the time it took her to outline her lips with a tiny pointed
brush and fill them in vibrant pink straight from the tube.
Then she added: "There are more places than not in this
world where they'll cut off your whole lower arm to steal
a cheap wristwatch, and from what I gather, Antwerp is not
exactly hallowed territory."

Nikolai knew then it would be futile to try to dissuade
her. He didn't say anything when she put her Beretta in
her purse, nor did he resist when she held up his shoulder
holster with his Sig in it for him to put on. He checked
in the mirror to make sure the pistol wasn't apparent be-

neath his suit jacket. If there'd been even the suggestion of a bulge he would have refused to wear it.

Now in Nagel's office he felt the hardness of the Sig against his side below his armpit and was rather glad he had it on. It was as though the pistol had assumed a certain responsibility. Nikolai was now also glad that Vivian had come along. Having her witness his closing this deal certainly wasn't going to hurt his stock. It was an event, something they'd recall any number of times in the future. Be sure to take in the details so they could be played back later, he told himself. He glanced at Vivian sitting there in her neat blue linen suit. She was squinting across the desk at Nagel. No doubt trying to focus on his irises. He probably thought she was myopic. As long as she didn't whip out her magnifying monocle.

"Well, let's get to it," Nagel said, limbering his fingers. "Did you speak to your client?"

"Of course."

Nagel appeared impatient, Nikolai thought. Perhaps that was his normal behavior whenever he got this close to profit. Nikolai snapped open his attaché case and took out the diamonds. He had them in ten separate oversize briefkes, five hundred pieces in each briefke, except for the one marked on the outside with a red x, which was nine pieces short. He placed the briefkes on the desk.

Nagel unfolded them and examined their contents. He stirred the layers of diamonds with a finger and cursorily scanned them through his loupe. As he finished with each lot he put it aside, without comment.

Finally, he was done with all ten. He sat back and locked eyes with Nikolai.

Nikolai didn't like that look. It had a smug, adversarial quality to it. "Satisfied?" Nikolai asked. Now he was the impatient one.

"Yes."

"Phone your client."

Nagel reached to the telephone and pressed one of its intercom signals.

At once the door on the left swung open.

In came George Pulver, head of the System's Security Section. And two of his men with their right hands partially inserted beneath their jackets, ready to draw pistols.

"I told you we'd nail you," Pulver said.

The reasons this was happening began coming together in Nikolai's mind, like the instantaneous reassembling of something that had been shattered. Nagel was a large part of it. He hated Nagel for it and wanted Nagel to see his hate, but the gray man was up now, standing at the window with his back to the room, as though what was happening in it was too distasteful for him. Nikolai had the urge to reach over and bash him on the head. Because of Pulver's two men he thought better of it.

"I'll take these, thank you," Pulver said, picking up the ten briefkes.

"They're not yours to take," Nikolai snapped.

"Just for evidence, Borodin. I'll be giving you a memo for them."

Nikolai glanced at Vivian. She appeared calm, as though she were no more than an interested observer. However, Nikolai knew her eyes and saw in them a mixture of futility and fury. He recognized it as the same emotion she'd revealed that day recently in the stream in Devon when she'd lost that huge trout. She had no idea who Pulver was. Probably she thought this was a holdup.

Pulver doubled a large rubber band around the briefkes and put them in his business case. He brought out a memorandum, the sort of receiptlike form used in the diamond trade when one dealer is receiving goods on consignment from another. "How many carats exactly?" he asked.

Nikolai told him.

"Why the odd number?"

Nikolai didn't tell him.

"Anyway"—Pulver exposed tea-stained teeth in a smile—"what a nice fat lot." He wrote in the amount of carats on the memo. Evidently the rest of the memo had been filled out in advance, because he signed it, tore off his copy, and left the original. "Ta," he said with mock sympathy, and the next moment he and his men and the diamonds were gone.

It hadn't happened, Nikolai told himself. It was something he'd feared that had manifested itself as an illusion. A blink or two would return him to the reality of Nagel phoning his client.

Vivian placed her hand consolingly on his arm. "The fuckers!" she gritted.

Nikolai picked up the memorandum. It was a printed form bearing the System's letterhead. He expected to see his name in the RECEIVED FROM: space.

But even worse.

The memo was made out to Almazjuvelirexport.

CHAPTER
❖❖❖**23**❖❖❖

SAVICH CAME OUT OF THE CRILLON, PAUSED A MOMENT TO survey the sky over Paris, and headed in the opposite direction from his destination.

Instead of going across the Place de la Concorde and into the Jardin des Tuilleries he'd decided to put the pleasures of some of the old lesser streets of the 1st arrondissement into his afternoon. He wasn't all that familiar with the area, but he'd chosen not to take along a map of Paris. What matter if he got temporarily lost, tricked by dead ends and alleyways? Wasn't that the amusement of any maze? And this one offered so many delightful distractions. He could hardly take a step without being diverted. A selection of silver-headed antique canes offered for sale, a beachscape as well done as a Boudin that he promised himself he'd return to and purchase, aged bushel baskets of silver-sided fish presented on beds of glistening seaweed, a glance from a very pretty twenty-year-old that was more affecting than a thousand spoken flatteries. Rue Saint-Hyacinthe, rue des Pyramides, rue Molière. Oh, how fond he was of this city that never merely tolerated him. Here he was assuredly accepted, often made to feel as desirable as a prize. A well-off older gentleman conscientious of his appearance, his agility and spirit lubricated by passion, not even the corners of his eyes given to ennui or fatigue. He was both teacher and taker, but never one more than the other. A purveyor of experience. To Savich, such self-value was not conceit. It was honest insight that being in Paris brought to focus.

Before traversing the frantic traffic on the Avenue de l'Opéra he stopped at the counter of a bistro for a *citron*

pressé. He didn't linger, downed the drink as though eager
to get to its pungent, saliva-inducing aftertaste. He smacked
his lips, ran his tongue across the fringes of his mustache,
decided not to tip the surly barman, and continued on his
way. After several more circuitous blocks he came onto
the sobering solemnity of the Bank of France, and took that
as indication he'd meandered enough. He crossed over the
rue de Rivoli and entered the Louvre end of the Tuilleries.

It took a moment for him to become acclimated to the
sudden change to openness and green. He spotted Valkov
fifty yards away in the parterres, waiting close by one of
the Maillol statues. Savich considered the contrast presented by Valkov and that blackened bronze of a nude
female, twice life-size, exaggeratedly robust, so powerful she
could recline on the merest axis of her hip. Valkov was
the perfect masculine foil for her dominant carnality. Valkov could crawl all over such a creature, caress her and
lick her and pump at her for a hundred years, and still be
baffled by her insatiability. Valkov was such an idiot, a
dreadful mechanic, when it came to women, Savich thought.

Last night Valkov had telephoned from Leningrad. He'd
tried at six and every hour thereafter until around midnight,
when Savich decided he might as well take the call. Valkov
said an unanticipated problem had come up. A minor
matter. He apologized for bothering Minister Savich with
it, but it required a bit of the minister's attention. Savich
understood that Valkov's tone and choice of words were
cryptic, that he was supposed to understand them to mean
there was a serious crisis. However, it was not the first
time Valkov had cried panic. Each previous time had
amounted to nothing, been actually a trifling matter or a
false alarm. As well, Valkov was not above inventing a
scurry to facilitate his personal wishes. Very likely, Savich
thought, there was no more to it than Valkov's wife, Yelena,
wanting to be in Paris at this time.

Valkov didn't see Savich approaching. He was at the
head end of the reclining statue. Savich came around the
opposite end and ran his hand along the musculature of
the statue's thighs, noting that the sun-struck bronze was

warmer than flesh. With the grass underfoot he was able to get close behind Valkov and purposely startle him with: "So, what's the urgency?"

Valkov spun around.

At once Savich realized this was a seriously concerned Valkov. The near-white blond brows were ridged with worry, the pale lips tight. Valkov didn't reply. He took a sweeper from his jacket pocket and held it aimed point-blank at Savich. The electronic device was about the size of a pack of chewing gum. Its tiny red light remained unlit, indicating that Savich was not wired with a recorder and did not have any sort of bug on his person. Savich just stood still and allowed it. Two years ago as part of their arrangement they had agreed not to be offended when either of them took such precautions. Savich had forgotten to bring along his sweeper, so he borrowed and used Valkov's. Thus assured, they could speak freely.

"Churcher called," Valkov blurted, as though those words had been so long in his mouth they'd become uncomfortable. "His security people intercepted a carry."

"Where?"

"Antwerp."

"Which did they get?"

"The June number one."

"How the hell did it get to Antwerp? I thought it was understood that we would steer clear of Antwerp." Savich was livid. Ninety million down the drain, half of it his. "You fucked up, didn't you? You saw what looked like an easy opportunity and went for it."

"I had nothing to do with it."

Savich had to look away. "At least," he said, controlling himself, "there's no way we can be connected."

"No, but Churcher has Almazjuvelirexport involved."

"Circumstantially, perhaps."

"Directly."

"I doubt that."

"The shipment was seized from Borodin."

"Who?"

"Our Nikolai Borodin. He was trying to sell it."

"Impossible. Churcher was fabricating, trying to suck you into admitting something. I trust you didn't go for it."

"I only told him I'd take the matter up with you. He said he'd been trying to reach you in Moscow but you were avoiding his calls. He's certain he has you red-handed this time. That was how he put it."

A scoffing snort from Savich.

"I don't think Churcher was making it up."

"He's not above that," Savich said. "In fact, he's attempted a similar tactic with me several times in the past. In the final analysis he had nothing but apologies."

"He has Borodin on videotape negotiating the deal."

"So he claims."

"Churcher let me hear a section of the audio of it over the phone. It was undoubtedly Borodin's voice. Anyway, Churcher is anxious for you to come to London and meet face to face with him to work things out. He said he'd be happy to play the entire tape for you."

Savich imagined being in a hot seat at 11 Harrowhouse, having to suffer Churcher's condescension. "How would Borodin manage to get hold of that shipment?" he asked, and, assuming Valkov did not have an answer, went on to make his point: "That impossibility bears out Churcher is bluffing, no matter what you heard over long distance."

"Borodin is a sneak."

"And you're an infallible judge of character," Savich said with sarcasm. For perhaps the thousandth time he regretted that it was Valkov with whom he was involved. As always before he forgave himself for that by thinking if not Valkov it probably would almost certainly have been someone similarly flawed.

"Borodin is also the worst kind of opportunist."

"He speaks well of you."

Valkov missed the wryness. "He should. I've never given him reason to feel otherwise."

Savich walked away, as though searching for more breathable air. Valkov followed. They stopped beside a large circular pool on which boats were being sailed. "Have you checked with Zuzana?" Savich asked.

"I phoned this morning from the airport."

"They should be able to discredit Churcher."

"All Zuzana could tell me was that the June shipment left Prague on schedule. They gave me the bill of lading number, and I'm having our broker here run it down. By now the shipment should be somewhere in customs. Normally it takes a few days, sometimes a week, to clear, and as you know, we've always taken care to be patient about that, not to attract attention by placing too much importance on a carton of crystal. Anyway, assuming the carton arrives, when it's opened we'll know."

"I already know. They'll break the crystal; the goods will be there."

"You seem to be defending Borodin."

Savich challenged him with a glare. "Is that your impression?"

A submissive shrug from Valkov. "I only meant that perhaps you believe Borodin incapable of such a thing."

"What I believe is that our methods are too sound for it to happen. Where's the hole? There isn't a hole anywhere along the line into which Borodin could have stuck his hand. Zuzana did its part; we know the shipment has been made. Churcher has to be bluffing."

"How do you explain the tape I heard?'

"Faked, probably . . . put together using bits and pieces of conversations Borodin had at various times during meetings there at 11 Harrowhouse. In this electronic day, something such as that is quite possible."

"And the videotape?"

"There won't be one. It will have been unfortunately lost, erased, destroyed, or whatever. Churcher will swear he had it and tell us how fortunate we are that he no longer does."

"The tape I heard did not sound assembled. It had a candid quality—the words weren't clipped or in any way unnatural."

"As well they could have gotten someone, a performer perhaps, to imitate Borodin's voice."

"No. I trust my ears. It was Borodin."

"All right, convince me. Where was the hole?"

"I know Borodin better than you do. I've been subjected to his attitude, his arrogance, and his cunning. All
you've gotten is his good behavior. Borodin is a sly one,
believe me. I think in his sneaking around he happened
to hit upon something and was able to figure it out. He
had all sorts of access."

"From out of the ground of Aikhal to the hands of our
buyers there's no paper trail, not one written word. Or is
there?"

"Not that I'm aware of. But then how the hell could
I know if one of our people is keeping a written account?
There are those in this world who can't keep large figures
in their head. It's as though they don't believe them unless
they can see them on paper."

Valkov had a point, Savich thought, but didn't let his
attention remain on it. He noticed a paunchy French father
sharing the amusement of a remote-controlled model speedboat with his boy of seven or so. While the boy operated
the control of the boat, making it perform sharp turns and
various zigzags, the father gulped from a bottle of beer.
They exchanged responsibilities and the boy took swigs.

"We should play it safe," Valkov said.

"How?"

"Have Borodin canceled."

Valkov took Savich's silence to mean he was considering
that course of action. Actually, Savich was loathing it. Up
until now he'd been only too glad that this ugly area of
their arrangement had been left entirely to Valkov. Valkov
had always seen to those expediencies, and Savich didn't
even want to hear about them. Now, however, it was imperative that Savich put his foot down in this, Valkov's
territory.

"We'll do no such thing," he told Valkov firmly.

"We must go on the assumption that Borodin has somehow learned too much. What he knows he can tell."

"You're being paranoid."

"I'm being prudent," Valkov contended, "and I don't

understand why *you* aren't. Why would you allow the risk, even if it's only a slight risk? You don't owe Borodin."

"That's true."

"After I received the phone call from Churcher, the first picture that came to mind was that bastard Borodin in a room with your most ambitious enemies, Kulinich, for example, helping himself to a deputy ministership by spewing what he knows. All they would need is a thread to pull on and everything could come unraveled."

A grunt from Savich sounded assenting.

"When you fall, I fall," Valkov said. He lighted a cigarette and took two long consecutive pulls on it. He exhaled the smoke through his nostrils.

For that moment Savich saw him as a creature with tusks saying, "We'll both rest easier with Borodin gone."

Savich lowered his eyes and nodded thoughtfully. "I'll handle Borodin," he said.

"What will you do?"

"Whatever is necessary."

"There's no need for you to—"

"Meanwhile you see that it's business as usual. Take a trip to Aikhal. Check our conduit all the way up the line. If you find a hole, patch it in any way you believe best." Savich got Valkov by the eyes to tell him unequivocally: "You're to leave this Borodin situation to me. Is that understood?" Taking Valkov's yes for granted, he turned and walked across the parterres.

Watching Savich go, Valkov thought it strange how a man he'd always considered an expert when it came to strategy could suddenly be so shortsighted. He supposed that was how certain people reacted to life-or-death pressure, no matter how level-headed they might otherwise be. What a catastrophe if *both* he and Savich were that sort. Good thing his natural obligation to survive had his mind honed sharp and decisive. Nothing Savich had said had changed his stand on how best to deal with Borodin. No second thoughts about having sent those three killers last night. They might already be in Antwerp; Borodin might already be dead. If so, Savich already owed him gratitude.

On his walk back to the Crillon, Savich thought he had adequately shortened Valkov's leash. The man had been only a degree or so from getting beyond control, but now he'd return to Leningrad and be just normally nervous. Churcher remained to be dealt with. Savich decided he would wait and allow Churcher's temperature to cool a bit. Contrary to what he'd led Valkov to believe, he didn't doubt that Churcher had the evidence he claimed. Churcher might be one to feint and jab lightly every once in a while just to make it known the fight was still on, but he would never attempt a bluff this aggressive. No, Churcher had Nikolai on tape, all right. Fortunately, in Churcher's mind Nikolai was Almazjuvelirexport. It would never occur to Churcher that Nikolai was acting on his own. Churcher was blinded by his eagerness to catch Almazjuvelirexport violating its agreement with the System, exceeding its marketing quota of finished diamonds. What a coup for him to finally prove the perfidy of the "bloody Rooskies." Yes, Churcher would now have his day, Savich thought, and in this instance he'd be only too glad to give it to him. In a month or so he'd go to London and confront Churcher, offer weak excuses, and appear contrite. He would ruefully admit he'd under-estimated Churcher's efficiency and patch up the rest of the affair by making trade concessions. No one would be the wiser.

But what of Nikolai? How much *did* he know? Did he know that he, Savich, was involved? If so, it was likely he'd had that knowledge the week before last in Moscow when he'd come to the apartment all concerned about the futility of his love for Vivian and about to give up on it. Was Nikolai so cunning that he could conceal such a thing so well, such an accomplished actor that he could sit there and seem to be humble while looking down his throat? Impossible, Savich decided quickly. He'd stake his life on it. Nevertheless, he told himself, Nikolai had managed some-how to get hold of the June number one shipment. How? The way he and Valkov had the thing set up, only the essential few along the conduit knew what sort of contra-band they were handling. There was the collaborator in

Aikhal, the two in Prague, and the recipients here in Paris. All were trustworthy, and by now, too deeply involved not to be. Savich wished Nikolai were there walking beside him so he could put it to him. Whatever Nikolai had done, it must have required ingenuity and risks. He'd enjoy hearing about it, and someday he would, straight from Nikolai's mouth. When that time came he wouldn't allow Nikolai to understate his resourcefulness. He believed he already knew Nikolai's motives: In one ninety-million dollar swoop a counter to his feelings of professional inadequacy in the West, and a solution to his Vivian dilemma. Savich smiled. It had been naive of Nikolai, though, to try to sell those diamonds in Antwerp. Evidently he wasn't aware that the city was rife with informants in the pay of the System. Except for that oversight, Nikolai probably would have pulled it off, Savich thought. Too bad he hadn't.

Savich entered the Crillon and went to the front desk for his key. As he turned to go to the elevator he spotted Yelena Valkova. She was seated in one of the lobby's gilded bergères. By far the most beautiful woman in sight, in some designer's afternoon dress of bold pink, which was good for her olive complexion. Savich believed Yelena must have noticed him when he came in, because now, even though she was looking in his direction, there wasn't a flicker of recognition in her eyes. On his way to the elevator he passed so close by her she could have reached out and touched him. At once she uncrossed her long, ideal legs and rose from the chair. Savich entered the elevator. The elevator operator started to slide the doors closed but then held them open—for Yelena to step in and face front, still aloof. The elevator doors were closed.

They went up.

CHAPTER

·•·•·24·•·•·

AN ENORMOUS SIGH OF RELIEF FROM VIVIAN. "FAREWELL to this place!"

Nikolai agreed with a reflective nod.

"And never to return!"

"It wasn't very good to us, was it?" Nikolai said glumly. He increased the pressure of his grip on the steering wheel.

"Don't start that again," Vivian warned. "If you go grim on me again I'll get out and walk."

Nikolai pulled the corners of his mouth up into a phony smile and did a few fast blinks to make his eyes look happy for her.

"Russians," she muttered, scrunched down so her chin was on her chest. "Give them an ounce of the dismals and they take a ton."

Nikolai believed the loss of nearly ninety million dollars would weigh on anyone more than an ounce, but he didn't say anything.

It was Saturday morning and drizzling. They were in the rented BMW headed west on N-617. Since Thursday and the Nagel fiasco they had remained in the suite at the Rivierenhof. Vivian had been ready to leave Thursday, but Nikolai got stuck in a chair in the sitting room. He wouldn't budge, just sat there in his anger and regret. The scene with Pulver and Nagel was like a loop across the front of his mind. He couldn't stop it from playing and replaying. He kept seeing his chance meeting with the slob Loodsen, at the Diamond Club. No wonder no one there wanted anything to do with Loodsen. They knew him for what he was, a *stukach* for the System. How slickly he'd been taken in by Loodsen and steered to Nagel. Loodsen with his poor-me and bullying-brother-in-law act. Loodsen probably did nothing but hang around the club every day on the lookout for anyone wanting to deal contraband diamonds. Churcher had often boasted about the covert network the System had going throughout the trade on every level. Nikolai had suspected that was an exaggeration, a purposely nourished rumor intended to keep diamond dealers on edge and in line. Now he knew it to be fact. Hindsight was indeed the informer of wisdom.

How gullible he'd been, Nikolai thought. Shamefully gullible. He could hear Loodsen and Nagel arguing their well-rehearsed lines about whether the diamonds were from Botswana or Namibia, knowing all the while they were Aikhal goods. And he, sitting there in Nagel's office in the euphoria of imminent Western-size wealth. What a comfortable, elated feeling it had been, though, to have all those millions within his grasp. A sort of enchantment, he realized now, a levitation. It had put a remarkable soft edge and diffusion on everything. How swiftly he'd become used to it, the prospect of never again having to ask the price, indulging old wants and new expensive impetuosities, buying for Vivian, being able to look straight across at Archer. He'd given quite a lot of thought to the dispelling of the castelike awkwardness between himself and Archer, had imagined them giving each other stock-market tips, things like that.

What could have been.

Now what was he left with?

Painful consequences.

The System now had a solid case against Almazjuveli-rexport. No longer mere allegations, but proof. With that advantage Churcher would be anxious to get to Savich. Nikolai imagined Savich's dismay when Churcher broke it to him. Savich would soon realize the no-win position Nikolai had caused. No matter that Savich deserved none of the blame, he'd have to suffer it, lose face, and eat as much crow as Churcher heaped on his plate. It would also be personally embarrassing for Savich, because he'd put such stock in Nikolai. How could he begin to explain to Savich the links of circumstances that had brought this on? Even if he was able to again get the minister's ear and told the truth from beginning to end it would still appear that he'd stolen five thousand carats of finished Aikhal goods.

He'd lost a friend, Nikolai thought sadly.

What was more, he'd lost a country.

He couldn't possibly return to Russia. If he went back the endlessly repeated question would be: *Comrade, from whom did you get those diamonds?* And he didn't know the answer. Another question would be: *Comrade, why were you trying to sell the diamonds?* That he could answer, but not without surely condemning himself to being tied to a rung on a post so he couldn't move and spoil the aims of those whose fingers would squeeze and send six hunks of metal tearing into his heart; or, at the least, to being transported somewhere so cold it didn't deserve a name, where, underfed and improperly clothed, he would die of exposure.

Like it or not, his only choice now was the West. If it would have him. What would he do for a living? He was unavoidably up against that now. He remembered Grandfather Maksim telling him about how after the Revolution Russian émigrés who were princes had worked as waiters in Paris restaurants. And they were the fortunate ones. Many dukes had literally gone begging, mere countesses took to the street. Well, he wasn't that bad off. He might put to use his linguistic talents, interpret or translate or do correspondence. His marketing background was too narrow to be considered valuable. Except, of course, to the System. Churcher would hire him in a second as an adviser. He knew the confidential ins and outs of the Soviet diamond interests. He knew, for example, that the Soviet Union was hoarding its large stones, squirreling away the really fine big ones for the day when the System might decide it no longer needed to rely on the Soviet Union as a primary source. If, for example, there ever really should be a major Australian find. He knew what the current Soviet inventory of gem quality amounted to, practically within a hundred carats. He knew the exact number of diamond-bearing kimberlite pipes discovered yet left untapped in the Yakut region. He knew precisely how many such pipes the Soviet geologists' projections said remained to be found. What he knew would make Churcher not sleep, would make every owner of diamonds in the world realize he or she had overpaid for a scarcity that did not exist—indeed, Churcher would hire him, keep him under wraps, pay him well for being an informer.

He'd rather be a waiter.

It was at this impasse that his thoughts looped and he recommenced with his "Russian" conversation.

At first Vivian had tried nonchalance. *"Tant pis,"* she said, "it was only ninety million." She went about brushing her hair as though nothing of all that much importance had occurred. "You'll probably lose more than that three or four times. Most men who are worth anything do."

When nonchalance didn't work she tried to tempt him out of it. First with sweets. She ordered about a dozen of the most elaborate creations room service could come up with. Peaches in kirsch, *gâteau millefeuille*, blancmange, profiteroles, and petits fours. Nikolai just sat there looking at them. She spoon-fed him vanilla Bavarian cream and he opened his mouth for her and swallowed it. He even smiled, but just fleetingly. That having failed, she tried to tempt him out of it with herself. She quick-changed into silk tap panties with camisole, without camisole, camisole without tap panties. A peach-colored teddy, a turquoise chemise. She pretended to be tending to her toenails with one leg up, she dropped some bobby pins on purpose so she could retrieve them stiff-legged with her bottom toward him. She lay on the sofa in an absolutely-alone-time sort of position, lay on the floor and did certain calisthenics, including pelvic lifts, wasted an entire repertoire of such enticing inadvertencies. When, Friday night, she put on a pair of tight antelope gloves and massaged him here and there without getting even a tiny spasm of response, she'd just about had it. "God, but you're shitty company," she said. "I'm going out." She dressed hurriedly, thinking any second he'd prevent her from doing so. She didn't get even a "Where?"

or a "Be careful" or a "When will you be back?" from him. At that point she was honestly angrier than she wanted to admit. But not angry enough. She gathered up her purse and went to the foyer. He was faced away, still in that chair. She opened the door, making sure the sound of the knob turning and the latch retracting was distinct. She remained in the foyer but slammed the door as though she'd gone. Hearing the unequivocalness of that, he'd rush to catch her, stop her, hold her. After two long minutes of just standing there waiting she came back into the sitting room, flung her purse in his direction, and went to bed. With all her clothes on.

That morning, Saturday morning, she'd been awakened by a sound that resembled bubbles gurgling up to a watery surface. Whatever it was, it was coming from the bathroom. She got up, looked in, and saw Nikolai seated nude on the edge of the bidet. He had both hands over his mouth, trying to stifle the laughter that was coming up out of him. He hadn't wanted to disturb her, but now that she was up he removed his hands from his mouth and let it come full force. It was an all-out belly laugh. Her first thought, because she was still half asleep, was that he'd gone mad, and how would he be able to hug her when he'd be hugging himself in a straitjacket? But then between outbursts he looked at her and she knew the siege had been broken. Thank the angels! No more the mope, he was seeing the amusing side of it all. Perhaps he'd at last learned from her that it was best to allow money to have its slippery way, that it wasn't even necessary for it to go in one hand and out the other, it could sometimes go right through any hand that tried to clutch it, so one might just as well accept it for the chicane that it was. His laugh was infectious. She caught it. She sat on the toilet next to him on the bidet and simultaneously began laughing and peeing. Soon they were both so weakened from laughter they tumbled from their perches, went to their knees on the rectangular bath-mat, and ended up like a couple of supplicating Muslims, but facing each other rather than Mecca.

Now on Belgian National Route 617 they were going

seventy through the cool drizzle. Nikolai turned on the demister to volatilize the ghosts that their warmths had attracted to the windows. To demonstrate that he was still in high spirits he hummed a bit and whistled a bit and sang snatches of a Noel Coward refrain from *Set to Music:*

> "*I've been to a marvelous party,*
> *Elise made an entrance with May,*
> *You'd never have guessed*
> *From her fisherman's vest*
> *That her bust had been whittled away.*
> *Poor Lulu got fried on chianti*
> *And talked about esprit de corps.*
> *Maurice made a couple of passes at Gus*
> *And Freddie, who hates any kind of a fuss,*
> *Did half the Big Apple and twisted his truss,*
> *I couldn't have liked it more!*"

Nikolai sang the last several lines with arch facial expressions and appropriate drollness. Vivian had never seen him more un-Russian. They had often sung Noel Cowards to pass the time while driving and tried to stump each other with obscure Coward lines. Vivian knew this one well but didn't join in, just enjoyed being Nikolai's captive audience. As a form of applause she smiled her best smile and thought how fortunate she was to be able to love him so much. Should she mention that counting today she was eight days overdue? She decided now wasn't the best time to tuck that into his carry. Quite possibly he might already know. All he had to do was figure the number of days since her last period, and he was the sort of man who might. Anyway, if she couldn't make it a topic, the least they could do was celebrate.

She broke out one of the two bottles of wine she'd had room service bring up at the last minute that morning. The most expensive wine on the Rivierenhof's list, Pétrus '43. She thought what the hell, as long as she was going to sign for the hotel bill using her Visa card, and as long as the Visa people were going to have to dun her interminably for payment, she might as well stretch the splurge that much more. To open the wine she used the corkscrew she'd "borrowed" from the hotel tray the wine had been brought on. She poured the wine into goblets also "borrowed" from the same source. So Nikolai could keep his mind on the road, she clinked their goblets for him and handed him his.

"*Nazdorovye!*" she toasted with growling Russian fervor.

"Cheers," he rejoined, very British.

They gulped.

She propped the bottle between her thighs and held it there with pressure while she dug into her carryall for the napkin-wrapped baguette from their hotel breakfast. She broke off a hunk of the bread, dunked it into her wine, and swiftly, to avoid dripping, extended it to Nikolai's mouth. He barely opened fast enough.

"Blood and flesh," she said, and after saying that realized what would have been more fitting. "Blood *or* flesh," she revised, and popped some wine-sogged bread into her mouth.

"You give good communion," Nikolai remarked.

"So the showgirl said to the bishop," she quipped.

"Are you sure you don't want to go down to Deauville?"

That had been the original plan: after financial success in Antwerp, as many days as they wanted in Deauville. A suite at the Golf, afternoon champagne at the Bar du Ciro's, the casino each night. It didn't matter that it was slightly off-season. They wouldn't ever let social timing dictate, none of that "It's August and we simply must be in Antibes" crap.

"We wouldn't have to stay in Deauville," Nikolai suggested. "We could drive right through to Le Touquet and catch the air ferry to Lydd."

"No," Vivian decided, careful not to sound disappointed. "Let's go to the tulips." A while back she'd read a travel-magazine article on Holland and had mentally put the tulip fields of Alsmeer and Lisse into her "perhaps someday" file. Now, if Nikolai had asked, she would have sworn that the travel angels had guided her to that article, because what side trip could have been more convenient—and less expensive? Less than a day's drive away, and, no doubt, bucolic accommodations. Seeing all those tulips was exactly the sort of parenthetical distraction they needed to recount their blessings, she reasoned. She took a road map from the door pocket. Earlier she'd folded the map to make it more manageable and marked the best route with a blue eyeliner pencil. "We go north when we come to Sixty," she said.

It was at that moment Nikolai first noticed the Saab, a maroon late-model sedan. He merely saw it in his rear-view mirror about a hundred yards behind, and thought nothing special of it. Within a few miles there was Route 60. Nikolai turned off. So did the maroon Saab. And only minutes later at the border, while getting passed through Dutch customs, Nikolai looked back and saw the same Saab pull over to the side of the road, which seemed a bit strange. It occurred to him that perhaps the reason it had pulled over was so it could keep its distance, thus preventing him from a closer look. Then again, the reason could be as mundane as taking a moment to make sure papers, pass-ports, car registration, and so on were in order. Nikolai believed he accepted that explanation, but as he drove away from customs he couldn't refrain from glancing back. The Saab had just then driven up to the customs station, right on cue.

Over the seventeen miles of minor road from the border to Perkpolder the maroon Saab made Nikolai increasingly uneasy. He pressed the BMW up to ninety. The Saab did the same. He slowed abruptly to thirty. So did the Saab, all the while keeping its distance.

"What the hell are you doing?" Vivian asked.

"Just fooling around," Nikolai fibbed.

"You've sloshed wine on me." Her white shorts were stained at the crotch, and there were red splatters on her white cotton knit cardigan. "Maybe I should drive."

He apologized.

"Okay," she said. "But no more of that."

By the time they arrived at the ferry landing in Perk-polder, Nikolai was convinced they were being followed, but he still kept it to himself. It was the System, he thought, some of Pulver's snoops. Keeping him under surveillance for a while, being routinely diligent after Thursday's contretemps. Well, he'd let them know he was aware of them, if they hadn't already gathered as much from his driving. The ferry was probably something they hadn't counted on. It presented them with an impasse. They could either come aboard and let him have a closer look or wait for the next ferry an hour from now and lose him.

Nikolai paid the required fare and drove across the treaded steel ramp and on into the belly of the ferry. He was directed to steer the BMW into a barely adequate space and pull it up until it came in touch with the bumper of the car ahead. Vehicles were being packed in all around. A scarred-up van got in directly behind the BMW, so when Nikolai looked in the rear-view mirror all he could see was some of its grill and windshield. The side-view mirror presented him only a raking perspective of various wet metals and glass. It was claustrophobic. He opened the car door. The car next over was so close it was a squeeze for him to get out. "I'm for some air," he told Vivian and assumed from her facial expression that she preferred to remain where she was.

Standing, he had a much better view of the cars jammed in behind. He scanned them, fought the reflections coming off them, and finally made out the roof of the maroon Saab eight cars back in the same line as the BMW. He went aft, sidling along the narrow space between cars. When he reached the Saab he glanced deliberately down and in. Its driver was a woman, an attractive blond in her twenties, a fair-complexioned Polish or Estonian sort. That was so unexpected Nikolai failed to get as good a look as he wanted at the others in the car. He only got the impression there *were* others, didn't even know how many, guessed two. He continued going aft until he was outside on the deck. The ferry was already under way, about a hundred yards out of its slip. The drizzle had stopped. The leaden clouds were breaking up here and there, allowing blue. The surface of the Westerschelde was scuffy. Nikolai stood at the thick chain that was strung across the edge of the ferry's on-and-off ramp, serving in place of a rail. He looked down into the roil of the wake and experienced a moment of hypnotic fascination. It seemed to be asking to be thrown someone it could drown.

That brought to mind the Lake Geneva incident Pulver had made a point of that day in Churcher's office—the errant dealer who hadn't known how to swim. Pulver was too well informed about the way the man had died. In fact, now that Nikolai recalled it seemed obvious Pulver had insinuated by his insensitive tone and choice of words that he himself was responsible for the man's death. It had been a macabre subject then, but now Nikolai realized it had also been meant as a warning. Perhaps these people of Pulver's were not merely following, he thought. It wasn't unimaginable that they might have more ominous intentions.

He stepped back from the edge and looked to his right. Standing at the chain about twelve feet away was the driver of the Citroën. She was in profile to him and the wind was whipping her hair forward, pressing it tight against the back of her skull, giving the illusion of a blond helmet. She was tall, with a strong, well-conditioned body. Just as Nikolai was thinking she didn't strike him as a Pulver type, she turned only her head his way and looked him in the eye. He met her stare. She smiled slightly. Not a friendly smile, but one he felt communicated with calm confidence that he would inevitably be killed.

Nikolai returned to the BMW. Vivian wasn't in it. She'd left the door on her side ajar. He reached to his carryon bag in the rear seat, and from it took out his holster harness. He put on the harness and, to conceal it, the cotton windbreaker he'd brought along. After adjusting the holster he got the Sig automatic from his carryon. Normally it wouldn't have been important to him whether it was loaded or not, but now he released the magazine, checked it, and shoved it back into position. He pulled back the slide to determine there was a round ready in the chamber. He holstered the pistol and zipped up his jacket. It disturbed him that he really didn't feel any safer.

Within a few minutes Vivian squeezed in. "I went to

the loo and ran cold water through my shorts," she said. "I thought I'd gotten out most of the stain, but now I see there's still a bit of pink. There's even wine on my knickers."

He apologized again for having caused that.

"Pas grave," she said. "I just wanted to give you something kinky to think about. Are you seasick?"

"No, why?"

"You look a bit peaked. That air you got must have been terribly polluted. I must say this tub has a very small loo. While I was in there rinsing my shorts an amply upholstered butchy creature came in and stood there practically panting down my back. Quite obviously what she had in mind was a Dutch treat. Have you got that pictured?"

Nikolai nodded.

"Shall I invent some details?"

Nikolai shook his head no.

"Perhaps all you need is an undemanding Vivian kiss and a bit of a hug." She leaned over and gave him a very light but long one on the mouth. Her hug felt the Sig. She studied him for a long moment before asking: "Why do you have that on?"

It suddenly occurred to Nikolai that he'd wanted her to discover he was wearing the pistol. So he'd have to reveal and share the threat he was feeling. Perhaps she'd convince him he was overreacting. He'd already explained to her who Pulver was and vaguely how the System took all sorts of measures to preserve its control over the diamond market. He'd intentionally not mentioned the drowning of that dealer in Switzerland, but he told her about it now, really opened up and told her how the System had a reputation for meting out its own justice to those who opposed it or violated its rules. He gave her some secondhand examples. That, he said, was the reason they were being followed.

"Swell people you're in business with," she remarked.

"Used to be in business with."

"Whatever." She thought a bit. "You know, it seems dreadfully melodramatic. Are you sure your remarkable Russian imagination isn't just getting a little too vivid?"

"I wish you'd stop attributing all these things to my nationality."

"It wasn't meant as a criticism."

"It's always my Russian this or my Russian that. You sound like a misinformed American."

"My, aren't we the touchy one!"

"I have an average, undistinctive imagination," he claimed.

Vivian disagreed with an almost inaudible scoff. "Are you really pissed?" she asked.

"Do I appear to be?"

"Not entirely. Maybe about forty percent."

"It feels like about ten."

"That's not enough to prohibit a smile."

He smiled for her, but his heart wasn't in it.

"So, you're certain we're being followed," she said.

"Definitely."

"And there's the possibility that they intend to do us harm."

"Not us, just me."

"As far as I'm concerned there's no such entity as just me."

"I think what we should do is drive up to Rotterdam. I'll put you on a flight there—"

"Like a piece of baggage."

"—then after I've dealt with this matter, settled it somehow, I'll come on to London. In a day or two."

His words seemed to go right past her. "How many of these blokes are there?" she asked out of one side of her mouth, suddenly a tough.

Nikolai sensed that Vivian had slipped into her obstinate phase and now it would be futile to try to reason with her. He hoped these people of Pulver's were only supposed to intimidate him. If it would get rid of them he'd act severely frightened. That would be easy. All he'd have to do was turn up what he was feeling half a notch. He told Vivian: "I don't know exactly how many there are, but they're not all blokes. At least one is a woman."

"You didn't see the others because you were so intensely noticing her, is that it?"

"Not quite."

"So, what did she look like?"

He told her but chose his words carefully. Instead of saying the woman was blond he said "fair-haired," instead of tight-bodied he said "solidly built." "I saw her face only for a minute."

"But you'd probably recognize her in nice low light. Did she say anything to you?"

"No," he replied, thinking how much the woman had wordlessly expressed.

Vivian dug into her carryall for her Beretta automatic. She attached the stubby silencer to it and put it on under her sweater. "Do you have your silencer on?"

"No."

"Better. That piece of yours sounds like a cannon without it. No need to flush all the birds."

Twenty minutes from then the ferry pulled into its slip on the north shore of the Westerschelde. The vehicles it carried were directed quickly off in double file. As soon as the wheels of the BMW had roadway under them it began showing its impatience, went around the cars and trucks ahead, maneuvered sharply in and out until it was relatively in the clear. Vivian was driving now. She'd convinced Nikolai that it would be a better arrangement if he "rode shotgun." He'd never used the term but understood it from the American westerns he happened to have seen on British television.

The highway they were now on was designated A58. It was four lanes, divided. Nikolai peered back through the rear window. "I don't see them," he said.

"That woman was probably some cheesemaker's wife and her lover on their way to the seashore," Vivian remarked with a tinge of disappointment.

Nikolai continued to look back. He sighted a mere black speck on the beige ribbon of highway. It turned into something that had color, which became maroon, which became the Saab coming on fast. "There they are!" he told Vivian.

"I'll bet I can lose the bastards," she said as she made the speedometer indicator climb. She remained in the left lane. Nikolai kept looking back. The Saab had steadied its speed, was now just following along about seventy-five yards behind. It must have been delayed by a traffic snarl at the ferry landing, he thought. He could see the silhouetted shapes that were the heads of its occupants. He counted three, including the driver, although a fourth was possible.

A green-and-white overhead sign said the turnoff to Route N18 and the city of Goes was a quarter mile ahead. Vivian was still keeping to the left lane, apparently intending to pass the turnoff. At the last second, however, she swerved across the right lane and took it. The Saab managed the right lane but was unable to make the turn. It went up onto the shoulder, slid to a stop on the grass. Immediately it backed to the turnoff.

"Lost them," Vivian said.

"No you didn't," Nikolai told her, sighting the Saab again.

"*Merde.*"

"Just drive at a normal speed and see what they do."

"What would be normal in these parts?"

"I don't know. Try sixty."

Vivian let up to sixty. It felt like slow motion. It was particularly irritating to Vivian because the sun was striking her face from the left and she hadn't thought to bring sunglasses. Even with the visor down and swung over the glare got to her. To make it even more excruciating, when she looked in the rear-view mirror she noticed the two identical dark ovals that were sunglasses being worn by the woman driving the Saab. And several much older cars, including a couple of four-cylinder weaklings, passed easily. Vivian endured it for a mile or two, then sighed a moan. "Maybe they'll give up on us out of boredom," she said.

After another six miles she couldn't resist a turnoff. She still kept the BMW at sixty, but now the road was only a regular black-topped two lanes with bumpy patches, unavoidable rises and dips, and no shoulders, and sixty seemed as though it were a hundred. The Saab, with its excellent suspension, was taking it with ease.

"I still think I can lose them," Vivian mumbled. A dubious grunt from Nikolai caused a reflex by her foot. It punched the accelerator pedal. The BMW responded like a racer breaking away. Nikolai thought losing them would be unlikely here in the lowlands of Holland, where the terrain was so level. There were no groves of trees or complexes of structures for the BMW to dart into and hide. It could only be straight flat-out, and the Saab had ample power to keep from being outrun.

"Hold on," Vivian said so calmly Nikolai didn't prepare for the sharp right turn she took onto a side road. His leg and hip was centrifuged against the divider. He grabbed the hand support above the door, and just in time, as, barely reducing speed, she took another hard right. How had she spotted that side road? Nikolai wondered. He hadn't. Now, the way she was driving, so confidently taking lefts and rights as they came, one might have thought she'd been over this course any number of times and knew exactly where she was going. The flat land, as it turned out, was a veritable grid, had all sorts of ways running through it, but none better than a dirt road, and some no more than crude double trails, evidently worn into definition by people or cows walking two abreast. A rutted road, heaved every which way, then suddenly, without any apparent reason, pinched down to a mere path. Committed to it, Vivian sped ahead, making buttercups fly. The path led to a narrow drainage ditch. Nikolai, hanging on, saw the flash of a silvery vein of water as the BMW hurtled over it.

All the while the Saab had been hounding and holding its own, losing distance in one place, making it up in another. However, when it came to the ditch it decided not to take it. The Saab stopped several feet short of the ditch, backed up a way, and, hoping to gain decisively on the BMW, chose to cut across a wide pasture. The pasture was close-cropped, appeared solid enough. In support of that impression the gray hips and spines of nearly buried boulders were visible in several places. The Saab was a third of the way across the pasture before it was made to realize how drastically it had ventured out of its element. The front wheels of the Saab were first to feel the pasture's soft spot, as though they'd come upon a deep-piled carpet. With their responsibility for traction, they were soon confounded. Immediately below the roots of the grass the earth was sog, and the front wheels worked themselves into it. They couldn't get anywhere, spun in place, whined, dug their own holes, and kept digging them until the Saab was hopelessly mired.

Meanwhile, the BMW was sending up a trail of dust on the dirt road that ran along the far edge of the pasture about a hundred yards away. From that distance Nikolai observed the stuck Saab. He saw two men get out and go forward and examine the buried wheels. He couldn't make out their features, just got a general impression of them. They had on business suits and hats, seemed even more out of place than the Saab way out there in the pasture. No doubt the muck was ruining their shoes. Vivian brought the BMW to a halt so she could enjoy a look.

"I suppose they'd consider it mockery if I gave them a couple of honks," she said.

"Don't," Nikolai advised.

"Not even a good-hearted adversarial wave?"

"No."

"All right, you drive now."

They exchanged places. Nikolai couldn't get away from there soon enough. He was fooled a couple of times by paths before making it back to the main road. He paused there. Vivian consulted her map. "This area is called Noord Beveland," she informed him. "Did you know that?"

"No."

"Well, now you do, and it's an island."

"How do we get off?"

"I'm hungry. Hang a right."

After driving an extremely fast twenty miles, Nikolai felt easier and told himself he could let up. For reassurance he kept picturing the Saab sunk up to its chassis in meadow mud. Neither he nor Vivian was in a talking mood. Her silence was punctuated every four miles or so with an uncomplaining reminder that she was still hungry. The first eating place they came to was in the village of Renesse. They ordered too much and ate too much, and afterward it was almost dark and they didn't feel like taking on the fifty miles yet to go to Lisse. When Nikolai inquired he was told the only nearby inn was a mile beyond Scharen-dejke village on the other road to Zonnemaire—mind, not the *new* road but the *other* road.

They had no trouble at all following the directions they were given. Nikolai expected Vivian to say she'd called upon her traveling angels, but for some reason she didn't. The *other* road was a tertiary road that seemed unfriendly the way it threw gravel up at the underside of the BMW. The inn, named Koopershaven, was situated shyly back from it at the end of a long unlighted drive. It was typically Dutch, a modest two-story brick farmhouse of simple lines with a steep-pitched roof and upper facades on each end to create the impression of greater height. The night pre-vented Nikolai and Vivian from seeing these features or the surrounding scenery. Thus when they were unloading their baggage from the car and lugging it inside, they experienced the feeling of having lost their bearings and being subjected to the mercy of some strange place.

They were welcomed by Erika Kooper, the fifteen-year-old daughter of the proprietor. With her straight, heavy flaxen hair and cheeks that looked as though they'd just been pinched, she couldn't have been more Dutch. While Nikolai was registering he called Vivian's attention to an enlarged color photograph hung prominently behind the counter. Erika and six youngsters in two rows. They so resembled one another that it could not be doubted they were all Koopers. "Breakfast comes with the bedding," Erika informed him with her thick accent, and choosing a certain key, she led the way up the stairs and down the hall to a rear corner room. She opened both windows a generous crack, filled a Delft blue pitcher with fresh water for bedside. Nikolai extended a two-florin tip. Erika declined it and wished a smiling good night.

The bed was a high one, and hard. Vivian tested it. "I'll wager anything that most of those Kooper babies were conceived right here," she remarked. She climbed to the middle and bounced vigorously. The mattress didn't bounce back, but whatever was beneath it gave off strident squeaks. "Well," she said, "if we do anything it will have to be quiet and passive. Are you for a quiet or a passive—or neither?"

Nikolai had removed his windbreaker. He was standing there caught on thoughts about beds: those that had been, those that might be. He told himself there were familiar ones waiting in London and in Devon and that this one would not be the last. He had taken so long to reply that he assumed now she didn't expect him to.

Vivian observed him wearing the weapon, the harness and the holster and the hard protruding butt of the pistol contrasting with the whiteness of his shirt. She wondered about the facet of her that was erotically stirred by the sight. Not an overwhelming stir but definitely that kind of stir. Marvelously perverse, she whispered to herself, and pictured him about to come to bed wearing nothing but that pistol and his new hat. He'd do it, for her, but she hoped she wouldn't have to ask. She rolled over and looked at the headboard. It was intricately marquetried, various light and dark woods arranged into a fine flower design. All the room's furnishings were of that type, she noticed, solid and sensible, aging but not yet valuable old. She got off the bed, balanced on one leg and then the other as she pulled off her canvas sneakers without bothering to untie their laces. "You sleepy? I'm not. We still have that other bottle of Pétrus. Quite a day deserves quite a night, wouldn't you say? What's out there?"

Nikolai had opened one of the windows more and was gazing out. It was a black night, clear but moonless. "Nothing," he replied absently, and then again with even less conviction: "Nothing."

CHAPTER
✦✦✦25✦✦✦

THE SAAB WAS NOW PARKED ON THE OTHER ROAD TO ZON-
nemaire.

The heavyset killer had the rear seat all to himself, so
he'd been able to get some sleep. His suit jacket turned
inside out and doubled up was better than nothing for a
pillow, although no matter how he folded it the buttons
were hard little lumps that troubled his cheek. The backrest
of the seat felt good to his lower spine. He couldn't sleep
well unless his spine was against something protective. His
regular bed in his apartment in Pskov was pushed into a
corner. The women who stayed overnight always assumed
the wall side of the bed was theirs, and he let them be
there until he was ready to sleep. There were times when
a woman would go unconscious from too much *chacha* or
sivukha and too many comings and he'd have to lift her
dead weight to the outside of the bed and the next day
when she awoke she'd wonder how she got there and be
disturbed that things had happened to her that she couldn't
recall and he would tell her nothing, just reach over her
roughly to get his cigarettes and after lighting up he would
make sure he crushed her a bit as he climbed over her to
go to piss. The fat ones complained less, if at all, about
that. Many of the fat ones laughed from their bellies and
parted their legs, thinking that was what he had in mind.
The thin ones, he supposed, were worried about their bones.
They usually made an ugly, painful sound as if letting out
their last breath. He often imagined himself dropping all
his two hundred and forty-five pounds upon a thin one and

hearing her ribs snap. He was glad there was such a thing as women. What would he do without them?

This woman who had done the driving, however, was not a woman he would want to touch with any part of him, not even a finger. When they'd met yesterday morning at the airport in Antwerp she'd said her name was Silvie. That was, of course, the name she was using, just as he was using Lotario. His choice of a name was more believable than hers. She wasn't fragile or helpless enough to be a Silvie. She looked more like a Martine or a Florence. He was curious about her, but he'd never know who she was or what she was. She'd never tell him, and even a look at the passport she was traveling with would be meaningless, just as the Italian passport he was using this time meant nothing. Beneath it all, though, he suspected she was some kind of German, most likely East. They were obsessed with physical fitness, the East Germans, especially the females. This one would have a belly and a rump like stone. He'd noticed her hands. They weren't the hands of a woman who'd rely on mere clawing. He remembered a masseuse in Leipzig who had a similar pair of hands. A good-looking woman, like this one, but she'd oiled him and pummeled him and as a finale had tried to shove three fingers up him.

Right away this Silvie had tried to establish herself as being in charge. No one told her to do the driving, she just got behind the wheel and told them to get in. No one was in charge. If she was supposed to be in charge the dispatcher would have mentioned it. When they were under way he'd let her know he didn't consider her in charge, and in response to that she'd handed him her two automatic pistols, ordering him to see if they were ejecting smoothly. She knew they were, had probably checked them out a half-dozen times. She'd just wanted him to see those two Mauser lugers, make it known that she wasn't going to be depending on some little purse pistol. He'd handled that by sarcastically asking her if one of the lugers was for her right and the other for her left, and, as though it were a serious, legitimate question, she'd replied, yes, one for each hand. Not to be outdone, he'd told her to take a look at his Galesi revolver, and he'd waved the blue-black .44 magnum with its ten-inch barrel around in front of her face, unintentionally clipping her nose with it. She'd jerked her head away and called him a *zhopa*, asshole. It disturbed him that she, an East German, had used Russian. It meant she'd figured out his nationality. He didn't want her knowing even that little about him. To even things he'd sat back and called her a *Votze*, a cunt, just loud enough for her to get it and realize he knew she was German.

By now he'd been in one position too long. His body wanted him to roll over, but if he did he'd be facing the backrest and his spine would be vulnerable. He sat up and lighted a Marlboro.

"I said before not to smoke in the car," Silvie told him. "If you must smoke do it outside."

Lotario dragged so deep on the cigarette its tobacco crackled. He didn't inhale. He blew out at the back of her head. The smoke wrapped around her hair and got to her face. He did it again.

Silvie got out of the car but didn't let her anger slam the door. It was the kind of place and kind of night that would carry sounds. She contained her fists with her armpits, pressed her crossed arms tight to her. She leaned against the fender of the car. It was wet, although the air didn't seem that damp. According to the map she'd looked at, this spot was only two or three miles from the North Sea coast. She listened. For a moment she believed she could hear the North Sea breaking, but then too many night bugs were making their noises. From what she understood, bugs did that by rubbing their rear legs together. It was their way of calling out for like company. She had fairly close acquaintances who did as much, she thought.

She'd never done this work with anyone before, and the arrangement wasn't comfortable. She much preferred having to be concerned only with the possibility of her own mistakes. Despite the larger amount that for some reason was being paid for this job, despite how easy it was apparently going to be, she kept being poked by the portent that it was going to turn out badly. These two did nothing to alleviate that feeling. One of them, the one who was going by the name Charlie but was obviously Russian, just sat there in the passenger seat like a mute. Not a word from him since that first minute when he'd said his name. Nor had he moved much. It was as though earlier, before Antwerp, he'd set himself on automatic, aimed irrevocably at the kills. At first sight she'd thought Charlie no older than twenty, with his slight build and clean, even features and light brown hair combed to the side. That impression was his stock in trade, of course, and when she'd gotten a better look at him and realized the hard corners of his mouth and eyes she revised her image of him from unlikely youth to lethal professional. No doubt if the job went as it was supposed to he'd get it done, she concluded, but how might things go if he had to improvise?

The other one, the one with the ridiculous name, Lotario, was worse. It was evident that his judgment was stunted. He had insisted they cut across that pasture, and she'd accommodated his stupidity, rather hoping for spite it would end up as it had. While he was cursing the mud and pushing futilely at the Saab, she'd set out for the farmhouse a quarter mile away and played the woman direly in need of assistance for the farmer with the tractor and winch. They'd lost an hour and a half in that pasture, and at that point Lotario had been for giving up. She didn't accept that all was lost. She'd thought like a woman and continued on and searched for a restaurant in Westenschouwen and Burgh and Haamstede and finally had come to a likely one in Renesse where she'd gone in alone and inquired after her sister, whom she was desperate to find, having gotten separated from her along the road. She'd described her sister and her sister's friend and was told yes, they'd been there, and possibly she would find them at the inn called Koopershaven. What luck, she'd said, and listened gratefully as she was given directions. She'd located the inn and parked out on the side of the road within sight of it but where some bushes would be concealing. Then she'd walked up the drive to the parking area on the far side of the place and seen the red BMW there. A part of her, a fractional, deeply suppressed part, had hoped it wouldn't be. She'd returned to the Saab and had an argument with Lotario, who was steaming with resentment because she'd been so smart and right. He wanted to be really messy, sneak into the inn and get it over with. No regard for who might be up and around. Charlie didn't say whether he was for that or not. He just sat there waiting for someone to push his button. She lied Lotario out of it, told him she'd tried all the doors of the inn and they were firmly locked and she'd also seen two huge dogs inside, Alsatians, obviously mean ones. The dogs would be noisy, rouse everyone, she'd said, and that had restrained Lotario.

Now the luminous numerals of her digital watch told her one forty-four. Hours yet to go. She looked to the inn and thought of the man and woman there sleeping a secure sleep, fitted against each other probably, front to back like a pair of spoons. She didn't envy them, although she felt a pang of self-pity because she was standing out there in the night of Holland with murder in her mind.

The window of the Saab whirred down. A cigarette butt flew close by her. Again she had the wish that she wasn't on this thing—or was alone on it. If it had been up to her alone she would have handled it differently from the start, been more discreet. Driving alone she wouldn't have been suspect. It would have been an acceptable coincidence that she happened to stop at the same restaurant. She would have been just aloof enough, smiled a cordial fellow-traveler smile, eventually struck up a conversation, joined them for dinner and later, bonded together by brandy and laughter, joined them in bed. From what she had seen of the woman that would have been delightful, a bonus of sorts. Then, during the night when they were sleeping sexually indulged sleeps, she would have shot them both behind their ears.

As it was, however, the killing would have to be more direct. It would be messy to some extent but not difficult, because in all probability neither the man nor the woman would be armed. She'd done some easy ones. The easiest ever had been last January in that godforsaken place in Siberia when all she'd had to do was shove that drunk out the hatch so he'd freeze to death.

CHAPTER
✦•✦•✦ 26 •✦•✦•

VIVIAN WAS IN THE SHALLOWS, JUST BENEATH THE SURFACE of consciousness. Her mind insisted that something wasn't right, that it was imperative she emerge, but her mind was ahead of her body, had to reach back and drag her body along with it, upward. She used her elbows for leverage, to prop up her shoulders and head, and then her body was ahead of her mind, needing to wait for it so she could clearly realize that Nikolai wasn't in the bed. The space under the bathroom door provided enough light for her to find the plane of his bare back. He was standing at that same window opposite the foot of the bed. She chose not to say anything but rather to try to reach him with the silent language she believed they shared. It would be a good time for it, she thought, gathering her thoughts like a sheepdog tending strays. Her will asked him to turn and see that her eyes were open and on him. She transmitted so intently that it seemed she could see her will splashing off the back of his head. Finally, she sat up on the edge of the bed and asked aloud: "Couldn't you sleep?"

"I got some."

He replied so calmly it seemed as though he'd been expecting her voice, and she accepted what satisfaction she could from that. "Come back to bed," she said. "Come hold me. I need the cave of you."

"In a bit." He still hadn't turned.

"What are you doing, anyway? Deep breathing?"

"Watching for the dawn."

She felt fully awake now. "It's reassuring to have faith in the inevitable, but I for one would appreciate a miracle now and then. I'm hungry again. I suppose it's too early for the breakfast that comes with the bedding. What time is it?"

"After four."

"I'd give my reputation, as paltry as it is, for a glass of milk and a scone or two. Why do you think I've been so hungry lately?" When he didn't answer she wondered how far away his thoughts were. Did they have a secret place they escaped to for a spell, as for a holiday? She hoped so. Secrets, especially secret escapes, were essential. She got up. The painted floor was cold. She yanked the white cotton coverlet from the bed, put it around her over her head like an Arab woman or an Italian saint. She padded to him. "When is dawn supposed to happen?"

"Any minute now."

"Tell it to hurry." Her hand found his, found it cold. She put the coverlet around him and herself against him, and thinking he could use the extra warmth she told him she loved him and he shouldn't ever doubt it. He didn't say anything, but her forehead was pressed to his cheek so she felt him smile.

By then a slight radiance was defining the horizon. The area of the sky directly in their view was changing from indigo to a purple with just a vague promise of fawn. There would be the green of the countryside, but all greens were still congealed and black, unawakened.

"How did you know that direction was the east?" Vivian asked.

"I didn't."

"Then possibly it's some instinctive thing that your bones and your soul knew. How about Mama Russia demanding that you look her way and do some longing? Couldn't that have been it?"

He slowly shook his head no but at the same time emitted a grunt that could have been taken for yes.

"Are you aware of how often you grunt? I think you must all be a bunch of bears. I noticed Savich also grunted a great deal. That night when we had dinner at Archer's, Savich must have grunted fifty times."

"Okay, no more grunting."

"No, I'd miss it." The coverlet slipped off; she pulled it back up around her. "Maybe we should go home today," she said. "We've got some pieces to pick up. We have to legally defect you and everything. From what I understand, it would be a huge help if you were my spouse. How would you like to be my spouse?"

When, he wondered, had she looked into the requirements for defecting? It seemed she was always a stride ahead while giving the appearance that she was only keeping up.

"What a disagreeable word, 'spouse,' " she went on. "Just a smidge of a sound different from 'mouse.' It should be struck from the language. Anyway, to hell with going to the tulips. Neither of us are in need of such repair. London will be good to us. Let's just catch a flight from Rotterdam. We could be in Rotterdam by midmorning and maybe home by noon."

London, Nikolai thought, was where everything might be set straight. He would go to 11 Harrowhouse and see Churcher, face up to it, lay the truth out. Churcher would trample all over it but eventually accept it. Churcher was, at rock bottom, a reasonable sort. Pulver worked for him. He could call Pulver off. Certainly it would be easier to straighten things with the System than with the Soviet Union. To his Soviet superiors he'd seriously misstepped, would have to fall.

The low sky was now definitely paling, going from mauve to pink. But everything of the land yet remained untextured, incapable of shadow or vividness. It was as though someone enormous carrying a lantern was ascending the sheer face on the other side of the world, would soon appear and come up over that distant edge. The hush that had prevailed during this dark time now gave way to chirps and trills, and a few of the more impatient birds reconfirmed that they could fly. Night seemed reluctant to leave, had to be chased, and when the sun took over Nikolai and Vivian were not prepared for what it revealed to them. Immediately below and for about a hundred yards out there was fenced pasture, but beyond that for as far as they could see on the left and as far as they could see on the right and all the way to a line of sentineled poplars in the distance—tulips!

Acres and acres of them, not all mixed up but planted in an orderly fashion according to color and species. Nearest was a regiment of intense scarlet. How many rows of those? It looked to be at least fifty. From them, a sharp demarcation to a section of soft golden yellows. Just as many. Then came those of a delicate pink shade, which had as their neighbor creamy whites. On the far side of the whites were countless rows of a salmon pink, and then oranges, cerises, and magentas laid out in swaths across the vast field, each color claiming its territory.

The higher the sun climbed, the brighter the tulips, the more impossible it became for Nikolai and Vivian to remain mere spectators. They felt drawn to participate. They dressed hurriedly. Vivian grumbled to herself now that she had to untie the laces in order to get her sneakers on. She didn't bother with socks or panties, put on yesterday's wine-stained shorts and the same T-shirt and oversize cotton knit cardigan. "Originally flowers didn't have color," she said while giving her hair a few swift strokes with a Mason-Peerson. "Did you know that?"

"No."

"I mean, they were all nothing but green. They became colorful to attract the insects they needed in order to propagate. Wasn't that clever of them? I think flowers think. What'll we do with these?" she asked, referring to their automatic pistols, which were on the dresser top.

"Leave them."

"One of those nice Kooper kids might come in and start fooling with them."

"So hide them somewhere."

Her first thought was to shove the pistols under the mattress. But what if someone came and made the bed? She glanced around the room. In the wastebasket? What if someone emptied it? No place seemed secure enough. She took off her sweater and armed into the shoulder harness, made sure her Beretta automatic was snug in the holster.

"Why don't you just put them in your carryall?" Nikolai suggested.

"I don't want to be bothered with lugging anything." She put her sweater back on, pushed its huge sleeves up to her elbows, and dropped two loaded clips into a pocket. "Why are you just standing there?"

A what-the-hell shrug by Nikolai. He put on the harness and the holster with his Sig in it, then his windbreaker.

Apparently no one at the inn was yet up and about. Nikolai and Vivian looked for a back way out. They passed through the impeccable kitchen. Vivian grabbed the heel of a black loaf from a basket of yesterday's bread. It was tough. She bit down hard and twisted it and feared for that one upper left front tooth she'd had capped. They were outside before she managed to be chewing on a chunk. "Tulips came from Turkey," she said with her mouth full.

"Ups em fa uky" was what Nikolai heard, but he nodded that he understood. He looked up at the sky and thought the day was going to be a pretty one. He inhaled deeply. The air had some of the North Sea in it. He should relax, he told himself, enjoy seeing things, such as the tiny grasshoppers that were being caused to jump by his and Vivian's strides through the grass of the wide pasture. People, including himself, should learn to appreciate each breath. He should be more like Lev. Maybe that was why Lev liked Gauguin so much; he identified with the artist's Tahitian laissez-faire. It occurred to Nikolai that he'd never asked Lev why he liked Gauguin, had assumed it was for the same reason his own famous favorite was Turner, the visual astonishment. What Turner could do with this tulip field up ahead!

They had reached the fence that marked the end of the pasture and the beginning of the tulips. There was no gate. It was a string wire fence of three tight strands, probably intended to keep cows or sheep from the tulips. And what tulips they were! The only others equal to them that Vivian had ever seen were in a mixed bouquet in the lobby of the

Ritz in Paris. They were a special hybrid, prized for their enormous blossoms that were like chalices, a good six inches long and four in diameter with stems that stood them up thirty inches or more. For a long moment Nikolai and Vivian paused to appreciate the tulips from closer range. They decided they would walk around the field or through it if possible. Vivian crawled between the upper and middle wire strands, and Nikolai was about to do the same when he saw concern cloud Vivian's face. She was looking back in the direction from which they'd come. Nikolai turned to see the three coming across the pasture: a slight young man on the right, a heavier-set and older man in the middle, and the woman he'd seen on the ferry, the driver of the Saab, on the left. Their intent was obvious by the way they were spaced well apart and the stalk that was in their pace. They were at the midpoint of the pasture about a hundred yards off.

There was no way Nikolai and Vivian could reach the inn and the BMW. Their only alternative was the tulip field. Nikolai climbed through the fence. Immediately, he and Vivian ran full out along the plowed-up edge of the field, stumbling over clods of dirt, one step sinking in, the next coming down on a hardened spot. Nikolai glanced back. The young killer had his gun out. He was sprinting diagonally across the pasture on a convergent course, making up ground, would soon be within firing range. The heavyset man and the woman were coming over the fence. They also had guns in hand now. Without letup Nikolai and Vivian cut to their right and headed directly into the tulips. The first few rows of the scarlet ones let them know how difficult it was going to be. Each row was thickly planted. Leaves and stems had shot straight up out of the soil close together, and the unusual length of the stems that before had been so admirable was now an impediment. Most of the stems stood crotch-high and were a half inch or more in diameter, tough as whips. They resisted being disturbed, lashed at Nikolai's and Vivian's legs, seemed to be deliberately trying to trip.

Forty rows in. Nikolai and Vivian dove forward into

the shallow depression between rows. They paused there, rolled over to catch their breath and decide their next move. After a moment they heard three forceful spits, each followed by a series of sounds like a razor blade slitting paper. Shots being fired at them from a silenced pistol, bullets tearing through the tulips. How close? The bright red blossoms directly above them had quivered, and several riper precarious petals had given up their hold and dropped. One petal fell upon Vivian's forehead. Deep red, it looked like a pooling of blood. Nikolai refused to accept that as a portent. There! How easily Vivian directed her breath upward from the corner of her mouth and blew the red away. From those near misses, however, it was evident that their location was exactly known. The swath they had trampled through the tulips gave them away, would lead to them. They had to go on.

Vivian led the way, down on all fours now. They kept to the bare dirt space between those rows of reds. The rows were planted so straight that anyone who came to the furrow they were in would surely spot them and have an unobstructed shot from behind. Any second Nikolai expected to feel the jolt and sear of a bullet going into him. They scrambled along for about fifty feet. Nikolai had Vivian remain there while he crawled across the row of tulips on the left. He forced his way through them and continued on across five more rows before reversing direction and crawling back to Vivian over the same course. The trail he'd made was conspicuous and convincing, with snapped stems, crushed scarlet blossoms. Now he gave his attention to the tulips of the row on the right. At mid-stem level he inserted his hands and arms through them and slowly pushed them aside. He took extreme care not to put too great a strain on the stems, not to disturb the blossoms, and both stems and blossoms seemed to respond to this gentler treatment, allowed themselves to be parted enough for the crouching Vivian and then Nikolai to step over and through. At once Nikolai and Vivian set about to help those stems straighten, to untangle those blossoms that had bunched and been caught by their throats. That done, it was not evident that anyone had crossed over the row; not a single petal had chosen to fall.

They crossed ten rows in this manner without leaving a discernible trail. That brought them to where the red tulips gave way to their sisters of yellow—a yellow so pale and pure it immediately persuaded the eye to respect its silent conceit. But no time to appreciate. Again Nikolai and Vivian hurried along on all fours, keeping to the depressed furrow between rows. Within a short distance they were presented with an interruption in the yellows, a narrow, nearly undetectable path that led off to their right, no doubt one used by workers to cut across the field. Without hesitation, Nikolai and Vivian took it, passed quickly through all the yellows and on through the adjacent section of pinks and on into the whites. The blossoms of the whites seemed larger. Was it an illusion that they seemed to be held higher? Were they compensating for their lack of color?

In the whites Nikolai and Vivian felt a degree of sanctuary and stopped. Nikolai pictured their position, using his memory of the total view he'd had of the tulips from the inn's upper bedroom. As he recalled, this section of whites was situated less than halfway across the field. Deep enough? He considered the evasive tactics they'd taken and decided at least for the time being they would stay put. It was, he thought, not impossible that they were already lost in this vast field—and wouldn't be found. They could, if they had to, remain in this spot all day, stay right there until after dark and then make their way out of the field and away. Another moonless night would be a help. Under no circumstances would they return to the inn or try for the BMW. There was also the possibility these three killers would soon give up, might well be more impatient than relentless. They might thrash around in the field for a couple of hours, then step back and take a look at it and consider how much of it there was to be hidden in and decide to hell with it.

Either way, Nikolai thought, it was going to be a long day, or, worse, a short one.

A breeze came up, a vigorous errant little breeze that

could not resist the tulips. Nikolai was momentarily startled when it scuffed across the whites and caused them to sway various ways like a fat, unsynchronized *corps de ballet*. The metaphor made him recall what Savich had said about the special sexual talents of ballet dancers. What a peculiar time for that to come to mind. He made the thought scurry back to its place in his memory and brought his look down to Vivian. She seemed to be studying the text of his eyes. In hers he saw what he believed was a mixture of anger and fright, but the anger was not yet a fury nor was the fright yet panic.

"Are you all right?" she whispered.

He nodded that he was and felt urgently the need to tell her he loved her, knew that his desperation to say that, to keep saying that as often as he could for as long as he could, was compelled by the proximity of death. He said it once and she smiled, pleased as much as if he'd said it countless times. It was then that he noticed her knees. While he'd had the advantage of trousers, her bare knees had been victimized by the soil and rubble. Dirt was ground into the caps of them and the skin was scraped raw. Yet she hadn't complained and didn't now. Like a child who'd just skinned herself during hard play she used her saliva to try to scrub the dirt away and better see the sore spots. Nikolai thought how removed she was under these circumstances from the beautiful London woman he'd known. She who had come walking down the aisle that day at the auction at Sotheby's to affect him forever. She didn't belong here crawling for her life. She belonged in a designer's afternoon dress with her feet in elegant shoes so barely worn they still had their maker's finish on their soles. She belonged at lunch on Archer's terrace tossing her laughter across the table, unconcerned about anything crucial. How could she be so displaced and yet so involved? He was to blame, but she'd never admit it.

She still had most of that heel of tough brown day-old bread in the pocket of her cardigan. She offered it to Nikolai, but if there was any hunger in him it was obscured by adrenaline. She sank her teeth into the heel of bread and held it clamped to her mouth while she took her Beretta from its holster. "Am nu ih uh iow a mal," she said around the bread.

"I'm not giving up without a battle" was what Nikolai thought she said. He watched her handle the Beretta with deft familiarity. She released the clip, examined it, rammed it back in smartly, then shifted the safety so a red dot was displayed, indicating the pistol was ready to be fired. Her mouth had soaked the bread soft by now. She tore a bite from it, chewed, and swallowed. "Do you think we should stay here?" she whispered.

"What do you think?"

"Good a place as any. Did you bring along your spare clips?"

"No."

"Maybe you won't need them," she said hopefully.

Nikolai took out his Sig. He'd checked it just yesterday on the ferry but he checked it again and took it off safety. For some reason it felt lighter to his hand now and the grip of it was a better fit. Quickly as that it had changed from stranger to comrade, from being a mere metal object to saying, *Use me, don't hesitate to use me.*

They sat back to back in the dirt between two white rows. That way they could see anyone coming up that corridorlike space in either direction. For a while they sat erect with not only most of their spines in touch but the backs of their heads. As the minutes passed, however, their shoulders became heavier and demanded slouch. It wouldn't be unbearable to sit like this all day, Nikolai told himself. The sun wouldn't poke along, it would see what was going on and sympathetically run across the sky.

Vivian jabbed him sharply with her elbow.

He held his breath to listen. He too heard it. Off to his right, to Vivian's left. Someone tromping across the rows, unconcerned about how much noise was made, carelessly wading through those tall tulips, forcing them aside with legs causing rustling and scraping sounds against clothing. How near? There was no way of telling. Nikolai guessed thirty rows, just a guess. He was tempted to crawl up for a peek but surely even just the top of his dark head would be distinguishable among all these identical whites. The tromping noises continued and didn't seem to be getting any closer. Perhaps whoever it was would pass right by. The tromping stopped, then started again. Evidently just then the person had decided to change direction, because now the tromping was louder, drawing nearer. And nearer.

Vivian stood up.

Nikolai had no chance of preventing it. What the hell was she doing?

She popped up suddenly with her arms raised in surrender.

The youthful-looking killer, the one who called himself Charlie, saw her at once. He was twenty rows away, about a hundred feet. He brought his pistol up to fire, but apparently, as expected, the woman was unarmed, so he waded closer through the whites to make a surer shot. Besides, he figured, if the woman was here the man would also be. It would be a credit to him if he got the both of them. The woman had given up, was just standing there afraid. He moved in on her, glancing aside, keeping an eye out for the man. He didn't see the man anywhere.

Nor did he notice that Vivian had the right sleeve of her baggy, oversized cotton cardigan stretched up over her right hand, concealing not only her hand but the pistol it held. In a single swift motion she brought the arm down and fired. At fifty feet if she'd been able to take careful aim it would have been an easy shot for her. As it was she had only the briefest instant to aim and squeeze off two rounds, so she was off her mark. Instead of hitting the killer in the center of his chest, both bullets went in a bit high. There was an expression of total disbelief on his face when the impact of the first bullet drove him back and the second bullet drove him back more. The first bullet entered him in the spot above his chest where his collar bones came together. It struck the top edge of his manubrium, that uppermost bone of the sternum, chipped a piece off that, and glanced upward at an angle to rip through the sheathing muscles of the neck. At a velocity of a thousand feet per second, the 105-grain bullet tore on through fibers and membranes, severed the right carotid artery and the internal jugular vein. The second bullet struck only half an inch lower than the first but was deflected more steeply upward and imbedded itself in the thickest area of the jawbone. The youthful-looking killer lay in a contorted position over a row of the whites. As though it had never liked him, eager to be relieved of its responsibility, his heart took less than thirty seconds to pump out his life.

Vivian dropped to her knees. She was stunned, like someone who'd just witnessed a horrible accident. She gazed at the Beretta in her hand, then looked to Nikolai, wordlessly conveying to him that she hadn't intended it to come to this. The Beretta felt as though it were now a permanent extension of her arm, grafted by experience. Even if she flung it away it would still be there.

"We can't stay here," Nikolai told her. The remaining two killers, the heavyset man and the woman, knew their location now. Also now the killers realized they were armed, would be cautious, coming on more slowly.

"I'm okay," Vivian said with forced confidence. "One offed, two to go."

She led the way, crawling along on all fours again. Down the space between those two rows for about fifty feet, then across the four rows on the right, careful, as before, not to leave an obvious trail. They were still in the section of whites. Nikolai paused and sighted ahead. These rows were extremely straight; they seemed endless on that flat land, went all the way to the sky. He caught up to Vivian. She was waiting where another narrow access path intersected. They took the path, and soon saw it was leading to some sort of structure. What a welcome sight. Practically anything would provide cover more substantial than tulips. It turned out that the structure was an open metal bin, twenty feet square by seven feet high. They crawled around to the far side of it and then felt concealed enough to stand. It was blessed relief to at last be upright, able to bow their spines and stretch.

The bin smelled terrible. It had a wide, heavy-hinged

gate that was slightly ajar. Nikolai looked in and saw rotting tulips, a mucilaginous heap being gone over by squadrons of huge blue flies and gnats. The buzz of the insects was acoustically amplified by the confines of the bin and sounded like an electric motor in the throes of going bad. Nikolai thought the inside of the bin might be good for cover. He pulled the gate open another foot. The huge hinges of the gate complained with a sharp screech, metal against metal. Nikolai was sorry he'd touched the gate, but there was nothing he could do about it now except hope that screech had gone unheard or been taken for the cry of a hawk or some other creature.

With the bin to sit against and serve as a shield, Nikolai and Vivian felt a few degrees safer. They were much deeper in the field now and most likely out of sight. Possibly they could wait out the day there. How many more hours until night? The sun wasn't even through with the morning sky. It was taking its time, not performing at all like an ally, more like an entertained observer, Nikolai thought. He watched Vivian giving attention-as-usual to her Beretta. Although she'd only used two rounds of twelve she replaced that clip with a fresh, full one. She appeared recovered from her recent reaction, getting ready to kill again if need be. Nikolai thought he should admire her resilience.

On that far side of the bin there were only about a dozen more rows of whites. Beyond the whites was a wide section of pinks, an intense, shocking shade. Quite a way out in the pink section was a tractor. A bright blue one. Evidently it had been left where it was at the end of yesterday's work. This entire field of tulips was ripe. It would be harvested a section at a time to make sure each color was kept separate. It was, of course, a business matter of bulbs, not blossoms. No solicitude for the blossoms; not a one would see a bouquet. Every blossom would be cut from every stem, so that as much as possible of each plant's potency would be forced down into its bulb. The bulbs would be turned up out of the ground, looking like onions but far more precious. They'd be gathered by a conveyor, sacked and tagged and taken north to the auction markets at Killegom and Lisse. The bulbs of this particular well-bred species, these extra-long-stemmed, gigantic-blossomed beauties, would be choice. They'd bring a pretty price. As for the blossoms, hadn't they by their compulsive display of vanity rather invited sacrifice? They'd be used for mulch or as fodder for cows.

Nikolai stood. Vivian remained seated. She leaned against his leg, hugged it, and that made him feel good, depended upon. He studied the blue tractor. It was, he noticed, not just a pulling-pushing thing but was equipped with special attachments. He couldn't make out what those were at this distance, but from the work the tractor had done in that pink section he could guess. The pink blossoms the tractor and its attachments had decapitated were strewn all along the rows.

Caws of crows, mocking.

A bumblebee, its legs already burdened with pollen, hovered indecisively over one of the nearby whites before diving into it.

Vivian's bare thighs had been streaked with the syrupy fluid from broken stems. Flaky dry now, it resembled semen. She scraped at it with a thumbnail.

Nikolai needed to assess the situation. He went to the adjacent side of the bin and peeked around the edge. His optimism expected to see only the expanse of tulips, but there little more than fifty rows away was one of the killers. The heavier-set man. He was moving swiftly in a crouch, alert but not searching, as though sure of his objective. His course was a roundabout sweeping one in relationship to the bin. No doubt the bin was what he had in mind. Meanwhile, approximately the same distance away on the far left was the woman. She was making the same sort of wide sweeping approach in the direction of the bin. They intended to pincer, close in from opposite directions and have Nikolai and Vivian caught in a crossfire. The fucking gate, Nikolai thought. The noise it made had given them away. He hurried back to tell Vivian. She got that angry-frightened look in her eyes again. She took her Beretta off safety, made sure there was a round in the chamber and that the silencer was screwed on tight. She was ready to make a stand, use the bin for cover and let the killers come. That was one option. Nikolai hastily suggested another. He'd go for the tractor. There was no way of getting to it without being seen, so he'd use that to advantage, make an obvious run for it. Vivian would stay, go into the bin and keep out of sight. No matter what, she wasn't to fire. The killers would be drawn to him. They'd run after him, and when they did, when they were committed surely to that and were far out in the pinks, Vivian would make a dash for the inn and the BMW. Did she have that straight?

Vivian nodded compliantly.

"Don't worry," he told her, "I'll make the tractor." To himself he added: And if I do I hope to hell there's a key in it.

He didn't kiss her; even a peck would have admitted to a farewell. He turned and bolted and let out a primitive attention-getting battle cry as he tore through the remaining rows of whites and on through the pinks, sprinting for the tractor. He didn't look back, just went all out for it. He figured the only edge he had was that the killers would either have to fire on the run or stop and take aim. On the run they'd be less accurate. While they stopped to aim he'd be widening the gap. Their bullets were smacking around him now, slitting through the foliage close by. He zigged and zagged like a foot soldier on the attack. He believed he felt a bullet brush the fabric of his windbreaker. He hadn't thought he'd get this far without being shot in the back. How much farther to the tractor? A hundred yards? The mounds of the rows and the depressions between the rows were fighting him. So were these pink tulips. The mounds seemed to be getting higher, the depressions deeper, the tulips thicker. He'd never run so hard. He wasn't used to it. The good London living had taken its toll. There was burning in his lungs because he couldn't get any air down to them. And now, suddenly, a sharp shooting ache in his right side. But the bullets were spitting at him from behind and survival was hung like a sweet out in front of him, compelling him on. He stumbled several times but refused to fall. He loathed the tulips by now. They seemed to want to play a part in his death, the way they grabbed at his legs as he forced through them. He'd never reach the tractor. He'd never reach it, never.

Then he had. He had some part of the bright blue metal of it in his grasp. It was glad to support him. It didn't mind that he brought bullets ricocheting off its hard body. Its other side offered protection. He drew out his Sig. His hand was shaking. He sighted back at his adversaries.

There was Vivian.

On the ground twenty feet from the tractor. She was slithering along reptilelike, trying to get to it. She appeared in pain. Nikolai feared the worst. He crawled out to her and dragged her in. Asked where she was hit. All she could do was shake her head to let him know she wasn't hit, only winded. As further assurance she managed an on-and-off smile. She'd run in his tracks, nearly kept up, would have made it had not fatigue and some of those bloddy blooming tulips caused her to fall.

Shielded by the tractor, Nikolai again looked back over the field for the two killers. That catch in his side was still bothering him. In fact, it was sharper now. It would go away when he got his breath entirely back, he thought. He reached in under his windbreaker to massage the spot, believing that might help. At once he withdrew his hand. It was wet, sticky wet and bright red. There was no way he could determine how badly wounded he was without examining his side. He didn't want to, didn't want to know, didn't want Vivian to know. What difference, anyway, would knowing make? If he was wounded seriously enough to die, then he was going to die. There'd be no rescuing ambulance and instant transfusions out there in remote tulipland. If he had to get hit, why hadn't he gotten hit in the leg or arm so he could have applied a tourniquet? Blasted luck. Anyway, he didn't yet feel woozy or weak. He felt even more ready than before to take these bastards on. Where were they? He scanned the pinks and the whites. They should be in there somewhere. No doubt they were.

Keeping down for the moment, deliberating their next move. Was it an illusion, or had a change come over the tulips? They seemed strangely inert. The near pinks explained the impression. The six petals of each blossom had opened as wide as possible to the higher sun and were basking, drowsing. Uninhibited now, their pistils and stamens exposed like genitals. The tulips that had been so involved in this confrontation were now disregarding it with insolent ennui.

The key was in the ignition of the tractor.

Nikolai climbed up onto the bright blue plastic seat. He glanced briefly at the controls, the foot pedals. He was supposed to know about tractors. Russians were practically synonymous with tractors. He'd driven one once. For a quarter of a mile from a beet field to a barn, because he'd been asked to and hadn't wanted to admit he couldn't. That was seventeen years ago during one of those summers when he'd helped with the harvest on a state farm in Vetuchna only because in the future it would look good in his *trudovaya knizhka,* his workbook. The tractor then had been a Chaika, cumbersome and simple—two speeds forward: slow and not quite so slow. This tractor he was now on had eight forward speeds and numerous levers and switches with no indication of which was for what. He couldn't take much time to figure it out. He was a sitting target up there. One of the killers would soon rise up and pick him off.

He shoved in what had to be the clutch pedal and turned on the ignition. The tractor exploded from its exhaust several times as though before doing anything it had to get rid of its flatulence. Nikolai eased the hand throttle down to race the engine and get it firing on all cylinders. Vivian climbed up. He moved forward on the seat to make room for her. She fit herself snug against his back, her pelvic mound pressed to his tailbone, her arms around his chest. Like a motorcycle moll, except there was no place to put her legs. She couldn't double them up, had to extend them ahead and hope they were out of the way.

Nikolai released the clutch. The tractor lurched forward and stalled. He had it in too high a gear. He quickly restarted and shifted the stick to a different position. When he let out the clutch this time the tractor lurched again but not nearly so much. He nursed it with some throttle and kept it going, and it rolled ahead slowly. Christ, but they were vulnerable up there. Only minutes ago they'd been crawling around hugging the ground for dear life and now here they were high up, flagrantly exposed. Why weren't the killers taking potshots at them? Nikolai wondered. Perhaps they weren't all that close, were hiding in wait for a surer opportunity, probably somewhere in the vicinity of the bin. In that case he'd steer clear of them.

He got as sharp a turn as possible out of the tractor, then straightened its wheels to be on a course that would skirt the bin by a good two hundred feet. He double-clutched and shifted to a higher gear. His intent was to make a run for the inn and the BMW, leave the killers thrashing about in the tulips. It would be a rough trip. Going straight across the humps of the rows at ten miles an hour the tractor pitched and tossed violently, seemed to be making a furious effort to throw them off. Nikolai hung on to the steering wheel and Vivian hung on to him. It was while her feet were trying to find something to brace themselves on that she inadvertently kicked the lever that lowered the cutting attachment. It fell and locked into a horizontal position straight out like an arm from the right side of the tractor. It didn't have serrations, teeth, or even any moving parts. It was like a razor about six feet long with a slightly curved steel blade contained in a holder so that its forward edge was the cutting edge. The blade was honed exceptionally sharp in order to sever blossoms from the pliant stems cleanly. It was now decapitating blossoms from the whites within its reach as the tractor bucked across one, two, three, four rows.

The heavyset killer sprang up.

Less than two rows, ten feet, away. Slightly off to the right, in perfect position to make the kill. He had both hands around his .44 Galesi magnum to steady it.

He didn't see the blade. It was coming at blossom level, somewhat obscured, and, as well, he was concentrating totally on making the shot. He had just squeezed the slack from the trigger when the blade reached him. It sliced simultaneously into both his thighs. Within a few hundredths of a second it was through his skin, the superficial and the deep fascia, through the abductor magnus, quadriceps femoris, and the other muscles there. Through the nerves and blood vessels, including the femoral arteries. It had no regard for bones, sliced cleanly through both femurs and all, and continued right on to literally cut his legs out from under him and leave him in three parts among the whites.

It was better for Nikolai and Vivian that it happened so swiftly. Neither saw much of it. In fact, Vivian thought the tractor had merely run down the killer and that it served him right. Nikolai knew better but would never tell her. He kept the tractor headed for the inn. There was still the last of the killers to contend with, the woman.

Nikolai spotted her.

Far off to his left between rows of whites. She was running away. Nikolai stopped the tractor and watched her diminish as she got farther and farther off. He wondered if she would look back. She reached the distant edge of the field that ran parallel with the road, scrambled through the fence, and disappeared into some bushes. A moment later there was the sound of a car door slammed, an engine turning over, tires making gravel fly. The maroon Saab sped out of sight.

Nikolai and Vivian climbed down from the tractor. He took off his windbreaker. His shirt on the right side was sopped with blood.

Vivian uttered a little *ooh*.

He gingerly pulled his shirt up out of his trousers. The wound was just below the rib cage and somewhat around back. He couldn't see it all that well. Vivian used the tail of his shirt to wipe and blot away the blood. He watched her face while she examined the wound. Her reaction would give the wound its due, he thought. He'd know by her reaction if it was terribly serious.

She looked at it for quite a while. Cocked her head one way, then the other as she considered and poked around it with a finger. Finally, she shrugged and told him: "It needs tending, but it's hardly a nick, Nick. Actually it almost doesn't qualify as a graze. You're a prolific bleeder, but I'll bet there won't even be a scar to show for it." Then in contradiction to her indifference she kissed the wound tenderly, and there was blood on her lips that her tongue came out and licked away.

It occurred to Nikolai that there where they'd stopped was in the vicinity of the youthful-looking killer's body. He found it four rows away. It was distasteful for him to touch it but he searched the pockets and found some florins and pounds and a British passport issued two years ago to Charles Smith of Liverpool. Nikolai came close to overlooking the tattoo. He just happened to notice it on the man's forearm. A blue heart with a scroll across it inscribed with one word: MATb. That the man had the word "mother" in Cyrillic on his arm and a Charles Smith passport in his pocket was certainly incongruous, and cause for thought.

CHAPTER
27

"AN APOLOGY SEEMS SO INADEQUATE."

"It shouldn't," Savich said. "Not when it's truly offered."

"What matters is that you realize your confidence in me wasn't entirely misplaced."

"Nikolai, why don't you come to Moscow? For a day or two. I know how much you dislike being away from your Vivian, but it might help if we could see each other's eyes while we speak."

"You already know the motive for my actions."

"I believe I do."

"Obviously I have no vindicating excuse. However, there are certain circumstances that I'd like to bring to light."

"So, come."

Nikolai was tempted. He imagined recapturing the feeling of being special and secure that he'd had when he'd visited Savich two weeks ago. He also imagined being met at Sheremetyevo Airport again. This time, however, not by Savich's limousine and driver but by a khaki-colored Volga sedan and two or three MVDs. A flight to Moscow now might never be a round trip. He came close to telling Savich that. Instead he told him: "I was hoping you might be coming to London soon."

"You know I could order you home."

"And I could refuse."

"Is that what it's come to?"

"Yes."

"Well . . ." Savich sounded resigned, more disappointed than displeased. "Then I suppose we'll just have to make do with long-distance. As anxious as I am to hear all about your recent affairs you must be careful not to reveal anything you might later regret revealing."

Nikolai caught the intent behind Savich's tone and choice of words. A warning that possibly their conversation was being monitored. Why, Nikolai wondered, should Savich be concerned with what was said and overheard? If anything, Savich should want him to run off at the mouth and implicate himself all the more. That Savich had even taken this call had been a surprise to Nikolai. He'd expected to get no farther than one of Savich's secretaries. The likelihood of such rejection and the anger it would signify was to some extent the reason why Nikolai had hesitated to phone. He'd dialed direct. Eight times he'd dialed all but the final digit and then hung up. He loathed his indecision. He tried to lose it by going out for a walk in Loundes Close. It was a misting London day but he hadn't bothered with a raincoat or umbrella, and within minutes he was damp clear through. He'd walked with head down, taking notice, for distraction, of how the wet brought out the surfaces of the cobbles. He hadn't ventured beyond the high-arched entrance to the Close. He'd given thought to going over to the hotel on Chesham Place only two short blocks away, where he'd go in and stand at the bar for a drink, casually, like a normal secure individual, but he decided he'd better not. Merely standing at the entrance to the Close he felt exposed. The cars and taxis that passed by every so often couldn't be absently viewed. Nor could that tradesman making a delivery to the townhouse across the way be left unconsidered. Paranoia had claimed him and he now viewed everything and everyone through it. Except Vivian, of course. She, apparently, wasn't so affected. She had the protection of her fatalism. And, even more, her belief that this was just a time around and not so vitally important because there'd surely be another. She'd come out of the tulip field psychologically unscathed, capable of exclaiming how delightful it was to be back in her own bed and of humming contentedly while submerged in a chamomile-oil bath and of ringing up Archer and promising lightly to bring him up to date and of being amused at something Archer said and of bidding a single, nonchalant good night to the whole world, as she usually did, before falling right off deep into a trusting sleep. Nikolai wished he was of such a fortunate nature. Perhaps then he might not feel that she was being injudicious and that he, the wiser, had to keep a raw edge for the sake of their safety. It had done no good for him to tell her that the prospect of peril hadn't been left in that tulip field, and their fending off of that assault would only bring on another more determined. He'd told *her* only once, but not for a moment had he stopped reminding himself. That was why he couldn't, as he wanted, take a stroll down to the Chelsea Embankment and ask the bilious Thames how best to go about making a living in the West. It was also what finally got him to punch in the last digit of Savich's telephone number in Moscow. He had no choice. Savich was his only resort. Only Savich could parry the inevitable, persuade Churcher to have Pulver call off his people. Savich had the clout and bartering ammunition to bring that about. But why should he?

Now there was Savich two thousand miles away asking: "What happened in Antwerp?"

Nikolai, heeding Savich's warning, chose his words carefully. He hoped Savich caught his cryptic emphases. "I tried to conduct a bit of personal business. The System didn't look kindly upon it."

"So I've gathered."

"Then you've already spoken with Churcher?"

"Not yet."

"But you intend to?"

"When I must. Is there any urgency?"

"Yes." Nikolai asked that single word to communicate a lot.

"Churcher always overreacts," Savich said.

"That's putting it mildly."

"Really? How unkind was their attitude?"

"Extremely."

"They tried to kill the deal?"

"They're set upon killing it. Churcher brought Pulver into it. You know Pulver, his way of handling matters."

"I understand. And all this came to a head when?"

"Yesterday."

"Evidently you coped with it."

"Just barely."

"How's your Vivian, by the way?"

"She's in good health."

"I'm glad to hear that. What makes you so sure it's Pulver you're having to deal with?"

"Who else?"

"I suppose you're right. How many of his people were in on the meeting?"

"Three."

"Did all three walk out?"

"One walked out."

"I've got the picture. You expect a resumption soon."

"Any moment. So, I thought perhaps you might be inclined to ring up Churcher and cancel the order. I realize it's asking a bit much of you, but I can't come up with any other way of resolving the situation."

"You sound very stressed. I'll tell you what I want you to do, Nikolai. Get away, go to the country and stop worrying about this deal."

"You'll see that they don't kill it?"

"I'll see that they don't kill it."

"*Spasibo.*"

Spasibo indeed, Nikolai thought. Thank you, yes, thank you, comrade minister, for showing so much understanding, having so huge a heart. He placed the telephone receiver back on its cradle gently, as though it also deserved gratitude. Deep breaths were now called for to release the tension that had been inhibiting his lungs, cramping his belly. He needed to tell Vivian about this marvelous change in outlook. He opened the bedroom door a crack and saw the shades were still drawn in there. She was still napping.

Nikolai drew in another deep breath, but this time to enjoy the air of the bedroom, the distinctive air, a blend of fragrances, lovemakings and sleepings, the combined smell of their belongings. Theirs.

He was definitely back on track.

CHAPTER
◆·◆·◆ 28 ◆·◆·◆

VALKOV TOOK A GULP OF THE TEA AND SPAT IT BACK INTO the gray plastic cup. "This is vile!" he exclaimed. "How dare you serve me such shit?"

The Aeroflot attendant took the cup from him. She knew him from having had him as a passenger on many previous Moscow-Leningrad flights. He was as usual arrogant, complaining. No amount of attention was ever enough. "Sir, may I get you another cup of tea?" she asked.

"I haven't yet had a cup of tea, so how could you possibly get me *another*?" he snapped.

The attendant's contrived smile said he was right but her eyes told him to go fuck himself. When she was certain he'd gotten that message she left him to attend to someone sane.

Valkov was of a mind to follow after her and give her a swift shoe in the ass. Everyone in the plane would laugh, he thought, and some would applaud. All these flight attendants believed they were something special. To hell with her. He wouldn't waste the energy. It was a shame, though, that he had to put up with such people. And at the same time he had to endure the odor of this woman in the seat next to him. Apparently instead of bathing like any civilized person she'd splashed her armpits and all with some dreadful Armenian perfume, all roses. She was literally acrid. Wasn't she aware of how she reeked? The blob of her sitting there in a ten-ruble dress reading Aeroflot literature? Didn't she know what cramped quarters there were in these Tupolev-154 jets? Most likely she'd never flown before. She was probably a *dezhurnaya*, a counter of linens, a watchdog who sat in the hall of a floor of some Intourist hotel to see who came and went.

Someday, Valkov assured himself, he wouldn't have to endure such traveling companions. He'd be going only roomy first-class on an airline that served champagne as routinely as this one served canned orange juice. Even better, then he'd have friends with large, private jets who'd be eager to invite him and enjoy his splendid sense of humor and intelligent conversation. The extremely wealthy Russian émigré, that would be he. How their ears would eat up his fabrications and opinions.

Valkov leaned out over the aisle for a breath of less tainted air. The Tu-154 had done its climbing. Valkov knew from the many times he'd made this flight, his genuflections to Savich as he thought of them, that the jet would fly at this altitude for about fifteen minutes before beginning its descent into Leningrad. Another half hour altogether. He reclined his seat as far as it would go, sat back, and closed his eyes. He wasn't at ease with his eyes closed. There was too much seething in him. He needed to have his eyes open, like a couple of flues. Otherwise he was brought to picturing too realistically his skull and being reminded that it was not much unlike all the skulls that no longer had flesh on them. With eyes closed he experienced the proximity of his teeth rooted in his jawbone, and the hole that accommodated his nose and those two that allowed his brain to peek out from its bony cavern. Usually he was easily able to deny that he was ephemeral, but at the moment he was having difficulty with it. When he got home he would manipulate Yelena into reciting all his superior qualities. He'd again prompt exactly the right therapeutic phrases from her. She would cooperate. It was easy for her to cooperate, because she believed in his brilliance. She often said so. For now, however, he was a captive there in a hardly adequate seat. He and his fury. Never in his life had he been so outraged.

Savich had summoned him to Moscow that morning. They'd met at Savich's office at the Ministry of Trade, where they'd spent a good hour discussing business in general and tending to a few specific details. Savich appeared to be in fine spirits, nothing heavy on his mind. He complimented Valkov twice, admired his necktie, even reached across and felt the fine silk of it, and Valkov was delighted to tell him it was merely one of the ties Yelena had picked up for him last week in Paris—at Charvet; most of his ties came from Charvet. Savich also complimented Valkov by asking for his assistance in deciding who should fill an administrative post that had become vacant at the new installation in Yakut. He even went so far as to allow Valkov to see a printout of his *nomenklatura*. In the course of looking over this list of candidates favored for advancement, Valkov had noticed the name Nikolai Petrovich Borodin—first in line for the next opening of deputy minister.

At one o'clock Savich had suggested lunch and lightly promised it would be considerably more than the Mc-Donald's over on Gorky Street. They ate at the Akademicheskaya Stolovaya, the dining room of the Academy of Sciences, had a sumptuous six-course meal with double desserts and trivial conversation. It was most enjoyable for Valkov. Afterward, Savich had suggested they walk it off. They strolled, a couple of business associates, down Dovogomilovsk Boulevard in the direction of the Kiev Station. That boulevard was heavy with traffic and rife with exhaust fumes, not at all a pleasant place for a stroll, and Valkov wondered why Savich had chosen it. He soon found out. On the bridge over the Moscow River, a noisy, isolated spot, Savich stopped, leaned nonchalantly on the bridge rail, and turned on Valkov. With a smirking grin he called him an idiot. Valkov thought it was a jest or that he'd misheard. But Savich, in that calm, sly manner, went on to say what an ignorant, irresponsible clod Valkov was, a devious heavy-handed wretch, typical of the peasant stock he'd come from, too dumb to be trusted.

Valkov wasn't used to being insulted. He assumed there was only one reason Savich would be subjecting him to such a personal onslaught. As soon as he'd regained his mental composure he defended his having acted contrary to Savich's instructions regarding the Borodin matter, claiming he'd done so only in their best interests. He pointed out, as he had in Paris, the risk they'd be taking as long as Borodin was alive. The damning information Borodin possessed would come out. Borodin's ambition would push it out, Valkov contended. He ran down the entire scenario of what would inevitably happen, all the way to putting the trapdoor of some government gallows beneath their feet. Savich seemed convinced. Valkov told him: "Possibly you're mistaking Borodin's competence for loyalty. I admit he's very competent, but that is only a camouflage for his self-serving. He'll give us up for no more than a couple of minor privileges."

That had only fueled Savich's contempt. Valkov was by no means a weakling, but he'd never come up against *this* Savich. It was perplexing the way Savich could remain composed, so calm, actually appear amiable while maligning him. All he could do was stand there and watch the subtle coordinations of Savich's bushy, sharp-peaked brows and try to block out the criticism, his dreaded enemy, criticism, that came from those lips beneath Savich's variegated gray brush mustache.

Valkov was trying so desperately not to hear Savich's words that he nearly missed those about not having any more contraband diamonds come out of Aikhal. They should shut down the chain, just shut it down at once and let its links disperse. Savich said that both he and Valkov had accumulated all the money they would ever need. Never mind that initially they'd agreed to give the thing two years and it had been only about a year and a half, they'd cash in now, defect by the end of the week. He would arrange for business that would require them to be in Paris or London. Other than that they'd make no preparations that might give them away. If Valkov was as concerned as he seemed about the Borodin situation, Savich said, this was a better, cleaner way of resolving it.

Clean, Valkov thought disdainfully. He got up and went down the aisle of the jet to one of the lavatories at midship. While urinating, he pretended this yellow stream of his waste would fall on the heads of Savich and Borodin. There was obviously something going on between those two, he thought. Otherwise why would Savich go to such an extent to protect Borodin? Twice now. Last week in Paris and again today, Savich had been for saving Borodin's ass. It seemed he valued it. They'd spent time together. They'd probably spent time in bed together. If that hadn't already happened, Savich was maneuvering to bring it about. Homosexuals were known to be dangerous, Valkov thought. And bisexuals were even more so. Bisexuals were by their own actions duplicitous, lacked the strength of self-definition. They only respected sensation.

Valkov shook off the last drops and rehid his penis. There was used scummy water in the sink, several miniature bars of soap turning to slime on its limited surface. Valkov decided he was better off not washing his hands. He returned to his seat. Within moments the Tu-154 shuddered as its speed was abruptly reduced. The descent had begun. Valkov hardly noticed. His mind was still so overcrowded with Savich. He thought of how Savich had concocted the day, started it out with being amiable, treating him like a confidant. Savich had carried that throughout lunch and then had sprung on him with all his claws. Why? Why had Savich bothered to set him up like that? No doubt he'd had an ulterior motive, Valkov thought, but what?

It came to him.

Sweeper.

He'd been so caught up in Savich's charm and taken so unawares by his attack that he'd forgotten to use his personal sweeper.

Savich had probably been wired.

That had to be it. The son of a bitch now had every word on tape. Valkov tried to recollect what had been said. Surely he'd incriminated himself. But then, so had Savich. Savich wouldn't hang himself with that tape. What would he do? Savich would electronically alter his own voice to make it unidentifiable. The conversation would sound as though it had taken place between him, Valkov, and some anonymous conspirator. Could that be done? Hadn't Savich remarked just last week that anything was electronically possible these days? What a crafty shit Savich was. All high officials were schemers, professionals in taking advantage of naive people. That was how they got where they were and were able to hang on to their privileged positions. Savich wouldn't go to the trouble of creating such evidence as the tape unless he intended to use it. At the very least Savich had the tape now to hold over his head and keep him in line. And, as well, to ensure that if their *na levo*, on-the-side, Aikhal enterprise ever came to surface, it would be he, Valkov, who'd take the fall—alone. He'd done all the recruiting, the organizing. It had been Savich's idea, but he had put it together and kept it together. He was exposed, not Savich.

No doubt Savich was sure he had him. Like an insect trapped inside an inverted drinking glass. Savich was sure he'd have to go along with defecting now. Savich hadn't merely suggested doing it now, he'd given it the ring of an ultimatum. This wasn't the time to defect, Valkov decided. Two shipments from Aikhal were already in process for the coming month. Larger shipments. It would be a waste to cancel them. Anyway, who was Savich to determine that they already had ample wealth? The West was expensive. One had to pay for everything. Millionaires were commonplace there. People who did nothing but swat and bounce balls around made millions. So did singers who couldn't consistently sing on key. The requirement for being categorized as one of the wealthy had escalated. There was even a new designation: the *truly* wealthy. Just recently he'd read that in America, for example, there were now ninety thousand individuals worth in excess of ten million dollars. It shattered the very concept of being rich. Nothing would be worse, he thought, than his defecting and then discovering he'd not helped himself to enough.

Valkov disregarded the seat-belt sign. He knew it always came on early. There was no reason why for the next ten minutes he had to sit there bound up like some disciple of de Sade. The woman seated next to him leaned toward him and asked was something wrong with the plane that seatbelts were being required? Puffs of garlic exploded at him through her rose-burdened atmosphere. Valkov ignored her, turned away. It was important that he resolve Savich and Borodin before landing. It was one of his ways— imposing such arbitrary deadlines on himself. He believed it proved his decisiveness.

Savich and Borodin.

They were inseparable, Valkov thought. He could no longer picture one without the other popping up. He really didn't need ten minutes of mulling to settle on how to deal with them. His foresight had seen to that. He was blessed with remarkable foresight. (He'd have Yelena add that to her list of his many attributes.) Long ago he'd bought his insurance against a Savich crisis such as this. Now it was just a matter of putting it into force. As for Borodin, he'd be even easier. This time it would come from in close where it couldn't miss. So unexpected Borodin wouldn't realize it had happened . . . until it had.

CHAPTER
29

IN KEEPING WITH SAVICH'S SUGGESTION, NIKOLAI AND VI-vian drove to Devon that Sunday night. During the drive down, Vivian was quiet, responding to Nikolai's attempts at conversation with as few words as possible, getting away with a mm-hmm or an uh-huh whenever she could. She didn't request that Nikolai touch her, not even the back of her neck, which was ordinarily her absolute minimum. She kept her eyes on the highway ahead and her hands on the steering wheel.

Nikolai thought she might just be in a little emotional dip and perhaps some music would help elevate her. He put on a compact disk of Debussy preludes. After only a minute of it she told him to turn it down. Without a please. Nikolai reasoned if she wanted less volume she really wanted none, so he clicked off the Debussy. He waited and suffered until they were a few miles beyond Bristol before asking: "Have I done or said something wrong?" He had to ask twice.

Her reply was sharp: "No."

When they arrived at the Devon house, Vivian made him a mug of hot chocolate and a toasted cheddar sandwich. Did so with silent, dutiful efficiency, as though she'd been programmed. She fixed nothing for herself, just grabbed a couple of green and bitter outer stalks of celery to chomp on and went up to bed. Twenty minutes later when Nikolai went up she was already turned onto her side and apparently asleep, which, of course, precluded the good-night peck and "Love you" that Nikolai liked to carry into his unconsciousness.

Monday morning her disposition hadn't improved. By then, however, Nikolai had decided on what it was that had her perturbed and how best he should cope with it. Although by mere proximity he'd be taking the brunt of her premenstrual stress at least he knew he wasn't the cause of it. He had only to weather it for its duration, which would be until she started flowing. That he be more patient than usual and not nearly so reactive wasn't much to ask of him, he thought. After all, she didn't have PMS every month. In fact, she'd had it only three or four times that he knew of since they'd been together. Those times there'd been some unprovoked lashing-out by her, but she'd also been able to temper it with telling him not to mind her, that at the moment she just had much too much water on the brain. "Slosh, slosh," she'd said, shaking her head.

So far this time Vivian was far removed from making light of her condition. At the breakfast table, whatever Nikolai said, no matter how neutral, got snapped at. The words that came from his mouth seemed to get attacked in midair—like friendly planes being decimated by heat-seeking missiles, he imagined. Even when he didn't say anything there was still some snapping. The safest thing was to get out of range. Vivian helped that by announcing she was going to an auction at a private estate in Wembworthy, some fifteen miles away. Not that she was thinking of going or did he mind if she went or did he feel like going with her, but straight-out intentional exclusion.

She left him the dishes to do while she went and got dressed. He waited until she was surely gone before doing them.

His hands in sudsy water caused him to think of how his father had never washed a dish, never once helped Irina with keeping the house. Grandfather Maksim had, often, but not his father. The most his father had ever done was rinse the brandy glasses after a visit by his party cronies, most of whom were local and district officials, ambitious and privilege-hungry. Unlike his father. It was his father's stance that being a man and being an architect were sufficient accomplishments—a man who apparently believed it essential that he view love as unessential and an architect who would draw whatever he was told to draw, denying that he had any appetite for invention. Perhaps, Nikolai thought, beneath all his helpless self-defeat, his father really had been ambitious. Certainly his arid personality and bitter outlook had been short tethers. Practically all his father's cronies were chosen ahead of him. It was sad. Nikolai enjoyed the squeak of the wet dishes in his fingers. He dried them and put them away correctly, wiped off the stove and countertop and hung the dishtowels neatly on their rack.

He went out on the terrace. It was the loveliest sort of Devon day. He considered taking a long walk, perhaps all the way into Pennyworth to the baker for a loaf of fresh bread and some scones, but then he thought he might miss Savich's call. Savich would probably ring up Churcher first thing that morning and settle matters with him, at least get them put on hold with promises of concessions. And what then, Nikolai asked himself, when this mess had been cleaned up? It was doubtful that Savich would want him to continue on his London assignment. Churcher might want him to stay, though. For tactical reasons. To have someone around he could point to as an example of misplaced trust in the Soviets. Churcher might for that petty reason stipulate that he remain on. That would be terrible servitude. On the other hand, even if he was promised, swear-to-Lenin promised, that there'd be no disciplinary measures taken, he couldn't return to Russia. Vivian and Russia were an impossible fit. Thus he'd be going back without his heart. Under that condition the best sort of life there, no matter how cushioned and convenienced by privileges, would be the same as exile. Savich understood that. When he and Savich briefly touched upon defection, Savich hadn't come right out and recommended it to him, but that was the impression.

Nikolai turned on the garden hose and washed bird droppings from the pavement of the terrace and the terrace furniture. He dried off the Lutyens-style teak bench and spread newspapers on it. Newspapers would be too confusing a background, he decided, so when he went into the house for the full vacuum-cleaner bags he also brought out a blue bedsheet. He spread the sheet on the table and dumped the contents of one of the bags onto it. Shards and fragments of Czech crystal. They were an impossible little heap. Nikolai used a wooden kitchen spoon to spread them into a single layer. Hunched over, he scanned them with a magnifying glass. Somewhere in the vacuum-cleaner bags of smashed crystal, he believed, were nine diamonds of a carat each. Ten days ago when he and Vivian had gleaned diamonds from the crystal they'd come up nine short of an even five thousand carats. Only by fortunate oversight had the vacuum-cleaner bags not been thrown out with the trash. In their hurry to depart for Switzerland and Antwerp they'd forgotten to put the trash out for collection, so yesterday Nikolai had salvaged the bags and brought them along, ten altogether.

It took Nikolai close to an hour to find one of the diamonds. At that rate it would be an all-day task. Nikolai encouraged himself with the fact that each diamond was a flawless Aikhal worth eighteen thousand dollars. Finding all nine would bring him one hundred and sixty-two thousand. He'd need the money for a bridge to a new life. He planned to be careful with it, not let it get within a mile of a roulette wheel. In addition to the nine there were the two diamonds he'd taken out on memorandum when he'd last met with Churcher. They'd been forgotten in a vest pocket of the business suit he'd had on that day and not worn since. Churcher would want those two back, or else payment of thirty-six thousand. Stickler that Churcher was, he'd probably send a bill for them. Why not beat Churcher to it and get those two off to him right away by registered post? Nikolai thought. No sooner had that thought entered his mind than, it seemed, Irina was there to veto it by pointing out that one hundred sixty-two plus thirty-six would be one hundred ninety-eight, a fairer figure. On second thought, Irina continued, as long as he had in mind becoming a British sort of gentleman, shouldn't he start immediately to get into the ways of one by not even thinking of doing anything about those two diamonds until the System had dunned him at least a dozen times? Her third thought was that, seeing all he'd been through he should consider those diamonds his and to hell with it. He deserved. Irina hovered around awhile and then went wherever it was she went.

Nikolai recovered only three diamonds from the next four vacuum-cleaner bags. Then the task took pity on him and allowed him to find all the remaining five in the sixth bag. He tidied up everything and deposited his small fortune in an envelope, which he sealed well and put in his business case. He'd go up to London in a week or so and sell the diamonds one at a time to dealers in Hatton Gardens, transform them into a balance in a bank account.

Why didn't Savich phone? Perhaps, Nikolai thought, Churcher was giving him a bad time, being overly demanding. One thing about the British: usually when they had a pound of flesh coming they wanted a whole arm. No matter. He had total confidence in Savich. Savich, in Russian fashion, would make it appear to be an arm he was giving but it would really be no more than a finger. He truly liked Savich, admired him. Evidently Savich had always been a roué, but it seemed he'd always been honest in that conduct, never hypocritical or vacillating. He hadn't cheated on anyone or on himself, so there were no chunks out of him where blame fit. It was difficult to imagine anyone being able to blame Savich for anything. As powerful as he was and with his self-declared personal immunity, blame would roll right off him. Nikolai wondered if Savich had ever in his life permitted blame to get to him deep enough to ripen into guilt. Was it possible to be that consistently invulnerable and remain enthusiastic? Perhaps that was one reason women were so attracted to Savich. They, with their embraces, saw him as a supreme challenge, not only someone they might erotically claim but also someone superbly resistant to the blames and guilts they were usually easily able to implant. All those women.

Nikolai stayed around the house all day awaiting Savich's call. In late afternoon, Vivian returned from the auction. Nikolai carried in the cardboard cartons containing her purchases. Vivian unwrapped them and placed them on the table. Three glazed procelain figures, each about a foot tall: a cockatoo, a squirrel, and a nude female riding a blue rampant bull. Also a pair of lamps that no new silk shade of any shape could help look less clumsy. Rather than comment, Nikolai cleared his throat and considered his shoes. Vivian put some distance between herself and the objects, studied them from across the room. Her facial expression went from hopeful to dubious to as though she'd tasted something bad. "How god-awful," she muttered. Nikolai thought then she might look his way for condolences, but she forgave herself with a shrug and went to freshen up and change.

Her mood was unimproved that night and no better the following day. Wednesday morning, after a mute instant-porridge breakfast, Nikolai's patience decided it was time for initiative. Her antenna must have picked that up, because as he was considering what to say that would be most forceful and yet sympatico, she looked at him dolefully and flashed a contrite pout that she turned into a hint of smile. Nikolai held her and gave her the kind of kiss on the temple that was called for. In the small of her back he felt through her robe the elasticized band of her sanitary belt. See, he told himself, just as he'd thought, she'd come around lovable as soon as she'd come around. He knew her so well.

Actually, Vivian's low was only about 30 percent caused by PMS. If that. She'd been mainly wallowing in disappointment because her "friend," as she usually referred to her period, had shown up. Brought on, no doubt, by all that vigorous crawling around in the tulips, not to mention the trauma of sending another person to the other side. She'd definitely been pregnant, she thought, not merely a little late, and it had taken her a while to be placated by the delightful fact that she and Nikolai would, at the rate they went at it, have thousands of chances to make offspring. That realization and giving in to the hugging had reverted her. She separated the racing section from the less important rest of the London paper and went out to be dappled in the hammock. She'd voluntarily promised to make only "mind bets." Looking out at her from the kitchen window Nikolai thought she was handicapping much too intently to let it go at that.

That evening Archer dropped by and was easily persuaded to stay for supper. Vivian cooked Veal Pojarski, which wasn't as much of an accomplishment as it sounded, merely a Russian version of breaded veal cutlet with mushroom sauce. Nikolai commented that he'd never tasted better, and that set her beaming.

Archer was talkative throughout dinner. He seemed to Nikolai to be considerably changed, more outgoing, as though for some reason he'd been moved to inspect many of his old habitual defenses and decided they were unnecessary. Nikolai hoped for Archer's sake these shuckings were permanent, because Archer's defenses hadn't served so much to keep people out as they had to keep Archer in. Archer was far more personable without them. His smile was quicker, his posture not so perpetually diligent, his voice more relaxed and a half octave lower for that. It occurred to Nikolai that the next step in Archer's evolution might be a change of tailors for unstructured clothes, softer shirts, and not wearing a tie most of the time.

It was during dessert, fresh strawberries and Crème de Chantilly, that Archer revealed the reason for his metamorphosis in progress. Offhandedly he threw in the name Tessa, using that person's opinion to substantiate his own low regard for a recent motion-picture version of a well-received novel.

Vivian caught it. "Tessa who?"

"Donaldson, Tessa Donaldson," Archer replied as though there were no other.

"Do I know her?" Vivian asked. "The name seems familiar."

"She makes the magazines quite a bit. *Tatler, Vogue,* and those. In their little black-and-white occasion photographs. You know."

"Is that where you discovered her?"

"Hell no. I met her at Nabantei, that new Jap restaurant

on Heath Street. We were both there alone for yakitori and just happened to be seated at adjacent tables, so naturally we hit it off."

"In stocking feet, I suppose."

"Matter of fact, yes, in our tootsies."

Vivian diverted her eyes for added indifference. "And I gather you've been seeing her since."

"Every night."

"That explains, of course, why we haven't been seeing much of you. How old is she?"

"Nineteen."

A little *oh* of relief from Vivian.

"But going on thirty." Archer grinned.

All through this Nikolai had observed Vivian closely. No woman enjoys such revelations, and Vivian was certainly not the best of losers. He could see her summon her interior forces to enable a soft smile for Archer. "Tell us all about your Tessa."

The Archer of before would have said there wasn't really all that much to tell, but this Archer went right into a description of Tessa that would have glowed in the dark. He spent five minutes applauding her physical attributes and twice that praising her intelligence and individualities. Only as an afterthought did he mention that she was ridiculously wealthy in her own right, having been provided for by her grandmother on her father's side, who, incidentally, had been titled. It was evident that Archer wasn't merely smitten with Tessa, he was captured by her. "She'll be down next weekend," he said. "You'll have a chance to meet her."

Nikolai raised his glass of port and proposed: "To Tessa!"

"Yes," Archer responded, "Tessa."

Vivian's sip was tiny.

Archer left soon after dinner. At once, despite the odd hour, Vivian got the largest-size green plastic trash bag and emptied all her baskets of dead flowers into it. Nikolai tried to understand the significance. It was something to do with Archer, but what? Vivian had always treasured her flowers as though she would have them live on, or at least remain useful, after their deaths. She dragged the trash bag around the house, upstairs and down, and got every dead petal. Nikolai heard her mumbling to herself. He couldn't quite make it out but it sounded as though what she said was: "I can't wait to get a look at that Tessa's irises."

At eleven Savich called.

"Enjoying your sabbatical?" he asked.

"Yes, thank you."

"And Vivian?"

"She's fine." Nikolai almost said "better."

"I'm sorry I couldn't get back to you until now. I trust you haven't been on edge."

"Not at all," Nikolai fibbed.

"I don't care to go into it now, but I want you to know I'm seeing to that matter we spoke of."

"That's good to hear."

"Rest assured. I'll phone you again Saturday, the latest. I may very well be phoning from London. Don't be surprised if I show up there for a visit."

"We'd like that."

"Take care."

"*Do svidaniya.*"

CHAPTER
·•·•·**30**·•·•·

THURSDAY MORNING THE KILLER, GEORGINE KRUGER, AR-
rived from Paris on Air France Flight 93. She came through
Heathrow with a French passport that gave her the name
Annette Detange. Her other credentials, including an international driving license, corroborated that identity.

Georgine spent what remained of the morning at Daniel
Galvin having her hair done. She had a serious, leisurely
lunch at the Savoy and then went shopping along Bond
Street. She found most of what she wanted at Saint Laurent.
At five-thirty she went to the car rental agency. There she
was confronted with a bit of a problem. The arrangement
she'd made in advance by telephone was for a Rolls-Royce
Corniche. She'd been assured one would be awaiting her,
but now the agency claimed she must have been mistaken,
as they never hired out Corniches. Georgine made a haughty
fuss but eventually compromised, accepted a Mercedes-Benz
560SL, a suitable dark blue one with only four hundred
miles on it.

She enjoyed the drive to Bristol, the smell of new car
and leather and the anonymous youthful engine responding
to the press of her foot. Although along one stretch some
misgivings reached her. With the surface of the M4 laid
out so predictably ahead and being consumed so easily by
the Mercedes it seemed that she was on a course that did
not permit turning back. Even if more of her than not
believed it wiser not to proceed, that was impossible. This
was all destined.

What lay ahead, she told herself, was merely a phase,
soon over and really not all that unpleasant. She'd already

given it enough thought. If she was going to dwell on anything, let it be what she would have after this. An entirely new self. The large amount saved from previous assignments would allow it. She had it well planned. She'd return to her apartment in Leipzig only long enough to gather up a few personal things. Among what she'd leave behind would be anything that might connect her to her childhood in Sassnitz. No mementos that might give her away. Fortunately the years she'd spent in that town on the Baltic had lost most of their clarity and nearly all of their value. She would also leave Krista behind in Leipzig. A shame, but there was no getting around it. Rapturous, clinging Krista, so dependent on passion and so effortless to arouse. Deserted, Krista would have a justifiable reason to cry. Rivulets of tears would stream down her well-boned cheeks and drip from her lovely jaws. She'd cry for a week or perhaps three days and then, libido stoked, give her arousal to another. That was how it went with *l'amour beige*, so why waste regrets on Krista?

There'd be no looking back. When she was situated in Paris, when she was no longer Georgine Kruger or anyone other than Baroness Carolina von Scherrer, her life would be finally under way. "Lina" to the coterie of new friends she'd make, socially powerful people. A few sophisticated understanding men would be her *copains*, her buddies. There'd be prominent wives to seduce in the afternoons and when their husbands were away doing business or with their mistresses. There'd be gifts from those women, not earned gifts, but rather hopeful inducements. Jewelry mainly. She would, for example, purposely wear a ruby-and-diamond ring she'd received from one when she was *with* another. Thus, the gifts of jewelry would become increasingly more expensive, more impressive, while she, like innocence spoiled, declared that it was impossible for her to control what people chose to do. What games she would play! Hurting everyone now and then, injuring no one. She'd be loved for it, sought. In Cap d'Antibes, Marbella, Gstaad, the Splendide in Lugano. It was wonderfully unfair what iniquities a baroness could get away with. She knew exactly how it would be. At the start she'd have an apartment in the Marais close to the Place des Vosges. Eventually she'd own a *hôtel particulier* on Avenue Kléber.

It was dark by the time she got to Bristol. The Hotel Unicorn was aware that she'd be a late arrival and had held a room for her. A clean if not charming one on the eighth floor overlooking the harbor. As she was registering she inquired whether or not a Mr. Mitchell had checked in. She was informed that he wasn't expected until sometime tomorrow.

When she was in her room she ordered up a bottle of Glenlivet, telling service that if it came with its seal broken she'd refuse it. She thought perhaps it was the prostitute hardness in her that made her so skeptical of everyone. She'd have to watch that when she was a baroness, but then even a baroness would loathe being taken. The scotch came as ordered. She poured a good portion of it into a tumbler and drank it down. While the bathtub was filling she tried on her London purchases for a preview of the impression she'd be making tomorrow. She put off looking at herself in the full-length mirror until she was completely dressed. She turned abruptly to it. For a moment the image in the mirror was like another person in the room. She was that much changed. Her hair, blond and long as it had been, was now deep brunette, cut short for a woman and somewhat long for a man. The stylist at Galvin had used gel to control it and combed it straight back. Georgine had always avoided anything that made her appear "butchy," but she thought this effect most attractive. She'd varied her makeup to go along with it, increased the arch of her brows a degree, darkened them and her lashes, painted a brighter-red, fuller mouth.

She struck attitudes for the mirror. Shoved her hands in the pockets of her dark blue trousers, undid the single mother-of-pearl button of her long-cut white flannel blazer. Her white silk crepe tailored blouse was best closed at the neck, she thought. She jerked down its cuffs to have them show. As she moved about, the unworn soles of her dark-blue-and-white lace-up, wing-tipped oxfords slipped on the rug. She nonchalantly crossed a foot over, exposed her white lisle cotton socks, poked at the puff of dark blue square in her breast pocket, adjusted her plain gold earclips, so large and dramatic, and put on her dark-framed, oversized sunglasses. She studied herself and approved and realized that unintentionally she'd already begun the transformation. Aloud she said: "Ça va, Baroness Scherrer?" and replied haughtily: "Ça va."

Nikolai Borodin would never recognize her.

When the dispatcher had wanted to know whether or not Borodin would know her if he saw her again, she'd lied, said he hadn't gotten a close look at her. Of course, on the ferry Borodin had really looked her over, would recognize her immediately. It would have been impossible for her to get close enough to Borodin to make the definite kill the dispatcher wanted. Now, however, she was no longer that woman on the ferry. She was a dark-haired French affluent, with that sort of superior bearing. How clever of her, she thought.

She hung the outfit carefully in the closet and went to her bath. She'd been so caught up with herself that she'd forgotten the water was running. It was barely an inch from overflowing, and she had to let some of the water out before she could get in. She lay back to soak. This was her first bath of the day. Normally she took three, sometimes four, depending. Once a lover on the way out of her life had spitefully remarked that the reason she took so many baths was that she'd been a whore. Perhaps that was true. It didn't matter. She preferred feeling clean. Men had soiled and sullied her early. Men. It wasn't as a rule in her best interests to let them know she disliked them.

What sort of man, she wondered, would this one be who was going by the name George Mitchell? She hoped to God he was brighter than those last two she'd been teamed with. What idiots they'd been! How badly they'd botched it! She'd had to clean things up. She'd driven back to the tulip field, dragged out what remained of them, and dropped them into the mouth of a canal miles away, so the tide would take them out to sea. This Mitchell, she thought, would probably also fuck it up somehow. If he did it would cost her dearly. There'd be no compensation, only expenses, no million Swiss francs for her and therefore no Baroness Carolina von Scherrer. She'd tried to convince the dispatcher to let her handle Borodin alone, but he wouldn't hear of it. He'd only have it as a recourse, if for some reason Mitchell didn't show up. Her instructions were to meet Mitchell at this hotel. He was to arrive Friday. She was to wait until noon Saturday before proceeding on her own.

"Foutre!" she spat resentfully. Fuck!

She got out of the tub. While still wet she lay on the bathroom floor and without hooking her feet under anything did a hundred sit-ups at a fast cadence. She got back into the tub. Her resentment had grown. She went to bed but the resentment was on the pillow with her. Around three she masturbated to pacify her mind. She tongued and licked the palm of one hand while fingers of the other performed the exact friction. Her orgasm was no shorter or less intense than usual. The enzymes and neurotransmitters that had come with her pleasure helped her to sleep.

She awoke at ten, ordered breakfast, and inquired after Mitchell. He hadn't arrived. She was relieved, admitted that she was waiting for someone she hoped wouldn't come.

At eleven she did her new makeup and got dressed in her new outfit, white flannel jacket, oxfords, and all. She checked to see that her backup Mauser and her compact Japanese binoculars were in her carryall and went out and down. As she passed through the lobby she didn't inquire after Mitchell, fearing he might have just arrived.

Before getting under way she lowered the top of the 560SL, so when she was southbound on the M5 and keeping within the speed limit the wind made it seem she was going faster. She took turnoff 27 to Tiverton and continued on over a secondary road to an even lesser road which brought her to Pennymoor. It was such a small village she had no difficulty locating the house. She understood it was the woman's house. She drove by it several times to get glimpses of it set back at the end of its drive. She would drive in and be the wealthy Annette Detange seeking some land in the area that she might purchase. They, the man Borodin and his woman, would offer information. She would ask to use a bathroom. They would be hospitable. She would accept their offer of tea. How much closer in could one get? Mitchell's presence would have made it impossible. Especially after the encounter in Holland they would be suspicious of anyone such as Mitchell. This was right, Georgine thought. She would simply place her cup of tea aside and take out her Mauser. Two practically point-blank shots would put them down. Other shots to their heads would definitely finish them. But first, to be prudent she should have a better knowledge of the house and its surroundings.

She explored several side roads in the vicinity before she found the winding one that took her up a nearby high hill. At the crest she pulled over and turned off the engine. From that vantage she had a perfect overview of the house and the lands around it. Through her binoculars she saw a gray Bentley parked in the circle of the drive, and another car, a black Ford. There was no one about. Only a cat moving along the side of the house, stalking and pouncing. The house couldn't have been better situated for such a killing, Georgine thought. The nearest house was a half mile off.

She continued to study the house, commending herself for being thorough. She had another reason for wanting to take it all in. So she'd be able to recall more of it in the future. This was such a crucial day, a turning point. Each year she would celebrate it and her good friends would wonder why.

Suddenly there was movement below. A man came from the far end of the house. It wasn't Borodin, but an older man in a dark, unstylish suit. A caretaker sort. He got into the Ford and drove away. She hadn't counted on there being a caretaker. Perhaps the caretaker had a wife and children. That would complicate. She would wait, see what else showed.

For a half hour there was no further movement around the house except for that cat. To pass the time she observed the cat. It seemed to be practicing various sorts of pounces. She was about to put away her binoculars when she saw Borodin emerge. And the woman. They were carrying fishing rods. The woman had on a complete trout-fishing outfit, waders and all. Borodin was barefoot, wearing shorts. Georgine followed them with her binoculars as they went across the field adjacent to the rear of the house and over a wall and into another more expansive field. All the way to where they climbed down a rather steep bank and waded out into a stream. What a perfect opportunity, Georgine thought. They were setting themselves up for her. They wouldn't have a chance.

She drove down to the house, parked the Mercedes in the drive, and went around to the rear. She could make out the subtle trail Borodin and the woman had made crossing the field, the grass not yet recovered from their trampling. She followed it exactly to the wall. She was careful not to scuff her new oxfords on the stones as she climbed over, but then she thought that soon, within minutes now, she'd be able to afford a hundred pair even better than these. She strode across the second, wider field. No need for stealth. She knew where they were. She could see up ahead where the field dropped off abruptly from having been incessantly eaten into by the stream. There was the sound of water on the run. She was approaching the end of their lives and the beginning of her own, Georgine thought. The dispatcher was going to be extremely pleased with her. He'd mentioned a fat bonus.

Now she saw fast water being played on by the sun. She proceeded slowly, believing that as she got nearer the shoulder of the stream would reveal them to her. She expected to see their heads first.

They weren't there. They'd entered the stream at this point, she could see their bootprints and footprints in the mud, but where were they now? She spotted them about two hundred feet downstream. Standing in the water, their backs to her. She kept them in view as she advanced along the edge of the high, grassy shoulder. She paused when she was about seventy-five feet from them. Not close enough, she decided. Although she was an expert markswoman and nine out of ten times she could make a kill at that distance she didn't want to chance it. This kill was too important. She went on another twenty-five feet. That put her practically even with them. They were still unaware of her. The downward angle would make the shots somewhat more difficult. Shouldn't she go down the bank to the edge of the water for a point-blank vantage?

While she was debating that, Borodin made a backcast. The tiny hook of the fly on the end of his tapered leader snagged upon a blackberry cane upstream. He turned and saw Georgine.

At that exact same moment Georgine peripherally sensed the presence of someone with her there on the bank. She glanced around. It was a man. A strongly built man with thick, light brown hair and features that looked as though they'd been beat up and healed numerous times. He fit the description she'd been given. "Mitchell?" she asked.

Lev nodded.

She told him: "You do her, I'll do the man."

"Yes, I'll do her," Lev said coldly.

Nikolai, when he saw Lev up on the bank with the woman, thought what a wonderful surprise it was—Lev and his latest come to visit. Lev was just what he needed. The sound of the running stream prevented Nikolai from hearing what they were saying. Shouldn't Lev be smiling? And then he saw the woman draw a pistol from beneath her jacket. And Lev, as well, had a pistol in his hand.

Lev had planned to kill her at the hotel in Bristol. He'd thought he would use his knife on her, about the same as he'd used it for the last kill he'd made, the French homosexual in Prague. But she'd left the hotel shortly before he arrived. That she'd left in her car led him to suspect where she had gone. Had she waited for him at the hotel as she was supposed to, everything would have been so much better. He wouldn't have had to expose himself like this to Nikolai. Such a loss wouldn't have been necessary. He would have merely been done with that phase of his life and gone somewhere other than back to Russia.

He judged from the back where her heart would be. Pressed the muzzle of his pistol against the cloth of her blazer. And fired. The bullet tore through two chambers of her heart, stopped it immediately. However, the oxygen in the blood in her vessels kept her alive just long enough for her to realize that it was she who would die.

Nikolai and Vivian didn't know what had happened. It was all so swift. They just saw the woman all of a sudden pitch forward as if she'd been shoved hard from behind, saw Lev reach around and catch her to keep her from plunging down the bank. There was the red, increasing splotch on the front of the woman's white jacket where the bullet had made its exit. They saw Lev put his pistol away and hoist the woman like a sack onto his shoulder. Lev didn't look at them. Just before he turned and walked away, he looked up at the sky.

As though asking it to explain.

CHAPTER
✦•✦•✦31✦•✦•

WHAT HAD GOTTEN INTO DO KIEN AND MAI LON? SAVICH
wondered. Normally, his Vietnamese couple were conscientious and orderly to the extreme. When he'd informed
Do Kien that he'd be leaving tomorrow for a week in
London, he'd assumed his packing would be done. On past
travels, whenever he got to his destination and opened his
luggage there would be everything he needed, not only his
personal toiletries and prescription medicines but clothing
both appropriate and in keeping with his tastes. Shirts and
ties would have tissue paper layered between their folds to
prevent crush. Jackets and trousers would be so meticu-
lously smoothed and folded they could be unpacked and
immediately worn. Savich had come to take such care for
granted.

That morning when he came down for breakfast, there
as he expected in the reception area was his black Morabito
luggage, five graduated pieces. He'd brought down with
him from his dressing room two favorite neckties that he
wanted to add to what he was taking. He opened the thirty-
six-inch case and could hardly believe his eyes. His things
had been just crammed in haphazardly. His silk neckties
were balled up and shoved down into the corners; his five
freshly ironed shirts had been treated like so much dirty
laundry. He opened the other pieces of luggage and found
the same mess. Do Kien and Mai Lon always both did the
packing. Both were to blame. Why would they do this?
Why would they do this *now*, unless—unless they didn't
expect him to return? Was it possible they'd overheard or
come across something to that effect? Savich doubted it.

He'd been especially careful never to mention anything related to his defection, and most certainly had never put anything about it in writing. Could it be that Do Kien and Mai Lon were merely intuiting his intentions? Was it within their oriental ways to put such strong stock in their senses? Not likely. Both Do Kien and Mai Lon, especially Mai Lon, had always struck Savich as being thoroughly Communist-pragmatic. It was most puzzling.

He summoned them to the foyer. Confronted them with the opened pieces of luggage. They offered no excuse or explanation. Their faces remained absolutely expressionless, not even a flicker of contrition. No matter how forcefully Savich demanded to know what had brought this about, they wouldn't reply. He finally gave up. They carried the luggage and its contents upstairs, evidently to make amends by packing correctly.

Savich dismissed the matter as a coincidentally timed show of rebellion. After all, Do Kien and Mai Lon had for so long catered to his whims and looked after his comfort diligently without ever a complaint. He didn't see how they'd put up with him all that while without letting out some rebelliousness.

After breakfast Savich wandered around the apartment saying goodbye to things. The elegant furnishings that he'd lived with and grown to think of as his weren't really his, he thought sardonically, not even those pieces that he'd personally purchased in Paris and elsewhere. He couldn't take them along. Even were he leaving with the state's blessings he wouldn't be allowed to take them. How unfair, he thought, as he imagined things of his taste being gone over and appropriated. That eighteenth-century Régence bureau in his study, for instance. Discovered and bought dearly years ago at a shop on Avenue Victor Hugo. What he was experiencing now, Savich realized, was a little of what Czar Nicholas II must have felt in 1916. He went down the hall to his study and sat at the desk. The inset brown leather top of it was very familiar. He felt he knew every inch of its gilt tooled and stamped border, all the different little scars on its buffed surface. He leaned far forward upon it so the near edge pressed across his lower chest and much of his upper weight was on his lateral forearms. He gazed past the miniature nude bronze of Herakles to the framed photographs of women on the table across the way. A final homage to them. He assured them all they'd be going along in his memory. Only one, however, would literally go with him. The one there in the center, more preciously framed by silver and rubies. Practically every intelligent woman who'd ever been in this room had asked about that photograph. They usually gave each of the many a brief look and made clever lacerating remarks, but without fail, that photograph in the center evoked lengthy, respectful regard. It was as though they knew this was the woman they would have to surpass. They usually wanted to know her name. And he would tell them, would say it as though its three syllables were an entire song.

"Irina."

That photograph wasn't the only one he had of Irina, but it was his favorite. He'd treasured it. She had been twenty when it was taken. And earnestly in love with him. He always thought he'd been saved from early matrimony by the circumstance that when he met Irina she was already married. Only six months married, but those were still Stalin times; annulment was unheard of and divorce was far more a man's prerogative. In those days a woman who sought divorce nearly always came away ridiculed and still married. Irina knew that, so, she never once mentioned divorce to Pyotr Borodin. She just accepted the irony that her marriage had been a badly timed compromise and was resigned to living with it. Only now and then, Savich recalled, a frown would cloud Irina's lovely face and she'd say aloud that something had told her she ought not to marry for a year. She chided herself for not having heeded that wise inner voice, that incorporeal being or whatever it was that could evidently see quite a way ahead in her life.

While she blamed herself for having married Pyotr Borodin, she never blamed Savich for seducing her. Most women would have sidestepped out from under some of the guilt by claiming they'd been taken advantage of, as though their sexuality were a component so vulnerable, so easy to ignite, that a man, especially a man such as Savich, should have mercy on them. Irina was never like that. She was her own person, as responsible for her infidelity as she was her forthrightness. Given the compromise she'd made, and taking into account her very private physical fires, she reasonably anticipated that someday she might have an affair. She just didn't expect it to occur so soon, nor did she expect to be so seriously affected as she was by Savich.

At the time they entered into it Savich was the head of the Department of Commerce with Western Countries, a position of importance within the Soviet command-political apparatus. His official duties required him to be in Leningrad several times each month, and it was during those visits that the affair was nourished. Only their very first lovemaking took place in his suite at the Hotel Astoria. On a summer Sunday afternoon when she was supposed to be out for a walk in the Kirov Central Park of Culture and Rest. Her light pale pink summer dress came off her like a chrysalis, Savich remembered. He'd watched her pair her shoes precisely and place them pointed away on the floor beside the bed, as though she might at any moment change her mind and want to jump into them. She waited until he was in her to let him know that he was only the second man ever to enter her. He liked it that she wasn't nervous, and hadn't afterward asked him to compare her with those who had preceded her. Because it had been such pleasure for them both, that it would happen again was taken for granted. But not at the Astoria. Savich arranged to keep a modest apartment near the Kirov Palace, and it was there that nearly all of their subsequent love-making took place.

He was honest with her, never promised a faithfulness that he knew he couldn't fulfill. Better an omission than a lie. Irina accepted that condition, although she often secretly wished Savich would lie huge, exhilarating lies. Before loving, she'd stare at him in the half-light and try to will lies from his mouth, and afterward, after parting, she was grateful that he hadn't said them. As time went on she came to understand how his honesty in this regard was one of the main things that kept their relationship from being bruised beyond feeling.

Her pregnancy was a crisis.

It changed their affair, let their secret out. At least out as far as Pyotr Borodin.

When Irina first learned that she was pregnant, she wasn't concerned. She had no way of knowing whether the father was Pyotr or Savich, and really it didn't matter. The cold reaction she got from Pyotr when she informed him she was pregnant she attributed to his natural insensitivity and the fact that at the start he'd claimed he wasn't fond of children, not good with them, would prefer they didn't have any. She'd thought that somewhat contradictory, because whenever they had sex he used nothing to prevent making her pregnant, nor did he request her to. During the first three months of her pregnancy Pyotr treated her with a quiet disdain. The only smile from him seemed more a castigating sneer. Irina thought that if her condition was causing so much friction she should get an abortion. She offered to do that, but Pyotr wouldn't hear of it.

He waited until her fifth month, until she was beyond aborting time, to tell her that the year before he had gone to see a urologist at Obukhov Hospital. He'd undergone a fertility test and it was determined that his sperm count was only eight million per square centimeter; a count of sixty to one hundred million was normally needed for conception. Not only that, but of his eight million count, 95 percent were immotile or deformed in some way. This infertility, the urologist said, was most likely the result of his having had the mumps with extremely high fever when he was thirteen. One thing he knew for certain: it was impossible for him to impregnate. So, he demanded, who was the father?

Irina refused to say, for fear that Pyotr would do something crazy. When she asked Savich what she should do he thought it best that she tell Pyotr the truth. She did so reluctantly and found that as much as Pyotr had ranted and threatened he wasn't about to get out of hand. For one thing, he didn't believe he was up to confronting someone as formidable in the Party as Savich, and for another, he didn't want everyone knowing he wasn't man enough to be a father. For face, he took credit for Nikolai's birth and then turned his back on the responsibility of raising the boy. He knew that whenever Irina announced that she was "going for a long walk" she was going to be with Savich. Pyotr particularly took silent exception to the emphasis she often placed on the word "long." She had a need to pique him and many times when she said that she actually did nothing more than walk.

In the next five years Irina and Savich were with each other less and less frequently. It was a mutual diminishing without any inflictions. The heat of their love gave way to a friendship that was warm. Meanwhile, Savich's career flourished. He was promoted to assistant deputy minister and, after a stint as deputy, was appointed minister. All along he assured Irina that she could rely on his influence, his *blat*. She held him to his word and got Nikolai admitted to those schools that normally were reserved for the off-spring of the very privileged. It was only fair, Irina reasoned, for Nikolai was the son of the Minister of Foreign Trade.

Pyotr Borodin resented every advantage Nikolai was given. The most violent argument he and Irina ever had was when Nikolai was accepted by the Institute of Foreign Languages. The more Nikolai attained, the more bitter and malignant was Pyotr's attitude. Savich warned Irina about that. She didn't heed him. Actually, it seemed she enjoyed her clashes with Pyotr, as though they exercised her mettle and gave her the chance to erupt and pay him back in kind for his perpetual rancor.

Savich never accepted it as coincidence that Pyotr had killed Irina and committed suicide less than a month after Nikolai was given the desirable assignment with the trade mission in London. Everyone acquainted with the Borodins knew of their chronic quarreling, but none knew the un-derlying reason for it. Some said that the Borodins had finally settled their differences in the quintessential Russian way. Without denying to himself the catalytic part he'd played, Savich tended to agree.

That favorite photograph of Irina at age twenty.

Savich, gazing at it now, remembered that he'd come close to leaving it in place when Nikolai had recently come to visit. At the last minute he'd removed it, because the timing wasn't right for such a highly charged revelation. He surely intended to tell Nikolai, but under more favorable circumstances, when he and Nikolai had more mutual equity, a better, stronger personal foundation. Then it would come out. Then it would be easier for them both. That event was now imminent, Savich felt. He'd be taking a huge step toward it when he put his feet down at Heathrow that night. Sunday he'd drive himself to Devon. Perhaps he'd be invited to spend a few days, maybe even a week. He'd take care not to crowd Nikolai and his Vivian. He'd put on old clothes and share chores. He and Nikolai would sit in the village pub and tolerate one another's philosophies. He'd become used to a bed in that house of theirs, and soon possessive of it. Vivian would put cut flowers from her garden on his nightstand and he would lie in the dark, breathe their fragrance, and fall gently to sleep with love in his lungs. He would sit with Nikolai and Vivian for meals and anecdotes. He and Nikolai and Vivian between them with arms around would walk the countryside. He'd feel that kind of being wanted.

Savich's "Russian conversation" was interrupted by the chirping of the telephone, a call on his most private line.

It was Yelena Valkova.

"The most horrible thing has happened," she said. She was crying. "Feliks . . ." She broke off, unable to speak.

"What is it? What's happened?"

"Feliks is dead. He poisoned himself."

"Accidentally?"

"He left a farewell note. Oh, it's so tragic. Poor, poor Feliks. I had no idea he was that depressed."

"I'm so sorry, Yelena. Is there anything I can do?"

"No," she sobbed. "There's nothing anyone can do."

"Perhaps you want me to make the arrangements. I

was about to leave for London, but I can change my plans and be in Leningrad within a few hours."

"I just have to get control of myself," she sniffled.

"Yes, you must," Savich told her pointedly.

"It makes me feel better to hear your voice. I know you and Feliks were close, in business and all."

"Of course."

"The note Feliks left was so pathetic. His handwriting is so clear and neat. He truly loved me, you know." She was again choked with emotion.

Savich waited for her to regain composure.

"The police are here," she said. "They've been very understanding, most helpful. Oh . . . they're about to take Feliks away. I must go."

"Please let me know if you need anything."

"I'll be in touch."

Savich placed the receiver down and shook his head incredulously. He hadn't thought Yelena would do it. She was one of the few women in his life that he'd underestimated. He recalled the embryonic stage of this development. Several months ago when he was alone with Yelena he'd only mentioned that in doing business her husband was often a problem. Apparently that was the sort of remark she'd been hoping to hear, for she latched right on to it, said that as far as she was concerned, Feliks was a stifling, unbearable problem, and that she for one would be far better off if he were to just suddenly evaporate. In fact, she went on, she'd been giving that very possibility a great deal of thought. Did that shock him?

Savich hadn't commented.

She knew exactly how it could happen, she said. Feliks looked to her to keep his ego inflated. It was getting so she felt like a damn psychological pump. It was a sickness with him, she believed, a narcissistic disorder. Why, whenever she withheld her worship he was like a man starved. Sometimes he'd demand she go on for hours praising and admiring him. If she refused he resorted to melodramatic extremes. He often threatened suicide. Three times, merely to cause panic, he'd left suicide notes for her to find. She'd saved those notes, shown them to no one, had them safely hidden away. Because it had occurred to her that they might be useful. Did Savich understand what she was proposing?

He understood well enough. With Feliks out of the way, all the money Valkov had accumulated in the West would be hers. It was mere talk, he decided. Brash she might be, but she didn't have that much nerve. Even when Yelena brought it up again the last time they were in Paris he hadn't believed her.

At that time she'd probably already made up her mind. Valkov always confided in her. No doubt he'd told her of the Borodin situation and all, and she'd seen it as a sign that everything was about to come apart. Yelena wasn't the sort to let her fortune slip through someone else's fingers, which was what she feared might very well happen with Valkov.

Valkov dead, Savich thought. It changed nothing, really. And how easy it was to accept. Fortunately he wasn't going to be called upon to grieve.

He still had three hours until takeoff.

Time seemed to be crawling.

He shouldn't sit, he told himself. He'd be sitting long enough on the flight. He stood and put all his weight on one leg for a short while. Then all on the other. His legs felt strong. Legs were usually the first thing to go, but his felt reasonably young, springy. Health and wealth, he thought, rhymed for a reason.

He used the intercom to tell Mai Lon that he'd have some tea. And, to nibble on, some of those imported shortbread cookies Raspredelitel, the food distributor to the elite, had delivered the other day. On second thought he'd also have a few slices of sterlet on some Carr water biscuits. Had she and Do Kien repacked his luggage?

"Yes sir," she said. "You are ready to go."

The tea and nibbles were brought promptly by Mai Lon. In her usual graceful and unintrusive manner she placed the tray down on the table that accommodated Savich's favorite chair. He sat and waited while Mai Lon fussed with the tray, correcting the position of a spoon, moving the teacup a half inch. The shortbread cookies were symmetrically arranged, and the slices of smoked sturgeon were identical. Sometimes Mai Lon's precision tired Savich's patience; however, better precise than sloppy. "I'll do my own pouring," he told her. "Has it steeped enough?"

"It is steeped."

Savich was so used to having Mai Lon around that he was hardly conscious that she remained in the room. She went to the window that was allowing stark afternoon light to hit upon the back of his head and shoulders. She adjusted the curtain to defuse the light.

Then from her ample sleeve she drew out a garrote. A simple device, merely a length of fine steel wire attached to wooden grips on both ends. She would do it for the huge amount of money Valkov had promised. There was no reason to doubt that Valkov wouldn't keep his end of the bargain. He'd been making regular generous payments to her and Do Kien for almost two years. They were in his pay much more than they were in Savich's. By tomorrow night she and Do Kien would be in Sri Lanka. People in this hemisphere had no idea what luxuries could be enjoyed by someone rich in Sri Lanka.

Mai Lon had used the garrote during the war in Vietnam. She'd learned by practicing on appropriately shaped squash and melons. Her hands and arms, delicate as they appeared, were quite strong. Actually, it didn't require great strength. Surprise, speed of hand, and sureness were more important. In a swift continuous motion the wire was looped over his head from behind and drawn tight around his throat, the wooden grips were pulled in opposite directions. Mai Lon hung on, maintained her hold, while he grasped vainly at the wire and the rest of him for a short while flopped like a fish.

CHAPTER
•◆•◆•**32**•◆•◆•

TWO WEEKS PASSED BEFORE NIKOLAI LEARNED ABOUT SAV-
ich's death. He happened to come across a small item deep
inside the section of the *Times* that Vivian usually disregarded. The item said, in effect, that according to an official
bulletin from Tass, Minister of Foreign Affairs Grigori Savich
had died recently of natural causes. It didn't say exactly
when or where or give any further details, merely said that
he'd died.

The news deeply saddened Nikolai. And Vivian as well.
She tried her best to be metaphysical about it, but she was
unavoidably heavyhearted. Nikolai vowed that someday, if
circumstances ever permitted him to return to Russia for
a visit, he'd seek out where Savich was buried and pay his
respects. He'd remember how much Savich appreciated
fine things, take along some delicacies and an excellent
wine and set table on Savich's grave slab. It occurred to
Nikolai that now he might also have Savich hovering around
giving advice and encouragement. He'd welcome it, of
course, he thought, but with Grandfather Maksim and Irina
and now Savich, wasn't it getting a bit crowded?

Nikolai assumed that before Savich died he must have
spoken to Churcher and made the concessions needed to
deliver him from the System's bad graces. A few days ago
a letter had arrived from Churcher. Not a typical, stodgy
piece of Churcher correspondence, rather a brief informal
one in Churcher's own hand, saying how much over the
years he'd found it pleasant doing business with Nikolai and
that if ever Nikolai was in London with an hour or so to
spare by all means to pop by. The postscript, Nikolai be-

lieved, was the letter's real purpose. In it Churcher inquired as to Nikolai's future professional plans.

Lev remained a puzzle. Nikolai tried various explanations for Lev's behavior but none were acceptable. That Lev had come there was not in itself remarkable. But that he'd shown up in exactly the nick of time was incredible. And that he'd known enough to kill the woman and then had walked away without a word was absolutely confounding. Nikolai hoped he'd be hearing from Lev soon, so he could get all this straight. Grandfather Maksim had something to say regarding that. He told Nikolai there were things better left unknown.

That year's summer was now peaking and Devon was at its most beautiful. Nikolai and Vivian awoke one morning, and after they had done rigorous facial exercises and laughed at each other, Nikolai told her he thought it would be a good idea if they became spouses.

Within the week they were married. The ceremony was performed by the vicar of St. James's Anglican Church in Pennyworth. Outdoors, beneath a sycamore close by the church cemetery, which was what Vivian wanted. She thought it nice to have all those old tombstones and, quite possibly, spirits in attendance. After reciting the traditional vows, including the for-richer-and-for-poorer one, Vivian pledged aloud to make a very earnest effort to live within Nikolai's means—whatever they might be. Archer gave the bride away. His Tessa was maid of honor. Tessa was not quite as beautiful as Archer had made her out to be, but she was surely a charmer. Vivian threw the bridal nosegay right at her.

Following the ceremony they went to Archer's to celebrate. Vintage Roderer Cristal and an elaborate cake that the four of them wouldn't be able to eat in ten years.

"Time for gifts!" Archer announced.

Two of his servants carried in a large carton. Vivian did the opening. She was very excited. The carton contained a *bureau de dame*, a makeup table.

"It's Hepplewhite," Archer said. "Genuine, dated 1753."

"It looks older," Vivian said dubiously. She placed her

hand on a corner of the table to get more familiar with it. That caused it to shake on its thin, inadequate legs. It had numerous tiny drawers, hardly large enough to contain a single lipstick. Vivian tried a few. Most of them stuck. The knobs came off some.

"Certainly an ugly little piece," Vivian remarked.

"Isn't it, though?" Archer said.

"It's not me at all."

"I thought it would be better than getting you a lot of little *tchotchkes*."

"That was sweet of you, Archie. But hell, I'll never put this thing to use, and I certainly won't want it standing around where I have to see it. I suggest you take it back."

"I can't. It was a final sale."

"Where did you purchase it?"

"A place on New Bond. They let me have it for a mere fifty thousand. They won't take it back . . . and neither will I."

"Oh, Archie. I don't know what we're ever going to do with you." A capitulating sigh from Vivian. "I suppose we'll just have to take the bloody thing home, but don't expect to see it there when you come to call."

"Righto!"

Vivian and Archer beamed fondly at one another. Vivian knew Archer would have liked to have given them a fat check. And they could surely use the money. But he didn't want to cause embarrassment. This was his way of getting around that. It was like old times.

"Now in order, a gift for the groom!" Archer exclaimed.

That was the cue for a servant to bring in another carton, this one smaller.

Nikolai opened it. Wrapped like a mummy in strips of cotton cloth was a carved gray chalcedony kitten with demantoid eyes. And a tiny desk clock of strawberry red guilloché enamel. And a carved stone figure of a soldier of the Imperial Escort. They were all there, all seventeen, Grandfather Maksim's entire legacy of Fabergé objects. They were the last thing Nikolai expected would ever again be his. He was stunned.

"I obtained them from a friend," Archer said.

"From that old fellow on Bruton Street? He was such an avid collector I would have thought he'd never part with them."

"Beckhurst was one of my mother's retainers, used to be her chauffeur," Archer explained. "He was quite convincing as a wealthy old fart, don't you think?"

Nikolai thanked Archer with a good, tight hug. He was tempted to show in a Russian way how fond he was of him by kissing him on the mouth. But he reminded himself that he was now in the West.

That day, Nikolai thought, was the happiest day of his life. Actually, he had another very happy day soon coming. The London solicitors Atkins & Pomeroy were at that very moment getting ready to notify him. They had to their satisfaction confirmed the death of their client Grigori Savich, and now would execute his wishes. Which were that the funds held in U.S. dollars in account number 13-6389 at the Foreign Commerce Bank, Bellariastrasse 82, Zurich, Switzerland 8038, be made available without condition to his son, Nikolai Petrovich (Grigorievich) Borodin. The solicitors had no idea how much money was being bequeathed. Nikolai would not realize how much it was until two months later, when, needing some capital to get into a business deal along with Archer, he went to make a withdrawal.

Three hundred and seventy-four million dollars.